TOUCH

To Heena

I'm sorry – no brown girls in this one... but there is a brown PR girl in the sequel.

– Gaylen.

Touch

Gayleen Froese

Library and Archives Canada Cataloguing in Publication

Froese, Gayleen, 1972 –
Touch / written by Gayleen Froese.
(Nunatak fiction)
ISBN 1-896300-93-6
I. Title. II. Series.
PS8611.R634T68 2005 C813'.6 C2005-903533-1

Board editor: Anne Nothof
Cover photo: Tobyn Manthorpe
Cover design: Ruth Linka
Interior design: Solo Corps

NeWest Press acknowledges the support of the Canada Council for the Arts and the Alberta Foundation for the Arts, and the Edmonton Arts Council for our publishing program. We also acknowledge the financial support of the Government of Canada through the Book Publishing Industry Development Program (BPIDP) for our publishing activities.

NeWest Press
201 – 8540 – 109 Street
Edmonton, Alberta T6G 1E6
(780) 432-9427
www.newestpress.com

NeWest Press is committed to protecting the environment and to the responsible use of natural resources. This book is printed on 100% post-consumer recycled and ancient-forest-friendly paper. For more information please visit www.oldgrowthfree.com.

1 2 3 4 08 07 06 05

PRINTED IN CANADA

To all the odd people who make the world interesting.

"Every contact leaves a trace."
—Edmond Locard, early forensic scientist

"Well, my life's back to normal now.
I do the things I always do.
'Cept once a week I meet with twelve
Other folks who've been abducted too.
I tell my story.
They tell theirs.
I don't believe them, though."
—Dan Bern, *Talkin' Alien Abduction Blues*

Never know where they're coming from.

Never see them until they're close, white wings on black sky, swooping in for the eyes.

Oh, God, not my eyes.

If I could lift my hands I could push them away.

My arms won't move, but maybe that's good.

Maybe if I keep very still, they won't notice me this time.

There was no feeling in Anna's arm, which wasn't a huge surprise. She slept on it whenever she lacked a decent pillow.

Enough light in the room to read a watch, so she grabbed the numb wrist and twisted until Snoopy's pinwheeling arms came into view. 7 AM. If she'd known she was going to have another nightmare, she would have put in a wake-up call for six.

She flipped the blanket over and looked at the tree trunks she used for legs. They needed a shave, but that seemed like work and unless there were courtesy razors in the bathroom, it just wasn't going to happen.

Hell, without some kind of a bribe, this whole morning was not going to happen.

"I promise," she said softly, coughing to break the seal on her throat, "if you make it to the coffee-shop by eight, you can have a white chocolate croissant."

As she swung her legs out of the bed, it occurred to her that there might well be razors in the bathroom, along with shampoo and a shower cap and enough other freebies to fill her travel bag. Curtis had actually put her into a nice hotel.

She reached under the bed for her purse and decided that it was well enough Curtis should choose a nice place, since—

Oh, goddamn it. Forget being in the coffee-shop by eight—she needed to be in the pool and sauna room, yesterday.

Anna made it down to the lobby in good time, considering the fogginess of the hour, but her momentum died when she caught sight of the gathering just outside the adjoining coffee-shop and pool room. If somebody had asked her what she did not want to see at that moment, a swarm of cops and reporters and hotel security guards would have been near the top of her list. She nearly turned and ran.

The only thing that convinced her to stand her ground was the dim realization that all this commotion couldn't possibly be for her. Not for one little gun.

She stepped closer. A tourist would. A tourist would be fascinated by the stretcher that had something person-shaped under that white sheet and sweet Jesus, what a cock-up. Anna was not, not impressed with herself.

She jammed her hands into the pockets of her sweatshirt and pushed forward.

"Excuse me, Ma'am . . . you can't go in there."

Security. Of course there'd be security. Can't have just anyone wandering into a crime scene.

Anna's first impulse was to show the security guard her very best smile. A fine idea, considering that she'd left her best smile upstairs with her toothbrush and make-up. She had no feminine charms this early in the morning. Good thing she was freakishly tall.

"I'm with the police," she told him, standing close enough that he had to crane his neck to meet her eyes. Close enough to notice she hadn't showered, but what the hell, her state of disarray went to support her story. "I've been called in as a consultant. Can you believe they called me at six thirty in the morning? Excuse me."

A tight smile, a quick shove, and he was easily moved aside.

She wasn't going to run to her purse. She wasn't even going to look to see if it was still there. She was a police consultant, very interested in what was going on at the deep end of the pool.

It wasn't interesting. The body was gone and you couldn't put a chalk outline on water, so it wasn't even possible to see where it had been. Not that she wanted to see that. She wasn't morbid.

Her hands pushed at her pockets until the seams began to tear.

The police were pulling things from the astroturf with tweezers, but whatever those things were, they were so small that Anna couldn't even see them from where she was. She tried to look thoughtful until the few people who had noticed her got tired of staring and looked away.

There were two people beside the chair she'd occupied the night before. One was a policeman who was wearily scrawling in a beat-up notebook. The other was a skinny ghost of a man with scholar's glasses and an intelligent face. He seemed to be doing most of the talking.

She moved slowly and quietly until she was able to sit in the chair. If she didn't move, they probably wouldn't even know she was there.

"You must have noticed," the skinny man was saying, "that this is one incident in a series of—"

"To be honest," the cop said, yawning, "I was too busy noticing the dead woman in the pool. What did she want to meet you about?"

"She didn't say."

The cop rubbed his eyes. "You go to a lot of mysterious meetings, Mr. . . . Echlin?"

"Of course I do. Do you know anything about what's going on at *The Rail*?"

"That'll be all for now."

Quickly enough that Anna was startled, spidery fingers shot out and grabbed the cop's jacket.

"What do you know about it?"

The cop stared at Echlin's hand. Echlin smiled nervously and relaxed his grip. "Um . . . sorry."

The cop sighed. "I don't know anything. I'm busy, okay? I have to tell you to stay in town for a few days. You gonna do that?"

"Are you kidding? I wouldn't miss this."

The cop shook his head and wandered off. As soon as his back was turned, Anna let her hand fall and felt for her purse.

It was there, which meant she could breathe again. At some point she'd given breathing up and not even missed it. Just as her fingers closed around the strap, the back of her hand brushed against a dark blue coat. She was suddenly furious, caught in an emotion so strong she could have sworn it was her own.

"You were late!" she hissed. She heard the words as if they had come from someone else. Echlin spun around, looking sick and pale. "What?"

"You were late," Anna repeated, but the anger was sliding away. She looked into Echlin's shocked blue eyes and bit her lip. She'd made an ass of herself in front of a stranger. Again. Funny how she never quite got used to it.

"I . . . uh . . . I'm sorry. I don't know why I said that."

Echlin's white lips were shaking a little, and she realized he was trying to smile.

"I was late. If I'd been on time. . . ." He shrugged and fell into the chair next to her as though he were a dropped marionette. "Do I know you? How did you know I was late?"

She was not there to discuss the mysteries of the universe. She was there to get her purse and get out, preferably without anyone remembering her.

"You don't know me. I'm a police consultant," she told him. "In behavioural sciences. I'm sorry I said anything. I have a big mouth."

From the way his eyes were gleaming, she guessed she'd chosen the wrong lie.

"That's amazing," he said. "How did you know I was late? The way I'm dressed? I got dressed in a hurry this morning."

"Join the club," said Anna, glancing down at her sweatshirt and torn jeans. "Yeah, I guess it was your clothes. I don't always know how I know things. We in the crime-solving business call it 'having a hunch.'"

Echlin laughed. His voice was a little reedy, probably from stress. Anna didn't hold it against him.

"That's funny. You're funny."

They sat in silence for a moment.

"I should go," Anna said.

Perfectly casual, she reached down again to grab the purse strap she'd dropped. Her eyes naturally followed her hand and she saw the coat she'd touched earlier. A woman's coat. Anna had a strong suspicion that it belonged to the woman under the white sheet.

No wonder she'd reacted.

"This is a rude thing to say to a stranger," Echlin said, rising to his feet as she rose to hers, "but you look sick. Have you had breakfast?"

That white chocolate croissant now seemed to be an especially vile form of torture.

"I'm not really hungry."

"Oh, you think so," Echlin said, putting one of his thin hands under her elbow, "but you're wrong. That sick feeling is your stomach telling you to eat. And this annoying voice in your ear, that's me telling you I'll even buy. You don't know me, but I'm so cheap I steal packets of Nutra-Sweet and strip bus tickets to make two out of one. Still, I'm offering to pay. That's how sick you look."

Anna didn't think she felt like laughing, but she heard herself doing it. "That's a hell of a speech. I guess breakfast wouldn't hurt."

Oh, God, where did that come from? Of course it would hurt. It didn't take a genius to guess that the man was after information, and she didn't know a thing about behavioural science. Anna pressed the side of her purse lightly, feeling for the outline of the gun. Still there.

Well, if breakfast went horribly wrong, she could always shoot the guy.

"What's so funny?"

Anna swallowed a laugh. "Nothing. I hope you know a decent restaurant around here. Seeing as how it looks right into the pool room, I'm betting the hotel's coffee-shop is closed."

"I'm not a coward," Anna said, "but still, I would never have come in here on my own."

"Not unarmed," Echlin agreed.

Anna quickly rammed a large chunk of cinnamon bun into her mouth and chased it with coffee.

Echlin nodded. "You see? I knew you were hungry."

He leaned back until his chair was resting on its hind legs and looked around the dingy café. "A friend of mine went to U. Vic. When I visited him, we always ate here. I don't like to think about the state of the kitchen, but you have to admit the food is good."

"Mmmph," Anna said, then swallowed. "That's a yes. Cheap, too."

"Cheap is my way of life. I'm Paul Echlin, by the way."

He thrust a hand across the table, and Anna shook it. The expected thing now was to tell him her name.

"Anna," she said, raising her coffee cup to her mouth. As she sipped, she considered the wisdom of giving a fake last name. It was probably a good idea, but for some reason the only name that came to mind was *Bond*, and she doubted it would fly.

"Gareau," she said. "Anna Gareau."

Echlin leaned forward, the chair's front legs hitting the floor with a thump. "Like *loup gareau*?"

Lord, what didn't attract this man's interest? Fat chance of him not remembering her name now.

"That's *garou*."

"Do you speak French?"

He was a terrier. She'd had one growing up; she knew one when she met one. So what if he looked like a person?

"Let go of my pant leg," she said. He blinked and looked under the table, presumably to see if he'd snagged her jeans with his shoe.

"What?"

"You're asking a lot of questions. Talk about yourself or something. I overheard you telling the cop you were supposed to meet that . . . um . . . that woman."

"Ah, yes. Esther Williams."

Anna looked at her crumb-filled plate. Would it be wrong to order another cinnamon bun? "Was that her name?"

Paul Echlin's eyes were very bright behind his glasses, but he didn't quite laugh. "No. That was just a joke. I have kind of a black sense of humour. Her name was Jocelyn Lowry." He pulled a notebook from the inside breast pocket of his coat and flipped through it with those surprisingly nimble fingers. "Lowry. Twenty-seven years old and not getting any older, but that's the way the ball bounces. The police didn't tell you her name?"

"That's not the way I work," said Anna, hoping he wouldn't pursue the issue. She sure as hell didn't want to get into a discussion of how she did work. "Sounds like you didn't know her too well."

"I didn't know her at all. She went to school with my assistant. I mean, my publicist."

Anna ran a finger over the crumbs on her plate. "You have a publicist?" She squinted at him, trying to figure out if she'd seen him before. "Are you an actor or something?"

"I'm Brad Pitt's understudy," Paul said, grinning. Anna laughed. "No, actually, I'm an author of sorts."

"Mmm." Anna licked crumbs off her finger. "An author of sorts. Have you ever thought about writing books?"

"Have you thought about a second cinnamon bun? I wouldn't normally offer, but I'm sitting pretty close to you, and I'm worried you'll start chewing on my hand."

Well, since he put it that way. . . .

"That would be great. Thanks."

"No need to thank me—it's pure self-defense."

He strolled up to the counter and placed the order, then dropped back into his chair. Anna had seen rag dolls with more tension in them.

"What do you write?"

Paul took off his glasses and rubbed at the lenses with his sleeve.

"I have a doctorate in Popular Culture. I started out in history, because I had a theory that historians attribute too much importance to political and economic conditions when trying to determine why historical figures made certain choices. If you think about why you do things, isn't it usually the people in your life, or your personal likes and dislikes, even your mood—rather than rational factors? I can see your eyes glazing over."

Anna blinked and shook her head. "No, what you see is me trying to keep up. You talk really fast."

"Sorry. Um—here's an example. Person X, let's call him

Hector, is a general in the American Civil War. Hector has to choose between attacking and retreating at an important moment. Historians will assume that he based his decision on strategy, that he was as cold and logical about it as we can be from the distance of a hundred years. But of course he wasn't. See, Hector was a real guy. Maybe he found out that his wife was having an affair and didn't feel like much of a man, so he decided to attack and prove himself. That's the kind of thing real people do. Always has been."

Anna pushed her coffee cup to the edge of the table. Maybe their waitress would get the hint. "I thought historians cared more about what happened than why."

Paul's face lost definition without his glasses, became something you'd forget the look of the second you turned away. It was as if his poor vision were contagious. "Some do, but for me the main purpose of studying history is seeing patterns, trying to figure out why things went the way they did so that we can avoid making the same mistakes. I guess what I've learned over the years is that people are always going to make the same damn mistakes, but at least once you know that you can take it into account when you're planning your life."

Anna steadied herself against the flow of words. When it seemed to have stopped, she grinned at him. "And still," she said, "the man has not said what it is he writes."

"I translated my historical theory into the modern day," Paul said, setting his glasses back on his nose, "and wrote a thesis about some of our pop culture heroes, why they made the choices they did. Then I turned it into a book called *A Simple Explanation*. It really did sell quite well."

The cinnamon bun arrived, along with fresh coffee. Anna would never have guessed that a café could seem so close to heaven.

"I've been living under a rock," she said. "You'll have to excuse me. What else have you written?"

Paul reached across the table and took a corner off the bun. "Right now," he said, dropping the food onto his plate, "I have a website. I invite people to email me with stories about powerful people and why they really do things."

"And you make a living at this, somehow?"

Paul gestured at their surroundings. "You see me living the good life, don't you? Actually, I have some advertisers. Between that and royalties from the first book, I do okay. But I'm a greedy bastard, so I'm working on a second book."

"What about?"

He shrugged. "Second verse, same as the first. Whatever Jocelyn Lowry was going to tell me, that probably would've gone into the book."

"Did she work for somebody famous?"

Paul's eyes widened. With the lenses magnifying his eyes, he looked oddly like a Grey. "Better than that—she worked at *The Rail*. I mean, considering the goings on at that place. . . ."

Anna read *The Rail* from time to time, mostly in doctors' waiting rooms, but she hadn't heard anything about any goings on. Still, she'd been in the States for almost a year. She spread her hands, palms up. "Rock dweller, remember?"

Paul looked into his coffee cup as though he expected to find a prize at the bottom. "I wouldn't know where to begin with this story," he said, frowning. He looked at Anna and smiled. "Collie would, though. She keeps good notes."

"Collie?"

"My assist—publicist. She's probably back at the hotel room by now. When we found Jocelyn's body she went for a walk. Like I said, they went to school together. Anyway, Collie could tell you what's been happening at *The Rail*."

Okay, yes, this was interesting. Anna had never been so close to an actual murder mystery before. She'd even seen the body, and that image wouldn't leave her mind. But this really didn't fit in with her plans for the weekend, and that was the bottom line.

"I appreciate the breakfast," she said. "It was really good, and I liked talking with you, but I have to go."

"If you're worried about your job, don't be. This is work related. I promise you, whatever happened to that woman has to do with *The Rail*. Do you really think it's a coincidence that she got killed the morning she was supposed to meet with me?"

"Probably not," Anna said, "but. . . ."

She couldn't think of a 'but.' He thought she was a police consultant. She had to pretend a professional interest in this case. Her errand was going to have to wait.

"Okay," she said. "You're right. Let's talk to Collie."

If Paul was a terrier, his publicist was a sheepdog. Not a collie, but one of those bundles of hair that made you wonder how the damned thing could see to herd anything.

She was, as Paul had predicted, back in her hotel room. Her bed was a faerie ring of newspaper articles and inked notes, with a small hill of rust-coloured curls at the centre. Anna could just make out a person behind all that hair, two crossed legs, and the side of one arm.

As soon as Anna had entered and Paul shut the door behind them, a voice made the curls sway. "The police are convinced it wasn't suicide."

"I think we knew that anyway, Collie," said Paul. He sounded amused. "I found someone who wants to be informed about *The Rail.*"

"Besides us?" Collie lifted her head, and the hair parted enough that Anna could see a white face and dark-rimmed green eyes. It was a good bet she looked better when she hadn't just seen the corpse of an old school friend.

"She hasn't heard anything about what's going on over there. She says she's been living under a rock."

"In the States, actually," Anna corrected. Collie grinned.

"Six of one," she said. "I'm Colette Kostyna, by the way. I handle publicity for Paul."

"Anna Gareau," Anna said, wishing she could turn back time. She'd been raised to believe that once she told a lie she was as responsible for it as she would be for her offspring. This morning's careless line was likely to be a problem child.

"Anna's a consultant for the police department," said Paul. "I thought she might find it helpful if you were to tell her everything we know about *The Rail.*"

Collie rested her elbows on her knees and set her chin on

laced hands. "I'm not a good source, Paul. I only know what's in the papers."

She said it without a hint of irony. Anna was amazed, not for the first time, by how common paranoia had become. Of course, the papers had everything wrong, and only a fool would doubt it.

"Tell me anyway," she suggested. As long as she was here, she might as well satisfy her curiosity. "I'll take it with salt."

"Oh, you'd better," Collie said. She patted the end of the bed, just beyond the last ring of papers. "Pull up some bed."

Sure. No problem. Anna gingerly settled herself, trying not to upset whatever order those papers were in.

Collie was studying the papers, chewing on her lower lip. "I guess," she said finally, "I should start at the beginning." She placed a copy of *The Rail* in Anna's hands.

"I'm very impressed you have that," Paul said. "I went on a search two hours after it hit the stands and it was already. . . ."

He kept talking as Anna turned pages. It was the second issue from March, and she couldn't see anything unusual about it. An international news story and a few national ones, Klebeck's financial column, movie reviews . . . someone named Trifa had taken over entertainment news, but that wasn't noteworthy. *The Rail* was a typical newsmagazine . . . a little superficial but largely painless, just the way she remembered it. She flipped to the last page to see Postnikoff's rant.

"You motherfuckers," it began. Anna could not possibly have read that right. She shut her eyes tight for a few seconds.

Paul chuckled. "I did that the first time too," he said, "but it's what it looks like."

Anna opened her eyes for another look.

> You motherfuckers. I know what you've been doing. I know. I know the things you say about me. And the women, they don't touch me, and I know you told them I'm unclean. You've turned them all against me. Do you think you can get away with this? I have my resources. I have my legion. The government would like to know the things I know.

> I'll tell them if I have to. You haven't reached them all. You can't buy a soul with money. You buy a soul with blood. Are you prepared for that? 308 is the number of your game. I found it in your last message. You thought you could hide from me. Now you know that I see you everywhere. I will be there when you turn around.

Anna dropped the magazine and stared at Collie, who had switched from chewing her lip to chewing the end of her pen. She raised her eyebrows when she saw Anna watching her.

"Weird and wacky stuff, hey?"

That was something of an understatement.

"Was this some kind of a joke?"

"Does it strike you as funny?" Collie answered.

"Well. . . ," Paul put in, the corner of his mouth turned up.

Collie glanced at him and shrugged. "Okay, in an *Evil Dead* sort of way I guess it might be funny. But it wasn't a joke. You know Postnikoff's stuff, right?"

Everyone did. *The Rail's* editor-in-chief had been writing that column for about a million years, kvetching about politicians and TV commercials and the fact that his neighbour's Christmas lights had been up all year. He was querulous, sure, but not crazy. He had not, for example, ever used the word *motherfuckers* in a column before.

"Yeah. I can't believe this made it to print."

Paul shrugged. "He's the boss. He was. He was the boss. Obviously, he found a way to do it. A better question is, why would he write that in the first place?"

He looked at Anna as if he thought she might know. She didn't, exactly, but she thought the general implication was pretty obvious.

"He was off his nut," she said. "Right? He's got Alzheimer's or something."

Paul shook his head. "Not according to his doctor. Nobody saw this coming. Collie has clipped dozens of interviews in which people say this came straight out of left field. A couple of his friends say he was maybe a touch paranoid about his privacy, but this was a man who made his living complaining in public. I like my privacy too."

Anna looked at the magazine again. She had the strangest feeling that it was a snake on her lap, something that would be happy to bite her. "What does Postnikoff say about it?"

"Nothing anymore," Paul said dryly.

"They found him dead the day that issue came out," Collie explained. "Slit his wrists and took a bath. I haven't seen the police records, but it was ruled a suicide." She had been steadily organizing the papers around her as they spoke and was now frowning at a newspaper clipping that didn't seem to have a home.

Anna's eyes fell on the magazine, still draped across her lap. She shoved at it until it wasn't touching her anymore. "Anything else I should know?"

Paul looked at Collie. She shook her head.

"Nothing public. Nothing we could put on the website, even. But Joce gave me the impression the place was falling apart, and Postnikoff's suicide was just part of it. For the past few months, whenever I talked to her, she seemed jumpy." She smiled, and Anna realized that there were tears at the corners of her eyes. "I told her she should quit. Doesn't she know I'm always right?"

Paul patted her arm. It didn't seem to be a natural gesture for him. "Some people don't listen," he said. He turned to Anna. "Last week she told Collie she wanted to give me something for the website—which was odd, because up to that point she'd always refused to talk on the record. She said she had a lot of interesting stories to tell us about *The Rail*."

"It's been a long time since Joce and I were close," Collie said, "but I think I know—knew—her well enough. She had something huge to spill." She shook her head. "Your fucking tie, Paul. We're up here looking for your fucking tie and, meanwhile, Jocelyn is. . . ."

Paul looked at his hands. He wasn't wearing a tie, but his shirt was buttoned all the way up as though he'd had every intention of wearing one. "I only spent five minutes looking for the damned thing. If you think those were the five minutes that she—"

Collie sighed. "Well, what if they were? I mean, how long does it take to . . . you know. Do what he did to her."

Anna wanted to slip out of the room and not come back, but it wasn't much of an option. She pressed Collie's cold hand and looked into those miserable green eyes. "She'd been gone for a while when you found her."

And as far as they knew, Anna was a police consultant—so they'd better believe her. From the looks on their faces, they did.

"I'm sorry about your friend," she added. It wasn't just a platitude.

Collie rubbed her eyes. "Oh . . . thanks, but it's not . . . I saw her last Christmas because we were both home, and I phoned her a few times last summer to dig for dirt, but other than that . . . I mean, we were close in school, but sometimes people change after university, and. . . . I don't think you said anything that sounded like 'tell me your life story,' did you?"

When she lost the bite in her voice and that twist of a smile, Collie also lost about ten years. It was hard to believe she wasn't still in university.

"I would've asked," Anna told her, "if I'd thought of it."

That earned a genuine smile.

"Well, some other time. I know it seems kinda cold to be going over newspaper clippings right now, but in spite of my many reservations about Joce, nobody had any business drowning her. You know? I'd like to find out who it was."

"I didn't know Jocelyn myself," said Paul, "so I don't have a personal stake, but I'm professionally interested . . . and obviously Collie has her reasons for wanting to stay on this. We're good researchers. I was thinking it would be good for all of us if we could work with you."

Oh, sweet Christ. She did have a gun in her purse; she could take it out and shoot the both of them. That would solve the problem. Or she could shoot herself, which would be appropriate. Anna forced a smile. "I'm sorry, but I'm really not allowed to bring anyone else on board. The police department is pretty strict about these things."

Paul had somehow managed to fold his legs up so that his feet were on the seat of his chair. He wrapped his arms around his knees and leaned forward. "Okay," he said, "here's another idea. I don't know how much the police are paying you, but I have a decent advance on the next book. I could hire you as an investigator. Just temporarily, until we've solved the case. I mean, technically Collie is supposed to be promoting my work, not scrounging for gossip. She's been nice enough to do research on this *Rail* thing for me, but I'm sure she wouldn't turn down help."

Okay, bad idea. Obviously. She wasn't a detective.

On the other hand, she'd been doing a lot of questionable things for money of late. And she was, God help her, uniquely equipped for detective work.

Then again, she was also uniquely equipped for committal to a nuthatch. Her hands belonged in her pockets.

"That's an interesting offer, but—"

"Two hundred a day . . . meals, expenses. . . . You told me you weren't from Victoria, so you'll need a place to stay. Is this hotel all right?"

The accountant in possession of Anna's body blinked a few times. "Your publisher must have deep pockets."

"Money's not so hard to come by."

Anna smiled. "If you say so."

"Aren't we wittier than the police? Aren't we better company? Do I need to mention that we are much better dressed? Join us, Anna."

Through all of this, Collie sat very still with her lips pressed together until they nearly disappeared. She was, Anna suspected, going to worry this case the way Paul worried everyone he spoke to.

That odd look in her eyes might be guilt over the fatal five minutes, or regret over something she'd said to Jocelyn years ago. It didn't matter. Anna was pretty sure that girl thought she had a debt to pay.

One of the newspapers took on a splash of colour, the change in appearance drawing Anna's eye to where it lay on the bed. No headline, for some reason. The front page was a photo of a corpse with its face hidden by the same thick red curls that confirmed its identity.

Anna blinked and saw the paper as it had probably been all along. No photo of Collie, just a lot of close text about Postnikoff's death.

Another of her little spells, and this one probably didn't mean anything . . . but damned if it didn't feel prophetic, like a trailer for a memory. Anna had a sudden attack of guilt so profound it might even have put Collie's to shame.

So, maybe Anna wasn't a detective. Maybe that would be a terrible career decision for her. But surely she was qualified to watch someone's back. Would it be so wrong to just do that?

"You're right," said Anna. "You do dress better than the police. I just have one errand to take care of, then I'm all yours."

"I beg your pardon?"

The porch swing creaked as the old man leaned towards her.

"I said," he said, "this isn't what I was looking for. It's a few years off."

Anna looked at the gun in his hands. Unbelievable. "Look. You told Curtis you wanted to buy this gun. We went to a lot of trouble to get it to you. I came all the way out to the end of civilization—"

"The name is Port Alberni, missy."

"Whatever—to bring you this gun. I snuck it over the border so you wouldn't have to worry about the damned paperwork. Curt told you how old the gun was when you agreed to buy it. How can you sit there and tell me you don't want it?"

"Your friend said it was from World War II, which it is, but not the right year."

Christ, what a piece of work.

"So, you speculated and you were wrong. You agreed to buy the gun. Pay up."

"Missy—"

"The name is Ms. Gareau."

"Ms. Gareau, I don't have to buy this gun. I don't want it. I won't buy it. You can take it back to your employer and send him my regards."

"I should take that gun away from you and shoot you with it."

Oh God, had she said that out loud?

His eyes crinkled at the edges and she realized this was entertaining him.

"You'd want to load it first."

She placed her hands on her knees and squeezed tight. It was important to keep her hands busy with something other than swatting this guy.

"I don't want to carry that gun back across the border. Once was bad enough."

He pulled a pipe and tobacco from his coat pocket.

"What you do with it is your business . . . but a lady in the city might have use for a gun. That's an old one, but it probably works just fine. I know a place you could get the ammunition."

"I'm tempted to go there and come straight back here," she told him. He laughed, then coughed.

"Don't take it so hard, my dear. Vancouver Island is lovely this time of year. Enjoy the drive back to Victoria."

There were a lot of things Anna wanted to do, but the only thing she really could do was take the gun and leave.

If there were enough deer in that forest that she had to stop for one every three miles, Anna couldn't see what harm there would be in hitting one. Sure, it would damage the car, but it was Curtis's car, so that would only be a bonus.

"Come on," she muttered into Curtis's cell phone. "Pick up, you bastard."

Not that, strictly speaking, this was Curt's fault, but she had every intention of taking her frustration out on someone.

"Hello, you've reached Millet Antiques and Collectibles. I'm not available right now, but if you leave a message at the sound of the tone. . . ."

Great.

"Curtis, it's me. I'm calling from your cellular phone to tell you that the customer decided against the purchase. Also, he kept calling me 'Missy.' I hope you understand that I still expect to be paid. What I want you to do is figure out who else around here might take this item off my hands, and then call me. You will want to call me at the hotel, and not on your cell phone. You take care, now."

Now she was stuck with that fucking gun in her purse while she pretended to investigate a murder. It was amazing how little time it took for her life to go south.

The phone rang as she stepped out of the shower. She ran for it, grabbing a towel and clothes along the way.

"What?"

"Anna. Nice weather up there, hey? I hear it's actually not raining. Small children are seeing the sun for the first time in their lives. What's all this about about the g-u-n?"

Anna didn't know what it would take to put Curtis out. She had never heard him sound annoyed about anything.

"That's clever," she told him. "Everyone knows the p-i-g-s can't spell."

She put the phone between her ear and shoulder and grabbed a tube of travel mascara that was in disguise as a toothpick.

"Look, Curt," she went on, "your customer refused to buy. He is not interested. Speaking as someone with a felony in her purse, I'm—ow!"

"You okay?" Curt asked.

"Yeah," Anna admitted. "Just poked myself in the eye with a sharp stick. Anyway, I'm wondering what I should do now."

"See a doctor?" Curt suggested.

Anna breathed in and out, slowly. "I don't need your special brand of humour. I need to get rid of the g-u-n."

She looked at the shirts in her hand, trying to decide between silk and cotton. That was a decision she was qualified to handle. Barely.

"I'll ask around," Curtis said. "See if anyone up there is in the market for a Luger. Do you mind staying a few more days?"

The silk looked better, but she knew she'd spill stuff on it and not be able to get it out.

"As it happens, no. I've got a second job."

"Waitressing?" Curt asked. "Whoring?"

Anna dropped the silk shirt on the bed and looked at the cotton one. It seemed a little plain. How the hell did you dress to question witnesses, anyway? "Homicide investigation," she said.

"This phone connection is terrible," Curt commented. He was starting to sound a little nervous. Anna smiled, knowing he'd hear the smile in her voice.

"I forgot my purse in the pool room last night, and some inconsiderate bastard decided to kill a woman in that room a few hours later. Just my luck."

There was a pause before Curtis spoke again. "Was the gun in your purse?"

"Certainly. If it makes you feel better, the victim wasn't shot. So, even if the police had found my purse—which they didn't, because I got to it first—I don't think I would've been arrested for murder. Oh, sure, illegal possession of a firearm, maybe some concealed weapons charges—"

"Would you mind," Curtis interrupted, "explaining how this involves you in a murder investigation?"

"I had to lie to the security guard to get into the crime scene and get my purse back. I told him I was there to consult with the police. Unfortunately, one of the victim's friends overheard me. So now this guy thinks I'm a . . . what the hell did I say I was?"

"I wouldn't know."

"Behavioural psychologist. I think that was it."

She'd put that particular lipstick in her travel pouch because it went with everything. How could it be clashing with her shirt?

"I can see where you needed to get the purse back. Okay? I'm grateful you got the purse back. But for Christ's sake, Anna, just because you told someone you were some kind of profiler or something doesn't mean you have to actually pretend to do the job."

Anna swiped at the lipstick with a tissue. "Mmm. I know, but he really wanted to hire me and it was awkward. He offered me money, Curtis."

"And you're broke." Curtis's voice was a little too friendly. "Well, I guess he's getting an okay deal. I know you're not a profiler and I'd still pay you to solve a murder, if the need ever arose. Did you tell this guy what he was really hiring?"

Maybe she could wear the silk shirt as a sort of blazer over the cotton shirt. And not button it. That might keep the silk out of the splash zone for salad dressing and motor oil and other stains in the making.

"I don't think we need to talk about that. Don't make me sorry I told you."

"Yeah," Curt said, sounding obscenely satisfied. "See, I knew you hadn't told him. Seriously, Anna, if you're going to be. . . . Who got killed, anyway?"

"Some chick," Anna told him. "It's a long story. I don't want to get into it over the phone."

"You're going to, ah . . . press your advantage. Right? Because you know damned well it's the only way in which you're qualified to do something like this."

"I'm going to keep my hands in my pockets," Anna told him. "I watch a lot of cop shows. I can fake my way through."

Curtis cleared his throat. "You are ridiculous. You are nuts. You watch a lot of cop shows? Jesus Christ. Anna, I don't care how much money this guy is offering you—if you're not going to . . . if you're not going to, you shouldn't be doing this at all."

She'd worn demure little gold earrings during her trip across the border in an attempt to look respectable . . . so where the hell were they?

"Anna, are you even listening to me?"

"Yeah. I just. . . ."

Maybe she'd taken them off somewhere, slipped them into her coat pocket. That was the sort of thing she did.

"What are you thinking?"

"I'm not, Curt," Anna told him. "I'm bad at it. I've decided to give it up."

"There's something you're not telling me," Curtis said.

"Usually," Anna confirmed.

Curt said nothing for a long time. Only the sound of distance on the line told Anna he was still there.

"Okay," he said finally. "Tell me half truths. Do something stupid. Get yourself killed. See if I care. But I'd like to know why in God's name you refuse—"

"I have to go," Anna told him. "I can't find my earrings. I'll talk to you later."

He said something else as she placed the receiver in its cradle, but she couldn't make it out. Whatever it was, she probably wouldn't have found it informative. He certainly didn't know where her earrings were.

"Hi," Anna said, straddling a chair in the hotel's coffee-shop. "Remember me?"

The security guard didn't look any happier than he had at seven thirty that morning. He nodded and reached for his coffee cup.

"Yeah . . . you're the police consultant."

Perfect.

"Can I ask you a few questions?"

He shut his eyes and dropped his face so that the coffee's steam hit his skin.

"I already talked to the police. For hours. Can't you just look at their files?"

Anna almost laughed, and resolved to get some sleep in the near future. She couldn't afford to be punchy. "I'm a behavioural scientist," she said. Scientist? Psychologist? Hopefully he didn't remember. "I need first-hand reports whenever possible. I'm sorry to make you do this, but. . . ."

"Aw, that's okay. Just give me a minute with the coffee."

"Sure."

They were the only ones in the coffee-shop, which looked out over the pool. Anna bit back a smile at the thought that the coffee-shop would make a record profit if it were open. People would be lined up around the block to eat next to a crime scene.

Not that there was much to see—the police were mostly gone, yellow tape blocked off most of the room, and a guard was posted at the door. Anna watched as he turned away curious guests and a member of the housekeeping staff who kept asking when they would be able to drain the pool.

"Strange world," Anna commented, mostly to herself. The guard nodded from behind his coffee cup.

"I could tell you stories," he said. "You ever work in a hotel? Probably not."

"No," said Anna, "but I've worked a lot of odd jobs. I mean, really odd. Are you the one who found the body?"

"No, thank Christ. I have a nervous stomach. One of the janitors found that woman, God rest her. She wasn't even a guest—just came in to meet some guy."

"You know anything about the guy?"

"Nah, I just heard him talking to the police. He said he's the guy who runs that *Simple Explanation* website. You been there?"

As if it were someplace she could get into a car and drive to. Anna tried not to look lost. She suspected a behavioural something-or-other would have to be comfortable with the internet.

"I don't have an account right now," she said. "Is it any good?"

"Sort of. He's usually right. But it's mostly businesses and politicians, and I don't know who half the people are. His thing about Universal Records was cool."

"The janitor who found the body, what's his name?"

"Trent something-or-other. I forget his last name. The night auditor would know."

What the hell did a hotel need with an accountant in the middle of the night?

"Auditor?"

His coffee disposed of, the guard had turned to stacking cream cups in a small and shaky pyramid.

"Yeah," he said, not looking up. "You know, the guy at the front desk? Last night that was Bryan, but I'm pretty sure he's gone. He'll be in around ten tonight."

Anna took a few packets of Nutra-Sweet and leaned them against the cream cups, putting walls around the structure. The guard nodded solemnly. When the light hit his brush cut, Anna could see that he wasn't more than a decade from bald.

"Careful," he warned. "It's not too stable."

"I'm always careful," Anna lied. "Is Trent still around?"

"He shouldn't be," the guard said, "but he probably is. I'm thinking he's into this violent death thing."

It was hard to know how to take that.

"You mean you think he did it?"

"Hmm." The guard sat up straight and looked over their construction. A voice behind Anna startled her badly enough that she shuddered.

"Look upon my works, ye mighty, and despair."

Anna turned to face Collie, who was munching on a cloudy pink popsicle and smiling wearily at the guard.

"It's just something you say when you construct a sphinx or whatever," she explained, waving her snack at the pyramid. "Hello again."

"Hi," the guard said, tentatively returning her smile. "You look better."

"I'm bad with surprises."

"You weren't in your room," Anna said, sliding to the inside of the bench to make room for Collie to sit. "I knocked, about an hour ago."

Collie shrugged and kept standing. "I went out for food. Found this instead. Who do you think he thinks did it?"

Judging from the look on the guard's face, Anna wasn't the only one who hadn't followed that.

"When I got here," Collie said with exaggerated patience, "you were saying to him, 'you mean you think he did it?'"

"Oh. I meant the janitor," Anna said. "Apparently he likes violence."

"I didn't mean it like that. He collects old weapons and stuff. I just figured he might get off on the atmosphere. I bet he's lurking around the hotel somewhere," the guard said.

Collie raised thin eyebrows. They were probably stylish. Anna wanted to search her luggage and take her tweezers away.

"This guy lurks?"

"It's not like he's dangerous. He just does it for grins."

Anna didn't know what this generation considered not dangerous, but she was pretty sure wondering about it meant you were getting old. Collie nodded thoughtfully as she licked a murky pink stream from the inside of her wrist.

"For grins. Good. What does he look like?"

This wasn't helping Anna's cover.

"You should leave my job to me," Anna said, "Ms. Kostyna."

Collie looked at her sharply, then caught on and plastered a bored expression on her face.

"Whatever," she said. "I was just curious. But if I were you, I'd want to talk with this janitor."

"I was getting around to that," Anna told her with a dark look. She was definitely going to have a word with her . . . uh . . . client. She turned to the guard. "What does Trent look like?"

"About six feet, maybe six one. Black hair in a ponytail, goatee. . . . I think he's thirty-two. He usually wears a black duster. You could check the smokers' lounge in the back alley."

"Thanks." Anna picked up the last packet of sweetener and the coffee-shop darkened. Collie and the guard started to fade from view. She shut her eyes, hoping it wouldn't happen. Maybe if she just squeezed her eyes shut she could head it off.

She opened them again and saw that the coffee-shop looked much the same. She could vaguely see Collie and the guard, if she tried hard enough, but they were overlaid with images of a waiter and waitress exchanging words as they refilled the caddies.

"Did you have her lined up?" the waitress asked. "Because you were out with that cooze less than a week after you dumped my ass. Wanna explain that one to me?" She turned to Anna. "What do you think?"

Anna's stomach clenched. She shook her head and felt the packet fall from her fingers. When was she going to learn not to touch . . . well, anything?

"Don't mention it," the guard was saying. His voice brought Anna back to the present, the actual. No waitress and waiter fighting next to her table. Just one Anna, one security guard, and one Collie.

Right.

"Yeah," she said, hoping it was somehow responsive.

Collie tagged along as Anna roamed the halls in search of the fabled janitor, slurping the last few drops of popsicle from her hand.

"What was that thing, anyway?" Anna inquired.

"Some strawberry-banana yogurt with . . . I don't know. They're on cheap in the confectionery across the street. Probably 'cause it's January. So what do you think? Did this janitor actually see anything or. . . ."

"I don't know. I'm going to ask him. I think he just found the, ah . . . your friend. Look, I thought you were more of a paper researcher. I don't think it's a real good idea for you to follow me around. I figure maybe you could do the computer work, go through newspaper morgues, whatever you research types do. And I'll do the interviewing. That's how I think we should work."

"You're supposed to be assisting me," Collie pointed out. "I'll follow you anywhere I want to."

Anna peered down the hallway, searching for a door that might lead to the back alley. "You probably will," she agreed, "but you shouldn't. Don't you think it looks a little weird—me questioning people with you standing beside me? I mean, they still think I'm with the police. I assure you, that's the only reason they're telling me anything. And for all these people know, you and your boss killed that woman. You have to know they're speculating about it."

"Let 'em," said Collie, pushing on a locked door. "Jesus, I should've brought a ball of twine with me. How can it be so hard to find a back way out of this hotel?"

"What we need to do is find someone who looks twitchy and follow them to their smoke break." Anna smiled a little, thinking that sounded very much like something a behavioural scientist might say. "Collie—"

"I have a fourteen-day waiting period on my nickname," Collie interrupted. "It's Colette until then."

This girl was a certified weirdo. Anna shook her head.

"Colette," she amended, "I want these people to speak freely to me. I don't think they will with you hovering over my shoulder."

Collie was looking at something down the hall. "See the way that guy keeps putting his hand in his jacket pocket? I bet he's a smoker."

So that was how it was going to be.

"Fine," said Anna. "Hobble me. Handicap me from the start."

Collie gave her an astonishingly sweet smile. "It's a pleasure to work with you."

"He's coming this way," Anna responded. "So shut up."

"It's a little nippy out here," Collie said. It was the first thing she'd said since Anna had told her to shut up, but in spite of that, Anna didn't think she'd taken it badly.

"You might feel better if you weren't sitting on metal," she said.

"True."

They'd been loitering in the back alley for a good twenty minutes, watching the smokers' lounge from what they hoped was an unobtrusive position. Collie, with complete disregard for her clothes, was sitting cross-legged on top of a dumpster. "What would my mother say," she sighed, "if she saw me now?"

Collie sounded oddly content. Anna raised an eyebrow at her. "Hard to say. I don't know your mother."

"Well, she—ah ha! Look—freakish janitor at three o'clock."

Anna looked. He was pretty much as the guard had described him. A little taller maybe, and a fair bit scruffier. Given a world of options, Anna probably wouldn't have chosen to meet him in an alley.

Collie jumped from the top of the dumpster and landed lightly behind Anna. Showtime.

"Excuse me," Anna said as they approached. The janitor was hunched over to light a cigarette and turned without straightening. Columbo with a black goatee.

"What can I do for you ladies?"

There was a gun in his hand. Anna's hand slipped inside her purse before she realized the gun was a cigarette lighter.

"Cute," she said, nodding at it. The janitor grinned, showing yellow teeth. It was a nice enough smile anyway.

"I know I am . . . and you're in luck, because I'm free tonight."

Collie opened her mouth. Anna cut her off. "We're here on business. The security guard says you're the one who found the body."

"Keith is absolutely right. I did indeed."

His expression was still friendly, but his eyes had narrowed a little. He leaned back against the wall and took a long drag on his cigarette. "Ahhh . . . I needed that. So, you want to know about the floater."

For a moment, Anna felt badly for Collie. Then she remembered that she'd told the girl to take a hike. Anything she heard and didn't like was her own fault. "Yeah. What time did you find the body?"

"Six twenty-five. My shift ends at six thirty. I cut through the pool room to get to my locker. I knew she hadn't been dead too long, 'cause she was still floating. See, a body will float for a while because it still has air in it. Then it sinks. Eventually gas builds up from decomposition and the body pops"—he demonstrated with his hands, raising the cigarette—"to the surface again. I knew she hadn't been there long enough to decompose, 'cause I did a pass through the pool room at a little after three and I would've noticed a body in the pool."

This detective work wasn't so hard.

"She was killed between three AM and six twenty-five, then?"

The janitor wiggled his cigarette. He seemed to think he was Groucho Marx. "That's not likely. Keith opens the pool room at six every morning, in case anyone wants a morning swim. Coffee-shop opens at six thirty. I hear the lovely victim was supposed to meet some people in the coffee-shop at six thirty, which explains what she was doing in the pool room at such an ungodly hour. Did either of you happen to see the corpus delectable? She was a treat. I would've liked to see her with a little more life in her."

"You weren't her type," Collie muttered. Anna lifted her

heel and rocked back until she was resting most of her weight on Collie's foot.

"Ow!"

"I beg your pardon, ma'am?" said the janitor. Collie smiled with tight lips.

"Nothing. Don't mind me."

"So," Anna put in, "you figure whoever killed her showed up between six and six twenty-five."

"That's what I told the police. Are you ladies private dicks? Because I personally think there's nothing more sad and lonely than a private—"

"Yeah, understood," Anna said quickly. She was rapidly getting a headache. The sound of Collie snickering at her shoulder did not help. "We're looking into this privately," she added.

"I won't tell anyone," the janitor whispered, looking over his shoulder. He was making a high-pitched wheezing sound that Anna realized was laughter.

"Do you know if anybody saw anything?"

"Oh, yeah," he said, his eyes huge. "The murderer probably saw the whole thing."

Anna nodded. This was clearly going nowhere. "In that case," she said, "I guess I'll have to ask him."

"Why doesn't somebody turn a hose on that man?"

Collie was pacing and chewing on a lock of hair.

Anna flopped down on her bed and stared at the ceiling. "Do you know any of Jocelyn's co-workers? Can you get us into *The Rail* offices to talk with people?"

"Finally," Collie said. Anna shut her eyes. That wasn't a damned answer.

"Finally?"

"Yeah." The bed moved as Collie sat on the edge of it. "Finally, you're going to do some behavioural scientist stuff."

Anna was surprised to feel genuine indignation. "I'm a consultant. I don't normally have to collect basic information about time of death and who might have seen something, but in this case I'm handling it all. You should just be glad I have a clue what I'm doing."

No question about it, she was going to hell with all the other damned liars.

"What were you doing at the crime scene this morning?" Collie asked. Anna considered her options, eyes still blissfully shut.

Trying to stay out of prison. No, that wouldn't sound so good.

"Yawning, mostly." She didn't have to open her eyes to know that Collie was glaring at her. "The Victoria Police knew I was in Victoria, so they asked me to take a look at the layout of the scene. I can usually see the difference between a ritual killing and something that was motivated by profit or revenge."

So now her story was that she was in Victoria on business, that the police had somehow known that, and, by an astonishing coincidence, she happened to be staying in this very hotel.

She'd told the security guard that she'd been called at six thirty, which turned out to be only five minutes after the body was discovered. And, to make matters worse, she'd then arrived at the pool room over half an hour later. She'd seen episodes of the *A-Team* with more internal logic than this mess of lies.

Collie had said something. Anna turned her head and opened her eyes, just a crack. "What?"

"I said, *and*? Was it a ritual murder?"

Anna tilted her purse so Collie couldn't see the contents and carefully fished for her ibuprofen. "Obviously she was killed because of her meeting with you and Paul," she said. Collie was drumming pale gold fingernails on the bed.

"But what did it look like to you, before you knew anything about it?"

Good question. Anna wanted the answer so badly that her stomach ached. "I couldn't tell," she confessed.

"Oh." Collie's shoulders slumped for a moment. Then she sat up and looked at Anna with bright eyes. "But that probably means something in itself, right? Maybe that the guy who did this had a motive, but he enjoyed it . . . or that he did it for pleasure, but it happened to work for him in another way?"

Anna found the ibuprofen and swallowed it dry. She offered the bottle to Collie, who shook her head. "Look, Collie . . . sorry, Colette . . . they call it behavioural science, but it's not an exact science. I don't know what anything means, yet. I'm just collecting impressions. If I figure anything out, I promise you'll be the first to know."

Collie was chewing her lip again, pulling off what remained of her lipstick. "Anna . . . are you sure you know what you're doing?"

Anna headed for the middle ground between the truth and a flat-out lie. "I've never done a real investigation. I'm not a cop. I just look things over, answer a few questions, and go home. But I have more experience than you and your boss do, and besides, you're a pair of loose cannons. You can hire a real private investigator if you want, but I recommend that the two of you be supervised."

To her surprise, Collie was smiling when she finished. "Is that your professional opinion?"

Sure—the opinion of a professional indigent.

"Yes, it is. Where is Paul, by the way?"

"On the phone with his publisher, last I saw him."

Anna took a good look at her face, but couldn't quite tell what she was thinking. "That frost you at all? Under the circumstances?"

Collie got a funny look on her face for a moment, then grinned. "Hell, no. I'm his publicist, right? Technically, I should be notifying the media that Dr. Paul Echlin is on the scene of this crime, ready to get to the bottom of things in his inimitable fashion. Actually, I should probably bail on you and make a few calls right now. I know that will break your heart."

Anna sat up and ran fingers through the hair that was stuck to the back of her neck. "Be careful what you tell the press," she advised. "Don't say he's investigating or that he's hired someone. 'Get to the bottom of things' is good. It's vague. I don't want to annoy the police."

"Okay. Anything else?"

"Yeah. You never told me if you knew people at *The Rail*. I mean, besides. . . ."

Collie stood up and straightened her blazer. "I do. Should I call them?"

"Make appointments, if you can. I want to talk with as many of Jocelyn's co-workers as possible."

Collie nodded.

"Okay. I'll catch you later. I'm not certain, but I think Paul would like us to make ourselves available for dinner."

"I'll clear my calendar," Anna said.

Collie was out the door and down the hall when it occurred to Anna to call after her. "Colette?"

She stopped and turned her head. "Yes?"

"Don't meet anyone without me. Or Paul, at least. Okay?"

Colette turned completely and stood like a gunfighter, hands on her hips. "This can't be a female thing," she said, "unless you're an exceptionally convincing transvestite. So you must think I'm a child. I'm not. I can take care of myself."

Anna leaned against the door frame. "Actually, it's an 'I'm-big-and-you're-little' thing. And this is personal for you, so I bet you're not being reasonable. This is a bad time to make bad decisions."

Collie kept perfectly still for a long moment. "I'm not that little," she said finally.

Anna smiled. "Everyone is, next to me. I'll be around the hotel. Find me when you're done with the phone calls."

"Okay."

Anna stayed in the doorway and watched her go until she was out of sight.

The pool room was visible from the lobby, just. From the overstuffed chair she'd planted herself in, Anna could see the closed coffee-shop. Next door, a forest of silk plants stood against the glass walls of the pool room and hid the pool from view.

Though she couldn't see it from where she sat, Anna remembered seeing a row of plants between the coffee-shop and the pool area. Those plants were too short to hide anything. The whole idea was that diners would be able to look at that tacky tropical paradise while they were eating clubhouse sandwiches and pretending they weren't in a strange city.

The pool room had opened at six. Jocelyn was supposed to meet Paul and Collie at six thirty in the coffee-shop. If she'd arrived early, say six twenty, she could easily have gone to the pool room to wait.

Was it possible that Jocelyn's watch was fast? Maybe Collie could arrange for them to get a look at her personal effects.

Anna went to the coffee-shop entrance. To see the pool, you'd have to be in the outer row of tables. It was possible that the staff were in the kitchen getting ready to open and missed the murder entirely. It was more than possible—it must be what had happened.

And that was weird. Anna had never worked in a hotel, but she had worked in restaurants. They were usually crawling with staff in the half-hour before opening. How could you drown someone in plain view of all those people and not be seen?

She flirted with the idea of taking some of the money Paul was paying her and hiring an actual detective, but she couldn't see what good it would do. She wasn't dumb. If this case could make sense to anyone, she'd be getting it.

She wandered to the pool room door. Still closed and, from the looks of it, locked. Maybe if she hung around long enough, the murderer would return to the scene of the crime.

Or maybe not.

There was something in one of those Nero Wolfe books about the folly of starting a hundred-piece jigsaw puzzle when you had only two pieces. That was the problem. She just didn't have enough information. After she'd—

"It's interesting," a soft voice said. Anna bit her tongue to keep from screaming and spun around to find Collie standing behind her.

"Christ on a sidecar," Anna spat out. It was one of her grandfather's expressions and it made her sound about a hundred years old, but she felt as though she'd aged that much in the past few seconds. "What is wrong with you?"

"My medical records are privileged," said Collie. "It's interesting that a person can stand behind this monstrosity and watch the door to the pool room without being seen."

She was pointing at a screen that was meant to look Oriental. It did, in the sense that it looked as though it came from a factory in Taiwan. It hid the spot where the outside wall of the pool room jutted out and became the front wall of the coffeeshop. Presumably Collie had been standing behind it as Anna walked right past her.

"This place," Collie went on, not pausing for breath, "has the worst collection of terrible decorating schemes I have ever seen. Since when were faux Oriental and nouveau Victorian complementary looks? They don't even look good by themselves."

"I take it," Anna said, not warmly, "you've wrapped up your publicity work. How did the phone calls go?"

Collie was moving fast to keep up with Anna's long legs. Anna considered slowing down, but she didn't make concessions for people who leapt at her from the shadows. Colette was just lucky she hadn't been shot.

"The receptionist wants to talk with us tomorrow. She'll meet us for lunch."

Anna patted her pockets for her room key. "Friend of yours?"

"I met her through Jocelyn," Collie said.

Having nothing to say to that, Anna held her tongue and followed Collie to her room.

"So . . . dinner?"

Collie nodded. She was glaring into the mirror and poking at her hair, apparently trying to find something she'd lost in it.

"One of *The Rail's* regular freelancers is an old friend of Paul's. As long as we buy, he'll talk to us over supper. I should say, as long as Paul buys. Getting Paul to pay for things is a hobby for this guy. I'm warning you now—Paul's friend isn't the world's best dinner companion."

Anna leaned against the door. She was starting to think a nap might be a good idea. "What do you mean by that?"

"You'll see." Collie gave up on her hair and flopped on

the bed, stomach down. Once the bed stopped bouncing, she rested her chin on folded arms. "I think Paul might want you to pretend to be his date or something."

Anna took her turn at the mirror and swiped at a streak of eyeliner that had dropped to her cheek. "His date. That's cute. Where are we eating, the Regal Beagle?"

Collie laughed. The bed shook again. "I'll tell him to come up with a better line." She cast an eye on her suitcase, resting half open on the dresser. "I'm gonna get changed."

Anna's lipstick was gone, which might be a good thing. It was frustrating, though. Other women's make-up didn't seem to blow off in a light breeze. "We're not going anywhere fancy, are we? I didn't pack for it, and I don't think I can exactly borrow your clothes."

"I repeat," Collie said, crossing to her luggage and tugging a blouse from its depths, seemingly at random. "Paul is buying." After a quick glance at the fabric, she headed for the bathroom and tugged the door shut behind her. Her muffled voice added, "Anyplace that cheap bastard is willing to pick up the tab . . . let's just say, I wouldn't worry about it."

Anna commandeered the bathroom after Collie was done with it. She thought maybe just being in a bathroom would do something for her appearance. Maybe her hair would be fooled into thinking it had been combed.

She gave that plan a few minutes to work, then went back into the main room to find Collie's door propped open with a garbage can and voices drifting through the connecting doorway to Paul's room.

Jesus. They were investigating a murder, maybe a few murders, and all the doors were wide open. If Anna really did manage to keep these people alive, she'd be an enemy to evolution.

Collie was on the phone in Paul's room, telling someone that she couldn't tell them anything yet. At the table, Paul was listening with rapt attention to a pudgy man who was delivering some sort of lecture.

". . . at least twenty seconds," he was saying as Anna entered the room. "Don't ask me how they know, but that's what I'm told. You really can take a decapitated head, hold it up, and let it take a good look at its body. It's not gonna say anything, unfortunately, so who knows what it's thinking. Maybe nothing. If you hooked that head up to an EEG, maybe—"

Anna coughed, trying to make it sound natural. To her relief, the pudgy man shut his mouth. Mission accomplished.

"Hello, Anna," Paul said cheerfully. "Roger, this is Anna Gareau. She's looking into this case for me. Anna, Roger Denton does some writing for *The Rail*. Maybe you recall his series on Canadian internment camps."

"Um, no," Anna said, turning to Roger. "Sorry . . . I've been out of the country. *The Rail* must be an interesting place to work."

"Well," said Roger, standing to offer a hand, "I don't work there, per se. But there's no denying it's been a wild year."

Anna shook his hand. Moist, as expected. God, she hoped that was just sweat.

"I guess we might as well get going," Paul said, and Anna saw that he was on his feet. There was something insectoid about the quick, convulsive way that guy moved. Anna pictured his arms jerking as he forced a woman underwater. She shivered.

"You cold?" asked Paul.

Anna shook her head. "Goose walked over my grave."

Collie finished her phone call and reached for a thick black fun fur coat. It put Anna in mind of a giant teddy bear.

"I'm cold," she said, "but that's not news. Where are we eating?"

"The Keg, okay?"

Collie grinned broadly. "Paul, that could be as much as thirty bucks a person. You sure that won't bankrupt you?"

To Anna's astonishment, Paul stuck his tongue out at his assistant. "I'm writing it off," he said.

Roger laughed, his voice dropping an octave to a deep baritone. Collie was smiling as she pulled car keys from her purse. Anna could see where the joke was, but it didn't really tickle her, since she'd never spent that much on a meal in her life. If they thought twenty bucks a person was a cheap meal, it was no wonder that moneyed people were always broke.

In any event, this was her chance to live large. She was definitely ordering the surf and turf.

There was no arguing with Colette's point, which was that she'd brought them to the restaurant in one piece. And yes, it was something that Collie had been driving for over ten years without an accident. But Anna would be damned if she was letting that road hazard drive on the way back to the hotel.

"I love Edmonton," Collie was saying as the hostess led them to their table. "I do, but the drivers there are pussies! Here in BC, people know how to drive."

"Where I come from," Anna commented, "Alberta drivers are considered maniacs."

Collie stopped in the process of unfolding her napkin and arched an eyebrow at her. "Where's that?"

"Saskatchewan. Prince Albert."

"Hah. I should've known you were a prairie girl. You're direct."

"If you mean I have no manners," said Anna, "that's a product of heredity, not environment."

"I hear that," Paul said mildly. He'd taken off his glasses to let them defog and was watching them as though they might try to escape. "I have the 'using the wrong fork' gene, myself."

"You're in luck," Roger told him from behind a menu. "There's only one fork in this place setting. I may not be able to eat my salad."

Paul snorted. "You've never eaten a salad in your life. They're just obstacles between you and your steak."

"Ah." Roger set the menu down. "Speaking of stakes, I'm reading a new book about Vlad the Impaler. It seems he—"

"Hold that thought for dessert," Paul advised. "When I pay for a meal, I want to enjoy it."

It was an interesting experience, sitting next to a man who could have killed someone . . . watching as he used a butter knife, thinking about where his hands might have been twelve hours ago.

Anna didn't have any reason to think Paul had done it. For all she knew it was just nerves. She wasn't accustomed to looking at people as suspects in a murder.

Of course, if she really wanted to know more about Mr. Echlin, his coat was touching her chair. Easy enough to just reach down and. . . .

And drive herself completely and irredeemably nuts. She lifted her hands from her lap and reached for a roll to butter. Idle hands did the devil's work.

The salad bar kept her occupied for a while, more with watching the others than with loading her own plate.

Paul was a devotee of rabbit food. Not a huge surprise.

True to Paul's word, Roger avoided anything that resembled salad. He covered a large plate with cheeses, olives, and filled a huge bowl of cream of mushroom soup. He'd brought a fork with him from the table and eschewed the tongs in favour of vigourously stabbing his selections.

Collie took one of nearly everything, from a slice of melon to a single baby corn, until her plate was a bizarre mosaic that didn't look a thing like food.

If she really had been a behavioural scientist, Anna probably could have divined something about their personalities from the way they approached a salad bar. Hell, she could probably have written a book on the subject. As it stood, all she could do was glance around at the other patrons to see if they'd noticed she was dining with freaks.

Happily, they seemed oblivious.

They'd been back in their seats for a few minutes when Anna noticed that Paul wasn't eating. He'd speared a piece of carrot and was slowly twirling it back and forth, staring at it as though it held all the mysteries of the universe. Anna put down her own fork and watched him. She was the only one who didn't jump when he finally spoke.

"Roger, do you have any idea what Jocelyn Lowry wanted to tell me?"

Roger choked on a piece of cheese and coughed until it

landed on his plate. "You don't waste time easing into things, do you?" He swiped at his mouth with a napkin. "I barely knew Jocelyn. She was in layout, wasn't she?"

"Yeah." As she spoke, Collie was slicing a radish with surgical precision. "She knew you. She said she photocopied you at last year's Christmas party."

Roger grinned. "You expect me to remember that? She probably did, but I remember her from a few years back. I was doing a story on neo-paganism for *Island Life* and somebody at *The Rail* pointed me in her direction. I guess she used to be into that kind of thing."

Something on her lap was suddenly very interesting to Collie. As she looked down, her hair fell to hide her face. "Yeah," she mumbled.

"Right . . . well, she gave me addresses for a nightclub and a couple of shops. I sent her a package of sage as a thank you. She seemed like a nice kid."

Paul had rocked back in his chair. He really did have terrible table manners. "This whole thing with Postnikoff's article, his suicide . . . you must have an opinion."

"Hmm. Blood and circuses." Roger finished his soup, slowly, before continuing. "I have opinions for a living, Paul. I can't give them out for free."

"You ordered a very large steak."

"That's true." He drummed heavy fingers on the table. "I'm not sure what to say. This business with Postnikoff was hugely strange, but I see it as a continent in an ocean of weirdness. Do you know that Eve Harris is taking a whacko break?"

"Collie?"

Collie looked up, brushed hair from her face, and offered Paul a shrug. "Someone else has been writing the lifestyle column for the past few months, but I didn't hear anything about it from Joce. I figured Harris was on mat leave or something."

"That's what you were supposed to think. Everyone who knew better agreed not to tell anyone, out of consideration for Eve. She's a little prim, but she's a good enough shit."

Their meals arrived before he could say anything else. Paul was actually squirming in his chair as he waited, and Collie looked as though she'd like to join him. Roger, who already knew the secret, took a bite of his steak before alleviating the suspense. "I shouldn't be telling you this, but since you're trying to solve Jocelyn's murder, Eve would probably okay it. Around the middle of August, the staff at *The Rail* walked in to find photographs of Eve Harris all over the building."

That was shiver-worthy, but it was hard to see how it could land someone in a nuthouse.

"Could it have been a joke?" Anna asked.

Roger's shoulders shook and she realized that he was laughing. "Pretty sick joke. These weren't your garden-variety pictures. For one thing, she wasn't wearing much in the way of clothes."

Paul folded his hands and brought them up to hide a smile. "Spicy," he said. Covering his mouth had been a waste of time, because his eyes clearly showed how much he was enjoying this story.

"Spicier than you know," said Roger. "She wasn't alone. Think of a position, think of a bed partner, think of a household pet—I'm telling you, Eve Harris has been photographed with it."

"Funny," Paul murmured. "I never saw her mention bestiality in her suggestions for gracious living. Do you have any of those pictures?"

"I think they've all been destroyed. If any of them slipped out of the building, I don't know about it."

"If," Collie put in, "I can interrupt Paul's fantasy life for a moment, I can't help wondering if anyone checked those photographs for tampering. You can do some pretty amazing things with Photoshop."

"I'm told they were the real thing," Roger said. "Not that it mattered all that much from Eve's point of view—it wasn't as if she could show her face around *The Rail* after that."

"So she checked into a mental hospital?" Collie asked, setting her fork on the table.

"No, that came after they verified the photos. Everyone figured, okay, she's a little uptight at the office, maybe she has a wild side in the off hours. But she says no. Even after they told her the pictures were real, she still said they had to be fakes.

She claims she's never done such things in her life."

That piece of lobster had been sitting in the butter for way too long. Anna fished it out. "She has, though," she said, glancing at Roger. "If the pictures are legit."

"She must have, but she doesn't remember it. Just like Postnikoff said he didn't remember writing that article. In fact, I'm pretty sure that's the last thing he said to anyone."

Paul was shaking his head and grinning with one side of his mouth. He probably thought he looked sardonic. Anna thought he looked more like a stroke victim.

"So," he said, "she's a liar, and Postnikoff was a liar. I specialize in knowing what people do behind closed doors. Everyone has secrets. I'm starting to think that Postnikoff simply slipped a gear and publicized the contents of his skull. Obviously, Miss Manners got careless. For those with large kinks, cameras should be verboten in the bedroom." He met Roger's eyes. "Explain to me why I'm wrong."

It wasn't a challenge. It was a command. The breezy affability had vanished from Paul's tone. He had what Anna's grandfather had called knife-smarts, and Anna could swear she'd heard the whisper of them sliding from their sheaths.

Roger's eyes widened. Collie didn't seem surprised. Most likely she'd been on the receiving end of that tone herself. She was calmly dissecting her stir-fry the way she had her salad.

"Why you're . . ." Roger shook his head. "Paul, you're obviously wrong, and you know it. Your theory doesn't explain why a large number of people at *The Rail* would go bugfuck in one year. I know a lot of stories I haven't told you yet. And it certainly doesn't explain why Jocelyn Lowry would be killed for making an appointment to see you. I know secrets are your stock in trade, but they wouldn't be if secrets could actually be kept. If there had been something this deeply wrong with Lou Postnikoff, somebody would have known. You, snoop that you are, would have known. And I'm prepared to change my stance on Eve Harris. You explain to me how she could parade around Victoria in bondage gear without somebody getting wind of it."

"Just so," Paul said softly. It was a sated, post-coital sound. "Tell me the rest of your stories."

Roger poked at his steak. "I'm not sure this is thick enough."

"I'll buy dessert."

Roger nodded and cut off another piece of steak. "Remember when Janet Trifa took over the entertainment news?"

"Took over for Mark Ling." Collie said.

Roger's shoulders shook again. "You really have been eating and sleeping this case, haven't you?"

Collie kept her eyes on her food. "What happened to Ling?"

"He took a leave of absence after his apartment building burned down. I don't know where he is now, but I'm guessing he signed up for a funny farm vacation."

That drew Collie's attention away from her food.

"Not," she said dryly, "I take it, because of the trauma of his stuff going up in flames."

Roger reached for his wine glass. "Who knows? Nobody knows anything, and I can promise you nobody asked, but I can tell you this—a week before the apartment building went up, the fire alarm went off at *The Rail*. No big deal, as it turns out. Just a small fire. But it was in Mark Ling's wastebasket."

That didn't sound coincidental, but it wasn't clear where the connection should be made.

"Somebody started a fire in his trash and then burned his house down?" Anna asked.

Roger shook his head. "No. A lot of people were in the room when the wastebasket fire started. Mark lit that fire himself."

That had to be the sort of thing that would interest a behavioural scientist.

"Any history of pyromania?" Anna inquired, hoping to God she was saying it right.

"Nope. No one knows why he did it. And if he torched his apartment building—which I kind of think he did—no one seems to know why he'd do that, either. Out of the blue."

Collie was chewing on her hair. It wasn't an attractive habit. "Jesus Christ," she said. "Has anyone checked out the ventilation system? The water cooler?"

"The building was checked three times. They brought some

high-toned specialist in and he said it was fine. No lead in the pipes, nothing. Besides, it's not as if there was a degeneration and then these people finally snapped. We're looking at absolutely no warning. Zero to sixty on the fruitcake highway in under a minute."

It had to say something about a guy, that he knew so many euphemisms for crazy.

"That's sensitive," she said, looking Roger in the eye.

"You've got to be sensitive," he replied, "if you want to get laid. Broads go for that crap."

That was the sort of thing Curtis might say, and Roger was displaying the shit-eating grin that Curt would wear while he said it. Anna felt a flash of kinship.

"If you do that 'sensitive guy' routine a lot, you must not get many dates."

Roger was running his tongue over his teeth, hunting down the last of his steak. "Don't need 'em. I've been married for thirteen years."

Anna looked to Paul for confirmation. He nodded. "She's a lovely woman. A saint. I believe she's paying for something she did in a past life. What is it she does again, Roger, besides live with regret?"

"She's a parasitologist. Her two greatest loves are me and trichinae, possibly not in that order. You notice I ordered my steak well done."

Collie pushed her plate away, looking slightly green.

"You can't get trichinosis from chicken," Roger said kindly. Collie brought her napkin to her mouth.

"I'd just as soon move on to dessert anyway. Unless there's something about cheesecake I should know."

Roger swallowed baked potato. "I wouldn't let it sit out," he said, "but I'm sure you don't have to worry about that here. Did Paul ever tell you about the time he and I were in Mexico City and—"

"I didn't," said Paul, loudly enough that other diners turned to stare. "I didn't," he repeated at a normal volume, "for a reason. I don't know what you and Sandy talk about at dinner, but for God's sake. . . ."

"Understood. I guess I should be singing for my supper anyway. Let me think." He shut his eyes and took a deep breath. "Mmm. The lawsuits."

Collie had twisted around to see the dessert display. At the word "lawsuits," she turned so quickly that Anna suspected she'd hurt her neck. "I didn't hear about any lawsuits."

"I know. They settled out of court."

Paul tipped the last of the wine into his glass. "It's not uncommon for a large magazine to be sued."

"No, but I can think of three incidents in the past year that were . . . unusual. Do you know what they have for pie here?"

Paul stared at him. "Do I look like our waiter? What do you mean by unusual?"

"They should never have happened. There was an article on child abuse in amateur sport where some guy was named as a convicted offender. Truth was, he'd never even been up on charges. Probably never touched a kid in his life. Bob Klebeck printed a bank president's unlisted telephone number claiming it was some sort of financial assistance hotline. What else? Oh yeah, *The Rail* published a lovely piece mourning the death of some scientist who is apparently very much alive."

"So, was anyone fired over this?" Collie asked, wide-eyed.

Roger shook his head. "No. The writers were . . . are reliable. Been there for years. They all claim that they can't fathom how these mistakes were made. Klebeck produced a draft of his column that had the correct phone number. If it hadn't been for Postnikoff . . . and Eve, and Mark . . . it would have looked like tampering. But given the circumstances, I'm perfectly willing to believe those writers just don't remember what they wrote."

"I missed all that," Collie said. She sounded miserable. "It never occurred to me to look at issues of *The Rail* from before Postnikoff's last article. Stupid."

Poor kid. It wasn't as if she were a professional detective.

"I hear," Anna said gently, "that a good piece of cheesecake can turn back time."

Collie smiled without much feeling and picked up her fork. "Okay, but I don't just want it to be yesterday, or six months ago," she said. "I want to be fourteen again. I liked fourteen. Is there anything else we should know about *The Rail*?"

Roger pursed his lips. "Three lawsuits, one suicide, one rash of pornography, one arson, and a partridge in a pear tree. I think that covers it. But I've got to say again, I don't work there. There could be any number of things I don't know."

"I never have a tape recorder when I need one," Paul complained. "Did everyone enjoy their meal?"

They said that they did, which didn't seem to please their host.

"Are you sure?" he asked. "Because if you didn't, if you found a cockroach or suchlike, they probably wouldn't charge us."

"Pay the damned bill," Collie said, reaching for her purse, "and we'll go, before one of you gentlemen does something to prevent me from ever coming here again."

Since Paul and Roger had decided to head to Paul's room with a case of Kokanee, Anna wasn't surprised to find company at her door just a few minutes after they returned.

"I'm sorry," Collie said. "I'm sure you just want downtime, but there are animals next door to me. I promise I won't get in your face."

"My room is your room," said Anna, stepping aside to let her in. Collie trudged past her, flopped down in a chair, and swung her legs up onto the table.

"Good old Saskie hospitality. When did you move out to Vancouver?"

"Not too long ago. I've been travelling for a while." She settled herself on the bed and eyed the TV remote. There was probably something she should be doing, but she couldn't think what. She was well and truly fried.

"The night auditor starts at ten-thirty or eleven," Collie said softly. Anna's shoulders tensed. She hated it when people seemed to read her mind.

"Yeah. What's his name, Bryan something?"

"I think so. So, you're a travelling police consultant?"

Anna placed a hand on the remote. Oblivion was just a

touch away. "You're in my face, Colette. Do you have any viewing preferences?"

"Does this place get Teletoon?"

"I don't know," Anna said, "but that is something I can find out."

She couldn't peg exactly when it had happened, but at some point Anna had switched from watching Johnny Bravo to watching her viewing companion.

Collie was low enough in the chair that her eyes were almost level with the table, and she'd moved her legs apart to see between them. Still, she managed to look comfortable as she blew pathetic bubbles with light blue gum and rocked a little in time with the music from the TV.

All of that hair was tumbling down the back of her chair, and Anna couldn't believe that the girl had left it down all day. The one year she'd chosen to keep her hair long, the stuff had been a constant torment to her. She'd kept it in a ponytail nearly all the time.

Of course, wrestling Collie's hair into a scrunchie might be more trouble than it was worth.

Unquestionably, Colette knew makeup and clothes. Anna didn't have those skills, but she recognized them in others. The tweezed eyebrows, the oversized blazer; they weren't choices she would have made in Collie's place, but there was no doubt that she looked the way she'd intended to when she put herself together in the morning. Maybe if Anna asked nicely, Collie would give her a few tips.

Her neck hurt, so she rolled onto her side for a clearer view. She had no idea why this stranger's presence was so comforting to her, but she wasn't going to kick. She was coming off a long stretch of homelessness, and she could use a little comfort.

That was the last thing she clearly remembered thinking before she fell asleep.

Sounds like a vacuum cleaner. Sounds like a womb. Sounds can't get through that other sound, because it fills the ears completely. Talking, crying, small wheels moving on linoleum, all of that isn't sound, but pressure.

Won't take much more pressure before what's left flies apart.

They lay on hands to shake what remains to dust, or to bind it together. It's impossible to know what angels want. They aren't like other people.

She knew that word from somewhere.

"Anna?"

Oh. Right. Her name. Anna opened her eyes to find Collie standing beside the bed, pressing one shoulder with a tiny hand.

"Sorry, I just thought, it's a little after ten, and we should probably talk to that guy. . . ."

"Uh . . . yeah. 'Scuse me."

Anna rolled out of bed, away from Collie, and stumbled into the bathroom to brush her teeth and wash the dream from her face.

"That was a hell of a dream you were having," said Collie. Anna sighed, fogging the mirror.

"I've had it four nights in a row. It's not exactly the same every time, but close enough."

She went back into the main room to find Collie sitting cross-legged on the bed.

"What was it about?"

"I'm not sure. It's in black and white, and I can't hear or see very much. I can't really move, either. I think I'm in a bed. And there are these terrible angels moving all around me. For some reason, they're really frightening. Is that a fucked-up dream or what?"

Collie tilted her head. "Hard to guess what Jung would say about it," she admitted. Anna was only dimly aware of who Jung was and didn't know what Jung would say about anything, but this didn't seem to be the time to bring that up.

"It's playing hell with my sleep," she said. "You wouldn't happen to know how I could make it go away, would you?"

Collie laughed. "Yeah, right. If I knew something like that, do you really think I'd need to work for Paul? Dreams are one of the great mysteries. They're a law unto themselves. What do the angels do in this dream?"

"I don't know. I don't know what they want. I keep hoping that they won't notice me if I keep perfectly still, but so far that hasn't worked."

Collie crawled off the bed and smoothed most of the wrinkles from her pants. "Try talking to them," she suggested. "That's all I can think of. Ask them what they want."

Anna smiled. "So, in other words, be direct."

"Yes," Collie said, eyes bright. "Show off your lack of manners. If you can't ditch your rough edges, you might as well work them. That's my philosophy, anyway, though I may just be crude and lazy."

"I'm not sure what you are. Whatever it is, it's not normal. Let's go talk to the auditor."

"No, I'm afraid you've got the wrong hotel."

The night auditor was on the phone as they arrived at the front desk, leaning on his elbows and gazing heavenward as if begging for salvation from idiots.

"Ma'am, I think I would know if a dead body had been found in the pool room of this hotel. You are mistaken."

Collie leaned against the desk and looked at Anna. She was laughing silently. Anna shrugged. In that poor guy's place, she would probably have done the same thing.

"Reporters get things wrong all the time. Did you still want to book a room?"

He met Anna's eyes with a grim little smile. Clearly, this wasn't the best night of his career to date. She smiled back.

"Fine," he told the receiver. "Thanks so much for calling."

He set the phone in its cradle, not gently, and regarded it silently for a moment. His jaw was twitching. "It's always the wrong fucking people," he said, "getting drowned in swimming pools." He shook his head, then seemed to remember they were waiting for him. "Sorry about that," he said. He didn't look sorry, but he did look reasonably friendly. "What can I do for you ladies?"

Anna studied his face and placed him at about twenty-five. Not nearly young enough to be calling her "lady," but she let it go. "I'm the police consultant who was here this morning. When I talked with the security guard, he said you were on duty last night."

"Yep. Lucky me. Ask me how little sleep I've had."

Collie raised an eyebrow at him. "How little sleep have you had?" she said.

He slapped a palm on the desk. "Thank you for playing. I have had so little sleep that I am considering eating this entire bag of java nuts." He reached into his pocket and lay a good-sized bag on the table. "Did either of you want in?"

"Actually," Anna said, "we just want to know what you saw this morning."

"Speak for yourself," said Collie, reaching for the java nuts. "I want the damn caffeine."

"Atta girl," the auditor said. "What did I see this morning? Same thing I see every morning. This freakin' lobby. The . . . um . . . victim came in around six fifteen and asked for directions to the coffee-shop. I told her the shop didn't open until six thirty and suggested that she wait in the lovely adjacent pool room, which, evidently, she did. I don't feel too good about that, because she seemed like a nice person."

He popped a handful of java nuts into his mouth, crunched, and swallowed. "While I was directing her to her death, the murderer came in and stood over there reading the coffee-shop menu. The victim did not seem to notice him. When you're reading that menu, as you can see, your back is to the front desk. So, no, I didn't get a good look at him."

He took a furtive look around the lobby, saw it was empty, and produced a can of Cherry Coke from the pocket of his blazer. "Ah, sweet," he sighed, popping it open. "The murderer followed the victim to the pool room, although he did not at the time seem to be following her. Otherwise, I would have said something."

The auditor stood a little over six feet, and though his weight was considerable, he wasn't flabby. He probably wouldn't have had to say much.

Collie had given up chewing java nuts and was instead staring at the auditor with her mouth open. There was a flake of coffee bean stuck to her left front tooth. "You actually saw the guy?"

"Yes, yes I did. Do this," he instructed, scraping at his teeth with a fingernail. She obeyed without taking her eyes from his.

She said, "What did the murderer look like?"

The auditor smiled tightly. "Lady, who are you?"

Maybe she could say that Collie was her assistant, but it was a good bet that wouldn't fly. Anna took a deep breath. "She knew the victim. She insisted on tagging along, and it's against policy, but she's very persistent."

He wasn't looking at Anna. His eyes were fixed on Collie, taking in her height and the colour of her eyes and hair. "You're one of the people she was supposed to meet."

"Yeah. You think you don't feel good about this. . . ."

He didn't move for a few seconds, just looked at her. Then, almost formally, he offered her his can of Cherry Coke.

Anna was surprised to see tears jump to Collie's eyes as she accepted the can and took a sip.

"Thanks." She handed it back, and he nodded.

"He was tall. Six feet, maybe. He had a parka with the hood pulled up, so I couldn't see his hair. He kept his head down. I think his eyes were brown. He needed a shave. It looked like his beard was going to come in dark blond. I couldn't tell his build inside that parka, but his legs were scrawny, so I'm guessing he wasn't Charles fucking Atlas. Believe me, I wish I could tell you something more. I've been kicking myself all day for not taking a better look, but I didn't know he was going to kill somebody."

"Well, for God's sake," said Anna, "it's not your fault. And it's not Colette's fault. It's the fault of the guy who did it. Can you think of anything else that would help us get him?"

"Ah, Jesus. I didn't see anything else. At six twenty-five Trent told me there was a body in the pool and I kept people out of the pool room and coffee-shop while he stayed with the body."

That didn't sound right.

"Where was the security guard?"

"At my desk, phoning the police. Guy's a marshmallow. He didn't want to get that close to a corpse."

"So he manned your desk and you watched the door until the police came."

"Right. It wasn't too long. Naturally, the one time they show up in a timely fashion the crime is already over. Anyway, I spent about ten minutes listening as Trent trampled the evidence, and then I went back to my desk."

Anna glanced at Collie, who was glancing at her. "Trampled the evidence?" they said.

"Trent's a good guy, but a ballroom dancer he is not. I heard him knock something over in there. I mentioned this to the police, by the way, so if they paid any attention at all to what I said, I'm sure they asked him about it."

"I think I'll ask him about it myself," Anna said. "Any idea where he'd be right now?"

"Hmm." The auditor scratched his chin through a sandy blond beard. "His shift starts in. . . ," he checked his watch, "five minutes, so he's probably in the supply room getting his shit. You want to go down that hallway and take the second-last door on the right."

"Thanks," Anna said, grabbing Collie's arm. "Colette?"

"No problem," said the auditor. He was looking at Collie as he spoke. "You take it easy."

Collie nodded and followed Anna down the hall.

One thing that could not be denied was that Trent was exactly where the auditor, Bryan, had said he would be. Of course, he hadn't said that Trent would be hanging from a rope above an overturned chair, but they hadn't asked if they'd find Trent alive, had they?

"Oh my God—"

Anna didn't have to see Collie's face to know what kind

of shape she was in. That was the sound of a woman who was about to unpack her groceries. Anna stepped backwards, pushing Collie out of the room as she went.

"You go in there," she said, shoving Colette towards the washrooms on the other side of the hall, "and do what you have to do. Then you go and tell that Bryan guy what we found. Got it?"

"Uh huh."

Collie opened the bathroom door by striking it with two white fists. Anna watched the door swing shut, then went back into the supply closet.

A real detective would have been able to tell if this was suicide or murder. There'd be something about the marks on his neck or the way the chair had been kicked over. Hell, this room was probably bursting with useful clues.

It was too bad that, as Curtis had observed, Anna wasn't a detective.

The room swayed before her and she angrily nipped her tongue. She could damned well save the fainting for a more convenient time.

Lacking any other constructive ideas, she decided to search the dead man's pockets. It seemed a detective thing to do.

She stepped forward, reached out . . . and the walls of the supply closet faded away.

* * *

She was in the pool room again, in early morning. No one there but her, the janitor, and Jocelyn's body. The janitor was holding Jocelyn under the water, almost casually. She wasn't fighting him anymore.

The janitor looked up and saw Anna watching him from the other side of the pool. He smiled his almost charming smile. "Long night," he told her. "Almost over, though. Just gotta put the cleaning supplies back, double check the locks, and drown this woman. Then I'm done."

* * *

"Anna?"

For the second time that evening, Colette's fingers were bruising Anna's shoulder.

Anna let her hand fall from the coat and swallowed bile. "You . . . uh . . . feeling better?"

"Better than you, from what I can see," Collie told her. "I thought you were used to seeing . . . this kind of thing."

"He did it," Anna said softly.

Collie pulled at her shoulder, turning her away from the body. "What?"

"He. . . ." Anna stopped, because her friend the security guard had appeared behind Collie. She hoped he'd gone home to sleep at some point if they had him working the night shift again. Judging by the circles under his eyes, though, she doubted it.

"Hi, Keith," Collie said. Anna almost smiled. God love the little PR weasel, she had actually picked up the guy's name.

"Hi," he said. "I'm sorry about this, but I'm gonna have to get you guys to step into the hall for a minute."

Anna put a hand against Collie's back and pushed until she moved. As they stepped out of the way, she heard Keith the Guard muttering to himself, "Son of a bitch. I don't believe it."

He moved forward until he'd taken Anna's place in front of the body and even reached for it before he caught himself and recalled his hand. "Did either of you move anything?"

"No," Anna said, not adding that she simply hadn't gotten that far. "Do you have any idea what happened here? Was this man suicidal?"

"Uh . . ." Keith blinked a few times, probably trying to remember what "suicidal" meant. Anna let it go. The poor son of a bitch was clearly having a tough week. "I don't . . . I mean . . . it's not. . . ." He took a breath. "Trent was a pretty happy guy most of the time, at least I think he was; I didn't know him all that well. Maybe the guy who killed that woman thought Trent saw something so he came back and killed Trent. Do you think that could have happened?"

It wasn't so much what to say as how to word it. Anna thought for a moment. "The guy who killed that woman could have killed Trent," she said finally.

"Oh God . . . do you think he's gonna kill everybody? Is he gonna keep coming back here? I'm not getting paid enough to get killed."

"I'd quit, if I were you," Collie said without much expression in her voice. "You can quit."

Anna would have sent her back to the room, but she didn't figure Collie would go, and she wasn't up for a fight. She had a crazy impulse to turn to Collie and say, "I told you not to follow me around," but she was pretty sure that wouldn't be productive.

She might have started something with Collie anyway, just to keep busy, if she hadn't seen the guard take something from the rim of the supply room sink.

"Hey!" Collie said sharply, the way she might have corrected a dog.

"Speaking of not moving anything," Anna added. Keith opened his hand to show them a plastic cigarette lighter.

"It's mine. He borrowed it from me about half an hour ago. If I leave it here it'll be evidence and I'll never get it back, right? And I really need a smoke."

"What happened to the gun?" Collie asked. Anna jumped, then remembered that Collie didn't know about the gun in her purse. She had to be talking about some other gun.

The guard's fingers tightened on his unlit cigarette, almost crushing it. "Huh? Did you say *gun*?"

"Trent had one of those gun cigarette lighters," Collie explained. "We saw it earlier today."

"Oh. Right. That thing. He must have lost it."

Anna didn't love that much, though she couldn't have said why. She looked at Collie, who seemed equally nonplused by the disappearance of that cigarette lighter and equally unsure of what to make of it.

"Maybe it'll make sense when we know more," Collie suggested. Any energy she'd collected from the coffee beans seemed to be gone.

"Yeah." Anna faced down the guard. "We'll be in our rooms if anyone wants anything. I guess the police will want to talk with us."

"You're not going to wait for your colleagues?"

Oh, sweet Jesus, her colleagues. Why did she keep forgetting that this guy thought she was with the police? It was a simple enough lie, wasn't it? She ought to have been able to keep that one thing in her head.

"Who knows when they'll get here?" she said, hoping that sounded reasonable. "You have things under control, and we're tired. If anyone wants to talk to us, we're in rooms 204 and 515."

The guard nodded. He didn't seem to find it suspicious that they were leaving. On the other hand, he seemed a little preoccupied and probably wouldn't have found it suspicious if Anna had sprouted wings. "Okay," he said. "Pleasant dreams."

"Go to your room, Colette."

Collie had planted herself just inside the door to Anna's room, and she didn't show any signs of leaving. "Why didn't we wait for the police?"

"Because I jumped ship, remember? I don't want them to find out that I'm working for you. Or that we're both working for Paul. Whatever. Go to your room."

"But—"

"Go."

Collie's eyes narrowed and her shoulders stiffened, but she left. Anna kept an eye on her until she entered the stairwell, presumably to ensure that Trent didn't come back to life and leap at her from the shadows. Then she shut the door, locked it, and put the chain on. She did not want unexpected company.

God knew what the police would think when that guard described her as a police consultant. It would probably make her look guilty as hell.

As she got changed for bed and hid the gun behind the air conditioner, Anna tried to think of a line she could use to dig herself out. All she came up with was a decision to wait until the police came knocking. She'd have to play it by ear.

The comforter smelled musty, but she pulled it up over her head anyway.

That humming and buzzing is their language. They're making plans to have everything their way.

Started out with a certain number of decisions. Eventually they were all used up. When the last decision was made, angels took the decider away and made all the choices forever.

It was important not to prefer anything now.

Knock knock knock.

"Ms. Gareau, please open the door."

They pronounced it Garr-ee-ooh, and Anna was tempted not to answer. That wasn't her name.

Knock knock knock.

"Ms. Gareau, this is the police."

Anna got to her feet and staggered to the door. In the grip of a strange impulse, she turned back to stick an arm into the bathroom and grab a toothbrush. She'd heard having a toothbrush was good when you were spending the night in jail. "Just a sec."

She fumbled with the chain in the darkness and squinted in the light from the hall as she opened the door. "Yes?"

There were two cops staring down at her, both male, both huge. Good thing they were huge, actually, since they were blocking a fair bit of that damned light.

"Ms. Gareau, may we step inside?"

"Um . . . yeah." She stepped aside, oddly surprised that her limbs moved. Those nightmares were going to drive her crazy.

They were kind enough to wait until the door was shut before asking if she'd told the security guard she was a police consultant.

"Hmm? Oh . . . yeah. I did."

The cops looked at each other. Obviously they hadn't been expecting honesty. She made up her mind to give them more of it.

"Ms. Gareau. . . ," the cop paused. He looked headachy. "Why did you do that?"

She sat down on the bed and yawned. "I'm sorry. I know that was bad. I forgot my purse in the pool room last night and I wanted to go in and grab it, but the guard was stopping everybody at the door, so I kind of lied. But I wasn't impersonating an officer per se. . . ."

The silent cop was writing in his notebook. For a second, Anna wondered if he was mute.

"That doesn't explain why you were questioning witnesses all day."

"Oh, that. I happened to meet up with Paul Echlin and we got along and he asked if I'd help him look into this. He's researching the whole *Rail* thing for his website. I don't think there's any law against someone looking into a murder privately, is there? I mean, I don't want to step on your toes."

The cop pinched the bridge of his nose. "Can we see some ID?"

"Sure." She pulled her purse onto her lap and dug out her wallet. "It's all from Saskatchewan."

The silent cop took her wallet and began looking through it, making note of her SIN and driver's licence number. "Your health card is out of date," he muttered.

Anna bit back a smile. The cop actually sounded as if he considered that one of her larger problems. "I know. The driver's licence is still good. I've been travelling. Right now I'm staying with a friend in Seattle."

"Uh huh. What are you doing in Victoria?"

She rubbed sleep from her eyes and wished she'd thought to wash her face before answering the door. "My friend owns an antiques and collectibles shop. He asked me to come up here and look around for him."

"So you're working in the States. Do you have a green card?"

"I have dual citizenship. My mother's American."

The strong silent type was on his radio, reciting her particulars in a low monotone. After a brief silence, he grunted and hung up. "She checks out. No record."

No record by the skin of her teeth, but good enough. The talkative cop looked her in the eye.

"Okay, Miss Marple. I take it you're not planning on going anywhere in the near future?"

"Not this week, anyway. I'll be right here."

"Fine. You may hear from us again. We'll see. It's true, you didn't precisely impersonate a police officer, but it was close enough that we could call it an obstruction of justice if we wanted to. Investigating a murder isn't a game. I recommend that you quit. And if you do persist, you'll know if you've stepped on our toes because we will charge you with being in our way and we will toss you in jail. Do you understand?"

Oh, boy, did she ever.

"Yes, officer."

"Good. Hopefully we won't see each other again."

Anna could get behind that sentiment. Once the door was safely locked and chained again, she flopped down on the bed and reached for the remote. She might as well watch a little TV, because until she found out what the cops had said to Collie and Paul, there was no way she was getting any sleep.

Knock knock knock. Knock knock knock. Knock knock knock.

"Give me a chance to get to the door," Anna snapped. She had a fair idea who it was, and they had every right to be pounding on her door even if it was two in the morning, but she was low on sleep and her patience was shot.

"Step on it," Collie answered. Anna could happily have let a million years pass before facing Colette Kostyna, but that wouldn't have been fair. She stepped on it.

She'd expected Collie's eyes to be shooting fire when the door opened, but to Anna's amazement she seemed almost amused. "Mind if I come in?"

"I . . . no. Of course not."

Collie didn't wait for her to move, just pushed past her and took up residence on the bed. She was wearing a T-shirt and boxers. She'd just wandered down to Anna's room in her nightclothes, without even grabbing a robe. Anna was starting to think that the girl had no shame.

"Tell me," she said brightly, "what is it you do when you're not pretending to be a behavioural scientist?"

"Mainly I tell lies," Anna admitted. "Particularly to people I like. I don't mean any harm by it, if you can believe that."

Collie slipped a hand into the pocket of her shorts and pulled out a lollipop. "They say," she said, while she worked on the wrapper, "that you can substitute food for sleep, up to a point. I learned that in a psychology class. Did you want one?"

For a moment, Anna was dazed enough to think she was being offered a psychology class. "What?"

"Did . . . you . . . want . . . a . . . lollipop?"

"Oh. No thanks." First the popsicle, and now this. "Did your psychology class mention anything about oral fixations?"

Collie took out the candy and smiled with pink teeth. "No, but you might be interested in what my professor had to say about pathological liars."

Anna leaned back against the door and slid down until she was sitting on the carpet. It wasn't as soft as it looked. "Did he say they should be lynched?"

"Only sometimes." Collie crossed her legs and rested her elbows on her knees. "You really should try one of these. They taste like Froot Loops."

Anna's stomach clutched itself in terror. "Maybe later. Look, Collie . . . sorry, Colette . . . I'm—"

Collie raised a hand, putting an end to that miserable sentence. "Chill. I don't doubt that you feel bad about this. I was going to give you a hard time, but you should see your face. I didn't have the heart."

"I only told the guard I was a police consultant so he'd let me into the pool room," Anna confessed. Bless me, Father, for I have lied like a cheap rug. "I left my purse in there last night, or two nights ago. Whichever it is at this point."

"Yeah, I know. The police told me. They wanted to know how much I knew about you."

Anna plucked at a loose strand on the rug. "What did you tell them?"

Anna couldn't remember half of what she'd said in the bizarre combination of lies and truth she had given Colette. She knew it was possible that Collie had cooked her good. Her only consolation was an oddly solid belief that the girl had done no such thing.

"I told them that Paul had hired you as a researcher," said Collie. "I made it clear that, as a lowly employee, I was not privy to the reasons behind his hiring decisions. In short, I told the police they would have to talk to Paul."

Paul. Now there was someone who might have cooked her. Not that he would do it on purpose, but. . . .

"What did Paul say?"

"I think he said 'gok.'"

"Excuse me?"

"It might have been 'vok.' Then he said something like 'snurfle chaaaaark' and horked something up. I'm not sure what the police made of that. I think they finally decided Paul was trying to say he was tanked and could they please come back in the morning."

Anna could see gooseflesh on Collie's arms from where she sat. "Don't you have a robe?"

"I always forget to wear it. Brr." She grabbed the comforter and wound it around herself. "Anyway, I didn't tell Paul because I don't like to tell people things when they're too drunk to flush the toilet. You wind up saying it about fifty times while they say 'Whaaaat?' and you have to repeat yourself in the morning anyway. It's a waste of energy. Aren't you cold?"

"No. I'm heated by fission. What are you gonna tell Paul when he sobers up?"

Collie squirmed farther down into the comforter. "That he'll never see twenty-five again and he can't hold his liquor the way he claims he used to. Also, that when he gets shit-faced with Roger and Roger passes out in his bed, that doesn't give him any right to climb into mine. He knows damned well he's not wanted. I don't know what to tell him about you."

"I'm worried about what he'll tell the police."

"Ah." She was studying what remained of her lollipop with a thoughtful expression. "Are you in trouble?"

"No."

Anna's first instinct was to stop there, but Collie was owed more than that. "I could be," she admitted, "if the cops made a hobby out of me. A friend of mine asked me to help him dodge some red tape. It's not anything all that bad and I'd actually have no problem telling you, but it's my friend's secret too. I have to keep my mouth shut."

Collie slid back on the bed until she could slip her legs under the blankets. "The problem is that Paul has to talk to the police. Otherwise, I wouldn't tell him anything. His employee screening problems are not my concern. I could tell him that you're a private detective, but the cops know you aren't because they checked out your ID. I have to think they'll tell Paul everything they told me. How did you let this go so far?"

Anna plucked another loose strand from the carpet. "When I met him at the crime scene I had to lie in case the cops heard me. Then I went for breakfast because . . . I don't know why. He's a bulldozer."

"Yeah. That's why. But you came to my room. . . ."

"I didn't want to fuck up my story by seeming uninterested in the case. And then it just never seemed polite to leave."

Collie gawked at her. "Polite? You're investigating a murder because you didn't want to be rude?"

Anna considered mentioning her premonition that Collie might die—her determination to keep Collie out of trouble. She considered it for exactly 3.5 nanoseconds before deciding to pass.

"I needed the money," she said instead. "I thought I could help. I thought it might be nice if you had someone watching your back. You should probably tell Paul I'm a fraud and get him to hire a real detective."

"I probably should," Collie agreed. She looked very comfortable in her stolen bed. "But sensible advice always gets my back up. I think I'd like for you to keep this gig." She cocked her head. "You never did tell me what you really do for a living."

"A lot of things. The closest I ever came to detective work was doing investigations for SaskTel. If there's anything you need to know about the phone company, I can give you five-year-old information from another province."

"Oh, hell, I can work the phone company angle. Making people look like bigger deals than they are is my life's work. No worries."

"Colette. . . ." Anna thought for a second about how best to phrase it, then gave up and ploughed ahead. "I don't mean to get your back up, but it's insane for you to trust me. I lied to you. I came to Victoria to do something illegal. You know almost nothing about me, and anything you do know came from my lying tongue. Do you always make decisions based on absolute whimsy?"

That sound coming from Colette's throat was suspiciously close to a giggle. "Oh, right, you're really bad news," she said. "I could tell that the second you fell asleep with me right here in the room. I'm sure Moriarty would've taken a nap while watching 'Dr. Katz' with a complete stranger."

Anna looked at her watch. Snoopy said it was nearly three AM. He seemed to be wondering when Anna was going to get her ass to bed, and she had to admit she was curious about the matter herself.

"Colette, you've really been great about this and I appreciate it more than you know, but I have to ask if you're planning to vacate my bed anytime soon."

"Oh," Collie said with a yawn, "I would, but like I told you, Paul's in my bed, and he's drooling. He smells like a bottle recycling centre. If you were willing to help me move him back to his room. . . ."

So that was how it was going to be.

"I think," Anna said, "that it would be simpler if you were to just shove over a bit."

"Yeah." Collie's voice wasn't too clear, but that was typical of someone who had her face buried in a pillow. "I think so too. G'night."

Good to be home. Sure, it's a little empty these days, but nobody else makes the rules in this place.

Don't need the upstairs anymore. Don't need all those stairs. Doesn't smell right up there, either.

That's fine, fine. Lots of room on the ground. The spare room beside the kitchen always stays warm.

This is the same room. This is the same damn room. Where did the goddamned kitchen go?

Someone moved it. Can't turn your back on a house for a second without everything being changed.

The walls are making a racket. They think there's something funny about the kitchen being gone. God, this house was never so dark before. And the rugs are wet. That's a terrible smell.

There's no kitchen because there's nothing to eat. The belly of the house is empty. That's why it's so glad that someone has come home.

Raining? No . . . wrong side of the room. Shower.

Anna blinked at her watch until her vision cleared. Nine AM. Most days she'd consider that next door to civilized, but most nights she wasn't awake past two. Suddenly she didn't feel quite so guilty about taking Paul's money.

Whoever designed the bathroom had been clever enough to put the sink in an alcove of its own, just outside the door. Anna saluted that idea by using the sink to clean up. It hadn't even been a full day since her last shower, so she wasn't going to panic about that yet.

A quick hunt through her luggage reminded her that she hadn't planned on staying more than two or three days. She was going to have to spend some of Paul's money . . . or Paul's publisher's money . . . on clothes.

She'd barely done up the last button on her shirt when the bathroom door opened and Collie came out, looking like a drowned sheepdog. She was wearing the shorts and T-shirt she'd slept in, with a bath towel slung around her shoulders to hide where her skin had soaked the front of her shirt.

"Nobody told me there was going to be a wet T-shirt contest," said Anna.

Collie grinned. She seemed perfectly happy to be up at this hour, which had to be a capital offence. "I'm going to run back to my room and get my clothes. I mean run."

"Uh huh. Keep a good grip on that towel. I'll come up in a few minutes."

"Give me half an hour. I need some time to lie to my boss."

"Okay. In that case, I'm going to hunt down a chocolate croissant."

Collie skidded to a stop in front of the door, which marked the first time Anna had ever seen anyone skid on carpet. "Chocolate croissant . . . thank you for asking, yes, I would like one of those. See you in a few."

Oh, Anna thought, *and by the way, the janitor killed your friend. I can't tell you how I know, but I do. I know it for a fact. I keep forgetting to mention that.*

Anna sighed and pulled on her boots. Sometimes it was not fucking easy being green.

"Anna!"

Oh, great. Lovely. Perfect.

"Morning, Paul."

She had to, absolutely had to pick the moment when Paul was coming out of Collie's room to enter the hallway. There was no way she could have deferred this until she'd found out what line Collie had fed him. That just wasn't the way the world worked.

"Anna, I was talking to Collie," he said, rushing up the hall to meet her, "and she told me about how you used to work for"—he looked up and down the hall, then leaned in close—"a government agency. I just wanted to tell you not to worry. I won't tell the police anything." He pressed her arm, gave her as broad a smile as could be expected from a walking hangover, and stumbled to his room.

Anna waited until he was inside before applying her fist to Collie's door. A government agency. Jesus.

"Door's open!"

Anna pushed the door and realized that it had been kept from latching with a piece of tape. She ripped the tape off and pushed the door shut, making sure she heard it latch.

"No, Colette, the door isn't open," she said. She pulled a brown paper bag from under her coat and held it up. Colette was doing something complicated to her hair and looked as though she was desperate for a third hand.

"Is that my croissant?"

"It is," Anna said, sitting on the bed, "if you promise to keep your door locked. You're investigating a murder. I'm sorry, at least two murders. At least. I want you to tell me that you understand the need for just a little security."

"You're bribing me with chocolate."

"Yes, I am. Will you keep your door locked?"

Collie returned her attention to the mirror.

"I guess. Yeah. I've never liked locking doors, but you're probably right. Is there anything else I need to do before breakfast?"

A French braid. She was putting it in a French braid. It looked tough, and Anna wished she could help, but she hadn't braided anything since the day she ditched Brownies.

"Colette, I . . . I'm pretty sure the janitor killed your friend."

Collie kept braiding her hair.

"That's goofy. She comes here to rat out *The Rail*, gets killed minutes before Paul and I are supposed to meet her, and you think her death was a coincidence? The janitor just got it in his head to drown somebody for kicks? It's possible that you really shouldn't be a detective."

"Look, I didn't say it wasn't connected to *The Rail*. I just . . . why would he kill himself like that?"

"I don't know. Maybe he felt bad about finding the body. Maybe he'd been planning to do it for a while."

"Did he seem broken up yesterday afternoon?"

"Okay." Collie was holding the finished braid with one hand while her other hand scuttled over the desk in search of something. "She asked us to meet her just over a week ago, and we suggested this place. From what Bryan told us, someone followed her here. I see this murder as a spur of the moment thing to stop the meeting, which sort of precludes the involvement of a janitor who's been working for this hotel for . . . well, a few months at least. Until yesterday, this hotel didn't have anything to do with *The Rail*."

"Maybe it did," said Anna, "or maybe the janitor hasn't been here that long . . . or maybe there's some other connection we can't see yet, but I swear there is one. There has to be. What are you looking for?"

"Barrette," Collie said. "And scrunchie."

Anna found the items in question and placed them in Collie's hand.

Collie dropped the scrunchie. "I need them one at a time," she said. "But thanks."

"Don't you get headaches from wearing a braid all day?"

Collie shook her head, carefully. "No. It's not in that tight. Why are you so convinced about the janitor? That security guard—now he probably had something when he said the murderer might have killed him. To keep him quiet."

"After he'd already talked to the police?"

"Maybe he was blackmailing the guy."

Anna snorted, which was no way to make friends, but she couldn't help it. "It's always the twisted path for you, isn't it, Kostyna?"

"William of Occam was a dick," she said, for no reason that Anna could ascertain. "At least my theory makes sense. I don't get yours at all."

Anna reclaimed her seat on the bed. "It's a hunch. A really strong hunch."

From the way Collie set down her lipstick and whirled around to face her, it was reasonable to assume that she was going to say something, but after a long look at Anna's face, she seemed to change her mind. "Okay," she said, turning back to the mirror, "you're the former government agent. Let's check out your hunch."

That was easier said than done, since Anna's cover was blown and she couldn't think of anyone who'd still want to talk to her.

She and Collie were standing in the lobby looking at the list of hotel managers and trying to find a name that sounded friendly when someone behind them broke into song.

"She's a hotel detective . . . you'd better—uh uh—check her owwwwwt."

Brian was still playing an invisible guitar when Anna turned around to see where the noise was coming from.

Collie was laughing. "Man, are we glad to see you," she said.

He set down his guitar down with exaggerated care, and grinned at them. "You've been naughty."

"Just me," said Anna. "I'm the liar. Sorry."

Anna wasn't sure if it was something she'd said, but that was the end of Bryan's good humour.

"As long as you're not the murderer, I don't care how many lies you tell. What was the point in killing Trent? Could either of you explain that to me? Someone walks into *my* hotel, my fucking domain, and kills my friend on my watch. I think I have a right to an explanation."

"Not to be rude," Anna said cautiously, "but are the police saying it was murder?"

"Not likely. Investigating a murder would be too much fucking trouble. They might be late for two-for-one donuts at Tim's."

Collie lifted her brows. "So what exactly did they say?"

"Well, let me think. They said, 'Did he have any history of instability?'"

As he spoke, his voice shifted into the voice of the talkative cop who'd visited Anna's room. It was a hell of an impression, though he'd have to start doing celebrities if he wanted to take his act on the road.

"They said," he continued, "'Did he ever talk about suicide?' . . . 'Do you have any reason to think that he knew Jocelyn Lowry?' . . . Oh, here's a good one—'Have you ever known him to have a girlfriend?'"

Anna sat down on the arm of a slightly grimy chair. Not that it mattered, her jeans needed washing anyway. "What did you tell them?"

He leaned towards her and spoke more loudly than was called for. "No. Fucking no, to all of the above."

"Including the girlfriend?"

He was thinking about belting her one. It was in his eyes. To be more precise, he probably didn't think about it so much as he felt a strong impulse towards violence. Anna looked him in the eye and tried to stay calm while he talked himself down.

It took a while, but when he finally answered her, he didn't look angry anymore. Just dog tired. "He never mentioned a girlfriend to me."

"And he would have," she said. No point making that a question. She didn't have a PhD in guys, but Christ, anyone knew that much.

"So all of a sudden, any guy who doesn't have a girlfriend is a murdering pervert? That's the only possible reason someone might not be dating? Because I have news for you—there are a lot of us. If we're all murderers, there's a serious problem."

There was something greyish-brown on her jeans. Anna scratched at it with a fingernail, hoping it was just a memento of some forgotten meal. "It's under control," she said. "I hear they're putting us single people in camps."

"No kidding," he said, with feeling. "Look, I'm not saying Trent was a completely normal guy, but who the hell is? He did not go around killing people, and there's no way he killed himself. I will stake anything you want on that."

You shouldn't, Anna thought, but there was no way she was going to say it. Collie didn't seem inclined to say much of anything, and good. Walking around a minefield was one activity where two people were not better than one.

"How long had Trent been working here?"

Bryan sat on one of the low coffee tables and placed his hands on his knees. "He started a month after I did. Almost two years. Oh my God, I've been working here for two years. Kill me."

Someone in a suit was pacing at the far end of the lobby. A manager of some description, no doubt.

"I think we're being watched," she said.

Bryan rolled his eyes. "So what? They wanna fire me? Let

'em. I'm sure people will be lined up around the block for this job after the last two nights." He stood. "Well, ladies, it's been lovely, but I have to go."

"Could you think about something," Anna said, getting to her feet, "and tell us when we see you tonight?"

"Provided none of us are dead," he said. "Sure. I'd love something else to think about. Right now all my thoughts suck."

"We want to know if Trent ever had anything to do with *The Rail*."

That was the first genuine look of surprise she'd gotten from him. She had a feeling he wasn't surprised too often.

"As in, the magazine?"

"Yeah."

"Oooh-kay. Whatever you say. You're the cop." He smiled. When Anna returned the smile, he tipped an invisible hat, shoved the front doors out of his way, and left.

Once he was a fair way down the street, Collie found her tongue.

"I notice you didn't mention your theory about the janitor," she said.

Anna nodded. "That's observant of you."

"Chicken," Collie said.

Anna didn't bother to reply.

"Is there any particular reason we're outside, freezing our asses off?"

Collie sounded genuinely curious. Anna spun around, boots sliding easily on the icy sidewalk, and stared at her. "You think this is cold? I thought you were from Edmonton."

"I am," Collie said. "Just because minus thirty is colder doesn't mean minus ten is balmy. I repeat—are we out here for a reason?"

Anna shrugged. She'd really only gone outside because she didn't want to be in the damn hotel for another second. She hadn't thought any further than that.

She looked up and down the street. They were about a

block south of the hotel. From the salt smell of the wind coming towards them, Anna guessed they were heading towards the ocean. "Thought we could soak up some rays at the beach," she offered.

"I'm going to my room," Collie said. Her face clearly showed just how funny she found Anna at that moment. "You'll want to be back by eleven thirty, because that's when I'm leaving for lunch with Rebecca. The secretary. *The Rail* secretary. I'm going now."

Anna put a hand on Collie's arm. "Don't. I actually came out here to . . . get a paper."

Yeah. A paper. That almost sounded reasonable. Collie, however, didn't seem impressed. "There are newspapers at the hotel. Free ones."

"Yeah," Anna admitted, "that's probably true. I'm used to staying in the kind of place where you park your car outside the room."

"I can't believe I'm still standing here discussing . . . anything . . . with you. We can talk about this at the hotel."

On the last word, Collie turned and headed back up the street. Anna fell in beside her, easily catching up before slowing to match Collie's pace.

"What are we going to do until lunch?" Anna asked.

Collie frowned. "To be honest, I've been obsessing about lunch. I don't—oh, you know what? We should go to a library."

"Holmes, we've got to get to a library!" Anna said. "Wolfe, I'm going to the library. Hi, I'm Sam Spade . . . and this is my library card. Nope. It's not cool, no matter who says it."

"Fuck cool," Collie said. "I want to solve this."

"You sincerely think a library is going to help with that?" Anna asked.

Collie smiled. "I sincerely do."

"Okay," Anna said. "The library it is."

"It's a dark day for journalism," Anna commented, shoving a copy of the *Times Colonist* across the dark wood table. Collie was working her way through a stack of *Rail* back issues, scribbling notes as she read.

"Read it to me," Collie said, not looking up.

Anna drew the paper back. "'Killer Stalks the Victorian.' There's a picture here . . . the hotel, cop cars, ambulance. No picture of Jocelyn."

Collie nodded. "And the horrifying purple prose of the article itself?"

"Yesterday, an unwanted guest walked the halls of the Victorian Hotel," Anna read. "Sometime between 6:00 and 6:25 yesterday morning, he visited Jocelyn Lowry, a twenty-seven-year-old graphic artist who had been working for *The Rail* magazine. Last night, he returned for Trent Hutton, the Victorian Hotel's thirty-three-year-old night janitor.

"That guest was Death, and he came to Jocelyn Lowry in the form of murder. Lowry was drowned by a person or persons unknown as she awaited a six thirty meeting with business associates from out of town.

"Her body was found by Hutton, who was later found dead by hanging in the janitorial supply room just before eleven last night. The police have tentatively called Hutton's death a suicide, leading to the obvious conclusion that he was Jocelyn Lowry's murderer.

"The man who found Hutton's body disagrees. Security guard Keith Siegerson denies that Hutton was inclined towards suicide . . . or murder.

"'Trent was . . . harmless. I never got the impression he was anything but happy with his life. He looked tough, but I never saw him do anything violent. I can't see him killing himself, God rest him, and I can't see him killing that poor woman, God rest her. There has to be some other answer.'

"That other answer may be a third party who murdered Lowry for unknown reasons and staged Hutton's suicide to keep him quiet about anything he might have seen. Or it may be that British Columbia's newest serial killer has found a home for himself in the lovely Victorian Hotel.

"Which is it? Undoubtedly, time will tell."

Anna dropped the paper to the table and looked at Collie's

face. She seemed to be chewing on something exceptionally bitter.

"Who's the hack?" Collie asked.

Anna squinted at the paper, searching for a byline. "Eilene Cebryk. You get the impression she's hoping for the serial killer thing?"

"Probably desperate for something exciting to write about," Collie said. "It's almost eleven thirty. I know I'll get lost at least twice on the way to the restaurant. We should probably go."

It was a nice enough little place, a few blocks from where the ferry left for Port Angeles. It was maybe a touch too convinced of its own preciousness, but Anna didn't consider that a hanging offense. Collie, on the other hand, was poking at their table's plastic flower arrangement and scowling.

"I hate tourist traps. This place—oh, that's Becca."

Anna looked where Collie was pointing and saw a stick-thin woman with short black hair and more makeup than was required. She was dressed somewhere on the Gothic side of professional, and looked about as rough as Collie had the morning before. Considering that, unlike Collie, she hadn't had a look at the body, it seemed clear this was hitting her pretty hard.

Collie stood as Rebecca approached the table. Anna was wedged into her corner fairly tight, but she managed to get to her feet as well.

"Hi, Becca. This is Anna Gareau. Anna, this is Rebecca Hildebrandt."

Anna shook her hand. It felt as though it was about to break. "Hi."

"Nice to meet you," Rebecca said softly. She and Collie slid into their seats, and Anna struggled into hers. The restaurant was designed to serve Munchkins.

"Collie says you're helping her find out who . . . what happened to Jocelyn."

Anna wanted to say they knew damned well what had happened to Jocelyn—she'd been murdered. She reminded herself it was only fair to make allowances for grieving people. Maybe, if Jocelyn had been Anna's friend, she wouldn't have wanted to say the word *murder* either.

"We're working on it," Anna told her. "We're going to have to ask you a lot of questions."

"Oh, I know. I brought Kleenex," she said, pulling a handful from her purse and giving Anna a shaky smile. Anna smiled back as her stomach turned over. Whose bright idea had it been to have this conversation over a meal?

"Just set those in the middle of the table," Collie said from behind her menu.

Rebecca's mouth twitched into something akin to a real smile. It wasn't happy, but it was friendly. "How're you doing, anyway?" she asked.

Collie set the menu down. "All right. I mean, you saw her every day. It has to be way stranger for you."

"Yeah. Work was pretty weird today. You'd think we'd be getting used to people being—." She cut herself off, looked at the Kleenex in her hand, then shook her head and directed her attention to her menu. "The veggie melt is good here," she said, and her voice was almost steady.

Anna took her cue and began searching for something to eat.

Collie waited until the waitress had taken their order and their menus, then folded her hands and set them on the table. "*The Rail* has been crazy all year," she said. "You must have thought, 'What the hell is going on around here?' You must have talked about it with people."

Rebecca was looking right through Collie. "I did," she said, narrowing her eyes at something. "I thought there was something in the water. The management brought people in to check for that, but they didn't find anything."

"You think you're being poisoned?" Anna asked, trying to catch Rebecca's eye.

Rebecca looked at the table. "It would explain things. Maybe. I don't know a lot about how poisons work."

"You think the poisoner is someone you work with?"

Rebecca slid her fingers around her water glass, then changed her mind and pulled her hand away. "I don't . . . yeah,

I guess so. I guess it would have to be, because whenever someone comes in to test the office, everything's normal. The poison's gone. You'd have to work at the office to know exactly when the toxicology people were coming in."

"Unless someone inside *The Rail* is working with your poisoner," Collie said. "Or maybe someone is calling people to confirm your appointments. You know? You call whoever does the testing and say you're calling from *The Rail* to check on the next appointment. They'll tell you."

One corner of Rebecca's mouth curved until she was nearly smiling. "You always think of the most dishonest things," she said.

Collie shrugged. "My ethics aren't on the table here. When you say you're being poisoned by someone you work with, is there a specific someone you have in mind?"

Rebecca shook her head. "No."

Anna watched her carefully and decided Rebecca wasn't lying. Either she trusted everyone she worked with and couldn't see any of them doing it, or, more likely, she had decided that no one was beyond suspicion.

Collie looked mildly put-out. "Do you have any other reason for thinking this is a poisoning by co-worker thing?" she asked. "Have the police said anything to support your theory?"

Rebecca's lips nearly disappeared as her mouth stretched into an ugly smile. "I've barely seen the police. They found Lou's . . . they found him at home and there was no point investigating because it was obviously a suicide. As for the rest of it . . . I guess you wouldn't know there was a rest of it, would you? Or did Jocelyn tell you?"

"She said it was a madhouse. That's pretty much all she said. She was saving the details for our meeting, you know? But a friend of Paul's told me about Mark Ling's fire, and those pictures of Eve Harris. Did the police look into those incidents?"

"Incidents." Becca shook her head. "Listen to Detective Girl. Yeah, the police were by. But from their point of view, Mark burned down his apartment building, so all they cared about was finding him. Which they still haven't done. I don't think they can prove it was him, anyway. And with Eve, you've got the . . . um . . . the crimes taking place in the pictures. Which the police kind of know she did, because they've got pictures of her . . . doing them. It. Them. Other than that—so someone put up some embarrassing pictures. They didn't try to blackmail her. They didn't threaten her. And—"

She stopped there, so abruptly that Anna thought she heard tires squealing in Rebecca's head. Collie sat up straighter. "What? What were you going to say?"

"Nothing," Rebecca said. She was looking at her cutlery as though she'd never seen anything like it. Couldn't tear her eyes away. "It just wasn't a big priority for the cops. I don't think they ever made a connection between Mark and Lou and Eve and Kate. . . ."

"Kate?" Anna asked.

"Kate Eby?" Collie asked.

"Who?" Anna asked.

"I shouldn't have said anything," Becca said quickly. "Never mind."

Collie actually laughed at that, just for a second before she got control of herself. Anna couldn't really blame her.

"Um . . . Becca, sweetheart," Collie said, "you have got to know that won't fly."

Rebecca sighed and looked suddenly older than the mid-twenties Anna had pegged her at. "I know."

The food came, and Anna was astonished to find she had an appetite. Somebody in the tourist trap's kitchen knew how to cook.

Rebecca seemed to have decided that putting food in her mouth was a good way to wiggle off the hook, and she was making damned sure that there wasn't a moment when she wasn't chewing on something.

Collie watched with undisguised fascination. "You gonna eat the plate when you're done?" she asked finally.

Rebecca mumbled around a mouthful of fries. "Thinking about it."

That was it for conversation until Rebecca's plate was clear. Anna didn't mind, because Collie's friend needed a good feeding.

It wouldn't have surprised Anna to actually see the bumps and shadows of Rebecca's bones through her chalky skin.

"Dessert," Becca said, putting her fork down and leaning back in her chair.

"Absolutely," Collie agreed. "Anything you want. But I want to know about Kate Eby. That's who you meant, isn't it?"

"I don't know who that is," Anna reminded her.

"She writes parenting articles," Collie said. She was still looking at Becca. "I heard she was on mat leave. If she's somewhere else, you should tell me. And I want to know what you were going to say about Eve Harris."

Rebecca sighed. "I know."

Collie slapped her palm on the table, rattling the ice in her water glass. "I know you know. Will you stop saying that? What were you going to say about Eve?"

Rebecca was rounding up the crumbs she'd dropped on the table and putting them back on her plate. "You know that the pictures were real, right? I mean, we have some really good graphics people at *The Rail*, and they were positive that Eve really did all those things."

"Yeah," said Collie. "That's our understanding. Did that surprise you? Really?"

"Well," said Rebecca, "some people would say she had a dark secret, but those pictures weren't it. Eve's big secret is that she grew up in a trailer park outside Winnipeg. She didn't come from money. The person she was in her column was who she wanted to be. That, if you can believe it, was her deepest shame. There's no way in hell I would've pegged her as . . . she made people use coasters in the lunch room, for God's sake."

Anna searched the floor for a hole she could sink through. She hadn't grown up in a trailer park, but anyone who had a problem with that wouldn't have liked her upbringing any better.

"She was ashamed of that?" Collie asked. "She must have lived a pretty dull life if that was her only skeleton. So she grew up poor . . . lots of people did. Jesus."

Rebecca was looking at the dessert menu with lust in her eyes. "I told her that I was still living in a bachelor suite and using an old Kraft Dinner box for a potholder. I told her I used Coke bottles for candle holders." She set the menu down. "Actually, I asked her once if she felt bad about making people who were as poor as she used to be believe they weren't living graciously enough."

Anna choked on a sip of water. "That's . . . what did she say?"

"She said they probably weren't reading the magazine, and that she hoped people who were struggling to survive had the good sense to put their priorities in order. She also said that some of life's little niceties were available to everyone. She said when she was a kid, she used to make dandelion bouquets. But I don't know if she totally believed that stuff, because the next morning I found a set of potholders on my desk."

Collie grinned. "Nice ones, I bet."

"Oh, yeah. Her taste was impeccable. Oh, I shouldn't make fun of her. She was basically a nice lady. She is basically a nice lady. Everyone talks about her like she's dead, and she isn't."

"What kind of state is she in?"

"I . . . it's embarrassing, but I'm not sure." Becca pushed the dessert menu to the edge of the table, signaling for a waitress. "I haven't been to see her. She was a mess the last time I saw her at work."

"We might have to see her," Anna said, fishing for a pen and paper in the bottomless depths of her purse. "Can you tell us where she is?"

"Well, I'm not sure that's a good idea. Probably she shouldn't talk about it."

"I'm not a behavioural scientist or anything," Collie said, "but that doesn't sound like good psychology to me. Shouldn't she be working through this?"

Anna stepped on Collie's foot, grinding her heel a little to scuff the leather on those expensive boots. Collie moved her foot away, but her expression didn't change.

"How do you work through something like that?" Rebecca asked. "Seriously, I can't figure it out. Eve says she never did anything that's in the pictures, but she must have, because they're not fakes. So management brought in a shrink to talk to her, and he spent the whole time trying to get her to admit she'd done what she swears she'd never do. That's, like, the goal of her therapy, getting her to admit she did those things. But I believe her when she says she didn't."

Anna looked at Collie, and was unsurprised to find that Collie was looking at her. Portrait of the blind leading the blind. "Rebecca . . . didn't you say that she must have done those things, because the pictures were real?"

Rebecca nodded. "Yeah."

Anna placed her fingertips against her temples and tried to rub her headache away. "Who was it that said the sign of intelligence was being able to think two contradictory things at one time?"

"F. Scott Fitzgerald," said Collie. "Fucking lush. Becca, you're going to have to pick a lane."

"I have. I'm in the poison lane."

Lord knew what the waitress thought, arriving at that moment, but Anna wasn't about to explain. She waited silently while Rebecca ordered chocolate paté and the waitress made her escape from the crazy table.

Collie leaned towards Rebecca. "What do you mean, you're in the poison lane?"

Rebecca set her plate aside to make room for the impending paté. The waitress had probably meant to take it, before she was distracted by the nightmare that was their lunch conversation. "I don't think Eve knows she did those things, and I don't think she was right in the head when she did them. Aren't there poisons that can make people go crazy? Like the Romans?"

Collie sighed. "All the heavy metal poisons can make people behave strangely, but you can't predict their behaviour. I mean, you'd have to know exactly what Eve was going to do and plan to be there with a camera. And she seemed normal the rest of the time, didn't she? Until the pictures went up?"

"She behaved perfectly. Annoyingly perfectly."

"Yeah." Collie took a slice of orange from her fruit salad, slit it down the middle, and hooked it over her Diet Coke glass. "I just don't think it would be that way if someone was poisoning her. Why would she only be crazy sometimes? And to do such strange things and not remember them, that's pretty extreme."

"You're not an expert on poisons!"

For the first time since the meal began, Rebecca sounded ready to cry. Collie reached across the table and covered her hand. "No, Bec, I'm not. You can try to find someone who is and ask them, but I've never heard of a poison that could explain Eve's behaviour."

Rebecca looked at her with eyes that were painfully red. "I don't eat anything at work. I wear gloves in the lunch room. I take my mug home and I don't ever leave it sitting on my desk."

Colette pressed her hand. "I don't think that's going to cut it, babe. I think you should quit. I told Joce I thought she should quit."

Her tone didn't change with those last words, but they had a force to them that stole the remaining colour from Rebecca's face.

"I like my job."

"No, you don't. You liked your job. You may like it again someday, if we put a stop to whatever's going on. But right now you fucking hate your job, because you don't want to go crazy or die. Christ, Becca, take a leave of absence. Tell them you have to look after your mother and go home for a few months. I don't want to watch the police fish you out of a goddamned swimming pool."

And that did it. The tears started, the Kleenex disappeared from the middle of the table, and at some point the waitress slid the paté into the spot Rebecca had cleared without any of them noticing. At least the woman had the good sense not to ask if everything was all right.

Collie was doing her fair share of crying, although she was making an attempt to keep it under control. Rebecca didn't seem to care who heard, and probably wouldn't have cared if they could hear her from the mainland.

Collie finished up with a Kleenex and tried to smile as she said, "Finality is so difficult to believe in. I think I must believe that if I find out exactly what happened, she'll step out from behind a door and congratulate me on solving the puzzle. That's so stupid. And have I stopped trying to figure things out? No. Will I stop? No, because I'm fucking stupid." Collie shook her head. "You know, Bec, she's not going to be there no matter how many times you walk into that office. Quit your job."

"I've hated all my other jobs."

Collie released her hand. "Tell them you have mono. That's good for a nice long sick leave. I can get you a note."

Rebecca didn't say anything to that. Colette pushed food around. "Joce would probably recommend it," she added. Rebecca reached for another Kleenex, but this time she was silent. Collie kept her mouth shut, and Anna couldn't think of anything she cared to say. They waited.

Finally, Rebecca took a shaky breath. "I can get my own note," she said. "My sister married a doctor."

"Okay, good enough." Collie's fingers were playing with a teaspoon, turning it over and over. "Do you think someone you work with put those pictures of Eve up around the office?"

"I don't think about it," Rebecca said. Her voice was oddly flat. "I'll tell you a detail. Whoever put up those pictures, they stole my Scotch tape. Sat in my chair and stole it from my desk."

Collie blinked a few times, slowly. "I understand, that must be upsetting."

"Yeah," Rebecca agreed. "Eve always wears too much perfume. Leaves it behind everywhere she goes. My desk smelled like her for three days afterward." She looked less happy than she had when she was crying.

"You think she put those pictures up herself?" Anna asked.

Becca turned dark eyes on her. "I told you. I don't think about it."

Collie's brow was creased. "Did you tell anyone about this?" she asked.

Rebecca shook her head. "God, no. Why would I do that?"

Anna waited a moment in case Collie wanted to continue asking questions, but she seemed to have lost her taste for it. It was easy for Anna to ask the tough questions, since she really wasn't personally involved—no matter how personal it felt. She had to remember that.

"Did you tell Jocelyn about your theory?"

"Yeah. She thought it was bullshit, just like Collie thinks it's bullshit."

"I didn't say it was bullshit," Collie protested. "I said I didn't think it was very likely."

Rebecca gave her a surprisingly warm smile. "I know what you said." The smile faded slowly, as if it were sad to have to go. "Joce was looking into things on her own, but she never told me anything. She said she'd let me know when she got something solid, but I guess she didn't. She called you."

Anna couldn't put her finger on it, but there was something in Rebecca's tone she didn't care for. Whatever it was, Collie heard and understood it. Her back stiffened.

"Joce wanted to talk to Paul. She didn't tell me anything on the phone, not even that it was about *The Rail.* I just figured it must be. You saw her every day; you had lunch with her on Friday. What do you think her theory was?"

They were fighting about something, but Anna didn't have a program and she was lost. It did seem, from the expression on Rebecca's face, that Collie had scored a direct hit.

"Obviously I wouldn't know," she said. "Which is too bad, because maybe if she'd told me we wouldn't be having this talk."

For a second, Anna thought Collie was going to get up and walk away. That would keep them from learning anything else of use, and it would stick Anna with the bill for lunch, but Anna wouldn't have resented it. Sometimes it was incredibly hard to sit there and take it, especially when you thought you had it coming.

But Collie did sit there, and she took it. "I wish she'd told you," she said softly. "Or the police. She could've told the police. If I could do this again, I'd tell her to get on the next plane out of town and call the cops when she landed." She picked up her napkin, crumpled it, and threw it on the table. "Can't, of course, do it again. I'd rather talk about something useful."

She'd found the magic words for Rebecca, who had discovered her chocolate paté and was hard at work on it. "Grab a fork," she said between bites, and Collie did so. Probably more out of a desire for rapprochement than actual hunger, since most of her lunch was still untouched.

"Not to upset anyone," Anna said, "but you still haven't told us about Kate whosit. Eby. Is she on mat leave?"

Rebecca paused over her dessert, then attacked it with even greater fervour. She couldn't have been tasting it. Collie sat back and watched, licking absent-mindedly at the remaining chocolate on her fork.

"There was a problem with the baby," Rebecca said between a bite of chocolate and a swig of water. "She was pregnant and she . . . had a miscarriage."

Collie's teeth were making white marks on her lower lip. "Either decline to answer or tell the truth," she advised. "You know I know when you lie."

Rebecca sat up straight. "That's what's on Kate's employment records. I should know; I typed them."

She actually sounded offended.

"Don't be a jackass," Anna snapped. Collie raised a hand to her mouth and coughed. It sounded suspiciously like a thwarted laugh.

Anna wasn't proud of herself. She was considering how to begin apologizing when Rebecca spoke.

"I don't know what happened to Kate's baby. What do you want me to do, repeat the things people are whispering in the washrooms?"

"Yes," Anna said, startled into speech by the stupidity of the question. That made her the left side of a stereo as the same word came from Collie's mouth in the same frustrated tone.

"Becca," Collie said, "tell us the rumours and we'll find out if they're true. We have to have leads. I promise we won't bother this woman if we don't have to. God, do you think we'd enjoy hassling someone who just lost her baby?"

"No," Rebecca conceded. "But I think you'd do it anyway."

Collie put her elbows on the table and leaned forward. "If Eve put up those pictures, if something happened with Kate Eby that you think she'd be ashamed of, maybe we can help.

Say you're right. Say someone gave them a drug that made them do things they wouldn't normally have done. Don't you think it might comfort them to know that? Don't you think Eve would feel better if she knew she wasn't crazy and it wasn't her fault?"

"Well . . . I think. . . ." Becca took a breath and started again. "I can't talk about it here. Maybe we should go for a walk."

"Fine," said Collie. Evidently she shared Anna's opinion. "I'll go settle the bill. You may want to splash some water on your face."

Anna followed Becca into the washroom, just to keep an eye on her. She watched as Becca expertly applied make-up that looked like paint against her ghostly skin. It made her wonder what Becca saw when she looked in the mirror.

Collie was outside when they left the washroom, standing with her eyes closed and her face towards the wind, taking deep breaths. Anna smiled. She wouldn't have pegged Collie as someone who loved the smell of the ocean

It was a shame to disturb that rapture, but this job had to be done before Rebecca changed her mind. Anna tugged on Colette's sleeve. "Collie," she whispered. She thought Collie would correct her, insisting on her proper name, but she just opened her eyes and smiled.

"Yeah, yeah. Where are we going, Rebecca?"

"Here's fine. I just needed air. I . . . okay. People say that she miscarried on purpose. That she did something to kill the baby."

"Do they have some reason for thinking that?" Collie asked.

"Someone said they had a friend whose cousin was a nurse and saw Kate at the hospital. But it's stupid. Kate really wanted that baby. I'm sure she's just devastated, and that's why she never came back."

Fittingly, it started to snow. The huge, soft flakes were perfectly designed to deaden all the sound in the world.

"Okay," Collie said. The snow was catching everywhere in her curls, making her hair white. "We'll need the name of that cousin, if you can get it. The name of the hospital and the day she went in, at least. We'd like to know where Kate is staying now, if you can find out. We'll also need to know where Eve Harris is, because I think we'll probably have to talk with her. I won't tell anybody who gave us the information. Could you have some of that for us by tomorrow? Also, is there any chance we could look through some desks?"

"I can have your information by tonight," Rebecca told her. "I said I was taking the afternoon, but I can stop by after office hours. If you want to search desks . . . I don't know. It's probably . . . I think I can sneak you in. Nine would work for me. Do you remember where the office is?"

Collie thought for a moment. "Yeah. I can look at a map, anyway."

"Okay. I'll meet you at the back door, so you'll have to be on time."

"While you're digging," Anna said, "could you find out if Trent Hutton ever had anything to do with *The Rail*?"

Rebecca frowned. "Who's that?"

"Kind of a suspect," Anna said. "We'll tell you tonight."

"You have a suspect?" Rebecca's sharp look was unnerving.

Collie blinked snow from her lashes. "When Anna says suspect, she means someone who's tangentially involved. She wants to make sure he's not connected to *The Rail*."

Rebecca cupped a hand over her eyes, holding it like the brim of a cap. "Where would I look for that?"

"He was a janitor," Anna told her. "Maybe he did cleaning there. Or he might have written a lot of letters to the editor, or he might have a friend who works at your office. He's the one who found Jocelyn's body."

"You're investigating the guy who found her body? That's kind of a reach, isn't it?"

Anna spoke quietly, just in case Collie had been thinking about opening her mouth. "We're being thorough. We intend to do this job right."

"Bec," Collie said, "do you need a ride anywhere?"

"No, my car's over there. The Nissan."

"Oh. Mine's the Tercel behind it."

Whatever hostility had come up between Collie and Becca in the restaurant was still hovering around, showing itself in the way they crossed the street to the cars. They were side by side but not touching, not even brushing shoulders. Anna had seen gymnastic routines that required less dexterity.

She couldn't say anything while Rebecca was with them. Once they'd sent her on her way, Collie got into their car and started the engine without saying a word to Anna, which indicated that she wasn't inclined to talk.

Anna had a policy of not upsetting people while they were driving the car she was in, so she wound up holding her tongue until Collie pulled in along the harbour and threw the car into park. "Fuck," she said.

With the snow melting on her hair and lashes, it took a minute to see that Collie was crying. She swiped at her face and slammed the heels of her hands against the steering wheel. "Fuck her," she said.

Anna nodded. "Thank you for elaborating. What was going on back there?"

"Stupid shit." Collie was running her hands around the steering wheel and giving the ocean a speculative look. "Old stupid shit. I don't know what's wrong with her."

"Grief," Anna said. "If nothing else. Grief makes a mess of people. If you're planning on driving into the ocean, you should know this little Tercel is not going to make it across the sand. If we were in my Jeep. . . ."

"Don't underestimate my car," said Collie, a smile touching the edges of her mouth. "If we were in your Jeep, we'd be driving something older then I am, and I have a rule against that."

The seat was most of the way back, but Anna could still bring her knees up and rest them against the dashboard. It was a clown car.

"I don't care how much Oil of Olay you use," she said, "I can tell you're older than fifteen. Are you telling me you have no respect for classics?"

"I believe in dignified retirement."

The snow was melting as it hit the beach. It occurred to Anna that it didn't snow in Victoria all that often, that they were probably in the middle of some weather emergency. That was pretty funny, since this was the most peaceful thing she'd seen in months.

"When did you see my Jeep, anyway?"

"The night Paul and I got here. Only Saskie plates in the parking lot."

"Ah."

Collie turned the stereo on and pushed lightly on the cassette that was sitting in the deck. It made an unhappy noise before clicking into place.

"Piece of shit," Collie said, without malice. A soft female voice was explaining that everything she touched ran wild. Whoever she was, she had Anna's sympathy.

"You have some old argument going with Rebecca?" Anna asked.

Collie's eyes were shut. Anna didn't know if she'd even been heard until Collie decided to speak. "She has an argument with me. But I don't think. . . ." Her eyes opened. The water on her lashes shone like stars. "Why are you so convinced about this janitor?"

At some point, Anna had started to rock in time with the music, moving the small car back and forth. She made herself stop. "What does that have to do with you and Rebecca?"

Collie's eyes were shut again, her head tilted back against the seat. She was grinning. "Quid pro quo, Clarice."

Anna shook her head. "I don't think so."

"I do think so," Collie said. "You tell me why you're stuck on the janitor, and I'll tell you what you want to know. I wouldn't be a hardass about this, but I don't think I'm going to find out your secret any other way."

"What makes you think I have a secret?" That was convincing. Anna felt herself turning red.

Collie looked at her and laughed. "God, I don't know. It's a mystery. You know, if I understand where you're coming from, you'll find me easier to get along with. I promise."

"Don't write cheques you can't cash," Anna said. She fixed her eyes on the ocean and did some thinking. Collie, thankfully, had the grace to let her do it in peace. The music had changed; now Tom Waits was running his sandpaper voice over the cold, cold ground. Anna couldn't imagine what kind of a mood Colette had been in when she'd put this tape together. "It's not fair not to tell you," Anna said.

"Nope," Collie agreed, her eyes following the path of a seagull.

"But I don't know if you'll believe me. I'm not sure I'll be able to demonstrate. I think I'll sound crazy. Lock-up-able."

Collie turned her head for a good long look at Anna's profile. Anna watched from the corner of her eye.

"Are you serious?"

That was best not answered.

Collie's eyes widened. "Like I would ever put anyone in a nuthatch. I'm all for rampant individualism. But see, now you don't have an option. You've got to tell me. I'll hound you."

Anna carefully pulled her legs in and crossed them, turning around in her seat to face Colette. "No need. But it's fucked up, I'm telling you. I need . . . can I have something personal of yours?"

Collie raised her eyebrows and shifted around to look at Anna. "You gonna tell my fortune?"

Oh, great. She thought it was a joke. Anna sighed. "Not exactly."

Collie kept her eyes on Anna's as she took the scarf from around her neck and dropped it into Anna's hands. It was soft, probably real silk, warm where it had rested against Collie's skin. It felt like nothing more than a piece of cloth. Anna set it down.

"That's not personal. Do you mind if I look in your purse?"

"Hm." Collie picked it up, clasping the shiny black leather with both hands. "Normally I'm particular about that but . . . go ahead."

Anna took it from her and pressed the latch. It was stiff. Collie couldn't have had it very long. She didn't bother to look inside, because looking wouldn't have told her anything. She slid one hand into the purse and shut her eyes. Her fingers skated over a compact and lipstick, a wooden pick, a change pouch . . . and something personal.

"It's not a lucky ring," Anna said. Her voice had as little to do with her will as the music from the tape player. "This is the worst birthday I ever had. My stomach is killing me and I don't think he believes me and I have to tell Mom I put a dent in her car. I'm sick on my birthday. He doesn't think I like it he doesn't think I'm really sick I took it off because it's not a lucky ring he thinks I just don't like it I don't like it I don't want his promise ring I can't promise I don't want him how do I get out of this?"

Collie was perfectly still, except for a flash of white teeth rolling over her lower lip. Anna took out the thing she'd touched. It was a tiny, delicate gold ring with a pearl set in it. Anna could never have worn it.

Apparently, for her own reasons, Collie couldn't wear it either.

"Well," Anna said, setting the ring on the dashboard, "you must have gotten out of it somehow."

Collie laughed once, harshly. The sound set Anna's nerves on edge.

"He dumped me. He gave me a promise ring on my nineteenth birthday. Said it would bring me luck . . . you know, like when he got me a real engagement ring and proposed to me, I'd be lucky? That's not as bad as it sounds. He was kidding." The words shot out like automatic fire. "He wasn't bad. He was nice to me. I was a bitch. I put on his ring, smashed up the car, and got stomach flu. I was really pissy about my birthday being fucked up, so I took off his ring. I said it was unlucky. Wouldn't wear it anymore. He dumped me, and, you know, fair enough. You can see his point of view."

Anna looked at the ring. It was a little worn. Not thinned from being on someone's finger—more scuffed around the outside. Probably from spending time being knocked around in a purse.

"He must have thought there was something wrong," Anna conceded. "And there was. You didn't want to be with him. You should have told him."

"I didn't know." Collie had found a stray thread on the sleeve of her coat and was picking at it. "I mean, I guess somewhere in me I knew, but not where I could get hold of it. I was nineteen. What the hell did I know? What did you know when you were nineteen?"

"Not enough," said Anna. Her nineteenth year had not been her best.

"I took him for a ride. The thing is, there was really nothing wrong with him. I couldn't figure out why I didn't love him, and then I thought I probably did and just didn't recognize it. Sometimes I thought I *would* love him, if I just stuck it out. That poor son of a bitch. It wasn't fair to him at all. He's got to hate me. He probably tells all his new girlfriends about me and they tell him how sorry they are that he had to go through that. Which they should, because I was awful."

"Nineteen," Anna reminded her. "I wouldn't hold it against me, if I were you. I bet he doesn't hold anything against you. God knows we couldn't see it at the time, but it's obvious now that we were children."

They watched the ocean again, listened to music. A woman with an aching voice was promising someone her presence and her breath in a rhythm that matched the movement of the waves.

"You got all that from touching my ring."

"Yeah." The snow had given up and switched to rain. It was drilling holes in the sand. "I don't know how. I know other people don't touch stuff and suddenly it's the Biography Channel."

"Some do. I mean, I've heard about other people who are supposed to be able to do it, for whatever that's worth. It's called psychometry."

"I didn't know my disease had a name."

Collie hunched down in her seat. It was amazing that she had room to do that. "It's not a disease, Anna. It's a gift."

Anna laughed. "Mary, mother of God," she said. Another of her grandfather's archaic curses. She wished she could take a pad of steel wool and scrub them off her tongue. "Try living with it. I have never found out anything I wanted to know. I never remember a trip to Disneyland. God, Colette, I have enough bad memories of my own."

Collie let that settle in. Anna studied her face and couldn't even guess what she was thinking.

"You don't wear gloves all the time," she said.

"No. It doesn't happen all the time. Sometimes people just . . . leave themselves on things. But most of the time they don't. I couldn't tell anything from your scarf."

Collie was running her fingers over her scarf, testing it out for herself. Anna tried not to smile.

"So it's just keepsakes?"

Keepsakes and sugar packets and coats people wear while they kill people.

"No. It's not really about the object so much as . . . the moment. Somebody feels something so strongly that it pours out and gets all over whatever they're touching. That moment and the way they felt stays there."

"Some people say that about ghosts—why people see ghosts. They say it's just passion hanging around." Collie dropped the scarf and placed her hands on her knees. "How can you live a normal life if anything you touch could mess with your head?"

"I keep my hands in my pockets a lot," said Anna.

Collie looked at her sharply. "You do. I didn't think anything of it. Stupid." She faced the ocean again, tapping her fingers in time with the music. "You aren't just guessing about the janitor. You know."

It wasn't a question, but Anna answered her anyway. "I wasn't thinking and I touched his coat."

"Uh huh. I saw that. You went all weird."

"I went all weird." Anna slid a hand under her seat and pulled at the lever, but her seat was back as far as it would go. "That's the kind of support that makes us freaks feel good."

"Don't whine about my word choice. At least I don't think you're crazy."

"He really did it, Colette."

The rain was coming down harder, making a steel drum of the car. Collie had to speak up to be heard. "If you say he did it, he did it. But. . . ."

"But what?"

"It's fucked up!" Collie wailed, punching Anna's leg. She probably didn't intend for it to be much of a punch, but it stung. "It makes no sense. It doesn't fit. I don't know what to do with it. Explain this to me, Anna."

"Why don't I leave that to my alter ego, Mr. Sherlock Holmes? Oh, wait, I can't do that, because he's not my alter ego. Look, Collie, are you stupid?"

"What the hell do you mean by that?" That marked two uses of the girl's nickname without a complaint. Anna was starting to think Collie's fourteen-day policy had been waived.

"I mean that I don't think you're stupid. You're not any dumber than I am. You're probably smarter. If you don't understand this, why would I? Maybe you should find yourself a real detective."

Collie was chewing on a loose curl. Anna hooked a finger around the hair and pulled it out of her mouth.

"That's a bad habit."

"I like having vices. It makes me a more interesting person. Why would I want a real detective when I have Frank Black? Or the guy from *Seeing Things*?"

Okay, that was way over the line.

"You ever compare me to some TV psychic again, I swear they will never find your body."

Collie put her hands in the air. "Your threat has been registered."

"Great," Anna said. "Now that we have that out of the way, in all seriousness, I don't want you thinking I can just go around running my hands over stuff and solve the case that way. I probably couldn't, and even if I could. . . ."

The look Collie shot her was a little hurt and a lot confused. "I wouldn't ask you to do that. The experience is really harsh, obviously. Besides, you've already given us a really useful lead. It's annoying and ridiculous, but useful. You put on some gloves and we'll follow it up. Okay?"

"I told you, I don't have to wear gloves. I don't have that much trouble."

Which was a half-truth or a white lie or something of the kind, but Anna didn't want to get into it. Not yet, anyway.

Collie pressed her arm. "We're investigating a murder. You're probably going to see a lot worse things than my miserable romantic history. I can't believe you touched a corpse."

Anna couldn't help smiling. "You'd do it. You'd have your hands on everything."

"Yeah, but I'm reckless." Her grin vanished quickly. "I don't know. After it happened once, I might wear gloves everywhere. Or I'd start telling everybody what I could do and wind up in a home somewhere. Or some secret CIA jail for psychics, like in *Firestarter*. Did you read that?"

"Yeah. It was food for thought."

Collie turned up the heat with a ghost-white hand. "I bet. Well, I'm not going to tell anybody. We're just going to solve this case like any two ordinary lying weasels who were pretending to be detectives would. You can let me search the bodies."

Anna laughed. "You want me to haul them into the bathroom so they're conveniently close to the toilet?"

"Finding him was a shock, all right? If I were a wuss, would I be doing this?"

Anna faced her. Collie's eyes were dark in this light, a rich green that coloured lenses couldn't fake. She hadn't had much colour since Anna had met her, but she was looking paler by the hour, and the determination on her face was unsettling.

"You would," Anna said finally, "if you were a stubborn little wuss who thought she owed somebody something."

Collie took her time answering that. In the meantime, a man with a wavering voice sang about something he'd been waiting on for a long, long time. From the sound of the song, it couldn't be anything good.

"Wuss or not," Collie said at last, "stubborn can take me anywhere I need to go. She put the car in reverse and swung out of their parking spot. "Where to now?"

If there'd been a third person in the car, Anna could have turned to them and said, "Well?" She could have asked them what they thought and waited for suggestions. Unfortunately, it was just the two of them. "If you think you can talk your way into Jocelyn's apartment," she said, "I guess we might as well go there."

“Look, her mom asked me to please just do one thing for her. Have you ever talked to someone whose kid just died? She’s a wreck. I don’t want to let her down.” The landlord eyed Collie with deep weariness. He’d probably been fending people off all day, and here he was faced with a woman who might start crying at any moment. Anna didn’t envy him.

“Ma’am, I don’t like letting people into my tenants’ apartments at the best of times, and the police told me—”

“Just a few minutes. I swear, we’ll be out of there as soon as we find the letter.”

It was an interesting lesson in confidence work. Collie’s story was that Joce’s mother had sent a letter about a week earlier, and wanted to know if Joce had read it before she died. Anna thought it was a hell of a line. Easy to sell, since Collie really did know Jocelyn’s mother, and poignant without stepping over into pathos.

The landlord breathed in deep and let it out, without opening his mouth. “Okay, I can give you ten minutes.”

He handed Collie the key. She gave him a teary-eyed smile and wasted no time getting into the stairwell. Anna stayed close on her heels.

It wasn’t until she saw Collie’s hand shaking as she put the key in the lock that Anna realized she was genuinely upset. “You okay?” she whispered.

“Never thought about Mrs. Lowry before. I always liked her. God, these are cheap locks.”

She jiggled the key and the lock gave with a click that made both of them jump. The door slid open, just a crack, and Collie stood perfectly still before it.

“We only have ten minutes,” Anna reminded her.

“Uh huh.”

Anna reached over her shoulder and lightly pushed the door until it opened the rest of the way. “Don’t make me step right over you, Colette.”

Collie smiled, and some of the stiffness left her shoulders.

"You're not quite that tall."

She stepped cautiously, leaning forward as though she were afraid someone would hear the click of her heels on the thick brown carpet.

Anna moved in after her and shut the door. "You've been in here before?"

Colette was looking around the room, her eyes constantly moving from one thing to another. She might have been trying to do a complete scan of the place, but Anna suspected she just didn't want to look at any one thing for too long. That might have led to thinking.

"Yeah. Just over a year ago. I don't think it's changed much."

It wasn't much of an apartment. It was small to begin with, and the dark brown of the rug didn't help matters. The kitchen and living room were joined, with one window along the far wall of the living room. It was a fair size window, but it didn't make up for the absence of light in every other corner of the room.

Apparently Jocelyn had decided that a rug the colour of mud dictated a forest-type decorating scheme, because she'd filled the apartment with plants. They were doing well, even if they had gone a few days without water, and some of them were delicate types. Whatever else Jocelyn had been, she must have been good with plants.

That was the benefit of having a home and living in it—that you could have house plants. Maybe even a couple of pets. Why not mull that over until the ten minutes were up? That would be productive. Anna bit the inside of her cheek to snap herself out of it and started checking out the scenery.

The dreamcatcher in the window made her smile. She'd had one as a child, a gift from her grandmother, but it hadn't been a fad at the time. And it hadn't been made to catch dreams.

There was a shelving unit beside the window, bending a little under the weight of the plants. Tucked in between the leaves, Anna spotted a row of books, a bookshelf stereo, and a stack of CDs. No television in evidence anywhere.

Looking at the book and CD collections of acquaintances

was a hobby of Anna's. Those collections said a lot about who their owner wanted to be. She stepped forward to get a closer look, then stopped herself. They were looking for clues, and they didn't have all day.

"They must have taken the rats to the SPCA," said Collie, pointing at an empty cage. Anna didn't think she'd heard that right.

"Excuse me, rats?"

"Yeah. She had a couple of black hoodeds."

Not just pet rats, but some fancy breed of pet rat. Where Anna came from, rats were something you hunted down with a pitchfork.

There was a notepad lying on the counter that divided the kitchen and living room. The top sheet was blank. Feeling intensely silly, Anna looked for pen indents. The top sheet was smooth. Maybe some other pretend detective had gotten to it first.

Anna looked at the archway to the bedroom. A bundle of dried leaves was hanging there, blocking the way in. It looked as though it had been put up in a hurry, without much concern for aesthetics.

"Collie, do you know what this stuff is?"

Collie set down the pile of letters she'd been rifling through and squinted at the leaves. "I don't know. Maybe she was drying an herb."

"That's not any herb I recognize," Anna said. She reached up to snap off a leaf.

"Hold it, Psychic Girl. I'll do it." Collie ducked into the bathroom and came out with a few squares of toilet paper. Very carefully, she took a few leaves, wrapped them, and put them in her purse.

"You find anything in the letters?"

"No." Collie looked over her shoulder at the letters. "There really is one from her mom. I guess that's good for our story." She didn't sound thrilled by that fact.

Anna went into the bathroom. It was uncomfortably small, with a drape cloth covering the bottom of a chipped green sink and a set of brown shelves straddling the green toilet. Adventurous bathroom colours were one of the worst legacies of the seventies.

Through the transparent blue shower curtain Anna could make out a shower basket full of Body Shop shampoos and scrubs. If she took a closer look, she'd know whether Jocelyn preferred Dewberry or Juba or what, but that probably wasn't a key to the mystery. The medicine cabinet, on the other hand—that was worth a look. From the way Anna had to tug to get it open, she suspected the original magnet had been replaced with a car-hoisting magnet from a wrecking yard, but she kept at it until it gave. Generic Neo-Citron, a tube of antibiotic ointment, Band-Aids, ibuprofen . . . all pretty typical stuff. There were a few dark bottles without labels. Anna opened them and found dried herbs. They looked as though you could use them to make tea, but in that case they'd be in the kitchen. Anna put them in her purse.

Collie was in the bedroom when Anna got there, making a mess of the nightstand. "I can't find her address book," she said without turning.

"The police probably have it." Anna opened the closet and found a collection of business clothes in earth tones, some with subtle floral prints. "Jocelyn was really into nature, wasn't she?"

"Kind of," Collie said absently. She had a book on her lap and was flipping through it. "She was into neo-paganism, which is into nature, but personally she got a little nervous when she ran out of pavement."

Anna opened dresser drawers and found more casual clothes, if fishnet stockings and fake corsets could be considered casual.

"Witch by day, vampire by night?" she inquired. Collie's mouth twitched. "Something like that."

The bed Collie was sitting on was black: black comforter, black pillowcases, black satin sheets. It didn't seem conducive to good dreams.

"Didn't she ever get depressed in this place?"

"Only happy when it rains," said Collie. "Do you think you can fit this book in your purse?"

It was an oversized paperback, but not as large as a hardcover. Anna opened her purse and held it out for Collie, who dropped the book in. Anna took a look at the spine. "*Amulets for the Coming Storm*. That was her bedtime reading?"

Collie stood up, which put her barely an inch from Anna. Anna stepped back to let her move away from the bed.

"I guess. She had it bookmarked about halfway through."

"What do you want with it, anyway? I mean, it tells you your friend was a kook, but I get the impression you knew that."

Collie moved to the makeup table and placed her hands on the edge. She let her head drop for a moment. "Yeah," she said softly. "She was a kook. She believed in people like you."

Before Anna could reply to that, Collie developed a strong interest in Jocelyn's jewelry box. It was a wood and glass deal, probably fairly expensive, with drawers for earrings and a cabinet for necklaces. Collie went through it quickly. When she was done, she examined it again. Finally she let her hands fall and turned to Anna. "That's at least ten minutes. We should go."

Considering that Anna had just been told not to keep secrets, that rankled. "What were you looking for?"

"Nothing."

Anna didn't know why Collie bothered to lie, since she wasn't even trying to sound convincing. "I think you mean we'll talk about it later," she said.

Collie chewed on her lower lip. "Yeah," she said. "I do. But I really, really want to go now."

From the look in her eyes it was plain that she really, really did want to go, immediately if not sooner. Anna put a hand on her shoulder and steered her towards the door. "We can always make up another sob story if we need to come back."

"You're a pronoun dyslexic," Collie told her as they went. "You misuse the word *we*."

Anna didn't know if Collie really had work to do for Paul. Maybe she did. Or maybe she was planning to have a good long cry and didn't want Anna to know. Either way, she'd begged off the moment they'd returned to the hotel and generously offered Anna a few hours of down time. "Take a nap," she'd suggested.

Anna thought instead she might find a lead or two, do some brilliant detective work, and solve the entire case. Of course, that nap idea was a solid backup plan.

Anna's room was in better shape than she'd left it in. It was probably the housekeeping staff, but she couldn't shake the feeling that her room just sorted itself out the moment she turned her back. Not that she cared how it got clean, as long as she wasn't the one doing the cleaning.

She unwrapped a tumbler, filled it with Victoria tap water, and took it to the bed. Her purse bounced when she dropped it on the quilted comforter. She flopped down next to the purse and tugged at the zipper, which was grating against the spine of the book. Fortunately, Jocelyn wasn't likely to complain if her book got scuffed.

The zipper gave all at once and the book slid partway out of the purse. Anna put her fingers on it and tugged and that shattering sound was glass.

The house she stood in was huge but old, drafts slithering through empty rooms and across bare floors to chill her skin and whistle in her ears.

It was creaking and cracking as tiny bodies hit it from every direction. As birds threw themselves into walls and windows, more glass broke and gave way. It scattered on the hardwood floor, adding to countless scrapes and marks.

The birds cut themselves open on the glass and fell dead to the floor. Each of them was followed by a dozen, a hundred more. Anna couldn't count them. She couldn't move.

They pressed inward as more birds came into the house, until Anna was surrounded. Suffocated by feathers. Her body extended into the bodies of the birds, reaching out through them to feel that the pressure had changed. Her bones were pulled painfully until they were thin and sharp as glass against her muscles. The birds were pushing at the walls of the house from the inside, now. The house bulged. It grew. It took on the shape of a giant bird and opened its wings to fly.

Anna dropped the book and gave her hand a quick shake, trying to scatter that memory as if it were water on her skin. It crossed her mind that if Jocelyn had been living with that feeling, it was a good thing she was dead. A merciful thing.

She carefully picked her purse up by the edges and overturned it. The book tumbled onto the bedspread. Anna moved away from it, not wanting it so close to her skin. She wasn't sure she wanted to touch anything in her purse again. She'd never known a moment to rub off from one object to another before, but she wasn't prepared to take the chance that this might be the first time.

Anna considered phoning Colette's room and finding out if Jocelyn had harboured a particular fear of birds. Or, possibly, *The Birds*.

She could do that, but if she did, Collie would want to know why Anna wanted to know. Anna didn't want talk about it. She did not want to describe the experience and then chew the whole thing over with Collie. If, instead, she pretended she had never touched that goddamned book, she might be able to convince herself that was true.

She crawled off the bed and went to the table, taking the phone from the nightstand with her. Distraction. That was what she needed.

Curtis answered on the third ring, sounding relaxed and happy. It was probably petty to wish he sounded less content.

"Hello, Curtis. I'm checking in from sunny Victoria."

"Oh, hey, Anna. I heard you got hit with a blizzard up there."

"Yeah. It's up to the window of my hotel room. We're drawing lots to see which guests will be eaten. Any luck finding a customer?"

"Hrm?"

It was a funny thing. Ever since Anna had acquired a gun, shooting people seemed to be the first solution she thought of when faced with a problem.

"A customer," she said, sounding it out the way they did on *Sesame Street*. "Cus . . . to . . . mer. Customer. For the thing I have and don't want to bring back to Seattle."

"Ohhhh. Right. That thing. I'm working on it."

Such a terrible liar. Anna sighed. "You're not. You are not working on this very pressing issue that is interfering with my pursuit of life and happiness. If I were just a tiny bit less happy with you, I'd get on the ferry to Vancouver and toss this item overboard along the way. I bet you'd rather I didn't do that."

"I would."

He didn't say anything for a while.

"Curt, are you there?" Do you know I'm putting this call on your bill and not my new employer's?"

She could barely hear him laugh, because his laugh was a quiet thing that involved blowing air through his nose and shrugging his shoulders a lot. "I'll make some calls, okay? I promise. You just . . . take care."

He sounded concerned. She thought she'd hid it, but she must still have had tension in her throat from touching the hell book. Well, he could sound as concerned as he liked. She wasn't about to go into it. "Is that a sincere promise, Curt, or your usual kind?"

"I swear on the graves of the turtles I got when I was five."

That being Curt's most significant loss to date, Anna was prepared to accept it. "Okay. Call as soon as you have anything."

"Yeah. You call if you need anything, okay?"

If nothing else, Curtis really was a sweet guy. Anna made herself smile so he could hear it in her voice. "I will. Thanks."

She hung up and went to the window. The sky was still a heavy dark gray. It didn't seem possible that anything so closely resembling steel could hang in the air indefinitely. It was only reasonable to think the sky was going to fall.

Anna drew the curtains, which were a light pink instead of the brown and orange she'd come to expect in hotels. The curtains dimmed the light, but they made what was left seem warmer, and that was a decent trade-off.

Anna decided to take a shower, see if maybe there was inspiration somewhere in the hotel's plumbing, just waiting to rain down on her head. As the water got around to being the right temperature, she convinced herself she needed a better understanding of the victim's character. Jocelyn was their guide, in a weird way. It might help to have a better grasp on what Jocelyn Lowry was all about. By the time she'd rinsed the last of the shampoo from her hair, Anna had made up her mind to get the full story on this mystical bullshit. Colette seemed to understand it. She didn't seem to want to talk about it, but she was going to have to get over that.

Anna took a hand towel with her as she left the bathroom and used it to grasp the book. Slowly, carefully, she placed it on top of the television. Nothing else was likely to touch it there. Then, still using the towel, she picked up everything else she'd dumped from her purse and dropped it back inside. She had just finished dressing when there was a knock at the door. "Who is it?"

"Oh, right, because there are so many people it could be."

Anna went to the door and ushered Collie inside. "I do know a few other people in Victoria," she said.

Collie grinned. "Would you have opened the door for any of them?"

"No," Anna admitted. She shoved the door hard until the lock clicked. Hopefully Collie would learn by example.

"Did you get that nap?"

Anna shook her head. "I'm trying to give up sleep. I'm thinking maybe I don't really need it."

"The big lie about people needing sleep, food, and drink," Collie said. She sat cross-legged on the bed and scooted back until she was resting against the pillows. "I've heard it at least a hundred times. Would you happen to have any idea at all what we should do now?"

Anna dropped into a chair beside the bed. "Tell me about Jocelyn."

Collie's open expression slammed shut. "What do you mean?"

Anna shrugged. "I don't know. I just don't get her. I don't get the whole pet rats in the living room and weird herbs in the medicine cabinet thing. What if this entire case hinges on me noticing some mystical piece of crap that means nothing to me?"

Collie raised her eyebrows. "Are you telling me you never practised the Craft? Didn't the other girls makes fun of you in school?"

Yeah, right. The other kids had hated her for not being a witch. Anna wondered if EC Comics was right, if irony really was good for the blood.

"I hope you don't talk that way in public," she muttered.

Collie grinned. "The mundanes need shaking up. Mind you, my act was better when I looked the part."

"Was that when you were in school?"

Collie's smile softened. "Yeah. Joce and I were doing the goth thing."

"Were you . . . that witch religion deal, what is it?"

"Wicca? No, that's different. It's more like what Joce was doing here, with all the plants and New Age crap. That was never my style."

Anna tried to picture Collie with thick black makeup and a choker around her neck, some ornate pre-Christian cross hanging from a strip of suede. She couldn't quite make the image work. And, though admittedly she'd only had one quick look at the girl, she couldn't see it on Jocelyn either.

"Jocelyn's party clothes didn't seem to go with the rest of her . . . uh . . . image."

"What, you mean the corsets and shit? Those are leftovers from her Goth days. She ditched the basic black a few months after she started at *The Rail*. At first I thought she was just trying to get into the West Coast spirit, but she stayed with it. Whatever turned her crank, I guess."

Now that Collie was talking about Jocelyn, her story that they weren't that close didn't fly. They probably hadn't talked much in the recent past, and Anna believed that Collie didn't think they were close, but some bonds never broke completely.

"But do you get this witch stuff she was into? Like that book you put in my purse, do you know what it's about?"

"You've been reading it," Collie said, raising her chin to indicate the book's new home atop Anna's TV. "You tell me."

"I can't make anything of it. I told you, I don't get this stuff. What is so damn funny?"

Collie was making a transparent and therefore pointless attempt at not laughing. Anna couldn't begin to imagine what was amusing her.

"You keep talking like Joce was from some foreign country and I've visited it a few times, so I know their customs. That's just crazy. This isn't foreign to you. It *is* you. It's . . . never mind. You're Zen, that's all. Say 'om' for me."

"I have no idea what you're babbling about," Anna told her. "Do you know what that book is about or don't you?"

Collie looked at her oddly, but let it go. "With the understanding that I have a superficial interest in the occult at best. . . ."

"Yeah, I get that."

"That book seems to be about protecting yourself from psychic or magical attacks."

Anna was starting to think Joce might not have been murdered after all. She'd just died of being a complete fruitcake. "Jesus. Does that book also tell you how to search your closet for the bogeyman?"

Collie grinned. "In a sense."

Anna shut her eyes and pinched the bridge of her nose. "Does that seem reasonable to you?"

Collie shrugged. "What I think doesn't matter. Joce was reading it when she died. Maybe it was just a good read, but she was never really into recreational reading, you know?"

Marlowe never had cases this nutty. Anna was almost sure of it. "You think Joce was under magical attack. Is that what you're saying to me? Think carefully before you answer."

Collie looked smug. Anna couldn't fathom what had brought that on.

"I told you. It doesn't matter what I think. What matters is what Jocelyn thought."

"So you think Jocelyn thought she was under magical attack."

Collie nodded. "It would seem so."

"The way Becca thinks the staff of *The Rail* are being poisoned."

"Exactly."

"And," Anna said slowly, "you think this is in some way helpful to our investigation."

Collie uncrossed her legs and shifted to lie on her back. She stared at the ceiling. "You," she said wearily, "asked me what the book was about. You keep asking people what they think is going on at *The Rail*. Don't blame me if you don't care for the answers you're getting."

There was nothing Anna could say in her own defense. Instead she said, "You think Jocelyn was planning to buy you and Paul overpriced breakfasts in the coffee-shop and confide that the staff of *The Rail* was being pelted with mystical mind rays. That would have disappointed Paul."

Collie shook her head. "Not everyone is as closed-minded as you, ironically, seem to be. He would at least have wanted to know why she thought that. And you have to admit, whatever she was going to say, there was someone who really didn't want her to say it."

Anna snorted. It wasn't ladylike, but it did express her feelings. "That doesn't mean anything. Consider: person X, whoever he or she may be, finds out that Jocelyn intends to talk with infamous busybody Paul Echlin. Person X has no idea what Jocelyn means to say, but doesn't want to take the chance that she really does have his number. He kills her just to be on the safe side. Do you have any ibuprofen or Aspirin or Tylenol or maybe just a brick I could knock myself out with? Because I'm working on a very ambitious headache."

Collie went through her purse, which didn't take long. How she got through life with a purse the size of a Chiclet pack was a mystery to Anna.

"Sorry. Tell you what—lie back on the bed, and I'll get you a facecloth."

That was the danger of waiting to have children. The maternal instinct just spilled out on anyone who was standing nearby. Anna herself had been known to tell grown men to eat their vegetables. Still, when your head was killing you and you felt completely lost, there were worse things than having a mother around. Anna climbed onto the bed as Collie rolled off the other side. She lay back and shut her eyes.

"Paul wants to debrief us over dinner," Collie said as she put a warm facecloth over Anna's eyes.

"Is 'debriefing' supposed to be some kind of euphemism? I thought you told him you weren't interested."

Collie laughed. "A man's reach has to exceed his grasp. He also wants to know how the investigation is coming along."

"This is not soothing my headache."

"Would you rather I'd told you at ten to six?" Anna felt the bed move as Collie stood up, heard her footsteps as she moved to a chair. "At least we have time to think of something to tell him."

"You're the imaginative one. Anything you come up with is fine with me."

"Great." There was a slight creak as Collie rocked the chair back onto two legs and a thump as her boots hit the table. "I'll say we can't tell him anything because he's your number one suspect."

"You bet he is. He got up at six AM, got dressed, ran down to the pool room by six fifteen, killed Jocelyn without getting a drop of water on him, came back up here, and delayed you by fiddling with his tie. It all makes sense."

"Sure, except that I was with him from ten after six until six thirty. He was in my room watching CNN while I did my makeup. It didn't occur to him to wear a tie until we were ready to go downstairs."

"That's convenient." The facecloth was starting to cool off. Anna pressed it against her eyes with the heels of her hands. "You're each other's alibi. Okay, if you're going to be difficult, let's go back to the janitor theory. How do you think he managed to drown an adult woman without anyone noticing while the coffee-shop was getting ready to open?"

"I don't know. I've thought about that too. There would have been people all over the place, setting tables, starting coffee . . . and, as you say, she was a grown woman. I'm sure she didn't just lie still while he did it. She would've made some noise."

It was interesting how Collie could intellectualize the problem. She might have been talking about something she'd seen in a movie.

"Maybe he hit her over the head first," Anna offered. "He probably did. Not that it would've been any less of a spectacle, but it would've been quieter."

The front legs of Collie's chair dropped to the floor. "Didn't Bryan say that he heard kind of a thumping sound while he was guarding the pool room?"

"Yeah, but that was after the body was discovered."

"Discovered by the janitor," Collie pointed out. "You know, the artist also known as our murderer? Did anyone else see the body before he closed the pool room and the coffee-shop?"

That was an interesting question.

"I don't think so." Anna sat up, pulling the facecloth from her eyes. "You could be right about that. She shows up at six fifteen, ten minutes later he closes off the area, then he goes back in to 'guard the body' and kills her in complete privacy. That explains why no one in the coffee-shop saw anything. They were gone before there was anything to see."

"Wouldn't they have seen Jocelyn standing around?" Collie asked. "Alive and well?"

"Sitting around," Anna said. "I found her coat when I was in there looking for my purse. She was sitting at one of the tables, behind that tacky garden thing they have set up between the coffee-shop and the pool. It's possible they actually couldn't see her at all."

"Okay," Collie said. "If that's the theory we're going with, how about this: the janitor had plenty of time to meet up with the guy who followed Jocelyn into the hotel. Maybe money changed hands or something."

"Um, I don't know a lot about hiring a hitman, but I don't think it's usually a spur of the moment kind of thing," Anna told her. "I mean, you have to assume that most people are going to say no. At the very least."

Collie put her arms on the table and leaned forward until her head was resting on them. Her face was turned to Anna, but nearly hidden by all the hair that had escaped her braid. "Maybe he used his magic evil eye and made the janitor kill her."

Where in hell did that come from?

"Where I went wrong," Anna said thoughtfully, "was when I decided to head west. I could've gone out to the Maritimes. I like it out there. Could've travelled down the east coast.

Could've gone to Quebec and worked on my French. But no, I had to wind up in Seattle running this stupid errand for my friend. And that errand was bad enough in its own right, but I never dreamed it would put me in a situation where I would hear someone seriously suggest that a mild-mannered janitor had been driven to murder by the evil eye."

Collie was smiling somewhere behind the hair. "Funny where life takes you," she agreed.

Anna didn't mean to laugh, but there was no avoiding it. "You're out of your mind," she said when she was done. "That notion of yours, is that what you're going to tell Paul?"

Collie sighed. "I don't know. Let's see if we can come up with something better."

"Yeah." Anna stood up, holding the facecloth in a tightly closed fist. "Just let me get some more hot water in this thing and I'll be right with you."

"We'll have a lot more to tell you tomorrow," said Collie. Their booth was next to a fireplace, and she was curled up like a cat beside the warmth. She'd managed to keep Paul at bay until they'd ordered and surrendered their menus, but now there was nothing to do until the food came and she'd run out of stalling tactics. Anna had to admit, she seemed amazingly calm.

"Why's that?" Paul asked. His drink of choice for the evening was the mighty Caesar, and his thin fingers were compulsively stirring one with an anemic stick of celery.

"Because Rebecca is letting us into *The Rail* office at nine tonight."

Paul did a trick Anna wouldn't have guessed he knew—he beamed. "A late-night visit to *The Rail*. I salute you." He did, raising his glass and taking a sip. "What else have you ladies done today?"

"We think something went wrong with Kate Eby's pregnancy."

Paul nodded. "That's hardly news. She had a miscarriage."

"Okay, so you knew that—but do you know why? There

are rumours that she did something to abort the baby, which as I'm sure you know is out of character for her. Rebecca's going to find out where she is so that Anna and I can talk to her."

"Good. Anything else?"

"Yeah." Collie was tracing the stems of her silverware. "We think the hotel janitor was involved in Jocelyn's murder."

Paul looked at Anna. She nodded, but kept her mouth shut. It had been agreed that this would be left to Collie.

"What makes you think that?"

"We were bothered by the fact that the staff in the coffee-shop didn't notice the murder being committed. You have to admit, that's strange."

"I do so admit," Paul conceded. "How does that implicate the janitor?"

"Well, what if he was lying when he said he'd found a body? What if he said that to get people out of the pool room and the coffee-shop and then he killed Jocelyn? The night auditor says he heard a loud thump while he was guarding the door to the pool room. He figured Trent just tripped over something, but he could have hit Jocelyn over the head."

Paul's eyes were gleaming. It was pretty clear he liked the idea. "That's good," he said. "That's devious. It may have actually happened. Let's run with it as an assumption. The only problem I have is the obvious one; why would the janitor want to kill Jocelyn Lowry?"

"We're on that," Collie replied. "We have two people looking for a connection between the janitor and *The Rail*. We also think there may have been an outside influence at the time of the murder. Jocelyn was followed into the hotel and later followed to the pool room."

Paul blinked. "Where in hell did you hear that?"

"The night auditor. He didn't think anything of it at the time."

The food arrived. Paul took a few bites of his steak before commenting. "You'd think, being a staff member and seeing a woman being followed in his hotel. . . . Well, for our purposes that's water under the bridge. Anything else I should know?"

"Not much. We were in Joce's apartment today, but nothing

jumped out at us. We may have to go back when we have a better idea of what we're looking for."

"Erm," Paul agreed from behind the baked potato he was swallowing. "Did you do the mail and the phone?"

Collie stopped winding fettuccine around her fork long enough to shoot him a dirty look. "What do you take me for? Of course I did. Nothing in the mail. When I hit redial on her phone it rang about fifteen times, so I gave up. I star sixty-nined it and got *The Rail* main switchboard, which I assume was Rebecca calling to see why Joce was late for work. I'll ask her to make sure. I tried to call forward to my hotel room, but her phone doesn't have that feature."

Paul smiled. "I apologize for doubting you, Colette."

"Damn right."

Anna couldn't get over their complete disregard for privacy. It was understandable in this case, but she had a funny feeling this was the way they always operated. Rather than discuss that topic, she concentrated on the very good pepper steak she was pounding back. Eating was much better than wondering, for example, what Paul had been doing all day.

"So, Anna," Paul said sociably, "Collie tells me you can't really talk about what you used to do. . . ."

Anna took her time chewing and swallowing before she attended to that. "That's true," she told him. "I can't."

Paul laughed. "Okay, okay. Can't blame a guy for trying."

Sure she could, but there was no point in it. Especially when you considered that he was footing the bill for dinner.

"I guess," Paul went on, "that I'm used to people wanting to talk to me. They seek me out to tell me secrets. I'm not good with reticence. You really don't like to talk about yourself, do you?"

The man was not so stupid as to need confirmation of that obvious fact, so the patter meant he was still trying to pry something loose. Anna speared a piece of green pepper and wondered how many tacks Paul would take before the meal was over. "Depends," she said. "I'm perfectly willing to tell you what I had for breakfast."

"Colette already told me that." He said it with slightly

smug confidence that Colette told him pretty much everything.

Anna told herself that it wasn't funny. Smiling would be bad. Laughing would be worse. "Then we're gonna need a new topic of conversation," she said. "If you want to talk about your doctoral thesis for an hour, I'm willing to pretend to listen."

"I'm not," said Collie. "Christ, Anna, you don't know what you're saying. He pulls out charts."

"Colette, my doctoral thesis is not boring. My book was a goddamned bestseller. It's gossip. Everyone's interested in that."

"'Cept possibly Anna," Collie told him. "She hasn't asked me anything."

Paul stared at Anna. "You do know that I have dirt on the best and the brightest in every field of endeavour?"

The waitress came by to warm up their coffees. Not wanting to draw her in with the irresistible lure of celebrity gossip, Anna waited until she was gone to answer. "I hope you're being facetious."

"Usually," Paul said, unruffled. "Aren't you interested in anything? Movies, music, politics, science . . . historical figures. I could give you my take on the Kennedy assassination."

"I would pay you not to," Anna said before she could stop herself. Collie almost choked on a piece of breadstick, then dropped her face to the table. Her shoulders were shaking. To Anna's immense relief, Paul laughed.

"Okay, I'll take that as a no."

"I'm sorry," Anna told him. "I really am. It's nothing personal. I'm just not interested in idle speculation."

Collie lifted her head from the table. "The past two days must have been really boring for you," she said, apparently forgetting that they were supposed to be making a good impression on their boss.

"That wasn't idle speculation," said Anna. "I mean, we're trying to get somewhere. That's different from talking about what fucking Prince Harry is doing when you have no idea and no way of finding out and it doesn't really matter in your life anyhow."

"The thing is," Paul said cheerfully, "most people are interested in idle speculation. It's a popular hobby. I make a very good living at it."

Anna wrapped a hand around her coffee cup. It was just on the right side of too hot to touch. "I know that, but I don't see what point you're trying to make."

Collie had a twist at the corner of her mouth. Anna had seen it a few times over the past few days. She was starting to think that it showed up exclusively when Colette thought she had somebody's number.

"Paul is saying you're a weirdo," she said. She presented it as a statement of fact. "And he's wondering why you are so very weird. It's a sneaky way of getting you to talk about yourself."

"But there's nothing to tell. I don't care for *The Enquirer's* prose style. I have better things to think about. I can't believe he's suggesting I have some kind of deficiency because I've never entered a dead pool."

"I can't believe you're talking about me as though I'm not here," Paul said. "What better things have you got to think about?"

Anna blinked at him. "Besides . . . anything?"

"No, seriously," Paul said, placing a hand on her arm. "I don't mean to offend you. I don't think you have any kind of congenital deficiency."

"I didn't say congenital," Anna snapped.

"All right, if I think you have a deficiency, it's a deficiency of free time. Most people get up, go to work, go home, there's food in the kitchen, all the basics are pretty much a given. What will I do today, how will I secure food, where will I sleep, what does my society expect of me. These are questions most people have answered before the alarm goes off each morning. Or within ten minutes after the alarm goes off, if you wake up as stupid as I do." He paused to take a sip of coffee. Anna took advantage of the distraction to take her arm back.

"In the life of your average North American," Paul went on, "the basics are settled, but the mind is still ticking. It needs something to work on. If you have a challenging job, fine, but most people don't. Instead, they have hobbies. Outside interests. Anything to occupy the active ten percent of that big old brain. Am I making sense?"

"Yeah," Anna said. "You've found the world's most long-winded way of saying that people are obsessed with trivia because they're bored."

"Absolutely," Paul said with a broad smile. Anna was starting to wonder if it was possible to offend him. "Maslow summed it up with his hierarchy of needs. Simplistic, yes, but a helpful guide to human behaviour nonetheless. Maslow believed that people don't develop an interest in art or religion—or entertainment, which is a combination of the two—until their basic needs for food and shelter and identity are met."

That was complicated, but it sounded suspiciously like a cut.

"I don't live out of a shopping cart," Anna told him, biting off the words.

"But you don't have a permanent address, do you?" Paul's smile was gone, and she realized he'd been leading her to this all along. "Certainly not in Vancouver, where you claimed to live. Now, I know what you told Collie about your background, and it may even be true. Regardless, you're keeping secrets. You've been on the road for a while, and there's probably a reason for that." He smiled, showing too many teeth. "You look tense, Anna. Relax. Collie likes you, and her taste is usually good. Also, I believe that 'takes one to know one' applies well to inveterate liars. Your survival instincts aren't packed away in storage—you have them up and running. As far as I'm concerned, you can stay on the job, I'll pay you what I promised, and officially I believe every word you say to me. I just wanted you to know," he added, leaning forward, "that I am not stupid. I'm vain."

Anna set her fork down so he wouldn't see it shaking in her hand. "I never did think you were stupid."

He smiled, perfectly friendly. "Good enough. Are we having dessert?"

Anna looked at Collie, who had lost interest in her meal. She was staring at Paul with a white face and bright red patches above her cheekbones. Paul looked right back at her, undisturbed by the sight.

"You should know by now that I do not let these things go," he said gently. "I'd apologize for upsetting you, but I'm not all that sorry. Did you want something with chocolate in it?"

Collie swallowed and moved her shoulders. Anna heard an unpleasant cracking.

"Yeah," she said. "Get me a menu."

Paul waved the waitress over and she gave them both dessert menus. It didnt take long for Collie to find something to settle her stomach, but Anna took her time looking the menu over. She was trying to decide if she'd get the most liquor out of a B-52 cheesecake or some sort of flambé.

Paul made a few attempts at conversation during dessert, but none of them went anywhere. By the time the three of them were packed into Collie's Tercel, he'd given up that idea and opted for a cheerful silence that involved a content little smile and fingers drumming perkily on his knees. Anna couldn't stop thinking about her gun.

Since it was close to nine, Paul was dropped off at the Victorian and they proceeded straight to *The Rail*. Anna waited until the hotel was a few blocks behind them before she dared to speak. "Seriously," she said, "are you sure he can't possibly have done it?"

Collie giggled. It had the ring of jangled nerves. "Not this murder," she said. "God, Anna, I'm sorry. That was awful. I had no idea he was going to come down on you."

"I think," said Anna, "he came down on us. And you don't have to apologize. I'm the one with the mysterious past."

"He's really . . . sharklike sometimes. Don't you think?"

"Yeah." Anna turned her head to watch the city lights move past her window. "He's very smart. Smart people—they're not just 'normal but smarter.' They're something else. Even you and I: we're not dumb, and we're not normal either. Your boss is that to the tenth. If I were a shrink, I'd say I thought his brain was hooked up funny. Better, in a lot of ways. Not in all ways."

Collie digested that for a few blocks. "I'm sorry I told him you hadn't asked about his work."

Anna smiled. "No worries. I think we had a ticket for that train no matter what."

A few more blocks passed, the neighbourhoods changing quickly to bad to bohemian to rich.

"Anna?"

"Yeah?"

"You didn't do anything terrible, did you?"

Anna shut her eyes. "This is something you want my word on?"

"I don't think you're an inveterate liar. I think you give it a rest sometimes."

It was impossible to figure out why Collie trusted her, but there was no denying that it did something to Anna. Even if she had done something terrible, even if she were wanted in a dozen States, she would damn well fess up if Collie asked her to. Wouldn't even consider a lie. She was relieved beyond measure that the truth was in her favour.

"No," she said. It seemed like a good time for simple human contact. She moved her left arm to a place where Collie would brush it every time she turned the steering wheel. "I didn't do anything terrible. I'm not in trouble. I'm not going to get you in trouble. Why do I keep letting you drive when I promised myself I would never take that risk again?"

"Because I know where we're going. And if you were driving, you'd be the one paying to put gas in your vehicle."

The Tercel was just reaching a comfortable temperature, the stereo was playing a pretty song from some eighties keyboard band, and for the moment Anna was at peace with the world. "I knew there had to be a reason."

They circled the block a few times looking for parking. It shouldn't have been a problem so late in the evening, but Victoria was crowded in spots. An unavoidable problem when a city was built on an island, as Anna has often heard from a friend who lived in London.

"We could just park in their lot," Collie said after the third drive-by. "It's past business hours. Becca could give us a visitor's pass."

"That would take away from the thrill of victory," said Anna. "I can see you have your entire self-image pinned on your ability to find a spot."

"Well," Collie said, pulling into *The Rail's* lot, "to save face, I should point out that this is a parking spot. I did find one. I won't hear anything else on the topic."

There was a thin line of light along the side of the building where Rebecca was holding open the back door. They went inside quickly and quietly.

"You're late," Rebecca said, pulling the door shut behind them. It hissed angrily as air was forced through the slow-closing hinge.

"Couldn't find parking," said Collie. "Do we need a pass for the lot?"

Rebecca shook her head. "Not at this hour."

The door they'd entered opened on a staircase: one set up, and one set down. Before Anna could say anything, Rebecca spoke. "Building has no main floor. How crazy is that? It's totally inconvenient, not to mention we have no wheelchair access. Collie, did Joce ever tell you her theory about modern architecture?"

She started to move downstairs, talking as she went. Anna looked at Collie, who shrugged and followed.

"She used to know some guys who were in architecture school, and I guess it's a bitch. Long hours, lots of big projects. Some of these guys came home every few days to shower, spent the rest of their time at the drawing tables, hardly ever ate. It was like some cult. So Joce figured, after four years of that, you've got to be pretty crazy. And you probably hate everyone too." Becca paused at the bottom of the stairs to fiddle with a heavy ring of keys. "So these kids graduate all psychotic and angry and make these insanely ugly buildings as revenge on a world that's done them wrong. That's the right key."

The door opened on a hallway lit by the red light on a security panel.

"Don't worry about that," Rebecca told them. "It's not turned on. They never turn that one on."

From the way Collie moved down the dark hall, Anna guessed she'd been in this part of the building before. When they rounded the corner, Anna saw a disorganized cluster of desks covered with stacks of paper, Macs, and huge monitors.

"Joce worked down here," Collie said softly. She headed straight for a desk that was surrounded by small plants. Gardening seemed to be what Jocelyn did when she was leaving her mark on a place.

"The police already did that," Becca said as Collie pulled open a drawer.

"I know," Collie said, "but we knew her and they didn't. Do you know the password for her computer?"

"I have everybody's passwords upstairs, in case they forget." Rebecca glanced at Anna, probably making sure she wasn't stealing the silverware. Anna helpfully clasped her hands behind her back. Becca didn't seem reassured. "I'll be right back."

Anna wandered around the office with no idea what she was looking for. There was a bulletin board near the largest desk, covered in Dilbert cartoons and updates on the staff hockey pool. A notice about Jocelyn's funeral was in the centre of the board. Just below it, there was a memo about office theft that listed eight missing items and asked that staff keep their valuables locked up at all times. Anna detached it and folded it until it fit in the pocket of her coat.

Collie was sitting in Jocelyn's chair with her head in her hands. Anna put a hand on her shoulder.

"She had a drawer full of Twix bars," Collie said. "Probably ate one a day, no more, that's the limit. She was really strict with herself about stuff like that."

"In spite of what some people say," Anna told her, "you can't live each day as though it were your last. You'd blow your bank account and clog an artery before the end of the week. Treats are more satisfying when there are limits, anyway."

"Provided you can be satisfied," Collie said. She shook her head and went back to searching the desk. Anna moved away, not wanting to crowd her.

The next desk over was sparse by comparison—no plants, no Twix bars, just a calendar with a photo of a businessman and a twinkie at an expensive restaurant. Beneath the photo, in large letters, was the word *Opportunity*.

Anna leaned closer to see the small print below that word: "Yes, that's your boss," it read. "No, that's not his wife."

Collie was moving plants around. It was hard to tell if she was looking for something special or just anything unusual.

"Do you think," Anna asked, "Jocelyn might have said something useful to any of her co-workers? I mean, besides Rebecca."

Collie had a sour expression on her face. Anna took a good look at it, but couldn't figure out what it meant.

"Not likely."

Anything Anna might have said to that was put on hold by the sound of the back door opening.

"Okay, I've got it," Rebecca was saying as she hurried down the hall. "Good thing there's no one near my desk right now. D'you know, they're talking about renting this building out at night?"

Collie held her hand out for the slip of paper Rebecca was clutching. "What do you mean, rent it out?"

"It's this new thing," said Rebecca, placing the paper in Collie's hand. "Do you know how to get on to her computer?"

Collie turned up the screen and pointed out the password prompt. "I'm thinking it's not rocket science," she said. She typed in the password and the computer kicked into gear.

"It'll take a while." Rebecca pulled up a chair. "They put in some cheap-ass security program, and it takes forever to verify the password. Anyway, speaking of cheap-ass, businesses have been trying to pick up extra cash by renting their office space to other companies at night. Can you imagine? You leave your desk at five; at six some other person sits in it until two AM, or whenever, doing God knows what. . . . I mean, you couldn't leave anything in your desk."

"You could lock it," Anna pointed out.

"I guess, but it's . . . I hate it when people touch my desk."

The monitor flickered and the desktop came up. The background photo was a close-up of thick green leaves.

Anna shook her head. "I'm starting to think your friend should have been a botanist."

"No," said Collie. She was moving an arrow across the screen, touching every folder as she tried to decide what to open. "If you'd known her four years ago, you would've said she should've been a mortician or something. Design is the obsession—the look is just a phase."

Rebecca stiffened and backed away from the desk. Anna didn't want to turn for an obvious look, but peripheral vision told her the woman was steaming mad.

"Fish or cut bait," Anna suggested, nudging Collie's arm. Collie picked a folder and began skimming. She called up pictures and opened articles. Anna didn't see anything that seemed relevant to the case and she suspected Colette didn't either, because her fluid movements never stopped or even slowed.

"The look is not a phase," Rebecca commented. The anger in her voice was poorly disguised. "Did it ever occur to you that she might have found her way? That maybe she had finally become the person she was meant to be?"

"Bec," Collie said softly, "you can give me shit later. I'm really busy at the moment."

Anna kept her eyes on the screen as Collie worked her way through the contents of Jocelyn's computer. It was a lot more pleasant than looking at Rebecca's face and wondering if she was actually going to cry.

It wouldn't be fair to say Jocelyn had nothing on her computer, because there was an astonishing amount of data. Programs, files, supposedly funny cartoons, even a knock-off of Tetris . . . but nothing that told them what Jocelyn had been thinking about during the last few days of her life.

"Did she have email on this thing?" Anna asked.

Collie nodded. "Going there now."

That was the difference between Anna and Collie's investigative techniques. Collie would look through Jocelyn's email.

Anna would think of looking at Jocelyn's email, then realize she had no idea how to operate an email program other than the one on Curt's computer. Sooner or later, she was probably going to have to give up and learn something about computers.

Since staring at the computer and trying not to look confused wasn't helpful, Anna disengaged and paid some attention to the surrounding desks. Most of them looked less lived in than Jocelyn's, and for a moment Anna felt she was looking at the desks of ghosts. They could be, for all the difference it apparently made in this place. The funeral notice on the bulletin board was the only sign that Jocelyn was away for longer than a weekend.

"Okay, this is interesting."

Anna went back to her post behind Collie's left shoulder. Apparently she'd found an email message that meant something to her:

> Hey there hi there ho there. Thought you'd vanished up your own asshole, but I guess everybody has to come up for air sometime. In response to your question, everything on that list is garage sale trash. Nobody with a hint of a clue would waste their time on it. If you're asking because you lifted that crap, shame on you. When we used to hang, you were a better class of thief. And BTW, I haven't forgotten about the fifty you owe me.
> Regards,
> the Waterer of the Moat

"I don't know who this guy is," said Collie, "but he's using a University of Alberta account. He sent this to her a week ago."

She was kind enough to point to the parts of the message that gave her that information. Anna nodded as though it made sense.

"Unfortunately," Collie added, "Joce seems to have deleted her Sent Mail—so I can't read the message she sent to this guy in the first place. Sucks."

"So," Rebecca said, "if this guy's from Edmonton, do you know him?"

Collie kept her eyes on the screen.

"Who knows? His real name isn't anywhere on this message. Not even in his return address. I could email him and ask."

"But you've got to have some idea who the Waterer of the Moat might be."

"She said she didn't," Anna said, looking Rebecca in the eye to make sure she shut up.

Personally, she thought Collie did know something she wasn't saying. Anna could understand not wanting to talk until Rebecca was gone. Hell, she was starting to wish she could be in cryogenic suspension until Rebecca was gone.

Rebecca ignored her and turned to Collie. "This is really progressive, Colette. Hiring a female thug."

She probably meant for that to sting, but it was the funniest thing Anna had heard in a long time. She laughed so hard she had to grab a desk for balance. Collie's shoulders were shaking, and Anna could hear her giggling. When Anna finally managed to stand upright, she saw Rebecca had retreated to a position near the front door.

"I'll be upstairs," she told them, "if you need anything."

Anna didn't feel any compulsion to stop her. She thought Collie might say something conciliatory, but Collie kept her mouth shut until the door closed behind Rebecca's stiff-backed exit.

"Oh, man," Collie said cheerfully, wiping tears away with the heels of her hands, "she's pissed."

"Yeah. Just let me know if she gives you any more trouble."

Collie grinned. "I can't believe she said that." She shook her head and the grin went away. "Oh well. She's a mess. I'm trying not to hold it against her. What else do we need here?"

"I wouldn't mind seeing some other desks. Postnikoff . . . Eve Harris. Who else are we looking at? That Kate woman, I guess."

"Right." Collie had a scrap of paper and was making notes. "Mark Ling, too."

Anna knew it really wasn't, but she couldn't help feeling that the echo from the door Rebecca had slammed was still shaking the air around them. "We're going to need Rebecca's help on that," she said. "Aren't we?"

"Yeah." Collie pushed back her chair and stood. "I don't know where those desks are. And I think you have to get past security to enter the other floors."

"Great. By the way, anytime you want to tell me what Becca's problem is with you. . . ."

Collie gave her an appraising look. Whatever this test was, Anna seemed to pass, because Collie finally let fly with her signature lopsided smile. "I'll let you know." She picked up the phone and dialed zero. Anna was a few feet away, but she clearly heard Rebecca's voice as she answered. Collie winced. "Hi. Sorry, but we need to see a few more desks." She nodded, for all the good that did, and hung up. "She'll be down in a minute."

That was the end of the conversation until heels clicked down the stairs and the door creaked open. When Rebecca faced them, Anna thought she saw red in her eyes. "Get this over with as fast as you can," she said. "You're not supposed to be here, and I'd like to get some sleep tonight."

"We need to see Lou Postnikoff's desk," Collie said.

Rebecca laughed shortly. "His office is still locked up. He hardly ever used it anyway. He preferred to work from home. Was that the only thing you needed?"

Anna cleared her throat. "No," she said. "Mark Ling, Kate Eby . . . and Eve Harris. We'd like to see their desks, too."

"That I can do. Well, not all of it. Mark's desk is on the second floor, and somebody's working up there. But Eve and Kate are on third. Were on third. Are. Were, are. No one's touched their desks, you know . . . it's as if everyone's pretending they'll be back in a day or so. Stupid. I'll take you up the back way."

She led them back the way they'd come in. The stairwell was grimy, not that you could see it well with so many lights burned out. If *The Rail* had ever been so lavish as to send janitors into every nook and cranny of the building, those days were gone.

Anna made a mental note to ask Collie how much money *The Rail* had made over the past few years. They might just be cheap; a lot of companies were. But it was possible they were in trouble.

Once they left the staircase and stepped into the third floor bullpen, there was no need for further directions to Eve Harris's desk. It was a showpiece of expensive and banal taste. Gold and crystal vases full of silk flowers, a fountain pen with what looked like real diamonds in the cap. Anna estimated the junk on that desk was worth more than her Jeep.

"You know," Collie said, surveying the landscape, "in a workplace where a lot of the staff is eating pot noodles and desperately trying to pay off student loans, I don't see it as classy for the television personality to wave her money in everyone's face."

"I'm surprised any of it is still here," Anna said. "I saw a memo downstairs that said there'd been a bunch of robberies."

Collie turned to stare at her. "You mean, like, with a gun?"

"I don't think so. I think somebody was just lifting stuff off desks."

"Yeah," Rebecca said. "We thought it might be one of the cleaners, which is why I thought it was weird you asked about that janitor."

"Technically that's not robbery," said Collie, "'cause there was no threat of force. It's just theft."

"Colette," Anna said, "I don't know how to tell you this, but nobody cares. Were you like this in school?"

Collie grinned. "I was worse. I've been socialized." She turned to Rebecca. "What did you find out about the janitor?"

"I didn't. I don't think he's ever been here. He didn't work for us, didn't apply for a job, he's not in the guest book for the past six months. Maybe he has a friend here or something, but I don't know how to find that out short of asking everyone. Which I won't."

"Well, of course not." Collie said. "We wouldn't want you to. His name was in the paper. People would wonder why you were asking about him."

Anna couldn't take her eyes off that desk. "So, getting back to Fort Knox here," she said. "All of this just sits in the open, and nobody touches it?"

"Somebody touches it," said Collie. "It's been dusted."

"Not around the vases," Rebecca pointed out. "The janitors are scared to move them. They're massively expensive. I wouldn't touch them either."

Anna didn't know a whole lot about decorating, but the way the paperweights and photographs and vases were arranged around the edges of the desk didn't seem quite right. There was a gap that even she would have noticed and filled with something.

"It wasn't left alone," she said. "Something was taken." Rebecca looked at her with wide eyes.

"How did you . . ."

"Something used to be here." Anna tapped the desk with one finger, and beetles were crawling over each other, shells and legs scraping. She was alone with them, in a small square room. The clicking was almost mechanical, almost meaningful. Like Morse Code saying that stuck-up bitch was going to get an education. Wings beat and hummed, making the sound of a transformer. The sound of power.

"Anna!"

Her arm hurt. She looked down and saw the reason for that—the small gold nails digging in as Collie held her arm a few inches from the surface of the desk. Anna tugged and her arm was released. She pulled it back, held it against her stomach and absently ran her other hand over the half-moons Colette had left in her skin.

"Sorry," Collie said.

Anna was about to say that it was all right, meant to say it as soon as she could get her mouth to move, but then she realized Colette's apology had been directed at Becca. "Anna has petit mal epilepsy. She just spaces sometimes."

Rebecca was staring at Anna. "Are you. . . ." She glanced at Collie. "Is she okay?"

"Oh, yeah," said Collie. She placed a hand on Anna's shoulder and gently pushed her into the chair that had somehow materialized behind her. "She'll be fine in a minute. It's no big deal. What were you saying about the photo?"

Anna listened as Rebecca described a framed photograph that had stood on the spot she'd touched. A picture of Eve's cats in a fifty dollar frame, probably the least valuable thing on that desk.

"But the most personal," Collie said. Anna didn't say anything. She was too busy brushing beetles off her coat. She couldn't see them, but she could feel them, and she could hear the clicking.

"Yeah, she really loved those cats. Loves. She loves those cats. Goddamn it, I have got to stop talking like she's dead."

Given the nature of the photographs that had been scattered around the office, Anna couldn't help wondering exactly how Eve had loved those cats. She managed to keep that thought to herself. "When did that picture go missing?" she asked instead.

"About nine months ago," Rebecca said. "If you want the exact date, I can get it for you."

"Maybe. I was wondering if all of the stuff that was stolen vanished on one night. The memo made it sound like it happened over a few weeks at least."

"Oh." Rebecca was running a finger along the base of one of the vases, picking up dust. "A couple of things went nine months ago, and a few more a month after that, and the last batch went five months back. Three different nights."

Collie leaned against the desk next to Eve's. "That's kind of weird. Have you figured out if any particular people were in the building all three times?"

Rebecca smiled. "We're not totally stupid. I checked everything, but except for the regular staff and the janitors, I couldn't find any one person who'd been here all three times. Not even the vending machine guy."

Unbelievable. Anna shook her head. "Is there some kind of law against our catching a break? Is it impossible that anything about this case might be simple?"

Rebecca stopped dusting the desk. "Do you actually think the thefts have anything to do with Jocelyn getting killed?"

"I don't know, but it seems pretty dumb to ignore it. No offense."

Rebecca had the expression of a woman who was taking plenty of offense, but she didn't say anything.

Anna pulled the memo from her coat pocket. "Could you mark down on here what things were stolen when, and who they belonged to?"

Rebecca took the memo and frowned. "You took this?"

Collie rolled her eyes. Anna bit the inside of her lip. Now would be a bad time to laugh. "I didn't see a photocopier. You want to make me a copy?"

"No." She picked up the million-dollar fountain pen and started to write.

Collie was watching Anna from somewhere near the end of her patience, and Anna had to bite her lip again. It was obviously killing her that she couldn't ask about the moment Anna had found on that desk. God knew, Anna appreciated Collie's silence . . . but it was still uncivilized fun to see the girl nearly curious enough to explode.

"Later," she mouthed, after checking to be certain Rebecca wouldn't see her. Collie nodded.

"Okay." Rebecca stood with one hand on the small of her back and set the pen back in place. "For whatever good it does, here's your list."

Anna took it. "Thanks."

"Yeah. I have to go downstairs and take care of a few things. Kate's desk is in the corner, beneath the window."

It was an ordinary desk. A little nicer than ordinary, since this place had real wooden desks instead of the usual steel and particle board. There was no reason for Anna to hate it. There was no reason to think she shouldn't go anywhere near it. She got to her feet. "Time's a wastin'," she said, grabbing a handful of Colette's coat sleeve and dragging her towards Kate Eby's desk. Behind her, she heard the door to the stairwell open and shut. For lack of reasonable alternatives, Anna kept trudging towards that desk. Strange that a tight looped carpet should feel so much like mud.

"I should," Collie said, pulling her coat sleeve from Anna's grasp, "go through Eve's desk. I mean, I don't know what you stumbled on, but we came here to look for clues."

"Okay," said Anna. Much as she disliked Kate's desk, she really didn't care for the thought of touching Eve Harris's desk again. "We can talk about the rest in the car."

"Yeah. I figured."

Anna stood in front of Kate's desk, listening as Colette rifled through Eve Harris's belongings. Kate's desk was surrounded by finger paintings and photographs of children, presumably her own. Anna had always assumed the people who wrote parenting columns were faking their extreme interest in the topic. Maybe she'd been wrong. She pulled the memo from her pocket and scanned through Rebecca's cramped handwriting until she found Kate's name. Apparently a small teddy bear had been swiped from her desk during the second haul. Again, nothing valuable. Just personal.

"Anna, if you don't think you should touch her desk, don't. I'll be done here in a sec."

Anna glanced over her shoulder at Collie. "It's okay. I think I've had my seizure for the night."

She pulled out Kate's chair to the sound of Collie laughing.

"It's not that funny," Anna complained as she searched for private notes along the backs of the photographs. "If you were trying to make me not look like a freak, I think you took a wrong turn at the lights."

"Oh, that's very enlightened. Lots of people have epilepsy. Oh, check this out. Eve Harris has a prescription for Zoloft that she never filled. It's from June."

"Swipe it," Anna said. "God . . . Kate Eby had her home phone, her kids' school, and her babysitter on speed dial. How many times a day do you figure she checked in on the little angels?"

"Maybe she was just bad at remembering numbers."

Anna spun the swivel chair she was parked in and gestured at the abstract art surrounding her.

Collie sighed. "Your point is well taken."

Anna turned her attention to the Rolodex. After a few turns, she found what she was looking for. "I've got a card with the name of her obstetrician," she announced.

"Swipe it," said Collie.

Anna could hear her smile. She slipped the card into her pocket. "Way ahead of you."

It wouldn't have been hard for anyone to guess this desk belonged to a pregnant woman. The pre-natal vitamins and crackers were in the top drawer, doctors appointments were all over the calendar, and a row of books for expectant mothers was lined up between bookends shaped like storks. Yet another argument for Anna's theory that pregnancy turned women into morons. To be fair, Kate Eby might always have been terminally girly. Probably grew up in a room with a canopy bed and had one of those porcelain dolls with her birth month written across its skirt and a birthstone in its precious little hands. Anna's childhood room had featured a stuffed badger and a .22. There were days when she missed that .22 pretty hard. She reached for the book of baby names. Kate might have used a prescription or some other juicy tidbit as a bookmark. No point searching a desk, really, unless you were going to be thorough. Anna laid her fingers against the top of the book and tipped it back. The spine was deeply creased from what had probably been compulsive reading. The book fell easily into the palm of Anna's hand.

The room was dimly pleasant, all cream-coloured wicker furniture and pastel cotton throws. There was a crib in the corner, empty for now. Waiting. And the movement of the rocking chair was soothing, but the dull pain in Anna's belly didn't stop. It kept on, gnawing and testing. It would be dull, because this baby was a long way from teething.

Beside her, Anna saw a woman rocking gently in an identical chair. She looked desperate for sleep. Her light brown hair was limp, the ponytail holder sliding out of place.

She had a book on her lap, below her round stomach. It was open to a chart about fetal development. Her short, clear-polished nails ran under the text. She turned to Anna with a puzzled expression on her face. She said, "What's the right age for a child to eat its way out?"

"That's crazy," Anna said, not sure where the words were

coming from. "Everybody knows babies don't do that. They don't eat or claw their way out."

"That's easy for everybody to say," Kate told her. "It isn't eating them. Do you think it's a monster instead? And not my baby at all?"

Anna nodded. She reached below her chair and found a pair of scissors. She placed them in Kate's hands. "It ate your real baby a long time ago."

". . . the goddamn scissors down right now!"

Anna took a good long look at what was going on in her stomach region before she really saw it. She was holding a pair of scissors to the button of her jeans, and Colette, God love her, was trying to take them away.

"Fuck," Anna said. She really, deeply meant it. She dropped the scissors and drew her legs up, resting her heels on the edge of the seat.

Collie sat down on the floor beside her, breathing hard. "Remember when I said you didn't have to look through that desk, and you said it was cool?"

Anna pressed her hands to her stomach. Not perfectly flat, okay, but she sure as hell wasn't pregnant. "Goes to show, I can be wrong too."

Collie picked up the scissors with two fingers, as if whatever had got hold of Anna might be lingering on them. "This is really stupid. Trying to stab yourself whenever you find a clue is not productive." She dropped the scissors into an open desk drawer and pushed it shut. "How old are you?"

Anna's headache was back. "That's a rude question, Colette."

"I can't help wondering how you lasted this long with such a self-destructive personal quirk."

Anna's mouth twitched. "I thought you said it was a gift."

"It's possible I didn't have all the facts. This is fucked up, though. You didn't act out when you touched my ring, or that janitor."

She seemed to think she was going to get to the bottom of things in a five-minute Q&A, which was pretty funny considering that Anna's "gift" had confused the hell out of her for a lifetime.

"Some things push my buttons and some don't. I don't know why. There's no pattern."

"I bet there is. But this isn't a good time to go over it."

There was no good time to go over it, but since Collie was prepared to drop the matter for the time being, Anna was going to keep her mouth shut.

"We should call Rebecca," Collie added, "and get out of here. You look brutal."

"It's my hair. I'm trying to grow it out."

"Ah. That explains it." She stood and reached over Anna's shoulder to use the unfortunate Kate Eby's phone. "Hi Bec. We're through here. Thanks." She hung up and took a step back from the desk. "Why'd you cut it?"

"Got some talons caught in it."

Collie opened her mouth, no doubt to make inquiries, but Rebecca's heels were already echoing in the stairwell.

"I don't know about you, but I would prefer to discuss all of this in absolute privacy."

That was, Anna guessed, an explanation for why Collie had chosen to head west, towards a less crowded part of the island. "I don't believe in absolute privacy," she said, "but it's nice country here. I think Rebecca expected us to tell her what we found."

"Of course she did, but she has to realize that you and I are the ones working on this case. We're just using her and throwing her away. She's an old J-cloth."

A glance confirmed Anna's suspicion that Collie was smiling when she said that, but that didn't make it any less true. "You can't expect her to like it."

"As long as we find out what happened to Joce and stop whatever's going on at *The Rail*, I don't care what Becca does or doesn't like."

No one would ever accuse Colette of dancing around an issue. Of course, Anna was no better. "Mainly what Rebecca doesn't like," she pointed out, "seems to be you."

Collie was scanning the road, happily undisturbed by that

revelation. "She likes me sometimes. She just has issues with me. Now, *you* she doesn't like. But I don't think it's anything personal."

"How could it be? I've known her for one day. Do you think she really thinks I'm a thug?"

Collie's smile was difficult to interpret. "Nope."

They drove in silence for a while before Collie saw fit to add to that statement. "She's upset about something she thinks I did. The fact that a friend of mine and stranger to her is hanging around means she can't take too many shots at me. It's annoying the hell out of her."

"Did you do what she thinks you did?"

"Nope."

That was the end of that. Anna lay her head against the window and watched the trees until the sight of all that green and brown flying past the car made her stomach turn. She shut her eyes.

"Tired?"

Anna didn't bother to open her eyes. "Getting there."

"Yeah. Long day." Collie paused. "How did you get talons caught in your hair?"

"I'm trained as a veterinary assistant. I was working for this place in Oregon, and somebody brought in a red-tailed hawk. Dumb thing flew right into their car. I was stupid enough to think it was out cold; it made a grab for me, and we got tangled up." She opened her eyes and looked into the passenger side mirror as she pushed her hair back into place. It never stayed where she put it. "Just the left side, but I had to cut all of it to make it even."

Collie gave her a quick look before returning her eyes to the road. "I didn't know you liked animals."

"I don't, especially. I don't dislike them; they're okay, I just . . . it seemed like a decent way to make a living."

"Wrestling with hawks seemed like a decent way to make a living?"

It was getting oppressively warm in the car. Probably the combination of heat and humidity. And what an amazing scientific breakthrough it was for Anna to come up with that all by herself. She turned the heater down a notch. "SIAST didn't mention hawk wrestling in its brochures."

The tape that had played while they parked at the beach was still rolling in the drive. It had to be at least ninety minutes, since Anna hadn't heard all of the songs on it yet.

"I wouldn't have pegged you for an Edie Brickell fan," Anna commented while Edie swore she remembered it that way.

Collie shrugged. "I like this song. It sounds like winter. If you hate it we can lose it."

"No. It's good for here. I just get curious about mix tapes. I used to know this guy who made soundtracks for . . . oh, God, sitting by the lake at night, one for driving to Saskatoon, one for walking to and from work, one for sex . . . he did nothing without music. I swear, he probably had a deck in the bathroom with some tape labeled 'music to take a dump to.'"

"'Ring of Fire,'" said Collie thoughtfully. "You'd definitely want that one. Oh, and that Frank Zappa song, 'How Come It Hurts When I Pee.' You could call it 'Music to Take a Dump To,' but how about putting a bunch of Ella Fitzgerald songs on the other side and calling it 'Scatology'?"

"Yeah, I was pretty sure you were his soulmate."

"No doubt." Collie drummed the steering wheel. "Where does this guy live?"

"He doesn't. He made up a tape called 'Songs For My Aneurysm.'"

"Your sense of humour is really dark, you know that? I bet not everyone finds it engaging. Did he really have an aneurysm?"

"Yeah." Anna rested her eyes on the highway's yellow line. "He was a good guy. Assholes never die when they're twenty-three, have you noticed? Had a good funeral, though. Nobody said anything; they just played songs. The Tom Waits song you have on this tape—they played that."

The way Collie was looking out the window suggested she was seeing something behind the fog. "Break all the windows in the cold, cold ground," she said softly.

"So, what's your tape for?"

"I don't know what you'd call it. You're a prairie girl. You know when you're outside in the winter at night and nothing seems real? I mean, you can't feel anything outside of your clothes, and you can't hear anything because all the sound gets lost in the snow, and the sky's glowing so everything's the same colour, and the air doesn't smell like anything. . . ." She slid a hand into her hair and rubbed the side of her neck. "I always get the feeling that there's something important I'm forgetting, but I can't stand the cold long enough to remember it. I thought if I put together some songs that made me feel the same way, maybe it would click." She smiled and put her hand back on the steering wheel. "Kind of psychotic, I know."

"It's not psychotic," Anna said. "Granted, I'm not actually a shrink . . . but I think it's just fanciful."

Collie laughed. "Fanciful? That's great. Maybe someday I'll wind up in a mental institution. Is she depressed, paranoid? No, it's much worse than that. She's fanciful."

"I wouldn't rest the whole issue of your mental health on my professional opinion."

Collie shrugged. "You're as good a shrink as any I've known. Is that one of those scenic view rest stop deals up there?"

Anna narrowed her eyes and leaned forward. "Yeah, looks like."

"Good."

Collie pulled in, parked the car, and turned the heater back up. "Are we in a national park or something?"

"I don't think so. There would've been a gate."

"That's true. Wouldn't want people seeing nature for free." Collie flicked the headlights to low beam. "This is nice country. Little claustrophobic, though."

"Hey, you wanted privacy."

"Yeah, but at home you know when you have it. You can tell if someone's coming. You can tell if they're coming and due to arrive in a week."

"You should turn those lights off before you kill the battery."

Collie turned them off. "What did you get off Eve Harris's desk? Or do you want to talk about it at all?"

"Want to? Christ, no. I will though. Just give me a minute to think."

“’Kay.”

It was more than a minute. It was most of a song before Anna had sorted the feelings well enough to create a narrative. “Whoever’s doing this . . . and for some reason I think it’s a guy . . . he touched her desk. He stole the cat picture. He’s a mess. He hears beetles in his head.”

“You can see where that would drive a guy,” Colette allowed. “Especially if he really has beetles in his head. Was it our janitor?”

“No. This guy was nothing like the janitor. When the janitor killed Jocelyn, that was all business. It was just one more thing he had to do before he could go home. This guy who stole the picture . . . he really wanted to hurt her. He had some thing about her being stuck up. He wanted to teach her a lesson. And you know what was really weird? He liked the beetles. He thought they made him powerful. He thought he could focus their energy into . . . I don’t know, whatever the hell he does.”

Collie was chewing on her lower lip. “This isn’t fair,” she commented. “Seriously. Most people, when they start doing detective work, I bet it’s following shoplifters. You know? Taking pictures through motel windows. Not tracking down some murderous freakazoid with bugs in his head. Did you get why he walked off with the cat picture?”

As if Anna’s spells were ever that useful. “No . . . but it was important. When he touched her desk, he felt he was accomplishing something.”

“You sure he wasn’t just trying to make her nervous by taking something of hers?”

“Yeah, I’m sure.” Anna placed the heels of her hands against the dash and pushed, trying to snap the kinks in her shoulders. “It was more than that. He had plans.”

“Okay. That’s good. I don’t have the first clue what it means, but at least we’re learning something.” She pulled a lever along the side of her seat and tilted it until it was touching the back seat. “You know what’s cool about this deal of yours? This guy has no way of knowing that you know anything about him.”

Anna’s stomach flipped. “I don’t know about that,” she

said. "I've always wondered if this thing didn't travel both ways."

"I didn't feel anything when you touched my ring."

"Maybe it's more subtle than that." Anna shook her head. "I could just be paranoid."

"Oh, possibly," Collie chirped. She laughed at the look Anna gave her, which was not the result Anna had been trying to produce. "Look, I'm sorry you had misadventures this evening, but I can't undo that. We might as well get everything we can from them. I'm still not suggesting you should do this to yourself on purpose."

"Good," Anna said, "because I'm still not going to do that. Maybe I will start wearing gloves."

"Whatever you're comfortable with," Collie said. "I can't deny that we don't know what we're doing, but we don't need to mess with your head to solve this. Somehow, we'll figure it out. I have to believe that. I mean, if only people with superpowers can accomplish things, where does that leave me?"

"Floundering?" Anna suggested. "Over-extended? Lost?"

"Oh, so now you're too highly evolved to hang out with me," Collie said, grinning. "You pity my mundane genes. You're one of Magneto's people."

Anna snorted. "You make it sound like Jerry's kids."

"Uh huh. I say genetic advantage, you say handicap. Wanna do some more word association?"

"No. I want to get back to the part where we're so very smart that it doesn't matter who has superpowers and who doesn't."

"We're not just smart," Collie said. "We're tenacious and creative and socially adept. Otherwise, we'd be Paul."

Anna laughed. "Still pissed off after all these years," she said. "I admit Paul has some character flaws, but I really do think he's a lot smarter than either of us. I think we are like unto bugs as far as he's concerned."

"Hmm." Colette considered that. "I don't think that's exactly right. I think he knows I'm not a dummy. He finds me useful. And he hired you, so he must consider you useful, too."

"Also," Anna put in, "he wants on you."

Collie laughed. "I just say that for fun. I have no idea what he really wants. Most guys have some letch in them, but I don't think he's all that serious about this pursuit. It's possible he pretends to be after me because he thinks it's funny. Besides the fact that he knows I'm not interested, I don't think I'm his type."

"And his type would be. . . ?"

"I've never seen him with anyone," Collie admitted, "so I don't know. But I picture him with one of those fire-and-ice women. Dedicated research scientist by day, wildcat by night. Nobody could guess the passion she hid behind coke-bottle glasses."

Anna could work with that. "He's desperate for her attention," she said. "So he stops by the lab and asks her to step into the specimen freezer with him."

"She won't, though," Collie added, "because her real passion is her work. She turns him away. . . ."

"Which only makes him want her more," Anna concluded. "I hear there's good money in writing cheesy romance novels."

"Yeah, but in the cheesy romance novel she'd have to realize love was more important than her work. This research of hers is way over my head, but I'm sure whatever she's doing is more important than a roll in the hay with Paul."

"I'm gonna tell him you said that."

Collie stretched out until she was using the dash as a foot rest. "Yeah . . . tell him we were gossiping about his girlfriend, who we made up. And his sex life, which we also made up." She closed her eyes. "Obviously, Kate Eby didn't just have a miscarriage."

Nice segue.

"That's the theory I'm working from, yeah."

"What did you get from her desk, besides a desire to stick a pair of scissors in your stomach?"

"It wasn't her desk. It was that book of baby names. She was crazy the last time she touched it."

"Pregnant women are often crazy."

"No." The windows were starting to fog. Anna cleared a patch with her shirt sleeve. "I mean, yes, they are, but this was different. She thought her baby was trying to eat its way out of her stomach."

That convinced Colette to open her eyes. She turned her head to look at Anna. "Trying to eat its way out."

"She could feel it."

"Huh." Collie folded her hands over her stomach. "There's this convenience store by my mom's house. I've kind of gotten to know the couple who runs it. They tried to have a baby for years. When she finally did get knocked up I thought she'd be ecstatic."

Anna tried to meet her eyes, but Collie was aiming an intense stare at the roof of the car.

"I take it she wasn't?"

"She looked awful. The whole pregnancy, she looked worse every time I saw her. I asked her if she was okay, but she wouldn't talk about it. She miscarried in the fifth month and I swear to God, the next time I saw her she looked relieved."

There was nothing moving in Anna's stomach. Really, there wasn't.

"Did you ever find out what was going on?"

"Yeah, about a year later we had coffee. She said that right from the start she felt the baby drawing the life out of her. Said she knew it was crazy, but she couldn't stop thinking about it. She was relieved about the miscarriage because she didn't think she'd be able to love the kid after it was born, considering. She figured she'd be a bad mom."

Anna shook her head. This parenthood business clearly wasn't for everyone.

"She was a nutcase."

"Not generally. Your hormones just get screwed up when you're pregnant. They adopted a kid and she treats it really well. The thing is," she added, rolling onto her side, "I wonder how many women feel like they're carrying a parasite and don't talk about it because they think they'll sound evil."

"That is evil. You're supposed to instinctively get all gooshy and want to buy teddy bears . . . which, by the way, is why you will not see me pregnant."

"Maybe it works that way in theory." Collie pushed hair

away from her face. "But there are a lot of hormones flying around. The end results aren't predictable. Some women get diabetes from being pregnant. Lots of them get food allergies. You have to expect that some of these women are going to go nuts in ways that aren't conducive to a good mother-child relationship."

That kind of thing was probably easier to say when you knew where your mother lived.

"It's not fair to the kid," Anna said softly. She could feel Collie looking at her, but she kept her eyes on the window's clear patch.

"Didn't say it was," said Collie. "I'm just saying, Kate Eby might have had one of those hormonal quirks. Might not be related to what we're doing at all."

That wasn't butterflies Anna felt in her stomach. It was beetles. She could feel the little claws on the ends of their legs. "This would have been her third kid. She had books about pregnancy all over her desk. If she went to all the appointments on her calendar, she saw a doctor at least once a week. I think her problem was something more than a hormonal quirk."

"You think she actually did what you tried to do?"

Why not? It wasn't her baby. It was some monster that ate her baby. Anna took a deep breath. "Probably not exactly what I did, or she'd be dead . . . but she did something. She didn't even think it was her kid anymore. She thought it was a cuckoo's egg."

Something about that idea caught Colette's imagination. "Maybe it was. Can I see that memo you snagged?"

Anna produced it. Collie grabbed it without any pretense of politeness and spread it out across the steering wheel. "Kate Eby had a teddy bear taken from her desk . . . Eve Harris had that photo. . . . Who else are we interested in? Let's see. Postnikoff's on here. His mug vanished from the coffee room. And Mark Ling—oh, this one gives new meaning to petty theft—someone grabbed his Batman Pez dispenser."

"I didn't notice that." Anna leaned over to look at the memo. "It doesn't say what year it was made."

Collie raised an eyebrow at her. "Um . . . Sparky? It was a Pez dispenser."

"People are willing to pay a lot of money for the right Pez dispenser . . . but Batman ones have always been pretty common. The expensive ones are the ones they never made lots of, like obscure villains and supporting characters. If you . . ." She noticed the way Colette was looking at her and decided that was enough of that. She really had to move out of Curtis's house soon. "I guess it doesn't matter."

"Uh huh." Collie returned her attention to the list. "Old pair of kid's ice skates, a 7-Up yo-yo, a 1952 penny . . . was that an off year for pennies or something?"

"Maybe," Anna said. "But I'm starting to think this is the list from Joce's email. Remember? The guy said something about how everything on the list was junk. And didn't Becca say nothing really valuable was taken?"

"That's true," Collie admitted. "That's a good point. So Joce was curious about these thefts. And out of eight or nine thefts, four of those thefts involved people who did screwy things in the past year. What do you want to bet it all matches up—somebody gets burgled, next thing you know, they're off the deep end? I'll have to check these dates."

Anna nodded. "It's starting to look like a hell of a coincidence. I've got a bet for you. Roger said there were other incidents. Just little things. I bet those incidents involved the other people who were robbed."

"Burgled," Collie said.

"What fucking ever," Anna said. "We can debate semantics some other time. Can you see any connection between the people on that list? I mean, any connection that existed before they all joined the Nutty Club?"

Collie's brow creased as she scanned the paper. "They were all writers," she said. "With bylines. They were all mildly famous. Maybe whoever did the stealing was just looking for mementos."

"You honestly think someone broke into the building for mementos?" Anna pinched the bridge of her nose. That hadn't done a thing for her headache the last fifty times she'd tried it, so why not try it again? "It's interesting, though, that they're all public figures. Jocelyn's the only one who wasn't publicly known."

"Except for her," said Collie, "you'd look at the victims and assume all this weirdness was being caused by a crackpot on the outside. Someone who was only familiar with those staff members who had bylines. Maybe a reader who wasn't happy with the content of the magazine."

"Except for Jocelyn," Anna repeated. "And don't forget that somebody had to walk into *The Rail* offices and steal a lot of trinkets. I don't think even the least gruntled reader would go that far. And even if someone tried it, I'm sure it wouldn't be easy to pull off. Maybe the first time stuff got stolen, but not after that."

"Yeah." Collie folded the memo and set it on the dash. "I think whoever's doing this must know *The Rail* from the inside. It can't be easy to get in there at night without knowing someone. I get the impression from Becca that there are staff members in the building almost every night. And it's a big company, fine, but not big enough that people don't know who belongs on the property and who doesn't."

"So someone with some unknown connection to *The Rail* is finding some way to get inside and steal stuff for some reason we don't understand. Choosing victims through some connection we can't grasp. We're really making progress tonight."

"At least we're asking the right questions," Collie pointed out. "I hope. I don't know. I still think there's something to that fame connection. Joce was killed because she was going to tell, that's all."

"So you steal stuff from quasi-famous magazine writers, and later find some way to make them go bonkers. Or at least make some kind of public mistake. And you do this because . . . why? Because you're crazy? I thought crazy people were supposed to have some kind of internal logic."

Collie rolled her head from side to side on the headrest of her seat. "I don't know. Maybe he has some crazy logic, but we can't follow it because we're not his kind of crazy. How about we just figure out who he is and ask him?"

Anna brushed a beetle off her arm. "Sure. And while we're asking him why he did what he did, we can also ask him what he did. Since we're still unclear on that."

"We're still trying to figure that out."

Collie sat up, not bothering to return her seat to the full upright position. "This is stupid. I don't know why we're talking around it when we both know damned well what this guy is doing. It's totally obvious, isn't it? Joce was reading a book on magical attacks. Magical attacks often involve the victim's personal items. Keepsakes. And you can't tell me you didn't know that, because everyone knows that. It's on TV, in movies . . . it's goddamned common knowledge. What else? We've been hearing story after story about people behaving out of character. Not like themselves. And then not remembering what they did or why they did it. Oh, and guess what? All of those wiggy people have lost keepsakes over the past year. Why are we pretending there's any mystery here?"

That wasn't good for Anna's headache. "You're saying this guy somehow controls or influences people by taking things that belong to them?"

"Personal items. Ones that mean something. Like my ring."

"That's ridiculous. People can't do that."

Collie gawked at her. It wasn't an attractive look. "You're crazy! You're plain nuts! People can't do what you do, either, but you do it anyway. How can you be the way you are and refuse to buy that somebody else might have something extra?"

Anna glared at her. "I think you're jumping to conclusions. Maybe this guy—if it even is a guy—called these people up to say he had their things and got them to meet him, and then he gave them some drug or hypnotized them or something."

"But it. . . ." Collie put her hands in the air. "No, it's fine. You paint it your way, I'll paint it my way, but we both have him doing essentially the same thing. Remember that the janitor's cigarette lighter was missing?"

"Yeah. I'd like to get my hands on it." She said it without thinking, and no one was more surprised than her to hear it come out of her mouth. Of course she didn't mean it.

Collie gave her a look she couldn't identify. "Well, I'm pretty sure we know who has it. We just don't have his name."

"We have a description though," Anna pointed out. "If he's

the guy that Bryan saw following Jocelyn into the hotel."

"Now you're thinking," Collie said approvingly. "I forgot about him. You're right. Our mystery man probably was our mystery man. We've solved the case. All we have to do is find this guy and prove he did what we think he did and make him stop. Our problems are over."

"Unless we're totally wrong."

Collie smiled. "Yeah, there is that. But the 'we're totally wrong' theory would leave us with nothing to go on. I prefer thinking we're right and trying to prove it."

"Also, if we assumed we were totally wrong, we'd have to explain our lack of progress to Paul."

Collie's mouth curved. "We're going to have to explain our theory to Paul."

"Now *you're* pronoun dyslexic," Anna said. "This is your crackpot theory. You, and I mean you, are going to have to sell this to your boss."

Collie grinned. "Not my boss. Our boss. I guess all we can do is bring him up to speed and see if he connects the dots the same way we . . . or I . . . do. Even you admit that the stolen items and the incidents must be connected."

Anna suddenly wanted to go for a walk. Get out of the car. Get moving. Of course, Collie wouldn't dream of leaving the car in the deadly cold of minus eight. Anna settled for shifting in her seat. "We can't bring Paul up to speed."

"Why not?"

"Because I'm not going to tell him what happened when I searched those desks . . . and neither are you."

"Look. . . ," Collie turned to face Anna. "I know you're not comfortable with this, and obviously I get the whole *Firestarter* thing, but Paul's not with CSIS. Hell, Paul thinks you used to be with CSIS."

As if Paul thought a lot of things that weren't true.

"I doubt he really thinks that."

"Whatever. The point is, he's not the enemy. And he won't think you're crazy. I told you, he's open-minded. All you have to do is demonstrate and—"

"*No!*" Anna slammed a hand on the dash for punctuation.

"First of all, I'm not in the mood to balance a ball on my nose. But even if I were, I will not demonstrate anything for that man. You think he can keep a secret? He doesn't believe in it! Look what he does for a living. He is, and I'm not exaggerating here, pretty close to the last person I would tell."

Collie took her time assimilating that. Finally, she smiled. "You're so hard to read, Anna."

Anna didn't think it was funny. "Are you going to tell him?"

"No. I see your point. And you asked me not to. Okay?"

As usual, though there was no good reason for it, Anna believed her. "Okay."

"You realize this creates a problem."

Anna shrugged. "Why not just tell him you have a hunch? You said he was open-minded. Maybe he'll go for the theory anyway."

"I said his mind was open. It's not, like, empty and deserted."

"So in other words, you don't think he'll buy it."

Collie bit her lip. "I have reservations about coming to him with this story."

"Maybe if the evidence builds up he'll come to the conclusion you want on his own. We could take him to meet Eve Harris or something."

"What?" Collie reached for the heater, realized the ignition was off, and pulled her hand back. "You think she's going to want to talk to us with him sitting there?"

"No," Anna admitted. "Maybe we'll have to do it and describe it for him later. Just as long as he gets a fair picture of what happened."

"Yeah, well, if we can give him the picture without speaking to any of the victims, I'd prefer it. Because I've changed my mind about wanting to see them. I don't want to look Eve Harris in the eye and ask her questions, and I don't even want to think about talking to Kate Eby. I do not have the stomach for this kind of work."

"We could ask Roger which ones screwed up their columns and talk to them. Maybe ask them about Eve and Kate. And we can tell Paul everything Rebecca told us." Which reminded her, Rebecca had given Collie an envelope as they left *The Rail*, and it still hadn't been opened. "Let me see that letter Rebecca gave you."

"In a sec." Collie took the envelope out of her purse, pulled an earring from one ear, and used the back of the earring to slit the envelope.

"Oh," she said after a minute. "Okay. This is the stuff I asked her for this afternoon . . . you know, the place where Eve is staying, and the name of the person who saw Kate in the hospital."

Anna held out her hand. "Give it to me."

"What for?"

"The mood you're in, you'll probably ditch it, and we might be sorry about that later. I'll keep it in my purse."

Collie handed it over. "It's not fair," she said again. "Not only is this case way too complicated and . . . nasty . . . it's also completely unbelievable. Even if we do find out who this guy is, I have no idea how to turn him in. How do we explain this to the cops? My head hurts."

Anna's head wasn't doing too well either. "We should go back to the hotel, get some sleep, and tell Paul everything we can in the morning. Get him to buy us breakfast."

"Yeah. Man, the next time I want to go on a diet, I'll have to remember to plan all my meals around unpleasant conversations."

"Just eat with Roger more often," Anna suggested.

Collie smiled and started the car. "His wife," she said, "is very thin."

"Good evening, ladies."

Bryan was at his post as they entered the hotel. Anna followed Collie to the front desk.

"What's new?" asked Collie.

"Oh," said Bryan, "nothing much. Ice machine's broken up on seven. Room 408 keeps running out of towels; don't ask me why. The police came by and asked to search your rooms. I told them to come back with a warrant. Still waiting on that. All in all, it's been pretty dull."

Well, that was all Anna needed. The gun was hidden from casual view, but anyone searching her hotel room wouldn't have any trouble finding it.

"Oh, Jesus." Collie turned to Anna. "Is there any reason we should be concerned about the police searching your room?"

"No," Anna lied, "but thank you for bringing it up in public."

"You're welcome. I wonder if Paul's here."

"Where else would he be?"

"I can't answer that," Bryan said, "but I can tell you that your boss went out two hours ago. Someone picked him up in a white Jimmy. It was about an hour later that the cops came by." He smiled, showing a lot of teeth. "Think there could be a connection?"

"If he's been arrested," Collie said, "after I bail him out, I am going to kick him in the nuts."

Bryan slapped the desk with both palms. "That doesn't incapacitate us. There's some time before it sinks in, and during that time we're really, really pissed."

Collie nodded thoughtfully. "That's too bad. Because I'm supposed to be his publicist, so, if he lands himself in jail for something embarrassing, it's my duty to kick him in the nuts. I guess my only hope is that I can outrun him."

"I don't think you can," said Anna. Before Collie could reply, her coat pocket started to ring.

"Right on fucking cue," Collie said, pulling out a cellphone that was smaller than a chocolate bar. She hit a few buttons and put it to her ear. "Yes?"

Anna leaned against the desk and watched Collie's face as she spat out a few words at a time. She didn't look pleased.

"I'm at the hotel. Where the hell are you?" Pause. "Uh huh. What a fucking surprise." Eyes narrowing. "No, I didn't know that, but . . . yes, I suppose they probably are. How do I go about getting you out of there?" Fingers tightened on the phone, knuckles turned white. "What do you—never mind. Your wish, my command. You have fun. Try not to make any new friends." Lips pressed together. "Riiiight. I have no idea what you're talking about, but I'm sure we'll discuss it tomorrow. Sleep well." She turned off the phone and jammed it back into her pocket with a force that probably tore the lining. "Anna, if you want to stop by your room, why don't you? And then meet me in my room."

She didn't wait to hear what Anna thought about that, and she didn't wish Bryan a good night. She just turned on her heel and went.

Anna looked at Bryan, who was still looking in the direction Collie had gone. When Anna cleared her throat, he turned around to look her in the eye. "Cops don't like to bother judges about warrants in the middle of the night," he told her, "but sometimes they do it anyway."

"True," Anna said. "I think I'll head up to my room."

The gun wasn't large. Anna knew that intellectually. Still, it looked huge in her hands as she tried to figure out what the hell she was going to do with it. Her room was no good, obviously. Paul and Collie's rooms wouldn't be any better. If they searched her room, chances were they'd search her person as well, so her purse wouldn't work. Her vehicle, Collie's vehicle, both out of the question. The only option seemed to be hiding it somewhere else in the hotel, but there was no way Anna wanted anyone else running across it. She wasn't sure it could be traced back to Curtis, but she wasn't sure it couldn't, either. Still, there was one place she could be pretty sure it wouldn't be disturbed . . . at least not until morning. She slipped the gun into her coat pocket and headed up to the seventh floor.

"You get everything taken care of?" That was the first thing out of Collie's mouth when she opened the door to her room.

Anna went into the room and shut the door before answering. "You're assuming there was something I had to take care of."

"You know what? You're right. I am. Did you?"

Anna sat down on the bed. This enchanted evening was

starting to make her tired. "I think so. It should be okay for the night, anyway. I take it that was Paul on the phone."

"Don't know. Could've been a pod person." Collie pulled up a chair. "He is, as he put it, in the clink. He told me to stop swearing over the phone because apparently there's some kind of law against it, and he thinks the cops were listening to our phone call."

That was a new one.

"No cussing over the phone."

Collie smiled. "Nope."

"What about 1-900 numbers?"

"Don't ask me, I just heard about this myself."

Anna kicked off her shoes and lay down on the bed. "Shouldn't you be bailing him out? Or is he stuck there 'til morning?"

"That's an interesting question. I don't know if he's stuck. It's possible that I could post bail tonight, but he doesn't want me to try it. He wants to stay there overnight."

It was hard to know what to make of that.

"Maybe this answers our questions about who his type would be."

"Funny you should say that. I told him not to make any new friends, but he said making a friend was what he had in mind."

Anna shut her eyes. "How long have you been working for Paul?"

"Too long. I don't know. If you're asking if he drives me fucking crazy, as a matter of fact he does. And don't even think about asking me what he's up to, because I don't have the first idea."

"Okay, I won't ask you that. Do you mind if I ask who you know that drives a white Jimmy?"

Collie was quiet for a long time.

Anna opened her eyes and sat up. "Don't know?"

Collie shook her head. "No, I think I do know. I think it was Roger. I'm just trying to decide if I want to call him at. . . ," she looked at her watch, "12:15 AM."

A pleasant thought came to Anna, and she snickered. "Maybe he's in jail."

"Heh." Collie pushed hair out of her face, then saw the futility of that and started taking out her braid. "Is there a distinction between 'jail' and 'prison'?"

With a mind like that, it was a wonder Collie ever accomplished anything.

"I think," Anna said slowly, "that jail is just lock-up. Whereas prison would be the clink. You know, stir. The cooler. Inside."

"Uh huh." She wasn't giving Anna her full attention, since the braid had become a mass of tangles and her fingers were trapped, but she'd heard enough to look amused. "You should go to bed. It's late. Paul's expecting us around nine-thirty."

"I might go downstairs and see if Bryan found out anything about the janitor and *The Rail*."

Collie wrinkled her nose. It made her seem about six years old. "Oh, yeah. I forgot we asked him to do that. I need to start using my day planner for this."

"Sure. Write it all down and leave it on the desk for when the police search your room."

"They'd just think I was a crackpot. Right? So what difference does it make?" She dropped her arms and rolled her shoulders. "I'll talk to Bryan. You go to bed."

Anna might have found that suspicious if she hadn't been so short on sleep. As it was, finding out what was going on in Collie's head didn't sound nearly as appealing as bed. She went.

Sounds flew into both ears, and there was no defence to keep them out. Lights and shadows moved over the eyes even when they were closed. That smell came in with every breath and heat and cold made an impression on every bare patch of skin.

Can't lock the door. Can't turn off the phone. Everything just keeps coming, and it won't ever stop. There's nothing that could make it stop, and even if they could the angels never would.

"Huhyeahhellowhat?"

"Ms. Gareau? It's eight thirty AM."

"Wha? Oh. Right. Thanks."

Anna didn't know how the receiver had gotten into her hand. She put it back in the cradle. Eight thirty. Because they were bailing Paul out at nine thirty. And besides that, some repair guys started at nine.

She got her shower out of the way, threw on jeans and a T-shirt, and went up to the seventh floor. Between the hour and the out-of-order sign on the door, there was no one in the ice machine room. Anna made sure the door was shut, lifted the panel, and dug around in the ice until she found her gun. She should've brought a facecloth from her room, some Kleenex at least. The ice in that machine had been melting all night, and the gun was dripping. She knelt down and dried it off on the carpet before dropping it into her purse. Now, because she couldn't leave the damned thing in her room, she was going to have the fun of taking it to the police station. Not that Curtis could really be blamed for the fact that she was playing private eye, but if he didn't find a buyer soon, she would have to consider taking the gun back to Seattle and shooting him with it.

She ducked into the stairwell and jogged the two flights down to Collie's room. The door was firmly shut and locked. It was an encouraging development that led Anna to believe that, on occasion, people might actually learn things. She knocked, then listened as Collie approached, stopped, and placed her hands on the door. Bracing herself, Anna realized after a second's thought, so Collie could go up on her toes and look through the peephole.

A moment later, the door opened.

"Good morning," Collie said. She turned as she spoke. She was heading back towards the television.

"Which movie is it," Anna asked, "where someone puts an eye up to a peephole and gets an icepick through it?"

Collie just kept staring at the screen. Anna watched over her shoulder. The local news. Collie was doing her real job.

"Anything about Paul?" Anna inquired. Collie shook her head.

Anna smiled. "Given that you're supposed to be his publicist, shouldn't you be on that?"

"Huh?" The news program went to a weather forecast. Collie turned to Anna. "Oh . . . are you asking if I want him on the news? 'Cause there's no such thing as bad publicity? Somebody said that once, and for some reason a lot of people believed it, but it's bullshit. Don't take my word for it, though—ask O. J. Simpson."

"Huh," Anna said. It was the best she could come up with, so early in the morning. "We should get going if we have to spring the boss at nine thirty."

Collie turned off the TV. "I'm tempted not to go. Can you imagine? That might put a dent in Mr. Suave's calm exterior."

"I wouldn't call him Mr. Suave." Anna grabbed Collie's coat and handed it to her. "I'd call him Mr. Bug. Son of Kafka. If no one bails him out, he'll leave through a crack in the floor. Do you know what he's charged with?"

Collie was putting the room key in her coat pocket. Given the size of that keychain, there was no way it would fit in her purse. "No. But he said he figured they'd drop the charges in the morning. You certainly got up on the wrong side of bed."

"There is no right side." Anna gave her a little shove. Nothing serious, just enough to get her moving. "Let's get this over with."

"Jesus. Okay, okay."

She didn't say anything else until they were out of the hotel and in the car. "Did you have another dream?"

It seemed like a non-sequitur until Anna remembered that she was in an unsubtly bad mood. So Collie thought she was out of sorts because of the dream.

Maybe she was. "Yeah. Second verse, same as the first."

"Little bit louder and a whole lot worse," Collie chanted back. "There must be something we can do about that. I bet I could find a good hypnotist for you."

"I think instead I'll become a lush," Anna countered. "I can pass out instead of sleeping. And jug wine is a hell of a lot cheaper than seeing a hypnotist."

"Well, you never know what Medicare will cover. Or Medi-Paul, for that matter. I bet he'd find your dreams fascinating."

"I can live without Paul finding me fascinating."

Collie didn't have a response for that. Not one she was inclined to share, anyway. Anna watched the buildings go by and wondered how Collie managed to navigate so easily. She'd been to Victoria before, okay, but just for visits. The fact that she could look at a map before starting the car and head straight to her destination without opening the map again . . . it was further proof that the girl's mind worked in mysterious ways.

"Anna?"

Anna turned her head. "Yes?"

"Do you think your dreams could have something to do with this whole . . . Jocelyn dying in the hotel and everything?"

That was a two-handed issue. On the one hand, the dreams had started the night before Anna left for Victoria. That did seem a little strange. But on the other hand, they didn't have any connection to anything from the case. They didn't feel the same.

"I don't know," Anna said, "but I don't think so. It could just be that I'm nervous. I had the first dream the night before I left Seattle."

"Hmm." Collie's eyes might as well have been shut for all the attention they were giving the outside world. Thankfully, they were sitting at a red light. "Do you ever know about stuff before it happens?"

"Oh sure, all the time," Anna told her. "This is exactly where I'd be in my life if I could do that. The light is green."

"Thanks. Look, you don't have to get smart with me. I was just asking. It's not as if you use your other gift for anything."

"I'd put it in a box, wrap it, and hand it over to you if I could."

"I'm sure you would. And maybe it's just because I'm ignorant, but I'd take it. Let me know if you see a parking space."

On their third pass, Anna thought of a beautiful way to keep from entering that building with a gun. "Pull up here," she suggested. "We'll switch places, I'll drop you at the station, and I can circle until a space comes up or they release him."

"Whichever comes first. Yeah, okay."

It was something like the thirtieth time around the block that they appeared on the sidewalk. Collie, Paul, and a young Asian man Anna couldn't quite place. She'd seen him somewhere before. They were moving fast, heading north along the street. A forty-ish woman with a microphone in her hand was in hot pursuit.

Seeing as how Collie was a trained weasel, Anna thought she ought to stand her ground and face the reporter. Still, it was possible there was a time to fight and a time to run away. Anna swung the car in beside a Geo about halfway up the block. She wanted to make sure Collie and Paul spotted her, and the Geo was the only car on the street that was smaller than the Tercel.

They played it well, pretending not to notice the car until they were right beside it, then diving in so quickly that the reporter didn't have a chance to follow. Paul dragged the Asian man with him by hooking an arm around his neck.

"Fuck us," Collie groaned as Anna pulled back into traffic. "How did she know you were arrested?"

"Don't be dense," Paul told her. "She probably has some paper-shuffling friend who calls her when something interesting comes in. What I want to know is, does she realize who I was arrested with?"

"She'd better not," the Asian man said. "I have enough problems."

"My friend," Paul agreed, "you really do. Anna, I think we could all stand a decent breakfast. Listen carefully."

He directed her to a small pizzeria in a strip mall, about eight blocks away. No one said anything until she parked the car.

Collie looked over her shoulder at Paul. "A pizza place? For breakfast?"

"Have faith, grasshopper," he said. "By the way, Anna, I don't believe you've met my cellmate. This is Mark Ling."

Anna had to wait until they were inside and seated before she could get a really good look at the guy. She'd seen his picture in *The Rail*, a typical magazine mug shot at the end of every column. Unsurprisingly, he looked better off the page. He also looked better than he had in her mind's eye, where he was covered in soot and clutching a gas can. She made herself smile. "I liked your column," she told him. "The last one I read before I went to the States was that article you did on Bill Farmer."

"An Edmonton boy!" Collie said brightly. "I hope you were good to him."

"By and large," Mark said, smiling. "I'm never glowingly nice to anyone." He stopped smiling. "I'm not anything these days."

"We're looking into that," said Paul. He was waving at the restaurant's sole waitress, who looked something less than half awake.

She yawned and came over to the table. "What can I get for you?"

"Coffee," Paul said. "For everyone. Lots of it. And the biggest breakfast pizza you have."

"Exqueeze me?" Collie asked politely.

Paul grinned at her. "A layer of hash browns. On top of that, an omelette. Onions, peppers, pineapple if you care for it. Top layer, melted cheese. Are you in?"

Collie was returning the grin. "I'm sorry I doubted you."

Paul nailed down the details with the waitress, then held his tongue until she entered the kitchen.

"As I was saying," he said to Mark, "we know something strange is going on at *The Rail*. I would have liked to discuss this with you last night, but the walls have ears and all that. We think whatever has been happening at your former workplace is connected to Jocelyn Lowry's death. Did you know she was at that hotel to meet with me?"

"Yeah. I visit your website a few times a week. I came home because I saw your press release on the murder."

"Did you know Jocelyn?" Collie asked.

"Not really. She was a nodding acquaintance. If you're trying to find out what she was going to tell you, I won't be any help."

"You might be," said Collie. "Indirectly. I hate to be so blunt, but did you set your apartment on fire?"

Mark's expression didn't change. "It was Roger who told you that," he said. "I'd lay money on it. I saw him drop you. . . ," he nodded at Paul, "last night."

"To be fair," Paul said amiably, "Roger didn't say you'd done anything except light up your garbage can, and there are witnesses for that. He said your apartment had gone up shortly afterwards and that he hadn't seen you since. I'll grant he was painting a picture, but he only did it by telling the truth. I take it you did set fire to your apartment building?"

Mark's eyes narrowed and he glanced at something over Paul's shoulder. The waitress was approaching.

They were silent while she set down the food and a carafe. Anna had always hated that when she'd been waitressing, the way people shut up when she came near. Though she'd known better, it had always felt as though they were talking about her.

"Don't ask me," Mark said once she'd left. "I have no idea. I remember going home from work that day, and I remember being on my way to the panhandle with burns on my hands and smoke in my clothes, but other than that I couldn't tell you where my evening went."

He said all of it in a clipped, almost angry tone. Anna interpreted that as scared, and who could blame him? He'd been a normal guy with a cool job one month, and an amnesiac arsonist the next.

"Did you see a shrink?" she asked.

"Yeah. I know a therapist in Juneau. Maybe that's why I was driving in that direction. She said that it was. . . ," he took a breath, then rattled it off, "an idiopathic fugue state incorporating pyromania."

He might as well have spoken Arabic.

"Idio-whatsis?" asked Anna.

Mark scowled. "Idiopathic. Meaning she couldn't come up with any reason why I would light up my home and run and then not remember anything. Or why I'd set my garbage can on fire. I've never had a thing about fire. I've never been crazy. My family isn't crazy. I was pretty happy. I liked my job. And

I haven't had a black-out since I got blind drunk on my eighteenth birthday."

"A fugue that was not idiopathic," Paul said between bites of pizza. "I don't suppose you set any fires back then."

"No. I threw up in my brother's car."

"Did you tell anyone at *The Rail* what happened?" Collie asked.

Mark smiled with thin lips. "I told Roger. He passed it along. The new editor said I should keep my head down for a while." He shrugged. "I think it's still a while. I shouldn't even have come here."

"I don't know about that." Paul grabbed a napkin and swiped at his chin, just in time to prevent a trickle of tomato sauce from landing on his shirt. "You may be glad you did."

"You had something stolen from you just before you set that first fire," Collie said. "A Pez dispenser."

That got a bigger reaction from Mark than anything they'd said so far. His eyes were huge as he turned to look at her. "What do you know about that?"

"We have a list of things that were stolen from *The Rail* over the past year. It's all personal stuff, not really valuable. I mean, no offense, I'm sure you cared for the Pez dispenser, but. . . ."

"It wasn't really worth anything," Mark finished for her. "I know. I had an antique dealer look at it a few years ago, out of curiosity. Actually, I was sort of relieved when I found out it was just another piece of plastic."

"Because you didn't want to sell it," Collie said sympathetically. "Or justify not selling it. I've been there myself. Look, Mark, we figure all of the things that were stolen were like your piece of plastic. Lots of sentimental value."

Paul was watching her carefully. "What's the connection here, Collie?"

"We don't know. But everyone who acted atypically and couldn't explain their actions also had a personal . . . trinket . . . taken from their desks. Or the coffee room, in Lou Postnikoff's case. I don't know what it means, but you can't write it off to coincidence."

"No," Paul said thoughtfully. "I'm not inclined to. Very odd. Mark, do you have any thoughts on this development?"

"I . . . don't know. Are you saying that someone made me behave the way I did? Put something in my food? And they marked me as a target by stealing something of mine?"

"We should fix him up with Becca," Anna told Collie. Collie frowned and shook her head. Ixnay on ecca-bay. Mark didn't seem to notice.

"This seems like a good time to ask," Paul said, "if you'd been seeing a therapist here in Victoria. A hypnotist, maybe."

Mark glared at him. "I told you—I was never a psycho. I never needed a therapist before last year. And I'm starting to wonder if I really need one now. You seriously think someone messed with my head?"

"It seems reasonable to assume that someone messed with a lot of people's heads," Paul answered. "The question is who, and why, and how?"

"Have you," asked Collie, "ever seen this man before?"

She took a square of paper from her purse, unfolded it, and passed it to Mark. As it passed Anna she saw that it was an Identikit drawing.

Unbelievable.

Mark took a good long look, but it didn't seem to ring any bells. "Sorry," he said, handing it back. "This drawing isn't very distinct. For all I can tell, it could be Mr. Dressup."

"Yeah," Collie sighed. "The witness didn't get a very good look at the guy. Someone saw this person following Jocelyn the morning she died. Mr. Dressup is dead, by the way."

"That's one person eliminated," Anna pointed out.

Collie smiled. "If I can change the topic for a minute, I would really love to know how the two of you came to be incarcerated."

"Oh," Paul said, leaning back in his chair. "That. Funny story."

He had the air of a man who was dining out on his wit, about to launch into his most popular tales. Anna wanted to point out that his clothes smelled of jail, but she managed to call up some restraint.

"You could say that Mark and I were in the wrong place at the same time."

Collie looked up from the deconstruction of her breakfast. "That wrong place being?"

"Trent Hutton's apartment."

"You broke into a dead man's apartment?"

Her tone wasn't quite indignation. It was more of a scold, probably stemming from the belief that it was risky to search a murder victim's apartment so soon after the crime. It was, for example, the sort of thing that could land a person in jail.

"This has been," Paul intoned in a deep FM-radio voice, "another great moment in hypocrisy." He cleared his throat and his voice returned to normal. "I know where you were yesterday afternoon. Besides which, I didn't break into anything. I hit buzzers until someone opened the security doors for me. And I'd like to point out that I never even made it to Hutton's apartment. I was arrested in the stairwell because the police saw me with him," he hooked a thumb at Mark, "and naturally assumed we were together."

"Naturally," Collie said. "And you didn't tell them you weren't?"

"Well, I recognized Mark, and I couldn't help wondering what he was doing there. So I didn't really mind that we were hauled in together. I may not have asserted my rights as strenuously as I could have."

"I did," Mark said. "I told them I wasn't trying to break into anything. I wasn't. I got into the building the same way Paul did, and I was trying to get one of Hutton's next-door neighbours to talk to me. I didn't even approach Hutton's apartment. But I'll tell you who did—that swamp witch from this morning."

"Eilene Cebryk," Collie said. "She had this horrible 'Death Stalks the Victorian' article in the paper yesterday. At least, I'm guessing that was her. While I was waiting for you guys I heard one of the cops call her Eilene."

"It was her," Mark confirmed. "She's a hack."

"Really?" Collie chirped. "She seemed so professional when she was chasing us down the street. I don't even know what she wants with Paul, considering that she thinks the Victorian has a serial killer."

"I'm newsworthy," Paul said, without irony. "I'm sure she knew all along that Jocelyn intended to meet with me, but she didn't mention it in the paper because it didn't fit her pet theory. Now that I've been arrested in Hutton's building, that will change."

Anna was working hard to keep up. "That reporter was trying to break into Trent's apartment?"

"Oh, yeah," Mark said. "I saw her. She pulled out a credit card and gave it the old college try for a couple of minutes before she turned and ran into the right stairwell. I figured she was running for a reason, and I didn't want to explain to anyone what I was doing there, so I ran into the left stairwell. Turns out there were cops in Hutton's apartment while she was trying to jimmy the lock. They came out looking for whoever had been trying to break in, didn't see anyone in the hall, and happened to pick the left stairwell . . . which meant the swamp witch got away and Paul and I got arrested."

Anna could see how the guy might be annoyed by the way things had turned out. "Did you tell the police who you saw at the door?"

"I described her, but I didn't spend a lot of time on it. I figured, the more time I spent talking to the cops, the more time they had to remember the whole arson thing. Which they never did, by the way."

"Right now," Paul explained, "we have leverage. We have something on that woman. I don't have a use for it at the moment, but I'm sure something will come up."

On that note, they returned to eating. Anna managed about ten bites before she gave in and asked Mark the thing she really wanted to know. "What was it like? Having those fugues? Do you remember anything?"

Mark set his fork down.

"No. One moment, I was living my normal life . . . the next, I was somewhere else and I didn't know what had happened to the intervening time. No memories at all. That day at the office, I went from dropping a gum wrapper into my trash can to being held back by two of my co-workers while a third shot off the fire extinguisher. My first thought was that I must be asleep and dreaming, because who would use a fire extinguisher on such a small fire? I accept that the incident really happened, but only because there was too much evidence for me to deny it. I still have a hard time believing I lit the thing up. And don't even get me started on my apartment building. That was my home. I lost all of my things. I don't think I'll have too much luck collecting my content insurance."

There was no arguing with that.

"That's interesting," said Collie. "That your stuff burned. That you didn't pack. I mean, on the one hand, you didn't prepare for the consequences of your actions . . . but on the other hand, you didn't die in the fire. You don't even seem to have had serious burns. You must have taken some precautions while you were doing it."

"Yeah. My therapist used to harp on that. I'll tell you what I told her—don't ask me about it, because I don't know."

"You're not crazy," Collie said. "At least, not inherently, organically crazy. I can see where you'd think that in a vacuum, but taking into account what else has been happening at *The Rail*. . . . Do you have all the details on your co-workers? Kate Eby and Eve Harris, especially. But I think Roger has a whole list of names."

"I've heard things," Mark said grimly. "There might be a reason so many of us have gone crazy. Something in the water, something in the air . . . but even if someone has been poisoning us, that doesn't make me feel any better. I'm still nuts. And maybe no one can fix it."

"Poisons are often reversible," Paul said absently. "You know, when you're making comparisons, you have to look at what's different as well as what's the same. You might learn a lot if all of you talked about this. I think you should."

"If I were you," Collie added, "I'd talk to anyone who might have witnessed your fugues. Your co-workers, people in your apartment building. You took a ferry to the mainland after you burned the building. Considering the way you must have looked, I'm sure people noticed you."

"Do that," Paul instructed. "Also speak to anyone who exhibited strange behaviour over the past year. I'll put you up at the hotel. Take a nap, clean up, then get out there and start talking to people. We'll meet back at the hotel tonight and you can tell us what you found out."

It had been a while since Anna had actually seen someone's jaw drop.

"Wha—you can't be serious!"

Paul smiled. It was a touch patronizing. "Mark . . . we may be the only chance you have to get your life back on track. You've been living with this problem for months and you haven't made any real progress. You should be happy to take advice from anyone with a sense of direction. If nothing else, the offer of a hotel room should be enticing to someone in your financial situation. You haven't worked in months."

"I'm doing all right," said Mark. He didn't pry his teeth apart to say it.

Paul shrugged. "If you say so. But *The Rail* won't keep you forever. Either they'll get tired of paying for your silence, or the burden of supporting so many unproductive people while quietly settling lawsuits will break their back. I don't think this has been a very good year for them. You should be saving the money you get now and working to clear up this mess so you can find a new job in the future. I can see you don't like being told this, and I realize I haven't been polite, but I recommend you look past that and serve yourself."

The two of them looked at each other for a good long time. Anna thought she heard the theme from *The Good, the Bad, and the Ugly* playing in the distance.

Finally, Mark dropped his eyes. "Fine. You want to pay for my hotel room, go ahead."

"We'll all be together," Paul said cheerily, waving at the waitress to bring the bill. "It'll be fun!"

"Gimme a minute to write some stuff down for you," Collie said. "Some of your colleagues are in hiding, so you'll need help tracking them down. One of my sources gave me addresses. Anna and I were going to follow up on Eve and Kate today, but I guess I can give you their contact info and you can take it from there." She managed not to sound relieved.

Anna had to admire the girl. Collie always seemed to get what she wanted in the end.

As they pulled up next to the hotel, Collie put a hand on Anna's arm to keep her from undoing her seatbelt. "Anna and I have some things to look into," she told Paul. "I'll just drop you and Mike here, and we'll go."

"Fine," said Paul, "but the three of us should confer. Will you be back fairly soon?"

Collie looked at her watch. "Noon at the latest."

"Okay. Have fun."

Anna didn't say anything until they were a few blocks from the hotel. She spent some time considering her best opening, and decided to be direct. Collie claimed to like it.

"Where did you get that Identikit picture?"

Collie smiled. "Our friendly neighbourhood night auditor. He sat down with the police artist a few hours after Joce was killed. Last night I had him phone the cop shop and say that he needed another look at it."

"I'm going to skip the part where I complain about you not telling me this," Anna said, "and go back to saying that picture is no help. I could probably find ten guys on this street that match it."

"I know. But I'm sure if I only saw the guy for a few minutes, I wouldn't have done any better. Hair colour, height and build, maybe eye colour. That's all I'd have noticed. I've got to work on my observational skills."

"Why not?" Anna said. "You need a hobby. While you were talking with Bryan, did you happen to ask him about Trent and *The Rail*?"

"I . . . damn it. I wanted that exit. Hang on."

Anna grabbed the oh-shit handle and shut her eyes. This was the reason she hadn't wanted Collie to drive. She'd almost forgotten. From now on, they were travelling by Jeep.

When the car straightened out and the honking stopped, Anna opened her eyes and repeated the question.

"Oh," Collie said. "Yeah. I did. He didn't find any connection. He said Trent maybe read *The Rail* in the dentist's office sometimes, assuming he ever visited the dentist. He also said that Trent had obviously been killed because he knew too much."

"In a sense," Anna commented, "I suppose that's true."

"I think Bryan was questioning our abilities."

That was pretty funny. Anna acknowledged it by grinning. "Why should we be the only ones?"

"Oh, that's a knee-slapper. I don't care if we know that we're useless. I just think we'll get more co-operation from other people if it isn't common knowledge."

"Bryan's not common. There's a brain in his head. Where are we going?"

"Metaphorically, or in real life?"

"For real. I have our metaphorical destination all figured out."

"I've been wondering about those leaves Joce had hanging outside her bedroom."

"So we're going to talk to a botanist?"

"Um . . . no. I have another idea."

"I'm glad you didn't say 'a better idea.'"

Collie laughed. More of a snicker, really. "We'll see. Ah . . . that must be the place."

She pulled the car out of traffic and parked it on a narrow strip of dirt beside a three-story building that was billing itself as "The Village Market."

"Did you know," Collie asked as they stepped out of the car, "there are stores in Alberta with parking meters on their lots? Private meters they put up themselves? Is that not insanely greedy?"

Anna kicked a beer bottle out of her way and into a clump of weeds at the edge of the lot. "I thought only cities could put up meters."

"I think she's on the third floor."

"Who is?"

"Someone Joce and I knew when we were in school. She moved out here last year."

They went into the building, which was going out of its way to seem rustic. Instead, it looked ill-tended. It was the indoor version of an open-air market, full of gift shops, hand-crafted jewellery stands, stores that offered about a dozen South American sweaters and nothing else. Most of the stores had walls that didn't quite reach the ceiling. Somewhere, someone was cooking soup with a healthy dose of fennel. It smelled good, but Anna was willing to bet the servings were ridiculously small and the prices insanely high. Also, she wouldn't care for the person doing the cooking.

She followed Collie up two flights of stairs that were so badly worn they curved down in the middle. Voices drifted up from the open shops below them, women describing overpriced baubles as "adorable" and "darling." Anna felt the contrarian in her acting up, making her wish she were wearing flannel and carrying the keys to a pickup.

"Oh, that's nice," Collie groused. "They stuck her all the way at the back."

The third floor was sparsely populated. The soup smell was coming from a tiny coffee-shop beside the stairs, and there was a gourmet popcorn shop beside that, but otherwise it was open space all the way back to where the shop in question stood. From the outside, it was hard to tell what kind of a shop it was. The walls made it to the ceiling, and the doorway was small. A sign over the door simply read "Estelle's."

"Estelle?" said Collie, wrinkling her nose. "Since when?"

She ploughed ahead, and Anna followed.

"Stella?" Collie said as they went through the doorway. "Did you get all snooty on me?"

Once they were past the doorway, Anna could see what kind of a shop it was. Incense, essential oils, loose stones in baskets, and shelves cluttered with items Anna had no idea how to use. Looking over Collie's shoulder, she saw talismans in a glass display case and a shelf full of books about Wicca.

"The Streetcar jokes were getting old," a voice said from behind the counter. There was a rustling sound and a husky woman in her mid-thirties stood up, pushing long black hair out of her face. "Sorry—I dropped a bunch of silver rings." She tilted her head and smiled. "It's been years, Colette. How are you?"

"Good," Collie said, "sort of." She went to the counter and gave Stella a hug across it.

"Careful," Stella warned. "I'm packing rat."

"Of course you are." Collie stepped back. "Anna, you don't have a thing about rats, do you?"

Did everyone in this town keep rats? Anna shook her head. "They're fine in their place," she said, not mentioning where that place might be.

"This little guy," said Stella, producing a black and white squirming thing from the pocket of her skirt, "is Jocelyn's. Was Jocelyn's. Since you're here, I take it you've heard."

"You could say that. I'm surprised you didn't hear about this in the news. Joce was supposed to meet me and Paul at the Victorian. That's why she was there."

"Paul. The mysterious Dr. Echlin. Jocelyn told me she was thinking about talking to him."

Anna looked at Collie, who had turned to look at her. Their choreography was getting good.

"That's interesting," Collie said, turning back to Stella. "Joce was playing that close to the vest. I don't think we've run across anyone else she told."

Stella set the rat on the counter and scooted it away. "You're trying to find out what happened?"

"Yeah. I'm naturally curious."

"And it's natural for you to be curious about this." Stella patted the counter. The rat, which had been exploring the cash register, returned to her hand. She scratched its back and it yawned, revealing long, curved teeth.

"You think her death had something to do with that strange business at *The Rail*?"

"Seems like a reasonable theory," said Collie. "We've been going with it. This is Anna, by the way. She's helping me snoop . . . or I'm helping her. Which is it?"

"I think we're supposed to say we're both helping Paul," Anna said. She offered Stella a hand to shake. Stella took it. Her hand was plump, but warm and dry. Anna tried to forget it had recently been petting a rat.

"Are you with Paul? I mean, are you dating him?"

Anna laughed. "Is that the only conceivable way I could be helping him? No, I'm not with him. He's paying me. It's a long story."

"I was hoping you'd know what this was," Collie said. She produced the leaves they'd taken from Jocelyn's apartment and spread them on the counter.

Stella swept the leaves towards Collie with the back of her hand. "It's rowan," she said. "Take it with you when you go."

"Why? What does it do?"

"It guards against witches. Prevents them from accomplishing anything. Where did you find it?"

Collie brushed the leaves into her purse. "Jocelyn's apartment. She had bunches of it hanging over the door to her bedroom."

"Really. I wonder where she got it."

Collie shrugged. "I thought you would be her one-stop occult shop."

"I thought so too, but I guess you never know a person as well as you think you do."

"No."

They spent a moment of silence with that thought.

"I don't sell rowan anyway," Stella said. "For obvious reasons."

"Yeah. Did you sell her anything else in connection with this? Maybe a book called *Amulets for the Coming Storm*?"

Stella looked at her bookshelf, but it seemed to be more a reflex than a genuine search for the title in question. "No . . . I don't think I've ever heard of it." She returned her attention to Collie. "Why?"

"We found a copy of it at her apartment. Look . . . it's pretty obvious she was scared. Did she tell you what she was scared of? Did she tell you what she was going to tell Paul?"

Stella thought about that. Her eyes unfocused as she thought, as if she had gone to the back of her brain to search for the answer. "She did talk to me about it, a little," she said after a minute. "But I don't think you're going to find this helpful."

Collie had picked up a piece of rose quartz and was rubbing it between her fingers. "Tell us and we'll see," she said.

"Well," Stella said, "obviously you've already guessed that someone is using magic to attack the staff at *The Rail*. If you didn't know that, you wouldn't be here asking me about it, right?"

"I don't know about that," Collie said. "I've been talking to anyone who might have talked to Joce, so I'm sure I would have come here eventually. But we have been working the magic angle, yes."

"Jocelyn told me she was trying to find out who was fucking with *The Rail*. As soon as she knew who it was, she was going to turn everything over to your boss."

Collie set the quartz down. "I bet she didn't say 'fuck.'"

"I don't remember. But she was pissed."

Obviously Stella meant that Jocelyn had been angry, but Anna couldn't shake the image of Jocelyn Lowry, stinking drunk, leaning on Stella's counter as she ranted about the increasing use of black magic at national news magazines.

"So she must have figured it out. Since she called me. Goddamn it." Collie stared at Stella, her eyes begging for help. "She didn't tell you who her suspect was? Or anything about them? Their name, gender, shoe size, favourite chocolate bar, anything?"

"The last I heard, she was still working on it," Stella said. "Sorry."

Collie looked disappointed beyond words.

Anna decided it was time to step up to the plate. "Did Joce say anything to you about stuff being stolen from *The Rail*? Small, personal things?"

Stella drifted back into thought for a moment. "She did mention that," she said as her eyes refocused. "I told her it probably was connected. Keepsakes have a lot of power."

"If you wanted to use someone's possessions to influence them," Anna said, "to make them do things against their will . . . would that be possible?"

Stella laughed. She sounded uncomfortable. "Well. Possible? Yes, of course. But I don't know anyone who has that kind of power. And even if you did have that kind of power, it would be very reckless to use it. What a violation of the law of three!"

That comment was enough to shake Collie out of her despair. "Did you just say 'law of three'?" she asked, sounding as if she couldn't quite believe it. "You have been way less fun since you got religion."

Stella narrowed her eyes. "You'd have religion too, if you'd seen the things I've seen. I know Jocelyn thought she had the answer to what was going on at *The Rail*, but she was wrong. You are wrong. The sort of ability you're talking about, that influence . . . it isn't common. If someone on this island could do that sort of thing, I would know about it."

"Are you sure?" Collie asked. "Maybe you're not plugged in with the dark side of the Force. You may not know the right people."

Stella shook her head. "You're obviously in love with this theory. That just shows how ignorant you are. Some Frank Oz wannabe sticks his hand up Grover's butt and makes him slash his fuzzy blue wrists? I don't think so. Real magic is more subtle."

Collie leaned forward. "What did you just say? I remember you telling me stories about. . . ."

"They were stories," Stella said. "I belong to a private club, and you were always a poseur. Poseurs aren't told the truth."

There was no warmth in her voice at all, and it probably stung, but Collie didn't back down.

"I'm not a poseur. I'm a hanger-on. I never pretended to anything. Do you have any idea where Joce might have gone after you turned her away?"

That certainly stung. Stella scooped up the rat and put it on her shoulder. It promptly began to wash its face with paws that looked far too much like hands.

"No. There was nowhere for her to go. Anyone else she spoke to was a fake."

Collie shrugged. "They knew enough to sell her rowan. Blessed be."

She brushed past Anna and left, not wasting any time. Since

the alternative was spending more quality time with at least one rat and possibly two, Anna hurried after her.

"I'm going to tell you this now," Collie said once they were safely surrounded by traffic, "because I don't want to discuss it in front of Paul."

"You know a lot of people in this town."

"Four people. That's not a lot. And I only know Becca and Roger through friends."

"How do you know Stella?"

Collie looked troubled.

"She used to be the wicked witch of Red Deer. She had a little store there. Sort of like this one, but it was more books and less . . . esoterica. She used to buy stuff in Edmonton, jack up the price, then turn around and sell it in Red Deer."

"A long-standing tradition for traders in the Northwest," Anna observed.

"Joce and I knew someone who owned a New Age bookstore in Edmonton, and we were in there one day when Stella came in, so he introduced us to her. Stella used to tell some wild stories."

"Or bald-faced lies. Whichever."

"Mmm." Collie was smiling with unreserved wickedness. "I didn't believe her at the time, but I do now. If they were just harmless lies, why recant now? She's trying to shut me out."

"That's one way of looking at it," Anna agreed.

Collie gave her a quick, dirty look before returning her eyes to the road. "Scoff away. But I'm going to prove you wrong. Stella is trying to hide something from me."

"Other than her hostility?"

Collie laughed. "Yeah, she was keeping that under wraps, wasn't she?"

"You don't know it was personal. This can't have been a good week for her, either. Do you think she and Jocelyn saw each other a lot?"

"I doubt it. About a year ago Joce brought Stella up during a phone conversation; said she'd moved to Victoria and opened a store. I said it was high time she got out of Red Deer. Joce agreed, that was about it. I don't think she ever mentioned Stella again."

"But you told Stella you figured Joce would shop there."

"Yeah." Collie ran her hands up and down the curve of the steering wheel. "We used to like her store in Red Deer. On account of how she stocked the place we didn't buy anything there, but it was a nice place to be. It was a lot more whimsical than the place she has here. She had books about faeries and stuff for kids, and actual wooden brooms and pointed hats . . . she even kept this little ceramic frog by the cash register with a note saying he was the store's most recent shoplifter. It was cool."

"Do you think Stella was lying about selling her the rowan?"

"No. Stella wouldn't stock that stuff. It would be like Superman selling Kryptonite."

"You didn't ask her about the powder I found in Joce's medicine chest."

"I know. Do you think we would've gotten a useful answer?"

"Lies can be informative."

"Questions are a burden to others, answers a prison to oneself," Collie said. It had the sound of a quotation.

"Huh?" said Anna.

Collie glanced at her. "That place we were just in? The Village Market. It's . . . never mind."

Anna broke the silence that followed with a question. "This Stella, you think she's an actual witch?"

"I don't know. It's like someone who has criminal friends, but they're not really a badass themselves. I've always thought Stella just knew the right people. Or the wrong people."

"So she used to be on the dark side?"

"Oh God, I just said that 'dark side' thing for her sake. I'm not sure the lines are so distinct . . . but I don't think she was ever a bad person. And I never said she was hanging out with bad people—when I said 'criminals,' that was an analogy. Here's a better analogy—say you have some lame power, like the ability to predict the outcome of a coin toss."

"Or what I do," Anna said, amused.

Collie grinned. "If you insist. What you do is useful. But if we lived in a comic book, would you go out and join the Justice League? You would not. Because the first time you went out to fight injustice you would get your ass kicked. Sure, you'd sort of belong because you had a gift, but it wouldn't be enough to protect you while you were living the day-to-day life of a member of the Justice League."

"So, you're saying Stella knew people in Alberta who could throw cars around and see through walls and fly."

"She told some wild stories."

Anna winced. "While drunk?"

Collie just laughed.

Anna shook her head. "You take it as it comes, don't you? No wonder you're all over this gonzo magical puppeteer theory. You have got to start questioning the things you hear."

"I do," Collie said brightly. "I think Stella was lying about lying. But that's okay—if she's here, she's probably trying to put it behind her."

Not that Anna believed in any of this, but that did raise an interesting question.

"Do you think Stella did put it behind her? Or could some of it have followed her?"

"Well . . . I don't know. But is that relevant?" Collie pulled into the hotel parking lot, choosing the spot next to Anna's Jeep. "This person we're looking for—"

"This guy we're looking for. I really think it's a guy."

"Okay, this guy. He only went after Joce when it looked like she was going to expose him, right? He wasn't after her to begin with. He was after *The Rail*. What has that got to do with Stella and her exciting past? Nothing. I sincerely doubt that any of Stella's Edmonton cronies would have reason to swear vengeance on *The Rail*."

"Maybe that's what we should be concentrating on. Who would have reason to hate *The Rail*."

"Maybe. Let's see what Paul thinks. We still have to tell him about that talk we had last night." Collie turned off the car, silencing the witchy and mournful voice that had been drifting from the stereo.

Anna put a hand on her arm. "Remember, this is your wacky theory, not mine. And there is nothing unusual about me whatsoever."

Collie opened her door, then waited for Anna to open hers before hitting the power locks. "Absolutely. You would not know a psychic power if it stood up in your soup. Let's go."

"The whole thing sounds voodoo-rific," Paul told them. He was lying back on the bed in his room, looking freshly showered and content. "Collie, you're a freak for the occult. You know people."

"Crystal-wearing hippies don't truck with people who sacrifice chickens. It's not vegan. I'm a long way out of my shallow depths with this magic puppetry thing. But I've got to know—are you, the world's most rational man, actually prepared to believe in something you can't touch? Or are you just going down this road to tease me?"

"I want it both ways. I think we're looking for someone who's adept at brainwashing, probably through the combined use of chemicals and hypnosis. But it's entirely possible that this person believes they have magical powers and believes they have to perform certain rituals to make their brainwashing work. Hence, the thefts." He sat up. "This Stella person—does she have a last name?"

That was a good question. Anna hadn't thought to ask.

"Hrybinski," said Collie.

Paul pursed his lips. "Another Ukranian occultist, steeped in the dark mysteries of the Eastern Orthodox Church. How many of you are there, Colette?"

"More than six. And we're feared. We kidnap people, draw on them with beeswax, and dip them in brightly coloured dyes."

"This theory makes it possible to see how the janitor might fit in."

"Yeah," Collie said. "And someone stole a fairly expensive cigarette lighter from him the day he died."

"Where'd you get the Identikit drawing?"

"The night auditor. He saw that guy who followed Jocelyn into the hotel just before she was killed."

"You've had this picture for a while now and didn't bother to tell me."

Collie smiled. "That's right. I learned this job from you."

"Okay, give me a moment. I'm going to let it slide, but that'll take effort." Paul scrunched up his face, made fists, and shut his eyes. After a few seconds, his features smoothed and he opened his eyes. "If you're giving me things now that you've sat on for days, you must be in search of guidance. You want me to tell you what to do."

"Didn't that *Globe and Mail* review I scared up for you last year say that you had a remarkable ability to find the salient points in any collection of rumour and innuendo? I want you to apply your talent."

Paul laughed. "Okay, don't admit that you came crawling to me for direction. I'll pretend I'm just thinking aloud." He moved the pillows to make a backrest and leaned against it. "There's no point investigating the mechanics of this brainwashing business, because Mark will take care of that this afternoon when he talks to his fellow victims. Someone with an Internet connection, such as myself, could investigate brainwashing in general. What this guy does goes far beyond anything I've ever heard of, especially if he can turn a janitor into a murderer in five minutes or less."

"It is pretty extreme," Collie agreed. "One might almost think it was magic. I'm still waiting for my orders."

"The obvious next step is finding out who would want to do this to *The Rail's* writers. But your conversation with Rebecca leads me to believe *The Rail* is aware they're under seige, and they've been working to uncover the problem. If all we do is look for someone—anyone—who might carry enough of a grudge to be our villian, we'll be walking in *The Rail's* footsteps. And since *The Rail* has a much better idea who they've wronged and offended than we ever will, I can't see us succeeding where they've failed."

"That's not a very helpful attitude," Collie said. "You're

implying there's no point in us doing anything."

"I am not," Paul objected. "There is another option, and I think it's what Jocelyn did. You can find out who in Victoria's occult circles thinks he's Reveen."

"I've already used up my occult connection in this city," Collie reminded him. "And she wasn't exactly helpful."

"Roger said Jocelyn gave him a list of occult shops and clubs when he was working on that neo-paganism article. That should give you an idea where she went and who she spoke to when she was looking for this guy. See if Roger still has the list."

"Sounds like a plan," said Collie. "We'll see you later."

"Say hi to Sandy."

"Yeah. Have a good surf."

"I always do."

"Roger's not here," Sandy Denton said. "He's buying magazines. He always picks up, like, twenty copies of everything he's published in. Did you want to wait for him?"

With pale blonde hair, white skin, and very fine bones, she reminded Anna of a weak and dusty sunbeam. It wouldn't have been surprising to see the things she touched pass right through her hands.

"We'll wait," Collie said. "If that's cool. Thanks."

Sandy led them into a bright kitchen without a spot of dirt anywhere that Anna could see.

"I was just going to make coffee. I'm working on a government report about parasites in pot-bellied pigs, and for some reason they think I should be handing over at least thirty pages. I could sum it up for them in five."

Collie laughed. "This is the government. No one will read it. You could turn in five pages of report and twenty-five pages of lyrics from Broadway musicals, and no one would ever know."

"Maybe I'll try that sometime," Sandy said. "Make yourselves at home."

Collie pulled up a chair at an oak table in the kitchen nook. Anna took a seat next to her. The wood surface of the table was completely unmarked, probably due to the fact that it was covered by a sheet of glass.

"Is your boss going to drag my husband into trouble again?"

Sandy smiled when she said it, but she didn't seem to be entirely joking.

"I don't think Roger needs to be dragged," Collie commented.

Sandy let out a huff of air. "True."

She took a Brita pitcher out of the fridge and poured the water into a coffee machine. Anna had never seen anyone use filtered water for coffee before.

"I'm only here to ask Roger for a list of names," Collie said. "I'm planning to get myself into trouble."

As Sandy took mugs from the cupboard, Anna cast her eyes around the bright kitchen. Everything was clean, and cleanable. Nothing was left uncovered. There was a bottle of antibacterial soap beside the sink, and beside it a small bottle of bleach. An unused J-cloth hung over the tap.

"Collie mentioned you were a parasitologist," Anna said as she waved a hand at the sink. "I guess you're pretty careful about germs."

Sandy glanced where Anna pointed, seemingly puzzled by her interest in perfectly ordinary cleaning supplies. "It doesn't hurt to be cautious."

"Is Roger the same way? I have to think, if you lived with someone who knew all about parasites. . . ."

"Roger's always had an interest in my work. He understands why I keep a clean kitchen. I don't know if you knew this, but the average kitchen is usually much filthier than the average bathroom."

"No, I didn't know that. Until now." Anna looked at Collie. "Do you think that's why Roger hasn't been affected by whatever's going on at *The Rail*? If he's really cautious about what he puts in his mouth, it would have to be tough to contaminate his food." Collie gaped at her.

"Anna, sometime we're going to have to discuss the value of having unexpressed thoughts."

"What did you say?" Sandy asked, though the kitchen was small and she couldn't possibly have missed it.

Anna turned to her. "Has Roger told you about the strange ways people have been behaving at *The Rail*?"

"Yes. Some of it, anyway. Everyone knows about Lou Postnikoff. And Roger told me about that stuff with Eve Harris. He said someone was starting fires. Mark something-or-other. Roger said some other people were making mistakes, but I'm sure they were just having trouble concentrating. You know, with the way Lou died and everything, they were probably just rattled. Are you saying you think these people are being poisoned?"

Anna couldn't see Collie's face, but she heard an angry huff from behind her and spoke before Collie could jump in. "That's one of the theories we've heard. If it were true, it would explain why nothing has happened to Roger. But I guess he's not really staff."

"No, he's not. He works for them maybe two or three times a year. Seriously, what do they imagine could have been put in anyone's food that would make them so . . . sporadically crazy? There are a lot of drugs that can induce psychosis, but the signs would have been there. I saw Lou about a week before he died. I didn't see anything wrong with him. Nobody saw anything wrong with him. Can I ask what this list is you want from Roger?"

Collie shrugged. "It's nothing exciting. We're looking into Jocelyn Lowry's death—she's the one who died in the swimming pool."

"Yeah, I know. I don't think Roger knew her very well."

"No, he said he didn't," Collie agreed. "But a few months ago he was writing an article on neo-paganism, and Jocelyn helped him out by giving him a list of some stores and clubs she hung out at. We thought it might help us find some of her friends."

Sandy stared at her. "You think that woman was killed because she worked at *The Rail*?"

"Maybe," Collie said. "That's the only real motive we can think of right now. But maybe her friends will have other ideas."

A rumbling outside told them the Jimmy had pulled into the driveway.

"I'll just be a minute," Sandy said. She went into the living room, towards the front door.

"She probably wants to warn him that there are lunatics waiting for him in the kitchen," Anna muttered.

Collie glared at her. "I can't believe you're still on that poison thing," she said. "What is wrong with you? I can see where Paul would need to believe in some bullshit brainwashing deal, but you should know better. I mean . . . look at you!"

"In spite of this gift of mine," Anna told her, "if you want to call it that, I have never run across anyone else who can do impossible things. Not one single person. And you have to admit, I am uniquely qualified to discover something like that."

"You haven't been looking," Collie hissed, keeping her voice down with an obvious effort. "You hate the idea of belonging to any group, but especially a group of people who have supernatural abilities. You're scared shitless of the supernatural. You are uniquely qualified to turn a blind eye."

"There's nothing to turn a blind eye to," Anna snapped. "You have an overactive imagination, which is fine in children but a little scary in someone your age. I'll give you this much—our villain believes what you believe, so your theory will probably lead us to him. Just remember, that doesn't make your theory correct."

"Did you ladies want to oil up?"

Roger. Anna turned and saw that he looked about as amused as he'd sounded. She hoped he hadn't heard anything more than what she'd said to Collie, because what Collie had said to her could lead to complications.

"Hi Roger," said Collie. "Did Sandy tell you what we're looking for?"

"Yeah, she did. And she told me why you wanted it. But that part was a damned lie."

"Is it so unreasonable," Collie asked, "that we would want to talk to Jocelyn's friends? Isn't that what homicide investigators do?"

"Maybe," Roger allowed, "but that's not what you are. You're the muckraker's apprentice. Your main interest here is the hijinks at *The Rail*. So why would you want to visit a bunch of occult bookstores and hocus pocus discos? Hmm?"

"I guess I might as well be honest with you," Collie said. "The truth is, Anna and I are really lost in this investigation. We just don't seem to be any good at detecting—possibly because we're girls. We were thinking maybe we could find a local psychic and get them to tell us who killed my good friend. Not that finding out who killed my good friend is a priority for me."

Roger put his hands up. "Cease fire. You're offended by my comments and I'm offended by your assessment of my intellect. Let's call it even. I know damned well that you're connecting Jocelyn's death to *The Rail*. Okay? So obviously you think her occult connections have something to do with the big picture."

"We might think that," Anna admitted.

"Hypothetically," Collie added quickly. "We might. So what if we did?"

Roger shrugged. "You tell me. Colette, I know you've always been a little flakey . . . but you don't seriously believe in this magic horseshit, do you?"

The question of the hour. Anna couldn't help smiling.

"Answer the man, Colette."

Collie looked at them, Anna to Roger and back again. It wasn't a friendly look. Faced with either taking Anna's side in the great mysticism debate or discussing her personal beliefs with Roger, Collie was twitchy and annoyed. "Fine," she snapped. She kept her eyes on Anna. "Yes, Roger. I do believe in this magic horseshit. I have good reason to believe in it. And I have at least some reason to think it's relevant to this case. Happy now?"

That last question seemed to be directed at Anna. She answered it with a shrug. Collie turned her eyes to Roger.

"Reasonably happy," Roger said. "You're flakier than I had previously believed. And so, I will give you the list."

Collie squinted at him. "What? You're giving me the list because I'm a flake? Is that what you're saying?"

"That is what I'm saying." Roger was at the coffee maker, mug in hand. "If, hypothetically, your friend had been murdered by some kind of magician, it would be dangerous to approach this murderer with no respect for—or even belief in—their abilities. That would be like walking into the middle of a shootout, unarmed and unconcerned, because you didn't believe guns were real. In your current situation, though you're still unarmed, at least you have some awareness of the danger you might be in."

So Roger was just as crazy as Collie. Maybe it was contagious. Anna glared at both of them.

"I don't have to believe a murderer is a magician to respect his abilities," she told them. "Obviously the person we're after is manipulative. I believe he's dangerous. Why is it vital to my safety that I also believe he can pull a rabbit from a hat?"

Roger gave her a look that was a subtle blend of patronizing and smug. "If you were on your own, Ms. Gareau, you would probably be dead by now. Fortunately for you, Colette seems to have a healthy respect for the fantastic. She knows enough to approach with caution."

Anna was surprised into laughing. "I've only known her a few days and I know better than that. Her idea of caution is carrying a rabbit's foot while jumping out of a plane with no parachute."

Roger smiled. "I think so, too. And still I wouldn't give you Jocelyn's list if Colette wasn't on the case with you. Food for thought."

"I was coming to the opinion," Anna said, "that you might be as crazy as Collie. But now I can see you're much crazier than she will ever be."

Roger nodded, unfazed. "That may be. But I have something you want, which leaves you no choice but to be nice to me."

"You have a nice house," Anna said testily. "Your wife seems intelligent. Your beard is clean and neatly trimmed. My admiration for your good qualities knows no bounds. Please get us that list."

Roger laughed and ambled out of the kitchen, leaving a full mug of coffee behind.

Collie transferred the liquid to her own mug and took a gulp. "And you thought I was the only flake in town," she said.

Anna snorted. "That is far from what I thought."

"Nobody likes to admit it," Collie said, "but there is a groundswell of belief in the supernatural. People are starting to see that it's a world of possibilities. Even you, Anna, even you are possible."

"There's always a groundswell of superstition surrounding a new millennium," Anna said. "Ask Paul about that and I bet he'll tell you. And anyway, shut up. You didn't have to bring up my . . . situation . . . in public."

"Roger didn't hear what I said. I was quiet. He only heard you."

"Still," Anna said, with finality.

"Okay," said Collie. "Fine. In future, we'll only discuss your . . . situation in the bathroom with the door shut and all the water running and a radio turned up really loud."

"If we discuss it at all."

Collie looked as though she had something else she wanted to say, but Roger was back with a file folder, so she clamped her mouth shut.

Anna put her hand out for the folder. Roger opened it, took out a sheet of paper, and handed the paper to her. It was dollar-store stationery with a light floral pattern. All part of Jocelyn's obsession with design. Four business names and addresses had been printed on the paper with a thick-nibbed fountain pen. The name at the top was Estelle's.

"Thanks," Anna said. Sandy re-entered the kitchen and went to the coffee machine. A few drops had fallen on the counter and she busied herself scrubbing at them.

As Anna slipped the note into her purse, her fingers grazed over the mysterious bottle of powder she'd taken from Jocelyn's apartment. She closed her hand around it. "Sandy?"

Sandy finished what she was doing and rinsed out the J-cloth before answering. "Yes?"

"I know you're not a biologist, exactly, but can tell what this stuff is? I think it used to be plants."

She held up the bottle.

Sandy stepped closer, frowning. "Just to look at it," she said, "it could be anything. Maybe if I smelled it—"

"I don't recommend that," Collie said quickly. "Never hurts to be cautious, right?"

Sandy smiled. "Good advice."

"Now, Anna, if you would be so kind as to put that stuff back in your damned purse. . . ," Collie said.

She was pissed off. No question about it. Anna looked at her. "What?"

Roger laughed. "You're not paranoid enough," he told Anna. "You haven't been working for Paul long enough to be appropriately paranoid. You see, Colette doesn't mind if Sandy and I are privy to your idle speculation about this case. She does, however, draw the line at showing us hard evidence. I don't know what that powder is or where you got it, but that's not good enough for Colette. She would prefer I didn't even know it existed. Why, you ask? Because this story belongs to the great Paul Echlin. He has a best-selling book to write. His exclusive must be protected at all costs." He met Collie's eyes. "Isn't that right?"

Collie smiled. Her heart didn't seem to be in it. "It's nothing to do with Paul," she said. "I just hate the idea of giving anything to you."

Roger hefted his expansive rear onto the kitchen table and set the folder down beside him. "Relax. I'm fascinated by your approach, but I wouldn't pitch it to editors. Wild speculation is Paul's thing. I discriminate between what I say in private conversation and what I'll put in print." He picked up his mug, found it empty, and set in on the counter. "Tell me something. What do you ladies plan to do once you've found your prey? Gut him? Strew his bloody remains hell to breakfast? Or just hand your findings over to Paul and let your murderer go on with his knitting?"

Collie set her coffee cup in the sink. "I'll give Paul the information," she said. "He probably will get another book out of it. But that doesn't mean I'm leaving a murderer to his business."

"Well," Roger said, "the police won't buy your story. I don't think you have it in you to strew his guts. And I doubt Mr. Bad Guy will quit or turn himself in or even feel a twinge of regret for your friend's death just because you pointed at him and said 'Gotcha.' So you'd better make plans for the future."

"Duly noted," Collie said. "Anna? Shall we?"

Anna had to move fast to leave on Collie's heels.

"'Strew his bloody remains hell to breakfast,'" Collie repeated. She sounded disgusted. It was the first thing Collie had said since they'd left the house and started driving. She'd waited a good ten minutes to say it.

"I can see," Anna allowed, "how you might not care for the question."

"Of course I don't. And I didn't need him to ask it. It's not as if it never occurred to me that justice might be a problem. I even said in the car last night, I don't know what we're going to do with this guy."

Anna nodded. "You did."

"I don't need that man talking to me as though I'm an idiot. Or a child. Or an idiot child."

"I don't think he was doing that."

"He thinks I don't care about what happened to Jocelyn. He thinks I'm just running and fetching for Paul."

Anna stared at her. "I don't think he really thinks that, Colette. He didn't ask us what we were going to do with the murderer. He asked you. He knows you're the one with a personal stake in this."

"You have a personal stake," Collie said. "You want to prove you're the only freak ever to walk the earth in the whole history of humankind."

Obviously she was spoiling for a fight. Anna sighed. "Can we drop it for now? If we keep on this case, that issue will sort itself out."

"And my position is easier to prove than yours," Collie said. The thought seemed to cheer her. "What's on the list?"

"Estelle's," Anna said. "Besides that . . . someplace called

The Word. Bookstore, maybe. Or religious cult. Could go either way. The next one I don't know how to pronounce . . . conjur-air, conjur-are-ay . . . conjur-something. And the last one's called 'The Healing Earth.'"

"Tree-hugging for fun and profit. Are there street addresses on that list?"

"Yeah."

"Okay, hang on. I'm gonna pull over and take a look at the map."

Anna clenched her teeth and shut her eyes until the car had come to a complete stop.

"If you're done your nap," Collie said, "there should be a map in the glove compartment."

Anna fished it out from beneath a travel packet of Kleenex, a blueberry Mr. Sketch marker, a Christmas ornament made from red and white pipe cleaners, and a black plastic switch labelled "kill."

"Who was Prime Minister the last time you cleaned your car?" she asked, setting the map on the dashboard.

"Very funny."

"No, I'm serious. Was it Campbell? Mulroney?"

The map rustled as Collie unfolded it.

"Turner? Clark?"

It rustled again as Collie smoothed it over her lap.

"Tell me it wasn't Trudeau."

Collie smiled. "I barely remember Trudeau. Give me that list."

Anna waited until Collie had read the list, picked their first destination, and planned the route. She waited until the map was neatly folded, an act of magic she had never been able to accomplish herself. She waited until it was safely back in the glove compartment and the car had started to roll. Then she said, "You remember Trudeau just fine."

It was one of those deceptively small bookstores that had been someone's house in a past life. Anna always admired the use of space in those places, the way everything from the basement to the bathroom contained bulging shelves, the way those shelves grazed the ceiling. You could put one hell of a lot of books into a house, if you were really dedicated to the idea.

There was no one behind the counter when they entered. A stocky man with short, tightly curled hair was pulling a book from one of the rough wooden shelves and cursing. "Fiction!" he spat, whirling around to face them. "This book has been thoroughly debunked. The author himself no longer defends it. Why does some revisionist malcontent insist on coming into my store to engage in the political statement of rearranging my shelves?"

Anna looked at the book in his hands. It was a thin paperback outlining a cloning experiment. She raised her eyes to the clerk and shrugged. "They put it in non-fiction?"

"They put it in medicine."

"We didn't really come here looking for books," Collie told him.

"Then you've made a mistake, because that's all I sell."

He walked away. Collie followed him. Anna followed her. Their procession wound into what had probably been the living room of the house. The books were confined to shelves along the walls, leaving space in the centre of the room for an aquarium the height and width of a card table. In spite of its size, it was about the dullest aquarium Anna had ever seen. Marine, judging by the barnacles and anemones, but devoid of any interesting life. An ugly grey plastic box was lying in one corner.

Collie frowned and moved so that Anna was between her and the aquarium. Apparently she had a bizarre phobia of water-filled glass rectangles. Anna let it go.

The curly haired man had found the shelf he was looking for. Collie stepped up behind him as he angrily rammed the paperback into place. "We came to ask about Jocelyn Lowry," she said.

He didn't turn from the shelf he was facing, but his arms dropped to his sides. "If you've come to pay her tab," he said, "it's in the neighbourhood of fifty bucks and change. I wouldn't have let her run it up that high if I'd known someone was going to drown her."

It wasn't offensive, not the way he said it, with his voice low and bitter. Anna opened her mouth to ask if he knew anything about the drowning, but she was cut off by the sound of Collie's voice.

"Son of a bitch!"

Anna turned to see Collie backed up against a bookshelf and gaping at the aquarium. It wasn't empty anymore. The side closest to Collie had spontaneously generated a small octopus.

"Don't worry about him," the clerk said. "Octopuses are curious animals. If you meet them in the wild and you're very, very patient, you can feed them. It's amazing, the level of intelligence they show. They're very advanced for molluscs."

"Yeah." Collie stood up straight, allowing the bookshelf behind her to right itself. "I hear the poison in the tropical ones is worse than a rattlesnake bite."

He moved to the tank, and placed his hand against the glass. The octopus went to his hand and tapped delicately at the glass with its tentacles.

"It's a lot worse. They're all poisonous to some extent. I once had to drag a guy to shore after he tangled with an octopus. The dumb asshole panicked—nearly drowned me with him. Drowning people are like that. If I came across either of you two ladies and you were drowning, I'd just keep walking."

"Thanks," Anna said. He gave her a nod and a crooked smile.

"On that topic," Collie said, "you know, the topic of drowning? We're trying to find out what happened to Jocelyn."

"She drowned."

"Besides that," Collie said. Anna could almost hear her molars grinding.

"She may have been a victim of urban violence," the bookseller offered.

Collie glared at him. "Inasmuch as she was killed in a city," she said, "that's true. But specifically, we think she was killed by someone in Victoria's occult community, and we know she went to you for occult books. So we were wondering if she had come to you looking for help. Or if you killed her. Did you?"

The clerk laughed. "Missy, if I had, would I say so?"

Missy. What was it with people on the Island and that incredibly obnoxious word?

"Who knows?" Collie said. "Some people can't keep a secret. Did Jocelyn talk to you about *The Rail*? Did you know she worked there?"

He looked at Collie and said nothing. The octopus detached from the wall and scooted towards an anemone. He said, "The topic came up. She thought someone was making a psychic assault on the people at her office. She asked if I could recommend any books on the topic."

"Did you?"

"No. I didn't have what she wanted."

Considering the sheer number of books surrounding them, Anna found that hard to believe. Granted, they weren't all occult books . . . but still.

"Did you recommend another store?"

"I recommended she develop a more realistic self-image. From what I've heard about *The Rail*, whoever is messing with those people has to be a pretty talented guy. Jocelyn recognized talent, but she had no talent of her own. I told her, you can hang out backstage all you want. That doesn't qualify you to pick up a guitar and join the band."

Collie's eyes narrowed. "Would it have done any harm to point her in the direction of some books?"

"As a matter of fact, I think books did her the ultimate harm. I don't know where she got her reading material, but judging from what she told me, she read some New Age happy-crappy about defending her psychic energy and got the idea she could stand up to this guy. Obviously that idea was a poor one. I told her the best way to defend herself against this magician would be to pack her bags and move to Seattle. Get lost in the crowd. Instead, she went for a swim."

"Did she," Anna asked, "mention this guy by name?"

"No."

That was all he said. No speech, no editorial comments. Just "no." Anna looked at Collie, but couldn't tell if she was buying it. "You have any theories?" Anna pushed.

He shook his head. "I do not ask talented people what they do for recreation. It's not my business."

"Not your business," said Collie. "Not even if these talented people are murderers."

The clerk smiled. "The only moral lapse I concern myself with is shoplifting."

"Okay." Collie reached into her purse and pulled out a tiny notepad. The notepad was quickly followed by a thin gold pen. "Give us a list of your talented customers, and we'll ask about their morals."

"You've got to be kidding. These people wouldn't be my customers if I gave their names to every ragamuffin who wandered in off the street."

Collie blinked. "We . . . wouldn't have to mention your name."

"That's right; you wouldn't. Talented people don't have to be told things. They already know. Now, if you're done wasting my time. . . ."

"I think we are," Anna said, putting a hand on Collie's arm. "For now."

It took a hard tug to get Collie moving, but Anna didn't mind putting her back into it. Anything to get them the hell out of that store.

"Did that man call us ragamuffins?" Naturally, that would have top billing in Collie's brain.

"He also lied when he said Jocelyn didn't give him a name. He knows who killed her."

Collie was caught up in adjusting the car heater, but that got her attention. "Are you just guessing, or do you know that? You didn't touch anything in there, did you?"

"Of course I didn't touch anything. He didn't open his mouth without lecturing us, not once, except when I asked if Jocelyn mentioned her suspect's name. Then we got a one-word answer. That one word was a lie. If we were equipped to go in there and beat the shit out of him, we could wrap up this case."

Collie laughed. "I think you could take him."

"Maybe. But I'm not used to fighting. Besides, he could sic his octopus on me."

"Yeah . . . he could paralyze you with octopus venom and drown you in the aquarium. And then he'd tell the police it was an accident. I'd know better, but they wouldn't listen to me."

"I'd be unavenged and have to wander that bookstore as a ghost," Anna concluded. "It's probably best if I don't fight him."

"I guess that leaves us with the rest of Joce's list."

"Guess so."

Neither of them said much on the way to The Healing Earth. Anna wanted to think that Collie was ruminating on the meaning of what the clerk hadn't said, but it was hard to tell. She knew perfectly well that they should phone Paul and tell him where they were going, as well as where they'd been. She suspected that Collie knew it too. Checking in was the cautious and reasonable thing to do. But they weren't going to call Paul. If they did, Paul would pretend to applaud their good sense, but he would also smirk and call them "ladies." He would call them "ladies" in the sweet and condescending way that one might call a couple of five year old girls "ladies." Death was preferable.

The Healing Earth was tucked into a strip mall with a florist on one side and a bakery on the other. It was impossible to see anything through the shop's front window, since it was full of hanging plants, bundles of leaves, stained glass ornaments, and large, crude dreamcatchers with twig hoops.

"They're in denial," Collie theorized. "If they can't see the pizza joint across the street, it doesn't exist."

"They're actually situated in the middle of a forest," said Anna. "Most of their customers are elves. Do we have to go in there?"

Collie sighed. "I'm afraid so. I'm betting they sold Joce the rowan."

Predictably, opening the door set off chimes. Anna had once

worked in a coffee-shop with chimes over the door. She'd lasted less than a month and made a point of swiping the chimes on her way out. Later, she'd backed her Jeep over them and tossed the flattened remains into the river.

"Helloooo!" The voice came from behind a curtain at the back of the store. The storage room, maybe, or the washroom. Anna wasn't any judge of British accents, but it didn't take an expert to know certain people's accents were fake. Keanu Reeves in *Dracula*, for example, wasn't fooling anyone. This woman wasn't quite that bad, but it was still pretty obvious.

The curtains parted and a woman in her early thirties emerged, wiping her hands on her jeans. "I was just repotting some plants," she said, all traces of the accent gone. Apparently that was just how she said hello. "All of the little roots were getting tangled and gnarly. . . ." On the last few words her voice changed again, this time into a passable imitation of the Wicked Witch of the West.

"Gnarly," Collie repeated with a slight smile.

"Dude," the woman answered cheerfully, her voice back to what Anna assumed was normal for her. "What can I do for you?"

Collie stepped forward. A hanging basket of sachets was brushed by the top of Collie's head and began to swing. Anna opted to keep perfectly still.

"We're looking into the death of Jocelyn Lowry," Collie said. "We were told she used to shop here. Do you remember her?"

"Oh. Shit. Yes, of course I remember her," the woman said. "Do you know . . ." she paused, face and hands twisting as she tried to find the right words. "Do you know what happened?"

It was amazing to Anna. They said they were investigating Jocelyn's death, nothing more, and everyone assumed they had some sort of official status. No wonder con artists made such good livings.

Collie shrugged. "We're working on it. I'm . . . we're working for Paul Echlin. He wrote—"

"I've read it," the woman said. "My ex thought he was brilliant." She paused. "I heard that Jocelyn went to the Victorian to meet Dr. Echlin."

"Yeah, she did. We think she wanted to talk to him about everything that's been going on at *The Rail*. Did you know she worked there?"

"I did," the woman said. Her face twisted again, drawing a cartoon of concentration. "How did I know that? I'm sure I didn't ask her. But when I read it in the paper, I already knew. So I must have known. I just don't know why I knew."

It would have been interesting, as a social experiment, to pull a gun on her and demand that she make sense. Collie was staring at the woman, blinking as slowly and deliberately as a lazy cat.

"Maybe she mentioned it in passing," she said. "Did Joce ever talk to you about needing magical or psychic protection from someone?"

"Oh, she *did*. She did. About a month ago, she came in here with that *Amulets* book. She said someone was trying to get into her head and controooool her thoughts."

Now her voice reminded Anna of a mad scientist from some terrible old movie.

"Did you recommend a shrink?" Anna asked. Collie turned to glare at her, a quick motion that set the hanging basket in motion again.

"I would never," the woman said, "recommend a shrink. We get some pretty special people in here, but Jocelyn was never . . . uh. . . ." The woman tapped her temple a few times. "I told her this psychic defense stuff was complicated. But, you know, she had that book and it said she needed rowan, so she was bound and determined to buy rowan."

"So you were the one who sold her the rowan," Collie said. She sounded just an eensy bit smug.

"Well, she wasn't going to get it from Estelle, was she? I'm surprised Estelle even sold her that book."

Anna glanced at Collie.

Collie looked suddenly unwell. "Which book?"

The woman waggled her head at them. It was an odd gesture that made her head seem like a ball on the end of a spring. "The *Amulets* book, hello? *Amulets for the Storm*. Something like that. Estelle sold Jocelyn the book and told her she'd have to find rowan somewhere else. And I was somewhere else."

"I bet," Anna muttered.

The woman looked at her. Just a glance at first, but it turned into a stare and finally into a bulging-eyed gape that made Anna twitchy.

"Am I wearing something of yours?" she asked.

The woman kept staring. "There's something different about you," she said.

"I have a third nipple," Anna said. "Are you sure about where Jocelyn got that book?" Collie's back was shaking as she tried not to laugh

"Not that it could possibly matter, but yes. Of course I'm sure. Oh! Oh! Estelle! That's how I know where Jocelyn worked. She was here with Estelle!"

"When she bought the rowan?" Collie asked. She sounded as confused as Anna felt.

"No, not then. Before. Ages ago. They came in together sometimes. One of those times, one of my customers knew Estelle, so they got to talking, and then Estelle introduced Jocelyn and said where she worked and *that's* how I knew." She sounded triumphant, as if she'd solved the whole case with that stunning bit of recall.

Anna rubbed some floating piece of herb from the corner of her eye and blinked wearily. "Mystery solved," she said.

"Haven't seen that man in a while," the woman went on. "Thank the gods."

"What man?" Collie asked. Something in her tone made Anna's skin crawl.

"My customer. The one who knew Estelle. He was rude. You should have heard him when he found out where Jocelyn worked. You would have thought *The Rail* was the root of all evil." She looked at Anna again. "Witches often have a third nipple."

"Yeah, and then turn people into frogs," Anna told her. "Getting back to this guy—you say he had a thing about *The Rail*?"

"The media in general, I think," the woman said. "He called her all kinds of names because she was working to produce a mind control device. That's what he called magazines and newspapers and TV stations . . . they were all mind control devices. I had to throw him out of here so many times. . . ."

"Did you throw him out that day?" Collie asked.

The woman shook her head. "No. He left on his own. You won't believe what he did. After he said all of that horse pucky to Jocelyn, he asked Joce out. Can you believe that? What on Earth made him think she would say yes?"

"His essential maleness?" Collie offered. Anna glanced at her, surprised by the venom of that statement. Collie definitely seemed put out by something.

"Whatever it was, it misled him." The woman turned to the shelf beside her and tidied it as she spoke. "But I guess he wasn't completely off base, because Estelle did start dating him a few months ago. I saw them together at Conjurare."

She said it con-jur-are-ay. Assuming she'd said it correctly, that solved one mystery for Anna. Pronunciation was a much nicer thing to think about than the whole question of what was going on with Estelle. Anna thought maybe she'd just stand around contemplating pronunciation all day.

"I didn't know Stella was seeing anyone," Collie said. Her voice was remarkably even. "I'll have to ask her about that. You wouldn't happen to know this guy's name, would you?"

"I never asked. I only ever saw him here and at Conjurare. I'm sure Estelle would know. Since she's dating him. Wouldn't she?"

"One would hope," Collie said. "Can I ask you one more thing?"

The woman set down the pack of incense she'd been dusting and smiled at Collie. "Go for it."

"Do you think rowan really works?

That wasn't a promising question. It suggested to Anna that Collie had a head full of bad ideas.

"Hmm," the woman said. "The fruit is excellent for . . . um . . . regularity. I don't know if it really fends off witches. But I try not to close myself off to the possibilities of plants."

Anna considered taking one of the powder vials from her purse. Collie had snapped at her the last time she'd done that. Also, showing this woman the powder would probably result in

Anna having to spend more time with her. All in all, it seemed to be a bad plan. Anna decided against it.

"Thank you," Collie said. "You've been very helpful."

"Service is a calling," the woman said cheerfully. "Have a good day."

"I want to talk to Becca," Collie said. She pulled the car door shut and waited as Anna got in the other side and did the same. "I need to know if Jocelyn mentioned this mystery asshole to her. Nothing personal, but I think she'll say more if you're not there."

"You're telling me to sit and stay until you get back, aren't you? You're telling me to go into that doughnut shop over there and suck back doughnuts until you find me useful again and therefore come to fetch me." Anna shook her head. "Where did I lose control of this investigation?"

"Is that where you'll be?" Collie asked. "Having doughnuts?"

"I could meet up with you there," Anna said, "but I have a personal errand I've been putting off. If you're ditching me, I might as well take care of it."

"I'm not ditching. . . ." Collie took a deep breath. "Semantics. If we're meeting up somewhere, it might as well be Stella's shop. You know and I know, we have to talk to her."

"I'll see you there in two hours," Anna suggested.

Collie nodded. "That should do it. Can I drop you somewhere?"

"You can drop me right here," Anna said. "I'll take a cab. Do you want me to go back into that store and show that woman our Identikit drawing?"

Collie shook her head. "I don't want her getting the idea this guy is a suspect. Identikit pictures kind of scream 'suspect.' I'll see what Becca says, then maybe we can come back here and get a description and stuff. I just have a feeling it would be bad to push things right now."

"A hunch," Anna told her. "Remember? We detectives call it a hunch?"

Collie smiled. "Get out of my car. I'll see you later."

Anna had barely left the car and slammed the passenger door shut when Collie put it in gear and squealed away. Probably she was anxious to get the whole thing over with. Two visits with Stella and a talk with Rebecca in one day. It was enough to make anyone edgy.

Anna went to a pay phone outside the pizza place and called herself a cab.

It wasn't much of a drive from The Healing Earth to Bill's Gunworks. Anna sat next to the driver, a custom that had disappeared from the largest Canadian cities but was stubbornly hanging on in smaller centres.

The driver asked what a girlie like her needed with a gun. He said he guessed she must not have a man to protect her. He suggested she ought to get herself a man.

Anna was starting to see the charm of sitting in the back seat. She said nothing and kept saying nothing until he finally shut up.

The cabbie dropped her off on the wrong side of the street, probably on purpose. She paid him with exact change, definitely on purpose.

Bill's Gunworks about three times the size of an average elevator. Anna had to duck to get through the front door. When she straightened up, she could see a small, balding man sitting on a high stool behind a glass counter full of guns. A sign below the cash register said, "When you're really angry, days can seem like years. Buy now."

"That's pretty black humour," Anna said, nodding at the sign.

The man smiled. "Call it humour if you like," he said. "What can I do you for?"

"I have a gun with no bullets in it. I'm starting to think that's silly."

"You're right," the man told her. He adjusted his glasses and smiled again. "Imagine you're holding a gun on someone and they realize it's not loaded. You'd never live that down."

"Yes. I'm very worried about being embarrassed. Do you have bullets that will work with this gun?" Anna could have shown him the gun itself, but she preferred not to. Instead, she took out a card with the particulars written on it in Curtis's careful hand.

He took the card and looked at it. Then he looked at Anna. After a good long look at her he looked at the card again. "Where in Christ's name did you get your hands on a Luger of that vintage?"

"I took it off a dead German soldier," Anna told him. "Do you have ammo for it or not?"

He looked at her for a while longer. It was the most intense look she'd ever received outside of a bar.

"As it happens," he said, "I do. You plan on doing a lot of shooting, or do you need these bullets for a special occasion?"

Anna had a wild notion that she should ask this man who might have killed Jocelyn. He seemed to take a lively interest in murder. "I guess you could say that I'm loading it on spec," she said.

The man blinked at her. His eyes bulged a little. Between the eyes, his large, thin mouth, and his claw-like hands, Anna suspected he was at least one-quarter chameleon.

"I have to have a look at your FAC," he said.

Anna took the card back and put it in her coat pocket. "It's in my other purse," she said. "I only want ammo. A very small amount of ammo."

"I still need to see your FAC," the man told her. Anna stood her ground and stared into his buggy eyes. "Unless," he said, "I get confused. I might think I saw it. It gets pretty crazy in here sometimes. A very small amount, you say?"

"I understand this will be more expensive than buying in bulk," Anna told him.

He nodded. "That's right." He reached below the counter and fished around. When he straightened again, he was holding a handful of bullets. "This will load that gun," he told her.

Anna was pretty sure he wasn't supposed to sell bullets by the handful, with or without an FAC, but she wasn't about to complain.

"I'd better not see you on the six o'clock news," he told her as she handed him some cash.

Anna smiled. "You won't."

"Still alive, I see."

Anna had been prowling the ground floor of The Village Market, scaring the hell out of middle-aged housewives with her inexpensive clothing and inappropriate height. It had been mildly amusing for a while, but the excitement had worn off in time. She was relieved to hear the sound of Collie's voice.

"How's Becca?" Anna asked, turning to look at Collie.

"Home sick," Collie said. "Mono."

"Wow." Anna smiled. "You gave her good advice, and she took it. Didn't see that coming."

"It did surprise me," Collie admitted. "Nearly into unconsciousness. I asked her about the asshole."

"And?"

"He was bothering Joce for a while. Wanted her to date him, quit *The Rail*. Becca saw him once. She said the Identikit drawing could be him, so at least we know he's a viable suspect. She couldn't give me a name, though."

"That's why we're here," Anna reminded her.

"True," Collie said. "Okay. Let's do this."

The second they walked into Stella's shop and didn't see her, Anna wanted to turn around and head straight back to the parking lot. She jammed her hands into her coat pockets and told herself to keep them there, no matter what they found.

"Stella?" Collie said it softly, as though Stella might be having a nap behind one of the shelves.

Anna wanted to give her a shake, but that would have meant taking her hands out of her pockets. "Collie . . . I don't think she's here."

"Well, her shop's wide open," Collie said, making her way down the rows of shelves. It wasn't much of a walk, since Estelle's only had room for three small rows. Three rows and a wide counter at the back.

"Maybe she went for coffee. Let's come back later."

"We can wait. We don't have to be at the hotel 'til . . . oh, Jesus."

Collie's search had brought her to the counter, and it was clear from her face that something unexpected was behind it. Anna leaned over and saw Stella on the ground. Or what used to be Stella, anyway.

Anna couldn't say she was surprised.

Collie ran around her to kneel beside Stella. She was checking for a pulse, getting ready to do CPR. It was a nice impulse, but an obvious waste of time.

"Don't touch her."

"What do you mean, 'Don't touch her'? I'm not a fucking psychic. I'll touch whatever I want."

Anna grabbed Collie's hands. They were colder than usual. "This has nothing to do with my curse. She's way past being helped. You don't want to touch anything dangerous, and I think we should be careful about prints."

Collie gawked at her, then dug into her pocket and brought out her phone.

"Colette, it's possible that we should just walk away from this."

"Fuck that. Jesus . . . what good is 911 if they won't answer the goddamned. . . . Hi. Hello. I need an ambulance at Estelle's in The Village Market. My friend has . . . she seems to have swallowed something."

That was an accurate assessment of the situation, as far as Anna could see. There was white powder around Stella's mouth, and her face was contorted.

As she watched, Collie bent to pick up a small cardboard box that was lying beside Stella's body. Anna planted a foot between the box and Collie's hand. "No!" she said. "Prints!"

Collie blinked owlishly at her, then the information clicked and she leaned forward to see what was written on the side of the box. "I think she took rat poison," she whispered into the phone. The operator must not have heard her, because after a moment she said it again. "Rat poison. There's a box of rat poison beside her." She rattled off the ingredient list from the side of the box, handling the unfamiliar words effortlessly. "But she wouldn't have . . . what? No, she's not. Yeah, I do. Okay. I'm gonna give you to my friend."

She thrust the phone at Anna. Anna put the phone to her ear, watching as Collie began CPR on the lost cause that had been Stella Hrybinski.

"Hello?" The operator sounded faintly annoyed.

"Hi," Anna said. "What do you need?"

"Just stay on the line."

"Okay."

It didn't take long for paramedics to arrive. About six minutes by Anna's watch, and that was with three flights of stairs to climb. It might have seemed a long time if there had been an emergency, but there wasn't, so what the hell.

"They're here," Anna told the operator.

"All right. I'm hanging up now."

Anna knelt beside Colette. "Collie . . . the professionals are here."

Collie responded by giving Stella's chest an especially hard shove. "Damn you," she muttered.

"Come on, out of the way." Anna grabbed her arm and stood, pulling Collie up to stand beside her. The paramedics moved in and went to work. They gave it the old college try; Anna had to give them that. When they finally stepped away from the body, even Collie could see that Stella was long gone. One of the paramedics said he was sorry. Collie just looked at the ground.

"Go wash your mouth," Anna said, nudging her arm with an elbow. Collie gave her a blank look.

"You might have some of that stuff on you. You should wash your mouth so you don't swallow any. There's a bathroom up the hall and to the left. See it?"

Collie nodded.

"Good. Go wash your mouth."

Collie went. Anna turned to the paramedics.

"The police are on their way," one of them told her. He was the one who'd said he was sorry.

Anna did her best to smile. "We got here about half an hour ago and found her behind the counter. I'm pretty sure she was already gone."

"Probably," he agreed. "You know her?"

"My friend does. Did."

"Uh huh."

They were saved from further conversation by the arrival of the police. Three cops, one familiar face. "You again," he said.

She nodded. "Me. Again."

"I thought I told you to stay out of this."

"Stay out of what? We came here to visit an old friend of Colette's and we found her dead. Are you saying this Stella person was part of your investigation?"

His mouth twisted as though he'd bitten into something nasty. "I don't know this Stella person from a hole in the ground. All I know is, here's another body, and here you are again. Is this one a suicide too?"

Anna looked at Stella's body. She didn't seem to have gone gently into that good night, but there was no sign that anyone had forced poison down her throat.

"I'm sure you'll think so," she said.

The cop snorted. "You disagree, do you? In your capacity as a police consultant?"

Anna shrugged "Who am I to blow against the wind?"

That was when Collie returned from the bathroom, pale and unhappy. The skin around her mouth was red from scrubbing.

"Where I find one," said the cop, "naturally I find the other. I hear your boss spent last night in jail."

"The charges were dropped," Collie said. She sounded short on patience. "He was arrested for being in the same building as someone who was committing a crime. Eventually someone looked it up and found out that wasn't against the law."

"Who knew?" Anna put in.

Collie leaned against her side. "Who knew?" she repeated softly.

The cop shook his head. "I'm going to get the particulars from the two of you," he told them, "following which, I want you gone. You do not want to run into me again. Not one more time. This had better be our last farewell."

Anna longed to say that she wanted that as badly as he did, but she had just enough sense to hold her tongue. Collie was silent as well, but Anna didn't think it was an exhibition of sense. Colette was probably just worn out.

In a beautiful display of great minds thinking alike, Collie told the same story that Anna had told the paramedic. Stella was a friend. They had stopped by to see her. Their visit had nothing to do with Jocelyn's death.

Collie added that they had come back for a second visit because Collie had wanted to ask Stella something. Again, it was nothing to do with Jocelyn Lowry. Collie didn't mention that Jocelyn had known Stella. She didn't mention that Stella was a witch. She certainly didn't mention the psychic assault book Stella had lied about selling.

Anna added nothing to Collie's account. Collie leaned on her through the whole thing, just long enough for Anna's arm to go numb. When the cop dismissed them, Anna moved her shoulder and watched as her hand flopped out of her coat pocket. Collie gave her an odd look.

"You pinched a nerve," Anna explained.

Collie nodded. "Sorry."

There was no point talking until they were well away from the police, so they didn't. They were blocks away, surrounded by traffic, when Collie opened her mouth again. "Would you like me to pretend I don't know you?" she asked. "You might live longer. I hear knowing me makes your insurance premiums go up."

"It's not knowing you," Anna said. "It's getting in a car with you driving."

"Oh."

Anna waited until they were at a light before speaking again. "I don't think the police think we did anything. I think they still consider that janitor's death to be a suicide. I bet they'll say the same thing about Stella."

"I'm at the centre of a rash of suicides," said Collie. "I'm trying not to take it personally, but I can't help wondering if it's something I said."

"It's not anything you said. It's something that guy said."

"What guy?"

The girl was losing it. Anna stared at her.

"The mysterious asshole? Stella's boyfriend? Our suspect?"

"Oh. Right. That guy." She looked at Anna. "You think he made Stella kill herself?"

"You're not normally stupid, so I'm going to assume this is shock. Let me know when you're ready for rational discussion."

"Don't hold your breath."

As it turned out, Anna could have held her breath. They'd driven a fair number of blocks before Collie spoke, but Anna had pretty good lungs.

"She wouldn't have had rat poison at the store," Collie said. "She would've used those no-kill traps. She wouldn't have killed a wild rat, and she wouldn't have kept rat poison where her pet rats might get into it." She turned to Anna, oblivious to the road. Anna grabbed the wheel and pointed ahead until Collie looked where she was going. "Sorry. I was just going to ask if you saw her rat at all. I mean, Jocelyn's rat. I didn't see it this time."

"It's a rodent," Anna said. "It probably hid somewhere."

"No, not a tame rat. I guess if it was scared it might have hidden, but most of them really like people. It would've come out when it saw us. I'm surprised it wasn't near her . . . uh, her body."

"Maybe it ate some rat poison and crawled off somewhere to die."

Collie shuddered, something she had not done upon finding either of the two corpses. "That's awful," she said. Anna sighed. Why not focus on the death of a rat? It would be nice to pretend that was the only thing that had gone wrong of late. Yeah," she agreed. "Awful."

"Aw, crap."

Collie had stopped dead just inside the front doors to the hotel. Anna stopped behind her and looked over her head to see what had brought that on. The answer appeared to be Roger, who was parked in the same dirty, pink chair Anna had occupied earlier.

"You should be relieved," Roger said. "At least you didn't find me dead."

"We must define *relief* differently," Collie hissed. She was rushing towards Roger, seemingly in an attempt to lower the volume of their conversation. "How the hell did you know we found another body?"

Roger smiled. "I should say I know because you just told me," he said. "But actually, I heard it from Paul. Don't ask me how he knows. I did hear something on the radio about the death of one Estelle Hyrbinski, proprietor of Estelle's. I assume she's the corpse in question. Do you know the police searched your rooms?"

"Is there anything we can do for you, Roger?" Collie asked. "By which I mean, is there anything we can do to get rid of you?"

"Sandy's coming by to pick me up," he said. "You're stuck with me 'til then."

"You know, I don't think that's true."

Collie brushed past him and went straight to the elevators. Anna sauntered after her. It wasn't seemly to be in too much of a hurry.

"What do you think he's doing here?" Anna asked. They were standing in front of the elevator doors, staring at them as if that would make the elevator appear.

"Had a meeting with Paul, obviously."

"Uh, yeah," Anna said. "I was leaving out the obvious part. What were they meeting about?"

"Fucked if I know," Collie said. "It's not as if Paul tells me anything."

The elevator doors opened, the soft bell blending with the sound of Collie's pocket ringing. They stepped inside to the sound of the phone. They cleared two floors to the sound of the phone. Anna was getting good and sick of the sound of the phone.

"You gonna get that?" she asked.

"You answer it."

It was poor behaviour for a PR person, refusing to answer a ringing phone, but Anna didn't want to fight about it. She snaked a hand into Collie's pocket and pulled out the phone. "Hello?"

"Anna." Paul sounded surprised, possibly a little amused. "You didn't take this phone off the dead body of my assistant, did you?"

"I don't know. Hang on. I'll poke her and see if she moves."

"Tell him to fuck off," Collie suggested.

"She says you should fuck off. I guess that means she's not dead."

"But Stella Hrybinski is."

Anna let her head fall back against the wall of the elevator. "You sure you want to discuss that over a cell phone? It seems to be a huge secret."

"Are you in any trouble?" Clearly he didn't know where they were.

Anna smiled. "Not that we know of."

"There's always a qualification with you."

In the lull that followed, Anna could hear the faint sound of people talking in Paul's hotel room.

"Do you have company?" she asked politely.

"I do. That's why I'm calling. When you get back to the hotel, go to your room and call me from there. I'll come up and see you."

"You mean both of us?"

"Yes."

Anna shut off the phone and dropped it in Collie's coat pocket. "Paul wants to hold a briefing in my room. He has people in his room, and I think he wants to prepare us to meet them."

Collie's mouth twisted. "Considering some of the people he's sprung on me cold, I shudder to think what he has waiting for us tonight. I can't remember him ever warning me about anyone."

"Except saying that Roger was a bad dinner companion."

"That's not a warning. That's like . . . when you're standing in line for a roller coaster and the guy you're with keeps laughing and telling you you're going to puke."

"Maybe these people aren't scary per se. Maybe Paul's running some kind of psychodrama to get information from them."

"Per se." Collie snorted. "Maybe they're the *ne plus ultra* of scary. Maybe they're the *sine qua non* of freakdom." She paused. "I thought we were meeting with Mark Ling."

"Ours is not to reason why," Anna told her.

"No. Ours is to fill our appointment books with funerals."

Collie stood aside, allowing Anna to open her hotel room door. Anna peered inside before crossing the threshold, looking for anything the police might have left behind. It looked about the same as it had when she'd left.

"Shit!" Collie said from behind her.

Anna froze. "What?"

"When is Joce's funeral? Please tell me I haven't missed Jocelyn's funeral."

"I doubt it," Anna said. "This was a murder. Her body won't be released until they've had a chance to . . . you know."

Collie nodded. "I wonder who's organizing the funeral. Probably Becca. Maybe she needs help. Maybe she's been wondering why I haven't offered to help. Maybe she doesn't want me to help."

Anna stepped into the hotel room, making room for Collie to enter. "Why don't you bring your neuroses in here and shut the door behind you?"

Once Collie had done so, Anna said, "I doubt anyone's given a lot of thought to the funeral yet. It's only been two and a half days since she died. If it'll make you feel better, call Becca and ask."

"Yeah. I'll do that. God, that was awful. Like those nightmares where you're back in school and you missed your final exam, only about a billion times worse." She glanced at Anna. "Has it really been just two and a half days?"

"Believe it or don't."

Collie shrugged. Undecided, apparently.

"I should tell Paul we're here," Anna said.

"Can we wait 'til later?" Collie asked. "Paul's older than we are. He'll probably die before us."

"Not the way things have been going," Anna said. "Are you seriously this worried about whoever's in his room?"

Collie threw herself onto Anna's bed and curled up with the pillows. Her expression was nearly a pout. "He's going to ride me about Stella."

"Oh." Anna thought about that. "Want me to tell him not to?"

Collie smiled. "Because you're my thug."

"Well, yes."

"Nah. I'll live with it." She picked up the phone and asked for Paul's room.

Anna took that opportunity for a trip to the washroom. When she came out, Collie was glaring at the room door.

"Why don't you save that look for the man himself?" Anna suggested. "The door hasn't done anything to you."

"He said he hoped he and I weren't friends, since my friends have such terrible life expectancies."

"Ah." Anna found a chair and sat in it. "Did you tell him not to worry about it?"

"More or less."

Paul knocked at the door. It was the perfect knock for a man of his temperament. Staccato, as if a woodpecker had perched on the doorknob. Anna opened the door without a greeting or a smile and stood to one side to let him pass.

"As you know," he said, settling himself in Anna's chair, "we're having dinner with Mark Ling."

"I hope you didn't come all the way up here to tell us that," said Collie.

"No. I'm aware you don't forget appointments. It's one of the reasons I hired you." He crossed his legs and wrapped his long, thin fingers around one knee. "I thought I should warn you that we're having a second guest. As a result, we'll be eating in my room tonight. I've ordered Chinese."

"You wanted to make sure we brought chopsticks," Anna said. "That's thoughtful."

"I wanted to make sure you were ready to talk to Eve Harris."

Anna looked at Collie. The last time the subject had come up, Collie had made it clear that she would never be ready to talk to Eve Harris. She didn't seem to have changed her mind.

"Are you serious?" she asked softly. Her eyes were huge and her face was dead white. "I thought I told you I didn't want. . . ." She stopped.

"That's why I'm here. I've talked with her. I understand why you think it will be difficult, but it's not as bad as all that."

"That's evasive," Collie snapped. "How bad is it?"

"She's been living with her situation for quite a while now. I don't think she's going to fall apart on us."

"Still, we're eating in the room."

Paul shrugged. "It's a private conversation. And she's emotional about her experiences, of course. When Mark suggested she might be a victim of brainwashing, she was pretty relieved. Even with all that implies."

"What's she doing here, anyway? I thought she was in a hospital or something."

"Mark got her a pass for the evening."

Collie shut her eyes. "It's always been my dream to interrogate someone who's out on a day pass."

"Did Mark find out anything useful?" asked Anna.

"Ask him yourself. We should go down there anyway. Dinner will be here fairly soon."

He stood. Collie sighed and rolled off the bed onto her feet. They followed him to his room without another word.

Anna had seen more of Eve Harris than she had of Mark Ling. Besides having her mug shot in the magazine every week, Eve had been on the CBC for a year or two with a half-hour etiquette and interior decorating show. It was the sort of thing Anna actively avoided, but she couldn't help seeing Eve's face from time to time. Still, if she hadn't been told who to expect, she wouldn't have recognized the woman in Paul's hotel room. Eve had gone from elegantly thin to desperately skinny. She was wearing an expensive wig that didn't sit right. Her expensive clothes bagged at her waist and looked about ready to fall from her shoulders. She was clean and fairly well-groomed, but her face belonged to the sort of women who slept beside their shopping carts in alleyways.

"Not as bad as all that," Collie muttered from somewhere behind Anna's left shoulder. Anna wanted to belt her one. Thankfully, Eve didn't seem to notice.

Eve was sitting at the table. Mark was in the chair next to her, going over a pile of notes. He looked up at the sound of Collie's voice and tried to smile. "Oh. You're back. Eve, this is Anna and Colette. I'm sure you guys recognize Eve Harris."

"Yeah," Anna said, offering a hand. "It's nice to meet you."

Eve's hand was hot, dry, and brittle. Anna shook it carefully and quickly let go. Jocelyn had said that Eve wore too much perfume, but apparently she'd given that up for Lent. Soap and hairspray and a faint mustiness were all Anna could smell.

Collie stepped into place beside her and took Eve's hand. She gave Eve a reasonably convincing smile. "Hello, Eve. Jocelyn said nice things about you."

"I didn't know her well," Eve said. Her tone was polite, but her voice had a rasp to it that set Anna's nerves on edge. "But it's good to know that. I was terribly sorry to hear she had passed away."

"Yeah." Collie's smile slipped a little and she let go of Eve's hand. "Me too."

Paul was moving chairs and a table in from Collie's room. Since it was an excuse to leave the room, Anna was more than happy to help. They pushed the two tables together and away from the bed. A little crowded, but tolerable.

"It's been a hell of a day," Mark said once everything was in place.

"Get anything useful?" Anna asked.

"I don't know. I think I've figured out how this guy is operating, but . . . okay, that's the wrong way to put it. I have no idea how this guy is doing what he does. It's not fucking . . . sorry, Eve."

Eve said nothing.

Mark cleared his throat. "Nobody can do what this guy seems to be doing."

"What did you figure out?" asked Collie.

"Well, I think I've got his MO."

Anna smiled. "His MO?"

Mark was nervously rapping the table with his fingertips. "I don't know what else to call it. He did the same thing with everybody. Two weeks before our science writer turned in her screwy article, she had a visit from a meter reader. She doesn't remember what the guy looked like or anything he said. What she does remember is that he stuck around and talked to her, and when he left half an hour had passed."

Collie frowned. "She has no idea what they talked about?"

"She remembers nothing except that they had a conversation. She couldn't even tell me which room of the house they were in. I could show her that Identikit drawing, but I'll tell you right now, I don't think it would do any good."

Collie was running her hand over her purse, no doubt considering the fact that the drawing was right there and Eve was at the table. Anna caught her eye and mouthed 'no.' Collie looked away.

"It was about a week later," Mark went on, "that the science writer's figure skates went missing from her desk. She told me to tell you, if you find this guy, she wants her skates back."

"It's not a priority," Anna told him. "But we'll see. Are you saying this pattern held for everybody who did unexplained things?"

Mark nodded. "Someone would show up that you'd normally have a casual exchange with . . . a meter reader, a courier . . . one of those people you just say 'hi' to and talk about the weather with and that's it. Except, right before things went wrong, all of the writers in question had a visit where this person stayed much longer than they should have. And they don't remember anything else about the visit."

"And after that," Collie said, "something was stolen from them."

"Yeah. I mean, a lot of things were stolen at the same time. But everyone got a visit before their stuff was ripped off. And everyone made mistakes or . . . well, whatever they did . . . shortly afterwards."

"Our bad guy thinks he needs personal totems to cement his influence over his victims," Paul said thoughtfully. "It's. . . ." The phone rang, and he shook his head. "That's probably the food. Excuse me." He took the phone, spoke briefly, and returned to the table. "Someone's bringing it up. We might as well put this discussion on hold for a few minutes, since we're about to be interrupted."

It occurred to Anna that Paul's decision to eat in the room might have more to do with his own desire for privacy than his desire to shelter Eve. He was getting very close to a very big story, and he had to be wondering how much longer he could hold on to the exclusive.

Paul got his wallet and stood by the door until the food came. There was a lot of it, which was fine with Anna. Chinese food had been a rare treat when she was growing up. As soon as the food was on the table and plates and cutlery had been distributed, Anna launched into the meal with enthusiasm.

"I can't believe you got them to deliver paper plates and everything," Collie said.

Paul smiled, pleased by the praise. "I paid for it, believe me."

Colette was in heaven, with a plate full of vegetables cut into tiny pieces. For once, she didn't have to disassemble her meal before eating. She quickly got down to the business of moving everything on her plate into a colourful spiral.

"Did your mother give out prizes for that?" Anna inquired. "Did the most interesting plate earn the biggest serving of dessert?"

Collie looked up from her food, eyebrows raised. "Excuse me?"

"You have strange eating habits," Anna told her.

"You really do," said Mark. "I noticed it this morning. My therapist would call you obsessive-compulsive."

"Unlike you," Collie said pleasantly, "I don't pay people to call me names."

Mark opened his mouth. Paul slapped a hand onto the table, making the plastic cutlery jump. "While I find my assistant's quirks fascinating," he said, "we have better things to talk about. For example, Mark . . . do you remember having the sort of encounter you've described?"

"I think so. I vaguely remember someone coming up to me in the parking lot and asking me questions about my car. I got home much later than I'd expected. I missed *Duckman.*"

Collie grinned at Mark. Something he'd done must have pleased her. "The thing I can't get over," she told him, "is how completely you've come around to our point of view. This morning you were convinced there was something in the water."

"I wasn't convinced of anything," he said testily. "I had suspicions. I told everybody what you people were saying and it seemed to jibe with their experiences. I'm willing to go with your theory until something better comes along."

"The heart of a scientist," said Paul, lifting a styrofoam coffee cup in salute, "in the body of an entertainment writer. I congratulate you."

Anna had a passing interest in the banter, since she expected Colette to start talking about murderous magicians at any second. But nothing at the table was half so interesting as Eve Harris's face. Eve was watching the conversation as though it were happening on a TV with the volume turned down. She stared at faces, studying them, not seeming to care if she was caught looking. Her expression was mild, almost dreamy, and it never changed. Anna suspected she could pick up her spoon and start flicking wontons into Eve's face without getting a response.

Just when she was beginning to wonder if Eve's programming had kicked in again, Collie asked Mark a question. "You didn't happen to talk to Kate Eby, did you?"

That put some life back into Eve. Her cheeks turned dark red, while the rest of her skin lost whatever colour it had had to begin with. She stared first at Collie, then at Mark. Her mouth popped open and stayed that way, but she didn't speak.

Mark dropped his eyes to his plate. "I . . . yeah."

Collie sighed. "We're gonna need details."

"I know." Mark pushed his plate forward and folded his hands on the table. "She couldn't be here tonight. They don't let her out of the hospital. They're worried she might. . . ." His fingers twitched. "I don't know exactly what they think she'll do, but she's not rational."

"You can hardly blame her," Eve said coldly. Collie shuddered.

"No," Mark agreed, "you can't. I'm just saying . . . she couldn't be here."

"Is it true," Collie asked, "that she aborted her own pregnancy?"

Mark shut his eyes. Eve looked about ready to lose her dinner.

"You could put it that way," Mark admitted.

"Uh huh." Collie's voice was shaky. "What other way might someone put it?"

"She had a kind of *Rosemary's Baby* thing going on," Mark said. "Even now, she's convinced she was carrying a demon or something."

"She thought it ate her child," Anna whispered. She hadn't intended to speak. As soon as the words were out she bit down on her lower lip and stared at her plate. She knew Paul was looking at her, but she wasn't about to look up.

Mark waited for a few seconds, then went on. "I don't know what she thought. Did you talk to her?"

Anna shook her head. "I was just . . . guessing."

"Anna's very empathic," Collie said. "Kate still thinks she was carrying a demon?"

Mark pursed his lips and took a moment before answering. "She didn't use that word. But she thinks something evil was growing in her. That's why she . . . decided to cut it out."

Anna remembered the point of the scissors against her stomach, the look on Collie's face as she took them away. She didn't dare look at Collie now.

"May the Lord have mercy on her soul," Eve said.

Anna looked at her. "Ma'am, I can't see why he wouldn't. If somebody got into her head, that wasn't her fault."

Eve's face took on a horrible intensity. To make it even

worse, she smiled. "And it wasn't my fault either, I suppose. All of those things I did."

"Philosophers and psychiatrists will forever debate the relationship between mind and body," Paul said, "but you have to make some kind of distinction between the two. Your body may have been taking directions from your brain, but your mind was under orders from a brainwashing expert. He drove the car while you slept in the back seat. You are not to blame."

Mark shook his head. "I agree that none of us were responsible for our actions," he said, "but I know a little about brainwashing and I just can't see it. One conversation and a stolen token? That's not how it works."

"The token is irrelevant," said Paul. "Our man only thinks he needs it. Geniuses are often superstitious. I don't know how he's doing what he does either . . . but I'm not going to argue with success. If he's getting these kinds of results, he obviously knows a lot more about brainwashing than we do."

Collie shifted in her seat. Paul caught it and smiled. "My assistant," he said, waving a fork in her direction, "believes our man is a practitioner of black magic."

"Isn't that obvious?" Soft though it was, Eve's voice had a remarkable tendency to carry. Everyone turned to look at her. "He's powerful and evil," she said. "He does things no human could ever do. I wouldn't be surprised to learn that poor Kate was bearing a demon. It might have been his child."

"I don't know that I want to go quite that far," Collie said.

Eve gave her another horrible smile. "You'll go as far as he takes you, my dear."

Collie set her fork down and wrapped her hands around her coffee cup. Even with such small hands, it was a tight fit. She didn't say anything.

"We're hoping," Anna said finally, "it won't come to that. Right now I think Colette and I are under his radar." She waited a moment to see if lightning would strike her. Since it didn't, she went on. "I think it's a mistake to attribute all kinds of powers to this guy just because he can do something we don't understand."

"Sufficiently advanced technology," Paul said.

Mark laughed softly, huffing air through his nose.

Eve looked at Paul. "I beg your pardon?"

"It's an old idea from science fiction. Sufficiently advanced technology is indistinguishable from magic."

"Do you really think this is technology?" Mark asked.

Paul finished his coffee while he thought that over. "I don't know. It might be. Might be sufficiently advanced pharmacology. I don't know a lot about this area. Obviously I'm going to learn."

Eve started to laugh. It might have been the most unpleasant thing Anna had ever heard. It made her want to bolt from the room, and she dimly noticed that Collie had pushed back her chair. She reached over to put a hand on Collie's arm.

Mark was clenching his teeth. Anna could tell by the way his jaw was twitching. The only one who didn't seem to care was Paul. He was calm and relaxed, gazing at Eve with boundless patience, waiting for her to stop. Once she had, he tilted his head. "I hear you're taking Zoloft," he said. "How's that going for you?"

Eve narrowed her eyes. "What good is a pill supposed to do?" she asked. "It's not going to change anything. It won't change the past."

"No," Paul agreed, "you're right. That medication works to cure depression when it's caused by a specific chemical imbalance. You're unhappy for perfectly rational reasons that have nothing to do with your biochemistry. I imagine they have you confined because you can't remember how those photographs came to be. I should point out that your situation won't change until either we prove that someone brainwashed you or you start lying."

"I know that," Eve said. "I don't mind staying at the hospital."

There had been times in Anna's life when a loony bin might have represented a welcome relief from stress. She sympathized.

"Eve," Paul said softly, "tell me something—before Mark came to speak with you today, what did you think had happened to you?"

She considered that question carefully, her eyes soft and unfocused. "At first," she said, "I thought the pictures must be fakes. I thought it was a horribly cruel joke. And I was quite frightened, because I couldn't think who would hate me that much."

"You're a media personality," Paul said. "Someone will always hate you that much. When did you realize that the pictures had not been faked?"

"They told me almost from the start that the pictures were real. They spoke to me as though I were . . . a liar, I suppose. Ashamed and lying. Of course anyone would be ashamed to have done such things, but I didn't and I will not say I did. I told them they must be wrong. I told them to go over the photographs again." She leaned forward and her eyes snapped into focus. She seemed to be trying to look straight into Paul's brain. "I wanted those horrible pictures burned. I wanted them destroyed. But instead I told countless people to look at them again and again. To study them. Would I have said that if I didn't truly believe they were fakes?"

"Obviously not," Paul said. "But some people just can't see these things. What finally convinced you?"

"A friend was visiting me at my home. She had a severe allergic reaction while she was sitting on my couch. I keep a very clean house, Mr. Echlin."

"I don't doubt it," Paul said. "What was she allergic to?"

"Feathers."

"I take it you don't keep birds?"

Eve stiffened. "I would never keep birds in the house. They're destructive, and the smell is intolerable."

"So where did the feathers come from?"

Eve didn't reply. Her short, perfectly polished nails were carving half moons into the sides of her coffee cup.

"Eve?" Collie said gently.

"I searched the couch," Eve said. She was staring at the unfinished food on her plate, but probably wasn't seeing it. "I found feathers. Pink feathers. Dyed. They were . . . they matched a feather boa from one of the photographs."

"That must have been a shock," Paul said. His voice was

even and steady, unmarked by compassion or curiosity. "How did you react?"

"I thought I must be crazy. I let them put me in the hospital."

"Did you remember anything?" Collie asked.

"No. I still don't, and I don't want to. But once I was in the hospital, I started to think. Why would I have done those things?"

"Did you have any history of mental illness?" Paul asked.

"No, nothing. And I certainly wasn't a deviant. I have never had such . . . inclinations. I was badly confused. But then I heard what had happened to Kate and I realized there was something unnatural at work in both our lives. What Mark said to me today made perfect sense."

"Your theory hit home with everyone," Mark admitted, looking at Collie. "Maybe it's because it absolves them, but it's very popular."

"It doesn't just absolve them," said Paul. "It means they—and you—weren't poisoned by the water. You aren't insane. You're no more likely to suffer long-term damage than a volunteer from a hypnotist's show."

"You don't believe that," Mark said. "You said a few minutes ago that you thought this guy might be using a drug. And we don't know what he's done to us. The effects could be with us for the rest of our lives."

"It won't matter," Eve said, "if I'm in the hospital."

So she wasn't just taking a break. She had made up her mind to stay somewhere safe and quiet for the next twenty or thirty years. She was probably doing everything she could to convince people she was irredeemably crazy.

"We'll find out what he did," Collie said. "If he drugged you, we'll find out how to fix it."

"That's a whole lot of promise," Anna told her. "I don't think we can guarantee any of that."

"It doesn't matter what you do," Eve said. "Some things can never be fixed. And you are certainly no match for whatever this creature is."

Collie picked up her fork, looked at it carefully, then flung it across the room. One of the tines snapped off when it hit the wall. "Fuck it," she said with a pleasant smile. "You may be right, but who knows? I'm in the mood to find out."

"It's probably time I got Eve back to the hospital," Mark said nervously.

Anna almost laughed. She thought Collie's sangfroid was charming, but it obviously wasn't for everyone.

"I'm feeling a bit tired," Eve said. Her voice had the too-polite tone of a gracious guest who desperately wants to leave. "Mr. Echlin . . . Paul. I thank you for the meal."

Paul's left eye twitched, and his mouth turned upwards into the shark-like smile Anna despised. "Beats hospital food, I bet," he said.

It was the end of Eve's attempt to pretend this was a simple social occasion, one more lovely dinner party in a life made up of little else. Anna realized that Paul didn't like Eve. She hadn't thought him capable of getting so personal, but apparently she'd been wrong.

Mark put a hand under Eve's arm and helped her up. He held her coat and opened the door for her. It was incongruous, this hipster with spiky hair and baggy jeans taking the part of a polished gentleman. Anna couldn't help wondering if Eve would have been seen with him in better days.

"I'll call you when I get back," Mark said once Eve was in the hallway.

Paul nodded. "You do that."

The door clicked shut behind them.

Collie pushed her plate forward and lay her face down on the table. "I quit," she said. The words were muffled.

Paul reached over and grabbed a handful of hair, tugging gently until she sat up. "I'm sorry, could I get that again?"

"Sure," Collie told him. "I quit. I resign. I'll try not to let the door hit me in the ass on my way out."

"You don't quit," Paul said placidly. "You just wish you could. Do you ladies have plans for the evening?"

"Aside from finding a new job?" Collie asked.

Paul laughed. "You can quit when this is all over, if you want. I'd rather you didn't, but you have to follow your path."

He began picking up cups and plates and tossing them into the garbage. "Regardless, you won't quit tonight because you haven't caught the man who killed Jocelyn, and you won't feel right until you've done that."

Anna considered helping Paul clean up the mess, but watching him do it was giving her some kind of perverse pleasure. She remained in her seat.

"We're going to a nightclub," Collie said. Anna had seen trapped animals with more hope in their eyes. "Jocelyn used to go there. We think it's where she met this magician."

"If you catch this guy," Paul said, "and he looks nothing like Rasputin, I'm going to be very disappointed."

Anna stood up. She moved very close to Paul, making it perfectly clear that she was taller than him. "If you make one more joke about this case tonight," she said, "I will rip out your tongue and hang it from the rear view mirror of my Jeep."

Paul studied her face. This close to him, it was possible to see that he was rattled. She could almost smell it. They stood that way for a few minutes. In Anna's peripheral vision, she could see that Collie hadn't moved.

Paul took a deep breath. "Give me the address of this club," he said. "And call in at least once an hour. If there's trouble, I want to know before it's too late to help."

"Done," Anna said. She backed away, giving Paul room to go back to his tidying. "Colette? Shall we go?"

"I have to change," Collie said absently.

Anna rolled her eyes. "Why?"

"So I'll fit in. You should change too."

"We're not going there to socialize. We're going there to ask questions."

Collie smiled. She was starting to look a little better. "Sometimes asking questions goes better when you socialize."

Anna had never considered that possibility, but it might be true. As a professional weasel, Collie would know. "Okay," she said. "We'll change. See you later, Paul."

"Later," he said.

Anna watched in fascinated disbelief as Colette threw two suitcases and a large travel bag onto the bed. Why would anyone pack that way for a week-long trip? Maybe Collie liked to be prepared, but cramming all of that into the back of a Tercel . . . it seemed a little ridiculous.

"Do you have anything to wear?" Collie asked. She was hidden behind the flap of the largest suitcase, only a few curls visible.

"I don't know," Anna said. "Maybe. We don't know what kind of club this is."

"I'm going with a cross between goth and pagan. I have an oversized silk shirt you could wear."

"Thank you so much," Anna said icily.

Collie laughed. "It'll be oversized on you, too. It's made that way. You have black pants, right? I could lend you some jewellery."

"That sounds great," Anna said. "Later, we could make popcorn and talk about boys."

Collie yanked a long black dress from the bottom of the suitcase and let the flap drop. She was grinning. "I'll do your hair," she offered.

Anna laughed. "Shave it. I was going to grow it out, but the hell with it."

"You should grow it out," Collie said thoughtfully, momentarily distracted by a compellingly trivial concern. "Just past shoulder length. Go plug in my curling iron."

Anna went into the bathroom and dealt with the appliance in question before returning to the bedroom. "What are you doing with a curling iron?"

"I use it to loosen my curls," Collie told her. "But it'll work for your hair too. The shirt's on the bed. Go change. I'll see you in a few minutes."

"Sir, yes sir!" Anna said, saluting.

Collie made a rude gesture over her shoulder and disappeared into the bathroom.

Back in her own room, Anna held up the shirt and decided it probably would fit. It was a dark wine, made of heavy silk that felt expensive. She changed quickly. Despite what Collie thought, Anna had more important things to worry about than her appearance. It had been a long time since she'd loaded a gun, and mostly she'd loaded hunting rifles. Handling an old Luger was different. She toyed with the idea of calling Curtis for a walk-through, but he'd demand an explanation she had no intention of supplying. Besides, the fact that he sold antique guns didn't necessarily mean he knew how to load one. She'd have to deal with it on her own.

As soon as she flipped it open, her hands felt cold. Painfully cold, aching to the bone. Her head hurt, and her stomach began to roll. She set the gun down and frowned at it. There were people who had a horror of guns, but Anna wasn't one of them. So why the hell was she freaking out at the prospect of loading the thing? And why did it look so . . . greasy? Curt had oiled it when he cleaned it, but that didn't make a gun look slimy. Kind of slithery. As if it were about to roil beneath her hand.

Now, that was truly stupid.

She swallowed hard and picked the gun up, intending to take another kick at the can, but this time her hands went numb and the gun fell back onto the bed, bouncing once on the comforter.

"Jesus," Anna said softly. She slid her hands under her thighs to warm them while she considered her options. She could sign up for therapy, but for someone as seriously crazy as she seemed to be it could take years. Since she only had a few minutes, that was out. She could call someone, maybe Collie or Paul or even Bryan if he was on duty, and ask them to pretty please load her unlicensed gun since she was too neurotic to handle the job. Or she could do something she'd like better, such as jumping off the roof of the hotel. Of course, nobody had to know the gun wasn't loaded. As long as she pretended very hard that she was holding a loaded gun, she should be able to convince other people that it was true. She picked up the bullets and dropped them into her travel bag. The odds were probably against the police searching her room twice in one day. She returned the gun to her purse, trying not to look at it. Then she grabbed her lipstick and made a cursory attempt at fixing her face before hurrying back to Collie's room.

"Good," Anna said simply when Collie opened the door. She'd had it locked and dead-bolted, and she'd looked through the peephole before opening it. "Make safety a habit."

"I'm learning to live in fear," said Collie. "That shirt looks good."

"I like your dress."

It was an understatement, actually. Collie's dress was phenomenally flattering, one of those dresses that seemed to have been tailored to fit. For all Anna knew, it might have been. It was black rayon with subtle dark green leaves embroidered into it, running down the slit on the left side and around the high neck. The back was crisscrossed with thin straps. With her curls hanging loose and gold-tinted makeup, Collie looked vaguely famous. Much too good for her surroundings.

"It might be a little dressy," Collie said. "I'm gonna wear granny boots with it, but I don't know."

Anna shrugged. "It looks good. Don't worry about it."

Fussing about clothes was much easier than worrying about the trouble they were in, so they kept it up. Collie took out a roll of jewellery and let Anna choose a necklace, then curled the ends of her hair.

"It won't stay," said Anna.

"Yes it will. Use hair spray, let it dry, and then brush it."

It was the sort of thing Anna's mother might have told her, had she been around to tell Anna anything. Anna felt a pain in her stomach, a touch of resentment for all the advice she'd never received.

"If you say so," she said, reaching for the hair spray. "Do we have any kind of a plan for tonight, or do you just intend to mingle?"

"People must have seen Stella and her boyfriend there. They might know the boyfriend's name. We can ask about Joce, too."

"And if we see anybody matching our magician's description?" Anna asked.

Collie shivered. "We avoid him."

"Right." Anna smiled. "I was checking to make sure you knew that."

"But we are going to get his name."

"Discreetly," Anna said. "We will get his name discreetly."

"Yeah. It's the better part of valour."

"It's interesting," Anna said. She patted her hair to see if it was dry yet and her fingers twitched at the tacky feeling. "The closer we come to getting ourselves killed, the less sense you make."

"That's because I've lost my mind," said Collie. "Don't poke at your hair. It'll be dry in a minute."

"I promise I won't believe you killed yourself," Anna said.

Collie's mouth dropped open and stayed that way for a few seconds. Finally she decided to laugh. "Okay. I won't believe it about you, either. But what if we both get killed?"

"Paul will know. I bet he won't care."

Collie thought about that. "It would be inconvenient for him, at the outset. He'd have to hire new people, and he knows there are things we haven't told him. That would bother him. But ultimately he could write in his book that his very own assistants were killed, which is a great human interest angle. It would get him on all the talk shows." She sat down on the bed and started to lace up her boots. "Now that I think about it, I'm surprised he hasn't killed us himself."

Anna picked up Collie's coat and held it out for her. Collie smiled and stepped into it.

"Are you really going to quit?" Anna asked.

"I don't know," Collie said. She picked up her purse, looked into it, and added a handful of Kleenex from the bathroom. "I think I've had it with Dr. Echlin, but I don't have anything else lined up."

"You could come down to Seattle and help me sponge off of Curtis until you find something." She hadn't expected to make the offer, but now that it was out it seemed natural. Of course Collie should follow her back to Seattle. What else were they going to do, just shake hands and say goodbye?

Collie turned around and looked at her. "Maybe I will," she said.

"Certainly you will," Anna said. She put a hand on Collie's shoulder. "Let's go do something stupid."

It was a plain building on the outside. Fairly small, with one unmarked door and a small painted sign that read, Conjurare.

"They don't seem too interested in new business," Collie said. "I hope we don't need passes or anything."

Anna rolled her eyes. Until she'd landed in Seattle, she'd had no idea that some supposedly public nightclubs restricted their clientele. It seemed asinine that a business would turn away customers, and equally asinine that customers would scramble for passes when dozens of other clubs would accept them without question.

People were perverse.

"Some of them want to be abused," Anna muttered.

Collie smiled. "If it's a problem getting in, we'll just tell them what we're doing here."

It wasn't a problem. Collie pulled the door open to find a sullen and effeminate bouncer who barely looked capable of ejecting a stray cat, let alone a difficult customer. He stood in their way until he'd looked both of them up and down. Mostly he looked at Anna, not hiding his curiosity.

"Go ahead," he told them. Anna could feel him watching them as they moved past him into the club.

"That was weird," said Collie.

Anna couldn't argue with her. "Maybe I was wearing something of his."

Anna could see why Jocelyn had liked Conjurare. It was decorated in green and silver and gold, all muted tones, lit mostly by tiny white Christmas tree lights. They were woven into silk ivy and strung along the walls. The furniture was curved metal covered in embroidered cushions. Not very original, but startlingly pretty nonetheless.

The crowd was about what Collie had predicted, a mix

of futuristic goth and neo-pagan. They were fairly young, and attractive if you liked that type. Anna, who didn't have a type, thought there was something a little waspish about them, though that might have been due to the way they were looking at her.

"Speaking of wearing something of yours," Collie said from the side of her mouth, "did you steal clothes from all of these people?"

"Why don't you go talk to the bartender?" Anna suggested. Collie nodded and moved away.

Anna reminded herself that she was a tall, broad-shouldered lady. She put her hand on her purse and felt the side of the gun. Nothing to be nervous about here. One by one, she sought out the eyes of the people who were looking at her and stared back at them until they looked away. For most of them, it didn't take very long. She moved farther into the room, listening to the conversations around her. Movies they'd seen, books they'd read, how much they hated their bosses. Nothing of any real interest.

Anna was about to join Collie at the bar when a hand touched her elbow. She turned and found a woman standing beside her, at least fifty years old and barely five feet tall. Her salt-and-pepper hair was waist-length and seemed too heavy for her tiny body.

"Your grandmother kept it," she said in a surprisingly low voice.

Anna took a step back. "Excuse me?"

"She kept your caul. She didn't really believe, but she kept it anyway. It was thrown away when she died."

"It may be time for you to go home," Anna said, though actually the woman didn't seem drunk. She didn't even seem crazy.

The woman laughed. "It's been time for years, but it isn't that simple." She patted Anna's arm. "Try to relax. You'll be yourself for a long time to come." She walked away, singing to herself. Her voice cut through the rarified Celtic dance music drifting from the ceiling. "Show me the way to go home . . . I'm tired and I wanna go to bed. Had a little drink about an hour ago and it's gone right to my head. . . ."

"She can get pretty personal," a voice said from behind Anna. "I don't think she knows it's rude."

Anna reluctantly turned around. A scruffy little man with bright red hair and torn clothes was grinning at her. A bumper sticker plastered across the front of his shirt proudly declared that he had driven the Coquahalla.

"You have a little accident?" he asked, inclining his head towards her hands. Prudently, Anna had jammed her hands into her pants pockets and was keeping them there.

"What? No. My hands are just . . . cold."

"Oh," he said. "I thought maybe we were in the same boat." He pulled his left hand from his jacket pocket and held it up. Impossibly, it glowed a soft orange under the Christmas tree lights.

Anna didn't know what could make a person's hand glow that way, but she didn't think it was a good idea to stand so close to it. She put a bit of distance between them. "Have you seen a doctor about that?"

"No," he said brightly, "just spots."

Anna couldn't have heard that right. "I'm sorry, what did you say?"

"It's an old joke. Guy tells his friend he's seeing spots in front of his eyes. His friend asks if he's seen a doctor. He says no, just spots." He shrugged. "No point seeing a doctor about this. You know how it is."

Anna wanted to say she didn't, but she was supposed to be undercover or something.

"Sure. Where'd you get the bumper sticker?"

"On the Coquahalla, obviously," he said, then laughed. "I had a teleportation accident. No biggie."

Another lunatic. Anna gave him what she hoped was a soothing smile. "I'm glad everything worked out."

He nodded. "It's cool. Hey—am I drunk or did you come in here with the redhead?"

"I wouldn't rule out your being drunk," Anna told him, "but I did come in here with a redhead. Why?"

"They're giving her kind of a rough time at the bar."

Anna looked towards the bar and saw that her new friend

spoke the truth . . . about this, anyway. Collie was engaged in a snarling, spitting argument with the fortyish blonde bartender. Anna couldn't make out what was being said, but Collie seemed about ready to crawl over the bar.

"I should go look into that," Anna said. As she got closer, she could hear the blonde talking.

". . . don't even know how you got in here."

"The bouncer let us pass," said Anna, moving into place at Collie's side.

The blonde shifted her glare to Anna and her face softened. She was wearing heavy, dramatic make-up that had seeped into the lines of her skin, making her look older than she probably was. "Oh," she said. "I see. That's all right." She looked at Collie again. "I'm still not going to discuss that matter with you. If you'll step outside, I'll talk about it with your friend."

Collie gaped at her. "Like hell!"

"Miss, I'm going to say this one more time—you don't meet this club's entrance requirements. If you came in with your friend here, that's fine. But there are private matters we will not discuss in front of you, and the death of Jocelyn Lowry is one of them. If you don't step outside, Carl will remove you."

"That little twerp?" Collie asked, hooking a thumb at the bouncer. "Tell him to bring it."

"Carl is more effective than you might think."

Anna didn't understand why she was getting the VIP treatment while Collie was getting the brush off, but if she had it—whatever it was—she might as well use it.

"Look, Jocelyn was a friend of hers. We're both trying to figure out what happened. I'd really appreciate it if you'd let her stay."

"I'm sorry," the blonde told Collie, her tone almost kind. "I really am. But we have rules. If it makes you feel any better, your friend was only allowed here as Stella Hrybinski's guest, and there were times when Jocelyn was asked to leave as well."

"I'll only be a few minutes," Anna said, meeting Collie's eyes.

Collie's mouth turned up at one corner. "You don't even know why, do you?"

What the hell did that mean? Before Anna could say anything, Collie put a hand on her arm and pressed it.

"Don't worry about it. I'll wait outside. We can talk later." Without a word to the bartender, she spun on her heel and strolled from the club.

"I hate to be rude," the blonde said.

Anna didn't believe that, but she nodded anyway. "It's okay. Did my friend tell you what we were looking for?"

"She wanted the name of Stella's most recent boyfriend. She also wanted to know if I had ever seen said boyfriend bothering or threatening Jocelyn Lowry. She showed me a drawing and asked if I recognized him."

"And?"

She put her elbows on the bar and leaned forward. "He's trouble. He believes he has remarkable powers, and he's always looking for an excuse to prove it. Frankly, I think Stella's crazy to be dating him. You know, she's the one you should really ask about this guy."

She hadn't heard. Anna froze. Should she spill it, or let the woman go on thinking Stella was alive?

"The thing about Stella. . . ," she said cautiously.

The blonde smiled. "She's kind of hard to talk to. I know."

Anna nearly giggled. She pressed her lips together until it hurt, then said, "You don't know the half of it." She slid onto a barstool, keeping her eyes on the blonde's face. "Did you ever see him bothering Jocelyn Lowry?"

"Jocelyn stopped coming here around the time Stella started dating that bastard. I didn't blame her. She did stop by once, on a Saturday afternoon. She wanted to talk to me. She believed Stella's new beau was making a prolonged and dangerous attack on her workplace."

Anna ran her fingertips over the perfectly smooth surface of the bar. "Was she right? Does this guy have something against *The Rail*?"

The bartender smiled. "He doesn't like the mass media in general. The first time I met him, he was ranting about media mind control. That's what he called it. He said *The Rail's* pretense of neutrality was an insidious disguise for their true agendas. He said other things, I'm sure, but I had stopped listening. I didn't think he was saying anything important."

Anna frowned. "Apparently he was more serious than you thought."

"Oh, I'm sure he doesn't like the magazine. But this was never about *The Rail*. He was just looking for a target. It could as easily have been government employees, or Asians, or . . . I don't know. Dog groomers. Whatever. The real point is showing off his power, proving to all of us that he's something extraordinary. An extraordinary monster."

The row of bottles behind the bar was starting to look good to Anna. She looked at her hands instead. "Is he extraordinary?"

"Unfortunately," the blonde said, "he is."

Anna sighed. "Do you have any idea how he does what he does?"

The blonde shook her head. "He's a better magician than I am. I gave Jocelyn a powder for psychic defense, but it's pretty clear how much good it did, isn't it?"

"Black powder? Quite fine?"

"Why do you ask?"

Anna opened her purse and pulled out the vial from Joce's medicine cabinet.

"This it?"

The blonde put out her hand and Anna gave her the vial. She held it up to the light and turned it around a few times. "Where did you get this?"

"Jocelyn's apartment. What's in it?"

The blonde laughed. "Eye of newt, toe of frog. You should know better than to ask something like that."

Was it rude to ask a witch for the details of a potion? Collie might know. Anna made a mental note to ask her. "Sorry. I was just . . . I guess it doesn't matter, anyway."

"No. Not with how things turned out. Excuse me for a sec."

She stepped away from Anna and served a few drinks while Anna stared at the little black vial. Jocelyn Lowry had taken it home, hoping it would protect her. Like the rowan. Like being pure of heart.

"I just have one more question," Anna told the bartender.

"What's that?"

"Do you know this guy's name?"

The blonde met her eyes. "Are you looking for him?"

Anna picked up the vial and put it in her purse. "I think he has something coming to him," she said. "Don't you?"

The blonde thought that over. After a few moments, she said, "Anthony Waal. Address unknown. At least, it's unknown to me. He doesn't give it out to just anybody. Again, Stella would probably be more helpful. And . . . that's almost all I know."

"Almost?" Anna raised her eyebrows. "Whatever else you've got, I'll take it."

Long red nails scraped at the bar, picking at something Anna couldn't see."I . . . uh . . . suppose you could talk to Anthony's brother."

That didn't sound right. Evil magicians didn't have brothers, did they? That was like saying an evil magician had a library card or an old kindergarten teacher. Anna couldn't picture it.

"His what?"

"Tim. Waal. I have some friends in the Vancouver community who've been keeping an eye on him, 'cause they figure he's probably a latent. But nothing so far."

"Latent?" Anna said.

"Yeah, I hear you. I can't believe Anthony Waal's brother hasn't so much as changed his luck. But my friends swear it's true. Anyway, Tim Waal should still be working at Nemo's, in Gastown."

"Nemo's in Gastown," Anna said. "Right." She didn't have the first idea where or what that was, but as a seasoned detective, she was confident she could find out. "Thank you," she added.

The blonde nodded. "I'm not sure you should thank me. But you're welcome, I guess. Good luck."

A name and a lead. Anna wondered if she should order champagne. Probably not a good idea to drink while on the job. She stood and headed for the door.

Collie hadn't exactly followed orders, which didn't come as a huge surprise. She was standing just inside the door, trading dirty looks with the bouncer.

"A stranger's just a friend you haven't met yet," Anna said once she was close enough for Collie to hear.

Collie cocked her head in annoyance. "What happened here tonight was not my fault. I can't believe I have to explain this to you. We can talk about it outside."

"Which reminds me," Anna said, "aren't you supposed to be outside right now?"

"I was outside," Collie said, rubbing her arms. "It's frickin' freezing out there. Did you get what we came for?"

"Got his name. Apparently he doesn't give his address to people . . . but I'm guessing his brother will have it."

"His brother?" Collie asked. "Rasputin has a brother?"

"Yeah. I got the brother's name, too. Our bartending friend thinks we can find him in Gastown."

"We kick ass!" Collie said, slapping Anna's hand.

Anna stared at her. "Did you just high-five me? Did someone forget to tell me that we're starring in the new Fat Albert show?"

"There's no life in you. No spirit, no soul," Collie said. She was grinning so broadly that her face just had to hurt. "So we're off to Vancouver."

"There's no guarantee the guy will talk to us." Anna said. "For all we know, he's evil, too."

Collie glanced at the bouncer, who was putting on an unconvincing show of not paying attention.

"Won't know until we meet him," she said. "C'mon."

The wind had picked up a little, but Anna still wouldn't have called the night "frickin' freezing." Collie's shoulders and head were hunched down against the cold. She was so intent on getting into her car that she nearly ran into the man standing outside the driver's door. She gasped and took a panicked step back, right into Anna.

Anna put her hands on Collie's shoulders. "No worries. I met this guy inside. I didn't catch your name, though," she told him.

"Ian," he said. "Everybody calls me Mandrake, but I really wish they wouldn't. Did I hear you say that you're going after Anthony Waal?"

Collie tilted her head back to look at Anna.

Anna nodded. "Yeah, that's the guy." She looked at Ian. "You know him?"

"We've met. I stay away from him. You probably should too."

"Probably," Anna admitted, "but we're not very bright. Do you happen to know where he lives?"

Ian smiled. "Anthony and I are not friends. I don't think he has friends. Nobody knows where he lives." He thought for a moment. "I see him at The Word sometimes."

"Okay," Anna said. "Thanks."

"I didn't do you a favour. Hey, you know what? He told me a joke once. Do you want to hear it?"

Collie was shivering. Anna expected her to say no, that she had to be going. Anything to get into the relatively warm car. Instead, she nodded. "Sure. What was his joke?"

"These two guys are sitting in a bar," Ian said. "The bar's on the top floor of a tall building. So one of them says to the other, 'This building has such a powerful updraft that you can jump off and you'll be blown right back onto the roof.' The other guy thinks this is bullshit, right? So the first guy says he'll prove it. He jumps off the side of the building. He falls a little ways and then, whadda ya know . . . he gets swept up and lands back on the roof." Ian stopped for a second to put his hands over his ears. The cold had made them nearly as red as his hair. "Bitchly night. Anyway, the second guy is just blown away. He has to try it himself. So he jumps off the building . . . and falls all the way down to the ground and dies. Kersplat."

Collie was tense under Anna's hands. Anna couldn't blame her. So far, it wasn't much of a joke.

"The first guy, he goes back into the bar and sits down. And the bartender says to him, 'Superman . . . you are one mean drunk.'"

Ian studied their faces and shrugged. "I didn't think it was that funny either . . . but Anthony laughed his ass off. For what it's worth."

"Everybody look what's going 'round," Collie chanted under her breath. "You should be getting inside, Ian."

"True enough," said Ian. "You ladies take care."

Anna meant to say something else, but she forgot what. It left her mind as suddenly as Ian left, vanishing before their eyes. Anna blinked furiously. Collie stood perfectly still.

"Did . . ."Anna stammered, "that's . . . did he actually disappear?"

"Only people who can do magic are allowed in that club," Collie said calmly. She turned to face Anna. "Don't you get it? I was only allowed in because I was with you."

Anna didn't say anything. Collie laughed softly, but her eyes were sad. "Let's get in the damn car."

Anna got into the damn car. Collie seemed prepared to let her ridiculous theory about that club drop, and good enough. Anna didn't want to discuss magic or where the hell Ian had gone or shoes or ships or sealing wax. She just wanted to get the bad guy.

"Did you want to catch a ferry in the morning or—"

She stopped, not because she was finished, but because she'd lost her audience. Collie was staring in terror at something in front of the car. Anna didn't see anything but swirling snow.

"Colette?"

She looked at Collie's face again and saw that Collie wasn't looking past the front of the car. She was looking at something on the hood. Anna followed her eyes to a glint of metal wrapped around one of the windshield wipers.

She opened her door, meaning to go out and see what it was. The sound shook Collie out of her trance.

"Don't," she said.

"I was just going to—"

"Don't. Don't touch it. I'll get it."

Anna raised her hands. "Okay. You get it."

That said, Collie proceeded to sit tight for a long time before placing her hand on the door handle and convulsively yanking it open. As soon as she was out of the car she nudged the door shut with her leg. Probably worried that precious heat might escape. She stood beside the hood, staring at the metal. Anna squinted at it but still couldn't see what it was. Collie took a deep breath and lifted the wiper blade with one shaking hand. With her other hand, she untangled the metal. It was a piece of jewellery, a bracelet or a necklace. Probably a necklace, going by the length.

Once it was in her grasp, Collie didn't waste much time getting back inside. She pulled the door shut with enough force to rock the car and gazed down at the object in her hand. Anna turned on the interior light for a better look.

It was a silver necklace, seemingly a choker. Nothing terribly expensive, but the chain was silver, and the light purple stones looked to be real amethyst.

"Collie?" Anna asked gently. "Do you recognize that thing?"

Collie put her hands together, trapping the necklace between them.

"Remember when we were in Jocelyn's apartment and I was looking for something in her jewellery box? I told you I'd tell you about it later?"

"You never did," Anna said.

"I know. I didn't want to talk about it." Collie rubbed her hands together lightly, careful not to damage the necklace. "I was looking for this."

"Well," Anna said. She liked it so much that she said it again. "Well."

Collie was watching her hands. She seemed to think they were going to make a break for it.

"Collie?" Anna said gently. "I don't mean to poke you, but do you have any idea how that thing wound up on your car?"

She didn't seem to hear, but after a moment she shook her head. "I don't. I don't know."

"It is kind of an important question," Anna said.

Collie dropped the necklace into her right hand and flung it onto the dashboard. "Him!" she hissed, not looking at Anna. "Obviously, it was him. Why are we even talking about it?"

Anna stared at her. "Because the implications are disturbing! He knew we were here. He knew which car was yours. How could he know these things? Where is he now? Why would he tip his hand to us?"

Collie was hunched down in her seat, glaring at the necklace. "I don't try to second-guess crazy people."

Anna waved a hand in front of her face. Collie shifted the glare to her. Anna met it without flinching.

"Colette . . . we have a problem. I could call ground control in Houston, but I thought I'd get a more useful response from you. Was I wrong?"

"I don't think there is a useful response," Collie told her. "Maybe he was at The Village Market when we found Stella. Maybe he was watching *The Rail* the night we were there. Maybe he saw us pick up Paul at the police station. We don't really know what he looks like; therefore, he could have been anywhere at any time. He probably came here tonight because he wanted a drink and saw my car in the parking lot." She shifted in her seat to face Anna. "You wanna know why he's pulling our chains with this necklace? I'm guessing because it occurred to him. I mean, we both know how much he hates upsetting people, but maybe he did something out of character just this once. What do you think?"

The anger in Collie's eyes was unsettling. Anna took a deep breath. "Remind me to never again mistake your defeatism for apathy." She gestured at the necklace. "Could that have been a personal token to Jocelyn? I mean, was it special to her?"

With startling speed, Collie's anger changed to tears. Whatever she'd said, Anna wanted to take it back.

"I'd kind of hoped so," Collie said. "That's why I was looking for it. Jocelyn was always sentimental about gifts."

Anna frowned. "Who gave it to her?"

Collie didn't answer. Anna put a hand on her arm. "Colette?"

"I did." She took another mistrustful look at her hands. "When Joce was really angry with someone, she'd throw away everything they'd given her. I thought she might have thrown the necklace away."

"Apparently not," said Anna.

"No," Collie agreed. "He had it. He touched it. This is the piece of her he stole."

She sounded sick. Anna didn't blame her. The amethyst was

glowing softly under the street lights, an easy thing for Anna to keep her eyes on while she spoke. "Why would Jocelyn have been angry with you?"

Collie bit her lip. "That's. . . ." She stopped.

Anna turned to find Colette looking at her questioningly, but she had no idea what Collie was trying to ask.

"You're going to have to give me some help here," Anna said.

Collie managed a smile. "You might as well pick the necklace up."

Anna didn't care for the suggestion. She kept her eyes on Collie's. Collie put her hand over Anna's. As usual, her fingers were freezing. "Go ahead. It's not a trip to Disneyland, but I promise it's not anything bad."

Anna slid her hand out from under Collie's. She moved slowly. She wanted Collie to have the opportunity to change her mind.

Her eyes were still locked with Collie's when her fingers touched the chain.

"It came off while I was on the bus. I almost lost it."

Collie put aside the book and lifted the necklace to the reading lamp, squinting at it under the light. Her hair was still wet from the shower, and Jocelyn could smell strawberries. From the corner of the bedroom, Anna could smell them, too.

"Get me some needle-nose pliers and I'll fix it," Collie said.

"Okay. Thanks."

But she didn't go for the pliers. Not right away. She leaned across the bed and placed her hand on Collie's, their grasp closing over the chain.

"It's my favourite necklace," Jocelyn said. And lay down.

The chain felt rough on Anna's fingertips as she let the necklace slide back to the dashboard. It was quiet in the car for the first time, the only sound coming from the heater. Somewhere in Anna's mind, it occurred to her that Collie's mix tape must finally have run out.

"It wasn't anything bad," Collie asked nervously. "Was it?"

"No. It wasn't anything bad."

They sat in silence. A few big snowflakes drifted onto the windshield and melted as soon as they touched.

"How long were you together?" Anna asked.

Collie kept her eyes on the windshield. "Nearly two years."

"Not just a fling."

Collie turned the heater up and held her hands out to the vents. "No."

Anna thought about Collie's face when she'd talked about finding Joce's killer, and her persistence in spite of everything. Her guilt. "You broke it off."

"Yes."

"Any particular reason?"

Collie snorted. She seemed amused, if darkly. "You must be getting the impression I'm a real heartbreaker."

"Did you dump your boyfriend because he was . . . a him?"

"Not directly. I didn't know what the problem was at the time. I shouldn't have dated him in the first place."

Anna shrugged. "Happens. You were very young. At least you didn't marry him."

"Yeah."

"So . . . what about Jocelyn?"

Anna expected to be brushed off again, but Collie surprised her.

"Our interests diverged. The whole goth thing was a lark, but after a while Joce developed a sincere interest in paganism. I'm too cynical for that. She wanted to move to the west coast. I wanted to stay in Edmonton. I think she knew there was no future for us, but Joce was . . . sentimental. She would've hung on until we were both miserable."

Anna thought about that. "It's no wonder," she said finally, "that Becca doesn't like you."

Collie smiled. "It is pretty easy to understand once you have all the facts. It really didn't help that Joce called me for help and didn't tell Becca anything."

"Apparently Jocelyn knew she was seeing a lower calibre of girlfriend," Anna commented. "I can't say that I would bring a serious problem to Rebecca."

"I don't know if that's fair," Collie said. Still, she looked pleased. She probably didn't like Becca any better than Anna did, but some ridiculous sense of guilt kept her from admitting it. "You're not . . . are you okay with this?"

"Why wouldn't I be?"

Bright red burned into Collie's cheeks. "Some people have problems with it."

"Some people are assholes." Anna picked up the necklace and held it over Collie's lap. Collie put her hand out and let Anna drop the necklace into it. "If I'm being weird, it's because you surprised me. I wish you'd told me earlier."

Collie looked at her, confused. "What difference would that have made?"

"For one thing, it would've saved you the energy you spent dodging the issue," said Anna. She paused, then met Collie's eyes. "For another, I like having time to think."

Before Collie could say anything, Anna reached over and turned on the Tercel's headlights. "We should get back to the hotel and get some sleep," she said, "if we're going to Vancouver in the morning."

Collie put her hands on the steering wheel. "Fuck that," she said. "Fuck this island. I say we go now."

The night air and salt spray were cold by the rails. The deck itself was coldly functional with wet steel and rust-resistant paint, but Anna found it more attractive than the passenger cabin. It was full of drunks and indoor/outdoor carpet, and from the smell of it she suspected one of the drunks had added a splash of colour to the carpet's dull brown.

"This boat is Stygian," Collie said.

Anna glanced down at her, surprised that Collie had abandoned the relative warmth of the indoors to join her in salty misery. "It was your idea to leave tonight," she said. "I understand the ferry attracts a much more respectable crowd in the mornings. Also, in the morning, we'd be dressed for it. We'd have slept and brushed our teeth. Do you seriously think Paul is going to spring for—"

"Okay, look," Collie said. "I'll make you a deal. When some mind controlling monster leaves your ex-girlfriend's jewellery on the hood of your car, I'll let you decide exactly when we get out of town. As for the clothing and toothbrush and accommodation problem, I'll take care of it. Out of my own pocket. Is that fair?"

"It's fair," Anna told her. Apparently, in a world bereft of justice, it was very important that the two of them were equitable about everything. "You should at least try to get Paul to cover it, though. Hey—about this Tim character. Anthony's brother."

"The impossible brother," Collie said. "I dimly recall your having obsessed about him. In the car. All the way to the ferry dock."

"I don't remember saying he was impossible."

"You kept saying how weird it was that this Anthony Waal guy, being a murderer, could have a brother. Like that was somehow inappropriate."

Anna looked to the east. Vancouver was a handful of stolen jewels at the end of the ocean, reflecting off the clouds. It was amazing how much glamour the right amount of distance could bring to an everyday town. "I just never picture evil magicians that way," Anna said. "You know. Having brothers and sisters."

Anna could feel Collie's coat moving against her jacket as Collie shrugged. "Everyone has a brother or sister," Collie said.

"Except me," Anna said.

"Or me," Collie said.

"Or us," Anna finished. She looked at Collie, who was wrapping gloved fingers around the rail and leaning forward to stare at the water. "You drop something down there?"

"I lost treasure here in a past life," Collie told her. "You were going to say something about Tim Waal."

"Oh. Yeah. The bartender said he worked at some place

called Nemo's in Gastown. Have you heard of it?"

Collie shook her head. The wind caught her hair and she stood straight to push it back into place. "Should I have?"

"I don't know," Anna admitted. "From the way that woman talked, I thought maybe everyone had heard of it and I just wasn't hip enough. As usual."

"You're hip," Collie said. She had a funny grin on her wind-stung face. "You're timeless. Like James Dean and Coca Cola glasses. You'll always be in style."

Anna looked down. Pearl black waves were slapping against the boat, moving in a rolling rhythm that somehow matched every song Anna had ever heard.

Timeless.

She crossed her arms and leaned forward, letting the rail catch her. "Speaking of time," she said, "Paul is probably wondering where we are. Unless he isn't."

"I was thinking we'd do this," Collie said. "Go to Vancouver, get a hotel, track down Tim Waal, interview him, go back to Victoria . . . and see if Paul actually calls to check on us before we see him again. We could even put money on it. I bet you fifty bucks he doesn't call."

"Sucker bet," Anna said. "You'd turn your phone off."

"I might," Collie admitted. "I might anyway." She gave Anna a gentle sideways shove. "I'm going inside, God help me. Are you coming?"

"In a minute." Anna shut her eyes and breathed. Clean air. Clean dark sky. Nowhere to rush to. No one to jostle her or honk or yell or demand anything of any kind. Considering where she was headed, she figured she might as well soak up a little serenity while she had the chance.

"I don't know what you're talking about," Collie said. "This is not some overgrown urban nightmare. It's a west coast city, for god's sake. It's all about the pursuit of hippiness. Dude."

Anna pulled the curtains shut, as if that would keep the sound of sirens and invective from entering their hotel room. "Sounds like peace, love, and understanding out there," she said. "I thought this was supposed to be a good hotel."

"It'll do," Collie said. She was lying on the right hand bed, nearest the bathroom. She hadn't bothered to change clothes or take off her granny boots or pull down the shiny blue bedcover. "You'll notice there are robes and toothbrushes and whatnot. Who could ask for anything more?"

Anna pulled a stray thread from Collie's bed and peered at it. "What kind of material is this, anyway? This faux-satin shit. I have never seen in it used in anything but hotel bedspreads. It is aggressively ugly."

"No uglier than your mood," Collie observed. "In the cab you were bitching about wanting sleep. Why don't you get some?"

Anna went into the bathroom and changed into the His half of the His and Her robes. Fucking His and Her robes. That was pretty damned tacky. If not for the twin beds, she would have thought Collie had booked them into the honeymoon suite. She would apologize when she went back out there. She doubtless sounded like a big baby, complaining about the noise and hassle and assorted smells that came from a city of any appreciable size. A big inconsistent baby, in fact, because Collie knew damned well Anna had been living in Seattle, which was far bigger and noisier than Vancouver. She might as well just admit that Vancouver, for some reason, never failed to give her a mother of a headache. Possibly she was allergic to large quantities of pot.

She went back into the hotel room with her mouth open to speak, but shut it when she saw Collie breathing deep and even on the bed. The apology was going to have to wait 'til morning. Anna went to the left hand bed and crawled in. It wasn't as comfortable as her bed in Victoria, but as Collie had pointed out, it would do.

She was nearly asleep when she heard Collie roll over, get up, and go into the bathroom to change. Had she been faking the sleep thing? Had Anna really been such bad company that it was better to fake her out than keep talking to her? Anna had always suspected that she wore on people. She was usually more careful about limiting the time she spent with them. Of course, if she had spent too much time with Collie, there wasn't a whole lot she could do about it now. You couldn't take time back.

With an effort, Anna shut her eyes and let it go.

Sleek and oily. Cold and hard and dead. But it has a pulse. It jumps and quivers with every beat.

Grab hold.

Anna sat up in bed. Awake for less than ten seconds, and she already had her traditional Vancouver headache. That, and a metallic taste in her mouth. This had all the markings of a banner day.

Collie was already up, wearing her dress from the night before. It looked out of place in daylight.

"You weren't overdressed last night. . . ," Anna began.

"Mrmph," Collie said, spraying croissant and blueberry jam over the phone book on her lap. "I know. I'm planning to keep my coat buttoned up. Hell, maybe I'll see some clothes I like in Gastown. Stranger things have happened."

"Is there more food and coffee where your food and coffee came from?" Anna inquired.

"Free continental breakfast," Collie told her. "They have trays set out in the lobby. I found Nemo's."

"Great," Anna said. She shoved herself out of bed and grabbed her clothes on the way to the bathroom. "You can tell me about it while I eat."

Just past eleven on a weekday morning, Gastown wasn't as busy as Anna remembered it. She'd only been there on weekends and evenings before. The sun was making a half-hearted attempt at breaking through wisps of cloud, but it didn't do much to warm the streets between the heavy old buildings. Anna looked up and down Water Street, taking in the trendy cafés and antique shops nestled into buildings that looked the way someone thought they should have looked a hundred years ago.

"I love this part of town," Collie said. "It's like Strathcona's older, cooler sister. I'm so glad they decided to restore it."

Anna snorted. "It was a loggers's drinking town. If they'd really restored it, you wouldn't want to be here without a weapon or a very large dog."

"Fortunately," Collie said sweetly, "I have you. Do you think Nemo's will be open before noon?"

Without waiting for an answer, Collie wove off the main path towards a shop full of wire jewellery and Indian dresses. Anna followed, keeping her hands in her pockets. She didn't think any of the gaslamps or building fronts were authentic, but she'd made up her mind not to touch them. Just in case.

"No," Anna said, trailing Collie into the store. "I'm sure it's closed. Might as well kill some time shopping."

"Good answer," Collie said. She was holding a necklace up to the light, turning it to see the play of green glass beads against copper wire. "Do you like this?"

Anna shrugged. "Doesn't look real comfortable," she said.

Collie smiled. "Talked yourself right out of a necklace," she said. "Too bad for you. Let me know if you see something you do like."

Anna wasn't sure she liked the symbolism of it, the idea of Collie buying her a necklace the day after Jocelyn's was returned to her in that particular way. It seemed like the kind of thing a therapist would chew on for weeks. She said, "I'm not really a jewellery kind of gal."

Collie looked at her. "No," she said. She sounded approving, though Anna couldn't fathom why. "Of course not. That's not you at all."

She turned to a rack of cotton dresses, delicately coloured with embroidery and tea stains. Her fingers moved quickly over the fabric, finding flaws in some, setting others aside for a better look. This was serious shopping. Anna showed her respect for that esoteric craft by getting out of the way.

Even with the address in hand, Nemo's wasn't easy to find. It took three circles around the red brick building before Collie suggested the restaurant might be inside, using whatever space the streetfront stores had left behind. They pushed open the only unmarked door on the block and found themselves in a narrow hall leading to the centre of the building. Collie's new dress rustled as it brushed the wall.

"Great location," Anna said.

Collie smiled. "Discourages tourists," she said. "I'm not sure that's a bad thing."

They rounded a corner and stopped in front of a thick wooden door with a porthole in the centre and the word *Nemo's* painted beneath it.

"This could be the place," Anna said. "My detective skills tell me so."

Collie turned sideways and shoved the door with her shoulder, waving Anna inside as it opened. Anna stepped past her into someone's idea of a nineteenth-century submarine. The walls were lined with curved wood and fit with a dozen tiny booths. Each booth had its own porthole. At least half the portholes looked out on some portion of a giant squid.

"Dear lord," Collie said. "Somebody had a very bad idea."

"And I thought fake nets and plastic lobsters hanging from the ceiling was as bad as a seafood restaurant could get," Anna agreed. "How nice to see I was wrong."

A short man with sleek dark hair scooted around the hostess station and offered them a professional smile. The word *Nemo's* was embroidered into his red and white striped shirt, just above the heart.

"For two?" he asked.

"Or three," Anna told him. "We're looking for someone who works here. Tim Waal."

The man blinked. The movement drew sharp lines in his tight skin. "It's the lunch rush," he said. "Tim's a little busy in the . . . you know, the kitchen. With vegetables. Is this . . . um . . . urgent?"

Anna looked over the man's shoulder. It wasn't difficult.

Of the ten booths, two were occupied. One held a man and woman in business suits, speaking quickly and quietly over bowls of clam chowder. Another housed an older man in a dingy saiwash. He was gripping a heavy brown mug that sent steam towards his face.

"It's kind of urgent," she said. "I'll tell you what—we just need a few minutes with him. If that winds up being a problem, we'll go in the back and help Tim with the vegetables. How does that sound?"

Anna thought she saw the man smile, just for a moment, before his politely cautious expression slid back into place. "I can ask him. Who should I say is. . . ."

"Tell him," Collie said, "it's about his brother."

The short man looked as if he wanted to say something. Instead, he turned and went through a door at the back of the restaurant.

"I don't know if that was the right thing to say," Collie said.

"It was non-committal," Anna said. "I guess we'll see."

It didn't take long. Anna guessed less than a minute had passed before the back door opened and a sandy-haired man gave them a nervous smile.

"I'm Tim Waal," he said as he approached. "Dwight said you were looking for me?"

"Yeah," Collie said, offering him a hand. "Is there anywhere private . . . maybe that booth over there?" She gestured at a booth towards the back, on the far side of the kitchen door.

Tim nodded. "Unless you think we'll be yelling at each other, that should do." He led the way, weaving gracefully past the bar and coat racks. Anna followed with her arms close at her sides. One of these days she was going to have to lay in a supply of Alice's shrinking potion.

They squeezed into a booth, Anna ducking to avoid the fake oil lamp hanging above it.

Tim gave her a sheepish smile. "The seafaring life isn't for everyone," he said. "Have you ladies had lunch?"

"Not yet," Collie said. "What's good here?"

"You might want to rephrase that," Tim said. "Ask me what's free here. The lobster bisque turned out a little watery, but I always say there's nothing wrong with lobster soup. I could have Dwight bring us some."

"That sounds good," Collie told him. "I think. Anna?"

"I like lobster," Anna said, "but maybe you should find out what we want, first. You might not want to feed us."

"That's true," Tim agreed. "I have a nasty temper. Anything you say could set me off."

Collie laughed. Anna didn't blame her. Tim looked like a cross between a boy band singer and a student librarian. Affable and mild. Anna wondered how much he looked like his brother. It was hard to picture an evil magician with spiky hair, Lennon glasses, and freckles across the bridge of his nose.

"So," Tim said, "since lunch is waiting on it, I guess you'd better tell me what you want."

Anna looked at Collie. Collie responded with a helpful shrug.

Anna turned back to Tim. "I don't know if Dwight told you, but we have some questions about your brother."

"Yeah," Tim said. He touched his fingertips to the frame of his glasses, giving them a push to some place they probably didn't need to be. "He mentioned that. Are you . . . friends of Anthony's?" He didn't seem to think that likely.

Anna shook her head. "We don't actually know him. Personally. We've never met."

"Oh." Tim looked mildly surprised. But only mildly. "You told Dwight you urgently needed to speak with the brother of a man you've never met. That's novel."

"It's weird," Collie said, "isn't it? Why would anyone do that?"

Tim's expression didn't change, but his shoulders tensed and his face took on a little more colour. "You tell me," he said.

Collie reached into her purse and took out her wallet. She flipped it open and showed Tim her driver's licence. "I'm Colette," she said. "My friend here is Anna. We're not cops or anything. We're doing a kind of private investigation because a friend of mine was murdered in Victoria, and I want to know who killed her. We think your brother might be involved."

"Involved," Tim said. There was a nervous laugh lurking behind his voice. "That's a hell of a word. It's like *interesting* or *different*. It sounds as if it means something, but damned if you can tell exactly what."

Collie looked at Anna. Anna caught it from the corner of her eye. She did not turn her head.

"Involved," she said, "means we think he killed her."

Tim pursed his lips. He looked down at the table, where his long fingers were twisting a cloth napkin. "I see." He looked up. "No, I'm confused. You want me to think you're just ordinary folks, right? If you think my brother killed someone, wouldn't ordinary folks want to tell the police? Why would you come here and talk to me?"

Anna didn't know what it was. Some look in his eye. Maybe just a trick of the light. Tim Waal wasn't crying or shaking or even frowning with anything more than confusion . . . but somehow she got the feeling he was miserable as hell.

"You know," she said, "there are things you can't tell the police."

Tim's fingers gave the napkin a twist before dropping it to the scuffed wood table. "I'm not so hungry," he said, "all of a sudden. I think I need a walk. Can I show you the waterfront?" Without waiting for an answer, he stood and swiveled until his eyes landed on Dwight. "I'm taking fifteen."

"But. . . ." Dwight looked at Tim's face and stopped himself. "Okay."

Tim moved quickly. He had a dancer's grace, that seeming ability to shift not only his balance but his shape and weight. Anna used long strides to keep pace with him. Collie bustled behind them.

"You know," Tim said, waving a hand at their surroundings, "Water Street used to be on the waterfront. Some of the buildings here are curved to fit the old coastline. Now we change the coastline to fit the buildings."

"We're assholes," Anna agreed. As they neared the smooth white lines of Canada Place, she felt a wind from the water and shrugged down into her jacket.

Tim stopped at a lookout point, a touristy little nook with a bench and a railing and a concrete trash can topped with flowers. Anna stood beside him, waiting for Collie to catch up.

"What is this," she said as she slid into place beside Anna, "with you and me and waterfronts? Why do we keep having important conversations beside water?"

"Maybe so that if the conversation goes badly," Tim said, "you can throw yourself in."

"What a funny thing to say," Collie said, "considering how Jocelyn died."

Tim looked at her without recognition, certainly without guilt. "How did she die?"

"Drowning," Anna said quickly. "It doesn't matter. The details don't matter. Mr. Waal—"

"Tim," he said sharply. "Please. Call me Tim."

"Tim . . . I feel like a horse's ass asking you this, but does your brother do magic at all?"

Tim turned away to watch a boat pull into a nearby dock. He watched intensely, as if the boat would crash into the shore if he dared to look away. "He does a flashy card trick. He's been doing it since we were little. Take a card, any card. Just make it *that* card." His mouth twisted. He probably thought it was a smile. "The force is the key to successful card tricks. I don't mean like in *Star Wars*. That thing magicians do, where they make sure you take the card they want you to take—that's called the force. Anthony always had a knack for it."

"I didn't mean stage magic," Anna said.

Tim looked at her, much the same way he'd looked at the boat. "For God's sake. Neither did I."

"Okay," Collie said, too brightly. "Good to know we're all on the same page."

Tim ignored her. He kept looking Anna. "You think he *killed* someone? Honestly?"

Anna met his eyes. "Yes. We're not sure why, but Anthony seems to have something up his ass about *The Rail* magazine.

Jocelyn worked there. We think he's been causing a lot of harm to the staff at *The Rail* for about a year now. And we think he killed Jocelyn because she knew what he was doing and she was going to tell someone."

Tim looked towards the water again. "What's the word for it, that word psychologists use, when you suspect other people of doing what you do yourself?"

"Human nature?" Collie suggested. To Anna's surprise, Tim laughed.

"Human nature. Yeah, it kind of is human nature to assume everyone's like you. Even when almost no one is. Anthony always thought people were trying to control his mind."

"Is he paranoid?" Collie asked.

Tim shrugged. "That's what the doctors said. The psychologists. They said he was a paranoid schizophrenic. He heard voices, he was convinced the media were trying to control his thoughts . . . what else were psychologists going to say? They gave him some meds and sent him home. Basically."

"That do any good?" Anna asked. "I mean, assuming good needed to be done."

"Considering that he really was hearing voices and the media really were trying to control his mind, no. Not a lot of good."

Collie raised her eyebrows. "The media really were trying to control his mind?"

Tim smiled at her. "No more his mind than anyone else's. Anthony used to watch TV . . . sitcoms, cop shows, the news, anything . . . and he'd say, there's the house you're supposed to want. There's the car you're supposed to go in debt for. That's the way you're supposed to live. He said most of the advertising wasn't in the ads. He really hated *The Rail*, because it pretended to be an unbiased news source. Anthony didn't believe there was any such thing."

Collie frowned. "There's a big difference between slanting the news and . . . you know. What your brother does."

"That's what I've been trying to tell you," Tim said. His brow was creased with the frustration of not making himself understood. "He doesn't see a difference. I'm sure he knows not everyone can do his force, but he feels as if everyone can. When he sees someone, or something, trying to manipulate him, he feels as if they're about to jump into his mind and start rearranging the furniture. I guess you could call that paranoid, but if you had some kind of psychic power, wouldn't you be a little nervous about what everyone around you might be able to do?"

Anna looked at the ground. The toe of her left boot was scuffed. She couldn't think when that had happened. She heard Collie say, "I suppose we can only speculate."

Anna turned her head to get a sideways view of Tim's neat and pleasant face. "Can you do what he does? Since you're his brother?"

Tim tilted his head, mimicking the way Anna was looking at him. "No. Never could. I thought I'd pick it up eventually. I mean, it's not like Anthony was this gifted from birth. It took years. But whatever mutant gene he got was his alone."

"Was that rough?" Collie asked. "I know brothers fight. Having a brother who could win all those fights. . . ."

"Nah," Tim said. He was smiling, looking at the water but focused on something else. "It was okay. He really wasn't much good at it until . . . well, puberty, I guess. When he was a kid, everyone thought he had a golden tongue. Mom and Dad said he should be a lawyer. They thought they had a brilliant son. I was the only one he told. He liked to practice reading my mind, or showing me what he was thinking. And when he started he couldn't know if he was doing it right unless he asked me, so I kind of had to be in on the whole thing. His confidant."

Tim looked perfectly happy as he wandered down memory lane. As if his childhood had been a lot of fun. As if the biggest problem with having a mind-controlling brother was keeping Christmas gifts a secret. Anna wasn't sure she could buy it. She looked at Collie but couldn't catch her eye.

Collie was staring at Tim. "We think he killed someone," she said gently. "A few people. Is that crazy? Is it crazy for us to think he could do that?"

Tim put his hands on the decorative railing. He gave it a shove, evidenced only by the movement of his shoulders and the tightening of his grasp. The rail didn't budge. "No crazier than he is, I guess." He sounded exhausted. He sounded worn clear through and stumbling to bed, hoping the words he said would make a pillow. He said, "I haven't seen him since he went to Victoria. And . . . I haven't missed him." He braced one knee against the support of the railing and looked across the Strait, as if he could see Victoria if he only stretched far enough. He shook his head. "Thing is, I've missed him forever. He's been leaving since we were fourteen."

Anna looked at Collie, and this time found Collie looking back. Sshing her. Don't interrupt.

Tim answered her question for her. "Fraternal twins. No more alike than any other brothers. But it's funny. In the beginning, he thought I was the only person whose mind he could read. Because there was something so mystical about doing that time together in the womb. There was something so mystical about everything."

"What happened when you were fourteen?"

Tim looked disappointed in her. Apparently it was a dumb question. "Puberty," he said. "I told you. I didn't mean fourteen, exactly. He was growing up, and he got so much better. A hundred times better. He didn't have to practice anymore. He heard people thinking all the time. He said no one thought anything nice. He suspected everyone of trying to get a hook into him."

"Including you?" Anna asked.

Tim shook his head. "No. There was always some scrap of him that liked me. He told me he didn't wish me ill. I felt like Hannibal Lecter had said the world was more interesting with me in it. That was when we were eighteen. He was pretty far gone by then."

He raised his coat to his face and rubbed the red tip of his nose against the sleeve. He looked cold, but gave no sign of wanting to go inside. "Might have been a blessing that he was crazy. He could've had anything he wanted. But he couldn't focus. He lashed out. When my parents put him in the hospital, he didn't even try to stop them. He was too busy worrying about the implications of satellite TV. I don't know—maybe he really is a schizophrenic, on top of everything. How do you like that for a cosmic joke?"

"It's not my kind of humour," Anna told him. "When did he leave Vancouver? When he got out of the hospital?"

Tim shook his head. "It was a few years after that. He actually stayed with Mom and Dad for a while. Took his meds. Made some fucked up friends. When I started at Simon Fraser, I moved into a dorm room to get away from all the fun."

"We might want to talk to those friends," Collie said.

Tim laughed. It was a choppy sound. "Oh, no. You don't. They were magicians. They didn't like . . . they used the word *mundane* a lot. I was a mundane. If you couldn't do magic, you were a mundane. At first I thought it had the same ring to is as . . . *nigger*, or something. Then I decided it actually sounded more like *livestock*. They didn't care what they said in front of me. I was just a mundane. They didn't think I'd be able to remember half of what they said." He turned around, putting the water at his back. "You know what's funny? I didn't. When they got into really weird shit, I lost the details somewhere. In all the incense, maybe. I got lost in the smoke."

He shoved his hands into his pockets, a gesture so familiar that Anna could have sworn she felt the ache from his chest. "It was around that time that he said he didn't wish me ill. I don't think he wished our dog ill, either. I moved out. And I don't know what happened; I never asked, but by the time I started my second year, his friends were gone."

"You don't sound as if you think they went away to school," Anna said.

Tim raised his brows at her. "I said I didn't know what happened."

"What about your parents?" Collie asked. "Would they know?"

"They're in Kelowna. They retired, so they had to move to Kelowna. It's practically a law." He sniffled. His nose was getting redder by the second. "They wouldn't know anything. They never did. Their memories are much worse than mine."

"He left when they moved?" Collie asked.

"Yeah. He could've afforded his own place, I think. Even in

Vancouver. Unsurprisingly, he always managed to have money. But I think something was ruined for him here. I don't know; I may have said something to him about a fresh start. I kind of hinted that he shouldn't call me. I really didn't want to talk to him anymore."

Collie's eyes were huge. She looked like a little kid attending a campfire ghost story. "Too creepy?"

"Too fucking sad," Tim said. He took a Kleenex from his pocket and grabbed at his cold, red nose. "He wasn't him anymore. He had so many people's thoughts in his head, you know, maybe there wasn't room for him. The last time I saw him I thought . . . well, crazy things. Like he was some big puppet himself, the way he made other people. The way he was always afraid other people would make him. Like he was playing the part of my brother and the only character note he had was that he did not wish me ill."

Anna couldn't think what to say. She couldn't come up with so much as a word.

Collie was shifting beside her as if words were jumping to get out and she was fighting to keep them in. "Tim," she said. Her voice was tight and high. "We need . . . we have to talk to him. We need you to talk to him. Find out if he did what we think he did. Convince him to—"

"To *what*?" Tim asked. "Turn himself in? Were you really going to say that? Turn himself in to who? Or should I say, into what? He's not a thing you talk to anymore. Go ahead and try it. You might live long enough to forget."

"Okay," Anna said, shooting a warning glance at Collie, "that was naive. But we're not wild about the idea of letting him get away with this. We're going to find out if he did it. If he did—and I think all three of us think that's a good bet—then we're going to have to figure out what to do with him. At the least, we could use some suggestions. We'd prefer to have your help."

"You people," Tim said. He was looking at the crumpled Kleenex in his hand. Anna wondered if he had ever seen one turn into a dove. "I asked him to leave and he went. If we never speak again, my last memory of him will be that he did what

I asked. Because I asked him. Because he had it in him to do me one last favour." He tossed the Kleenex to the ground and kicked it towards a garbage can. "I will not see this end any other way."

Collie took a deep breath, as deep as the breaths she'd taken the night before when she pretended to be asleep. "Could you write that down?" she asked. "I was thinking I could read it at Jocelyn's funeral."

Tim shut his eyes. "Fuck you," he said.

"Yeah," Collie said. "I heard you the first time."

She shoved past him and started walking. Anna looked at Tim. His eyes were still shut. He didn't move. Collie was making good time on her way back to Water Street. Anna hesitated, then followed her. She wasn't in the mood to do this on her own.

"Wait," Tim said. His voice had enough strength to reach Collie, and it stopped her. Anna stopped and looked at him. "What?"

"I don't know where to find him," Tim said. "I . . . come back here, please. I don't want to share this with the neighbourhood."

Anna took the few steps back to him. Collie took longer. She approached slowly, with caution. She didn't look as if she cared to hear what Tim Waal might have to say.

"You're not the first people to ask me about him," Tim said. "After his friends disappeared, I got the third degree from a bunch a magical types. They showed up at my dorm room. They didn't say they were magicians or anything, but they had the air. They said they suspected Anthony of . . . I don't know. I forget exactly what they said. But they wanted me to help catch him. They said, if I could get them some proof of what he'd done, they could do something about it. They said the magical community looked after its own."

"What did you say?" Anna asked.

"I told them go ahead. Look after your own. I said they should know better than to discuss that kind of thing with a mundane. And they started with this whole spiel about how Anthony was dangerous. He had to be stopped. But I figured they didn't know that, not if they needed me to find them some proof. I'm not French. I'm not into the whole guilty until proven innocent thing. So I sent them packing, and then I sent him packing. But the thing is . . . they kind of left me their card. And if he did kill your friend, and you know it, and you have real proof . . . that might be different."

"Can you give us the number for those magicans?" Collie asked. "Some way to get ahold of them?"

Tim smiled just a little, with the far edges of his mouth. "I couldn't if I wanted to," he said. "It wasn't an actual card."

"So you're saying you want proof," Anna said. "You want us to bring you proof that he killed these people . . . and if you think it's convincing, you'll get in touch with people who are equipped to deal with him."

"Well," Tim said, "it's more like, when I know, they'll know. I told them I would really have preferred a card."

"And you don't know who these magicians are or what they do."

"No," Tim said. "Not really. But I believed them when they said they wanted to keep him from hurting people. On this, my nerve endings are all I have."

"You don't think this makes for a kangaroo court?" Anna asked.

Tim shrugged and sniffled. He was probably catching a cold. "I have thought about it," he said. "This scenario. I try not to think about him, but some nights I can't sleep. And this is where I always end up. It's not perfect, okay, I'm the first to admit that. But it's what I'm prepared to do. If you have any better ideas, I promise I won't stand in your way."

Collie looked ready to say something. Anna jumped in first. "Okay," she said. "We'll see you. Or we won't."

Tim nodded. Anna took Collie's arm and gave her a good tug in the direction of Water Street. Collie took the hint and moved. Tim watched them go. His fifteen minute break had to be up, but Anna got the impression he really didn't care.

"Where are we going?" Collie asked. She was keeping up with Anna, but her voice said it wasn't easy.

"We're leaving him," Anna told her, "with his thoughts."

"Why? I don't think we got everything we could from him. We didn't even ask him if Anthony had any weaknesses, or if he knew of any friends who might have Anthony's address, or. . . ."

"Were you there for that conversation?" Anna asked. "We got exactly everything we could from him. Now we're done. Do we have any other business in Vancouver?"

"I. . . ."

Whatever that was supposed to be, it died in Collie's throat. Anna nudged her shoulder. "I'm asking you—where are we going?"

"Victoria," Collie said. "Might as well go back. Since we're all done here."

Though the ferry was different in the day, Anna wasn't sure it was better. The sky had clouded over and there wasn't much to see but grey. Grey air, grey water, grey faces staring into cups of grey-brown coffee. Collie wasn't giving her the cold shoulder, exactly. Nothing so clean and crisp. It was more of a grey shoulder—muddy and slow to respond. Did Collie want a cup of coffee? Huh . . . oh . . . okay. Were they going straight back to the hotel when they got to Victoria, or did Collie have somewhere else she wanted to go first? Oh . . . whatever. Hotel's fine. Anna sat across a table from her and put up with it, because there was nowhere else to go. There was the deck, but Anna had had her fill of the ocean for a while.

Victoria was starting to form out of the haze when Collie finally broke up the party. She shoved her chair back without comment and strode past the half-empty tables to the ladies room.

Anna gave her a thirty second head start before going after her.

As Anna had suspected, it was a sham. Collie was at the sink, killing time by splashing water on her face and making pointless adjustments to tiny wisps of hair. Anna pushed the door shut and slid a convenient trash can in front of it.

Collie gave her a look. "Gonna kick my ass?" she inquired.

Anna shrugged. "We'll see how this goes. Look . . . I don't pretend to have social skills. I've figured out you're mad at me, but if you want me to know anything more than that, you're going to have to clue me in. How long have you been mad? What are the top five things I did to make you mad? Is this about Tim Waal?"

"I think," Collie said, "you might be losing sight of the big picture, here. I realize you feel sympathy for Anthony Waal, but—"

"You realize *what*?"

Collie leaned against the sink and folded her arms. "Growing up with something special . . . maybe it's not as easy as I imagined it would be. Okay? I get it. It was tough for you; it was tough for him. Maybe there are even reasons to feel sorry for the guy. But we can't forget that he kills people. We have got to make him stop."

"Jesus Christ," Anna said. "Did you pull a muscle leaping to that conclusion? You think I feel some kind of kinship with this guy because we're both freaks of nature? Or do you think I'm a paranoid schizophrenic evil magician murderer, too?"

Collie was frowning. "Well . . . why else would you just walk away from Tim Waal like that? I get the impression your heart just isn't in this anymore."

"Tim Waal is the one I feel sorry for," Anna said. "He's been living a nightmare. Do you really believe his childhood was as pleasant as he made it out to be?"

"I don't know. Should we believe anything that guy said? Did it even occur to you to not believe him? For all we know, he's working for his brother. For all we know, that *was* Anthony fucking Waal we just talked to."

Anna sat on the domed top of the trash can. To her relief, it seemed prepared to hold her weight. "We have no particular reason to believe him," she admitted. "But I don't think that was Anthony Waal or one of his Muppets. I think it was Timothy Waal, and I think he told us the truth as he knows it. I, like him, have decided my nerve endings are all I have to go by."

"Uh huh," Collie said. "Well. Obviously I don't know about him, but that sure as shit is not true for you. If you'd brushed some lint off the guy's shirt, maybe we'd know what we needed to know right now."

Anna looked at the ceiling. It was tile, stained with age and less agreeable things. "Maybe the world would be a better place," she said, "if Anthony Waal had kept his hands in his pockets more often. Figuratively speaking."

"Maybe that wasn't an option for him."

Something in Collie's voice made Anna look at her. She was out of bluster and suddenly seemed too small for her clothes.

"No," Anna said carefully. "I don't suppose it was."

"Did you . . . I mean, this psychometry thing . . . did you get better at it when you . . . you know. . . ."

Anna stared at her.

Collie shifted uncomfortably. "Never mind," she said. "Forget I asked."

"No," Anna said. "Puberty had nothing to do with it. You're pretty damned determined to wrap me up in a package with this guy."

Collie shook her head. Her eyes were too green, the bathroom lights reflecting off water. "I don't have to. You are wrapped up with him. He reads people's minds, you see their histories. You know all these secrets, whether you want to or not. And I think you both keep catching people at their worst. When we started to find out about this guy, you know, I thought it was a power corrupts thing. Like he wanted to push people around. I thought, how can he be so intimate with people and treat them that way? How can he be the kind of person he is? But you know something funny?"

"I'm dying to hear something funny," Anna told her.

Collie blinked, nearly spilling the carefully balanced tears. "I don't wonder about that anymore, how he turned out the way he is. I think I understand that now. What I mostly wonder about is how you turned out to be you."

Anna didn't know how to take that. Her nerve endings said it was a compliment of some kind. She raised one shoulder and let it fall. "Mystery for the ages," she said.

Collie smiled, nervously. "Guess so." She leaned over to grab a paper towel from the dispenser.

Anna watched as she fixed her face, dabbed moisture away. "Collie," she said, "were you just pretending to be asleep last night? Was there some reason you didn't want to talk to me? Because, you know, I was going to apologize for being a whiny bitch, and you missed it."

Collie laughed. "You weren't that bad. It's not as if we don't have reasons to be cranky, right?"

"So, why?" Anna said.

Collie wadded up the paper towel and tossed it to Anna. Anna was confused for a moment, then realized she was sitting on the garbage can. She reached down and threw it away.

"I thought you might ask me about Jocelyn," Collie said. "About me and Jocelyn. Or you might tell me what you saw. And I know you said it wasn't anything bad, but I didn't want to think about her. I mean, any more than I already was. I have this act to keep together, you know? I have this crazy guy to catch. I just don't want to remember too much until the job's done."

"Okay," Anna said. "I won't ask."

Collie nodded. "Okay."

Anna stood up and shoved the trash can back to where it belonged. "Buy me a coffee," she said, "and while I'm drinking it, we can figure out what we are and are not going to tell Paul."

"I vote for nothing," Collie said. After a moment she added, "You know . . . all this money Paul has, it doesn't come from a publisher. And I'm not really . . . well, I could be a publicist. I learned how in school. But that's not what I do for him."

Anna looked at her, waiting.

Collie gave her a crooked smile. "You don't know what the hell I'm talking about, do you?"

"Not really," Anna admitted. "I know I don't like your boss. That's as much thought as I've given it."

"He has a lot of money," Collie said, slowly and distinctly. "He knows secrets about people. Yeah, he writes stuff. I think he even does intend to write a book about *The Rail* and he thinks it will make money and it probably will. But if you really want to make money off people's dark secrets, it's much easier to write letters than books. I hope you're caught up now, because that's all I'm going to say about it."

And to think Anna had been feeling like a dirty criminal because she'd carried a gun across the border and lied to a couple of cops. She breathed in deep and let it out, taking her time about it. Then she said, "You plan to keep working for him?"

"Not after this," Collie admitted. "No."

"You want to resolve this first? Give him his book? Take his money and run?"

Collie nodded. "That was what I was thinking."

"Then," Anna told her, "we have to tell him enough that he keeps us on the payroll. Until we're done."

"Right." When Collie smiled this time, it looked sincere. "Let's go back out there and talk about how much is enough."

They'd opted to lie, quickly and cleanly. More an evasion than a lie. They would say they had a few leads. They intended to follow one up that night. They were getting close.

Neither of them had words for the precise reason why they had not wanted to put Paul onto Tim Waal's trail, but Anna could think of a few words that came close. Compassion. A dash of spite for the great Paul Echlin. And some cosmic sense that letting Paul pester someone as beleagured as Tim Waal would make for very bad karma.

Collie had offered to do the evading. She had other things to discuss with Paul, pursuant to her resignation. She wanted to talk money. Their talk might touch on the mysterious ways in which Paul made the lion's share of his money. Anna knew better than to ask for details. She bided the time thinking and planning. They had a name. They had a lead. Anthony Waal was somewhere in a small island city. How hard could it possibly be to find him? She lay on her bed, careful not to fall asleep. The last thing she needed was another dream. She got up once to load the gun. She didn't even get so far as her purse before her stomach rolled and she had to run to the bathroom instead. On her way back to the bed, she checked to make sure her purse was latched. It seemed, somehow, important.

By the time Collie showed up at her door with the agreed-upon dinner of burgers and fries, Anna thought she had an idea they could work with. "Come on in," she said, shutting the door behind Collie. "I've figured out how to get Waal's address. That Mandrake guy, the teleporter? He was right. We need to go back to the bookstore. Did they include ketchup with that?"

Collie set the food on the table and gave Anna an uncertain smile. "Does the entire plan fall apart if I say no?"

"No," Anna said, pulling up a chair. "It will only break my heart."

Collie grinned and pulled ketchup packets from her coat pocket. "Can't have that," she said.

Collie pulled into the lot beside the bookstore and killed the engine.

"How long will you need?" she asked.

"Not long. About ten minutes."

"You'd better be sure," Collie said, "because if you say ten minutes, that's what you're going to get. I don't want to spend any more time with that creep than I have to."

"Creep is a relative term," Anna reminded her.

"That's what I needed to hear," Collie said. She opened the car door and shivered. "See you in ten minutes."

Anna gave her time to get rolling before sidling up to the door. Even through the heavy wood, she could hear Collie's voice.

"Good," she said softly. She crouched down and pushed the door open with her shoulder, peering in to see if there was anyone in the front room. Satisfied that it was empty, she moved inside and eased the door shut behind her.

Somewhere in the bowels of the shop, Collie was berating the store owner at the top of her voice. She was accusing him of everything from not caring about Jocelyn's death to holding her under the water himself. She sounded like an escaped mental patient. Anna wanted to applaud.

Instead, she went quickly and silently to the desk and began her search.

The desk was tidier than Anna had expected, and pleasantly free of computers. Nothing to boot up, no passwords to figure out. If this guy had a customer list around anywhere, it was on good old user-friendly paper.

It was in the second drawer she checked, a binder in imitation leather with gold leaf initials on the cover. The names were in chronological order by the day they'd set up charge accounts. Anthony Waal was about halfway through, a regular subscriber to a few occult journals and something called *Blue Blood* magazine. His account was currently forty dollars in arrears, but none of his debts had ever gone unpaid past thirty days. His address and phone number were neatly written at the top of the page.

Collie was still ranting, but her voice was starting to sound hoarse. Anna grabbed a sheet of notepaper and copied the information down, then shoved the book back into the drawer and left with as much alacrity and as little noise as possible. She got into the car and waited. A few minutes later, Collie found her way into the driver's seat. She opened her mouth to say something and immediately started to cough.

"You did a good job," Anna told her, patting her back. "I got the address. And a phone number."

Collie stopped coughing, swallowed hard, and nodded. "Good," she croaked.

Anna rubbed her shoulder. "Would you like me to buy you an herbal tea or something while we figure out what we're going to do with it?"

"That," Collie coughed, "would be lovely."

It took Anna's eyes a while to adjust to the dim light, but once they did, she appreciated the surroundings. They were in a pub on the second floor of a downtown building, a dark place with oak bookshelves lining the walls, soft leather couches, and old jazz and blues pouring from the Wurlitzer. Across the room, a noisy young crowd was playing pool. Where she and Collie sat, it was quiet enough for conversation.

Collie had her hands wrapped around a large mug of fennel tea. She was breathing in the steam with her eyes shut. Anna sipped at a decent cup of coffee and waited for Collie's ecstatic trance to end.

"I'm surprised he had the address," said Collie.

"You remember he said Jocelyn had an overdue account with him?" Anna said. "I figured he probably kept accounts for most of his customers. And that guy, Mandrake, he said Anthony was a customer. It looks like the owner special orders a lot of magazines and stuff. Like in a comic book store."

Collie grinned. "What do you know about comic book stores?"

"Nothing," Anna said. "I've never set foot in one. Hey . . . have you ever heard of *Blue Blood* magazine?"

Collie laughed in mid-sip, spraying tea onto the arm of the couch. She set the mug down and wiped it up with the sleeve of her coat. "Why would you want to know that?"

"It was on Anthony Waal's order list."

"Oh." Collie shook her head. "I guess I shouldn't be surprised. It's a porno magazine for vampire fetishists."

Anna smiled. "I won't ask why you know that."

Collie was absently running her fingers up and down the side of her mug. "You know I'm a sexual deviant," she said mildly. "So . . . I'm thinking we can't just walk into Anthony's apartment. Is it an apartment?"

Anna looked at the address. "Duplex, I think. His suite has a letter instead of a number."

She showed the slip of paper to Collie, who nodded. "In that neighbourhood, duplexes are called townhouses. Tim wasn't kidding when he said his brother had ways of making money."

Anna nodded. "I hear there's very good money in mind control. Tax free, too."

"Paul would be jealous," Collie muttered.

"You were right about us not being able to just walk into his apartment," Anna said. "Since he's paranoid as all get-out. And judging by that little gift he left on your car, I suppose I'm not going out on a limb when I say he knows we're looking for him."

"If we go anywhere near him, we should take your Jeep," Collie said. "I assume he knows what we look like, too, but the Jeep's a start."

"I don't think it matters which vehicle we take. I think he knows all about us," Anna said. "You forget that Anthony and Stella were an item."

"And?" Collie said.

Anna looked at the scuffed wood of the table in front of them. It was better than trying to look Collie in the eye. "I don't think either of us thinks it was her idea to date him, so that leads us to the obvious conclusion that she was working for him. Do you really think he didn't ask her about us?"

"That's a nice thought," Collie said. "You know, I hear Jamaica is nice this time of year."

"I hear there's a lot of crime," Anna replied.

"There's very little crime under my bed. Maybe I should go there."

Anna set her coffee down. "If you're serious, I'm willing to discuss leaving town."

Collie's mouth curved. Her eyes were suspiciously bright. "You know better than that. If you want to go, go."

"You know better than that," Anna countered.

"If you say so," Collie said.

Anna sipped her coffee. Collie sipped her tea.

"What did you say to that guy at the bookstore, anyway?" Anna asked.

Collie's eyebrows shot up. "How could you not hear me?"

"I was concentrating on something else."

"I did what you said. I accused him of knowing who killed Jocelyn . . . and I think you're right, by the way. I think he does know."

"It doesn't matter anymore. So do we."

"I got loud. I got hysterical. I kept him from leaving. When I ran out of things to say, I started suggesting he was in on the murder. That really pissed him off." She said it with more than a little satisfaction.

Anna smiled. "Did he wonder where I was?"

"I don't know," said Collie. She paused for another sip of

tea. "He didn't say anything, but I didn't really let him get a word in. I think mostly he was wondering if I had a gun."

It occurred to Anna for the first time that she had never asked. "Do you?"

Collie laughed. "You've been living in the States too long."

"Yeah." Anna held her empty mug up for the waitress. "It's okay if you wear a lot of kevlar."

"I used to have pepper spray, but now it's illegal." Collie flipped open the lid of her tea pot. "I bet people don't bother you."

"No," Anna admitted, "not usually. I don't think it's because I'm tall, though. I think I just look extremely angry."

"Only because you are," Collie said. "Wanna call Anthony Waal and tell him you're angry?"

"Or," Anna said, "we could call and tell him his refrigerator's running and he'd better go catch it."

"We could have twenty pizzas delivered."

"That'll teach him a lesson," Anna said.

The waitress refilled her coffee cup and took Collie's tea pot for more hot water. Once she was gone, Collie sighed. "Fuck Tim Waal for not coming with us. You and me? We have no way of confronting this guy."

"Well," said Anna, "we have this." She took the vial of black powder from her purse and set it on the table. "The bartender gave it to Jocelyn as some kind of protection."

Collie picked up the vial. "What does it do?"

"Nothing. Obviously."

Collie glared at her and dropped the vial. It rolled to the edge of the table and stopped.

"That was staggeringly useful."

Anna put the vial back into her purse. "What can I say? We're talking about a guy who can control people's minds. We go in there and tell him to give himself up. He tells us to play in traffic. Tomorrow our accidental deaths are on the front page of the paper. If there's any defense against that, I don't know what it is."

"Maybe we should put tinfoil on our heads," Collie said. With impeccable timing, the waitress leaned over her shoulder with a fresh pot of tea. She didn't say anything, but her face left no doubt that she'd heard. Collie smiled at her. "What do you think? Is wearing tinfoil on your head a good defense against psychic attack?"

The waitress straightened and put her hands on the small of her back. "Excuse me," she said, stretching. "It's been a long night. I think tinfoil only works if you're trying to keep out the orbital mind control lasers."

"Oh," said Collie. "That's too bad. Thanks anyway."

"Sure." The waitress stretched again and went back to the kitchen.

"I'm not certain she's an expert," Anna said.

"We could go through Jocelyn's book. The one you refuse to touch."

"I'm sorry," Anna said. "The one I what?"

"I'm not stupid," Collie said impatiently. "I'm thick sometimes, but I have noticed that you won't go near that book."

"Jocelyn had some nasty things on her mind while she read it," Anna said. "You're right. I don't want to touch it. If you want to read it, go ahead, but let me remind you again that Jocelyn is dead. If the things she tried had worked, we would not be having this conversation."

Collie didn't have a response to that. Anna let the silence go for a while. Then she said, "We won't get anywhere until we decide what we want to do with this guy."

Collie gave her a blank look.

Anna slapped her palm on the table, shaking the dregs in Collie's mug. "Don't act dumb now. Are we going to call the cops? Are we going to convince Anthony to leave the country and never come back? Are we going to put a bullet between his eyes? Or are we going to get some evidence against him and go back for another talk with his brother? Until we have a definite goal in mind, we should not be making plans."

Collie lifted her mug and dipped her head forward until most of her face was hidden.

"Well?" Anna prompted.

"Do you really think we could have him arrested? By actual police?"

There was a weird note in her voice, a high wavering that sounded a little hopeful and a little crazy at the same time.

"When we find him," Anna said, "I'm sure we'll find that woman's figure skates. He'll have all his little tokens. He probably has scrapbooks. But none of that even comes close to proving to real police that Anthony Waal killed anyone. By current legal standards, I don't think he did kill anyone. Not even Jocelyn. Unless you'd like to have him arrested for petty theft, I recommend that we either dump this in his brother's lap, or go back in time and try him in Salem."

Collie looked at her speculatively. "I don't think you would have enjoyed Salem."

Unbelievable. Anna stared at her. "Colette, I am not the fucking issue here. Leave me out of this."

"People like you are exactly the fucking issue," Collie snapped. "If you were willing to believe what's right in front of your eyes. . . ." She shook her head. "Never mind. We keep coming around to trusting Tim Waal."

"You noticed that too, did you?"

Collie dropped her eyes to the table. The waitress has somehow managed to return the teapot without Anna noticing. Collie poured tea and held her mug near her face, but didn't drink from it. Anna watched the steam taper off and finally stop. Collie didn't even seem to breathe.

"There's the bullet between the eyes thing. But I don't think I have the stomach to kill him," Collie said at last.

"I have the stomach," Anna said, "but I don't think we'd get away with it. Too many people know we're gunning for Anthony Waal."

"I wonder," Collie said, "what would happen if we got him to confess. If we got a confession on tape. And gave that to the real police."

"Provided we could convince them it was a real confession and not a joke . . . I guess they'd think he was crazy," Anna said.

"And they'd lock him up. Like he was locked up before. Right?"

Anna considered that. "Possibly. Unless he talked them out of it. But what would happen then?"

Collie looked confused. "What do you mean?"

"They wouldn't toss him into an oubliette. He'd be in a mental hospital with lots of sick people who couldn't get away from him. God knows what kind of shit he pulled the last time he was in the looney bin. Hell, maybe this time they'd even put him in the same place as Kate Eby. How does that sound?"

"Awful," Collie admitted. "Not acceptable."

The waitress was carrying a plate of cookies to a nearby table. Anna waved her over.

"We'll have what those people are having," she said.

The waitress smiled. "If you think you can get it away from them."

"Maybe I should just order something similar," Anna said. She glanced at Collie, but Collie wasn't listening.

The waitress inspected Collie's tea pot, found it nearly full, and returned her attention to Anna. "I'll be right back."

"And we're back to the brother again. Do you think those magician guys will kill him? Or do they have an oubliette for him somewhere? This could all be some big scam so we hand over the evidence to them—provided they even exist—and they help him get out of town. Or hire him to assassinate someone. The possibilities are—"

"You know what I find sickening?" Anna said, cutting her off. "We just met a whole club full of people who seem to know what he's been doing and completely believe it . . . and they haven't done a damned thing to stop him."

"It is sickening," Collie agreed. "And discouraging. Maybe they're afraid of him."

The cookies landed on the table. Collie grabbed one and pounded it back with alarming speed. "Okay," Collie said, spraying cookie crumbs onto her lap, "nobody wants to deal with him but us and the mystical kangaroo court. So I guess we have to hope they're on the level." She pushed the plate of cookies towards Anna. "Do not make me eat alone."

Anna poked through the cookies, trying to decide between peanut butter and chocolate chip. "We get evidence," she said. "Or a confession. We do what we can here, meet our obligation to Paul, and leave the problem in Tim's shaking hands. Then we'll go to Seattle and forget the whole damned thing ever happened. How does that sound?"

"Seattle." There were cookie crumbs at the corners of her mouth, but somehow Collie managed not to look silly. "Did you still want me to come to Seattle?"

Anna reached over and brushed the crumbs away. "The invitation stands."

Collie met her eyes. "Okay."

Anna picked up the lone chocolate chip cookie and set it on Collie's knee. "While you eat that," she said, "think about how we're going to get the goods on Anthony."

"Mmm." Collie swallowed and set the remainder of the cookie down. "When I'm done eating—and not before—I'd like to go for a walk. I'm jumpy."

"We can do that." Anna went to settle the bill while Collie finished her cookie and tea. When she returned, Collie was putting on her coat.

"Are you sure about this?" Anna asked. "Because I hear it's about a billion degrees below zero out there. As is usual in Victoria."

"I have nervous tension to keep me warm."

It was snowing and the wind was sharp, but Collie didn't seem to notice. She walked slowly, weaving dreamily around people and street lamps, narrowly avoiding collisions. "You know," she said, so softly that Anna had to lean in to hear her, "I bet we could get him to talk."

"How do you figure that?"

The tips of Collie's ears were starting to turn red. She pulled her hair down over them. "This whole thing with *The Rail* has been a dramatic production. I think he'd love to brag to someone about everything he's done."

"Could be," Anna conceded. "The bartender's convinced he's been trying to prove something."

"Okay. So we give him an opportunity to talk, and he'll take it. Why wouldn't he? When he's done, he can tell us not to remember."

"Or he can tell us to hang ourselves."

"Sure," Collie agreed cheerfully. "We're not a threat. I bet he'd tell us everything."

"And we get it on tape," Anna finished. "Except he takes the tape away from us before murdering us and dumping our bodies in the ocean. Or whatever he decides to do."

"Yeah." Collie was chewing on her lip again. "We have to make sure he doesn't do that."

Anna's purse bumped against her leg, the weight reminding her that she was carrying that gun. Under the circumstances, she should have felt better about it than she did. She put a hand on Collie's shoulder. "I'm eager to hear your ideas."

"Hmm." Collie stepped off the curb against the light. Anna grabbed the collar of her jacket and yanked her back to the sidewalk.

"Watch where you're going," said Anna, "or find a place to sit down."

"Sorry." Collie rubbed her eyes, melting the snow that had gathered on the lashes. "Do you think Waal can control two people at once?"

"Sure. If my theory is right, he had Stella going at the same time as he made the janitor drown Jocelyn."

"True," Collie said. "But he'd been working on Stella for a while. Maybe that makes a difference."

Anna lifted her hands and shrugged. "Who knows? We could talk about this all night and get nowhere. All we can do is guess. And I don't really think that's good enough."

Collie mulled that over for several blocks. "It's not," she said finally.

Anna tried to remember the last thing she'd said, and failed. "What's not what?"

Collie smiled. "It's not good enough to just guess what Anthony Waal can do. We need to know more. And since you won't let me beat it out of his brother, I guess we're left with breaking into Anthony's house."

Anna stared at her. "I bet you think the sentences 'We need to know more' and 'We're left with breaking into his house' are naturally connected."

"Of course I do. He's paranoid and probably friendless. If

we're going to uncover his deepest secrets, it'll be in his home. His den. His fortress of solitude. We need to get inside. We might even get acceptable evidence while we're there."

The wind screaming up the street made the thought of being inside anyone's house almost appealing.

"I like the idea of not meeting him face to face," Anna admitted. "But I don't know if we're going to get him out of his house, and I don't know how we're going to get in once he's gone."

"Oh, we get him out of the house by saying we can prove he killed Jocelyn, meet us in some dark alley with ten thousand dollars, blah blah blah. He'll bite. Even if he's not scared, he'll be curious. Anyone would be. We'll make it sound as though it would be incredibly easy to bump us off."

"Which it would be," Anna said. "Provided this plan works, how do we get into the house?"

Collie's cheeks, red from the wind, darkened further. "I was kind of hoping you could handle that."

Anna raised her eyebrows. "I beg your pardon?"

"I just thought. . . ." Collie stopped and turned to face her, tilting her head back and narrowing her eyes against the snow. "You're sort of a bad ass. You came to Victoria to do something illegal. I thought you might know how to pick locks."

Ye gods.

"Sort of a bad ass?" Anna said. "I might know how to pick locks? What is it you think of me, Colette?"

Collie looked embarrassed, but she stood her ground. "I think you're having an unusual life. If you're not a bad ass, I apologize, even though I didn't mean it to be derogatory. Lots of people know how to pick locks. I wish I were one of them."

Anna looked at the ground. A few snowflakes were bravely trying not to melt against the wet concrete. They'd never make it to morning. "We'd be better off going in a window," she said. "The wind is making enough noise that we could probably break one without anyone hearing. But he might have an alarm. We wouldn't be able to stay in the house very long."

"Okay," Collie said, nodding. "Do we need a baseball bat or something?"

From the tone of her voice, she might have been a child on Christmas eve.

Anna smiled. "If you have a tire iron in your trunk, that'll be fine."

"Cool. Let's do it."

Collie bounced up the street towards her car. Anna trudged behind her, considering the twists and turns of her life. She was about to go from carrying an illegal weapon to breaking into a house while carrying an illegal weapon. She hoped Curtis would write to her in prison.

The car was unnaturally bright, covered with water from melted snow. A few snowflakes dotted the windshield. Collie swiped them with the sleeve of her coat. "My goodness," she said, showing the flakes to Anna. "And me without my scraper."

Anna nodded. She tried to look serious, but she knew her eyes were giving her away. "This may be the worst storm in Victoria's history."

"That's good," Collie said, sobering. "Means the neighbours won't notice us."

Anna placed her hand on the passenger side door and waited for Collie to turn the key. "Oh, come on," she said. "You know you'd love prison."

Collie laughed and opened the doors. She was still laughing as she settled herself into the car and pulled her door shut behind her. "I would," she said. "I have this thing for rough types."

And bad asses, maybe. People who could pick locks. Carriers of illegal weapons. Of course, this was not a good time to follow that comment to its logical conclusion. Anna held her tongue. It was too quiet in the car. Collie asked for the address a few times, and Anna recited it with increasing condescension. Other than that, they didn't speak. Anna thought about finally flipping the mix tape over, starting the whole thing again. She decided she didn't want to do anything so overt. She wanted to sink into herself and hide under her own skin. She wanted the night to be over. She kept her eyes on the road.

"This is perfect!" Collie said.

Anna had to agree. She couldn't have designed a better setting for their crime. The house was surrounded by a tall fence and thick trees. Windows circled the building, all of them large and some of them resting on the ground. To top things off, the power had gone out in Mr. Waal's neighbourhood. Even the street lights were dark.

Collie had driven by once, then parked around the corner. Between the blowing snow and the darkness, Anna suspected they could have parked on the front lawn and not drawn attention, but it didn't hurt to be careful.

"Pretty mundane house," Collie commented, "for such a mystical guy."

"Can you see his front door?" Anna asked, peering through the windshield. Every time she found a gap in the snow that she could see through, the wind shifted and she was blind again.

"Just barely." Collie pulled out her cel and dialed Anthony Waal's number. Anna had a crazy feeling that she was sixteen again, calling the cutest boy in grade eleven physics because Collie was going to ask him on a date.

When Collie jumped a little, her breath catching in her throat, Anna knew someone had answered the phone. "Is it him?" Anna whispered, barely breathing the words.

Collie nodded and shoved her to shut her up. "Mr. Waal, I want to talk to you about the death of Jocelyn Lowry. And I think you'll want to talk to me."

That was some terrible dialogue. Anna pinched the bridge of her nose and tried to will her headache away.

"I know what you did," Collie went on, "and I can prove it. I'll meet you in the parking lot beside The Village Market. I'm sure you know where that is."

That was a nice touch, pointing out that she knew he'd known Stella. Still, that 'I know what you did' line was a problem.

"I'll be there at midnight," Collie said. "If you show up with five thousand dollars, I'll give my evidence to you instead of to the police."

She looked at Anna and shrugged. Anna leaned back in her seat. They waited. After a long minute, Collie smiled. "Wonderful. I look forward to it." She clicked off her phone and set it between the front seats. "He should be leaving any time now."

"Sure," Anna agreed. "Unless your terrible eighties TV show dialogue made him die laughing."

"Mock me all you want," Collie said. "I get results."

"Did he sound like Tim?" Anna asked.

Collie frowned. "No. He was kind of frosty. He didn't waste words."

Anna nodded. She looked at Collie, who was staring at the house with undisguised delight. As if this were some game, as if it was something they could laugh off when it went wrong.

"Colette? I should probably tell you something."

Collie looked at her sharply. "This sounds confessional."

Anna looked at her hands, which were pushing against the dashboard. Apparently her subconscious was trying to enlarge the vehicle. "I wasn't exactly honest when I told you why I took this job."

Collie made a sound. If Anna hadn't known Collie to be such a dignified lady, she might have called it a snort. "Don't be silly. You would never lie."

"I didn't lie. Everything I told you was true. I just didn't tell you everything."

"And you know," Collie said, not unkindly, "I had sort of assumed that. Look . . . whatever it is, don't worry about it. I don't care what inspired you to take this on. I think you're doing a hell of a job."

Anna took a deep breath. "I might be. Or I might be about to screw up in a big way. You know what the biggest problem is with having a . . . gift, power, whatever?"

Collie shook her head. "Considering the education I've been getting over the past few days, I'd have to say I wouldn't know where to start."

Anna almost smiled. Why did small victories always come when she was in no position to enjoy them? "You get hunches, just like anyone. And some of them don't mean anything. Some of them are pure fiction. Even a psychic can have an overactive imagination."

"And you're telling me this because. . . ."

The wind howled. For a moment, Anna took it personally. She wanted it to shut up and die. "Sometimes you envision a dead person on the front page of a newspaper. It's this redhead who's basically a good person, if kind of flaky. And you get this feeling that, if you don't help her, she's going to die. Or maybe the feeling is that she's in danger of dying, so you want to try to keep that from happening . . . even though you might not be able to. And you make some decisions based on that feeling, which may be a psychic flash or might be nothing at all. And then you don't know when to step in. Should you tell her not to go into the crazy guy's house? Should you send her back to the hotel? Should you convince her to pack in the whole thing and move to Guam? You just don't know when you're being prudent and when you're being ridiculous. It's very confusing."

"Oh," Collie said. She didn't seem distressed. Just thoughtful. "I see."

"*I* see," Anna said. "I'm the seer. Get off my turf."

"So you had a vision I was going to die and decided to look out for me. That's actually really sweet." She looked at Anna. "Thank you."

"Don't thank me yet," Anna said. "On second thought, yes. Thank me now. You may not have a chance to do it later."

Collie shook her head. "I don't know about that. This feeling you had, that I was going to die—have you had it since you started working with me?"

Anna thought about that. "I think it's a fair bet we're both about to get killed," she said. "Since all we have is my weenie power and absolutely no idea what we're doing."

"Yeah, but that's logic," Collie said. She was perversely cheerful. "What do you feel about it? Do you still have that hunch?"

"No," Anna admitted. "I only had it the one time."

"Great," Collie said. She was smiling broadly. "If I really was going to die, you must have changed that by helping. Otherwise, you'd still feel greebly about the whole thing. I feel way better now."

Anna gawked at her. "You're nuts."

"And you're a freak," Collie said fondly. "Any other hunches you want to tell me about?"

Anna pulled the lever at the side of her seat until it gave, letting her seat sink into a blissful recline. "If you need me," she told Collie, "I'll be asleep."

"I won't need you," Collie said.

Anna shut her eyes. The wind rocked the car and kept up a steady background noise that blocked out all other sound. She had to be as crazy as Collie, maybe crazier, because she felt more comfortable than she had all week.

Cold metal feels so good after feeling nothing for so long. It's a promise. It will drive the angels away. And it doesn't hurt to forget when you can't remember that you've forgotten anything.

"Nightmare."

One sharp word from Collie and Anna was awake, blinking with confusion.

"You had another nightmare," Collie elaborated. "We have seriously got to do something about that."

"Some other time," Anna muttered. "Has he left yet?"

"No, he's . . . oh, wait! I think that's him."

Anna tried to see the door, then gave up and looked at Collie instead. "What do you mean, you think?"

"I can't see his face or anything. But someone is leaving his house."

"He's not supposed to have any friends," Anna pointed out.

"True." Collie kept staring down the street. "He's heading for that car, on the corner. Do you see it?"

Anna shook her head. "No. Your eyes are better than mine."

Collie squinted through the snow. "He's in the car. I say we do this."

Anna sighed. "You would. I'd love to get someone else's opinion."

Collie handed her the phone. "Feel free to call Paul."

Anna set the phone down. "I'd rather go inside."

"Great." Collie gave her a cheerful grin. "Then it's settled."

As they got out of the car, it occurred to Anna that she didn't smoke. She was a big girl who could use cigarettes as currency. That would make prison a little better, anyway.

Collie popped the trunk and handed Anna the tire iron. It fit nicely up the sleeve of Anna's coat.

"You look very comfortable," Collie said. "At ease. Almost as if you've done this before."

Anna waved her arm threateningly. "Shh," she said, smiling. Collie nodded once and started for the house.

"Side window," Anna whispered once she'd caught up. "I think, anyway."

"It's your call, bad ass."

The window in question was about a metre wide and half as tall, hidden from sight by a fence nearly two metres tall. Anna crouched beside it and leaned in for a look at the room behind the window.

Some of the rooms in the house were lit by the distinctive orange glow of candles, but this room was perfectly dark. Collie took out a small flashlight and aimed it at the window, then cursed as most of the light reflected off the glass. She angled it down and the beam picked out a latch.

"Okay," Anna said softly. "Stand to the side."

Collie did as she was told. Anna managed not to comment on the novelty of it. She got to her feet and braced herself, then took a swing at the window. The glass cracked over the latch, but didn't break. Anna kicked it with the heel of her boot and it shattered. She stood and looked at Collie, who was starting to look cold. She wasn't dressed for this. Neither of them were.

Anna didn't even know she was going to speak until the words left her mouth. "Don't tell anyone I have this," she said, opening her purse. She took out the gun and put it in Collie's hands, trying not to think about what a relief that was. "It's not loaded, but it might come in useful anyway."

Collie looked at the gun, then at Anna. "We can talk about it later," said Anna. "We don't want to be here any longer than we have to."

Putting that philosophy into practice, she crouched beside the window again and pulled her coat sleeve down to cover her hand. She carefully slid her arm inside, then pulled the sleeve back enough to let her fingers find the latch. Once it caught, she pulled the window open. She rolled onto her stomach and grabbed the sill. Slowly, she lowered herself into the dark room. She would have preferred to know what she was getting into, but she couldn't always get what she wanted, could she?

Her feet hit something soft about a metre down. "There's a couch or something," she told Collie before letting herself drop the rest of the way.

Collie followed her, then turned on her flashlight and ran the light around the room. It was unremarkable and uninteresting. A plastic and plywood desk, a ratty brown couch that probably doubled as a hide-a-bed, a brown coil rug on the linoleum floor. They stood in silence and listened for movement upstairs. If there was any, they couldn't hear it. If anything, the wind was louder now that they were inside.

Anna crept to the door and opened it, reaching behind her for the flashlight. Collie placed it in her hand and Anna swung it around to light the hallway. It showed her a narrow flight of stairs with another closed door at the top. They moved up the stairs one cautious step at a time. At the top, Anna stopped. Collie bumped into her and quickly went down a step. They waited and listened. Hearing nothing but the wind, Anna took a deep breath, held it, and eased the door open a crack. Faint orange light poured in around the edges of the door, giving the stairwell an eerie glow. Anna leaned in close and tilted her head, then squinted through the gap until her eyes adjusted and she could see what was on the other side. Another hallway, from the looks of it, with candles burning in a room at the far end. There were two closed doors on the left side of the hall, one on the right.

Anna pulled the door shut. "You look behind the closed doors," she said, returning Collie's flashlight. "I'll check out the room at the end of the hall."

Once the door was open, there was no point wasting time. Anna moved quickly. Behind her, she could hear Collie opening one of the left-hand doors. The hall didn't end at the candle-lit room. Just before the room, another narrow hallway branched off to the right. Anna left it for later and stepped into the room. It was small, maybe a quarter of the size of her hotel room. A set of emergency candles stuck in saucers lit it easily, if dimly. Of course, the room might have seemed bigger if it hadn't been so full of other people's belongings.

The figure skates were the first things Anna saw. They were hanging from a coat rack just inside the door. Eve's cat photograph was on a table in the far left corner, along with a Batman Pez dispenser and a small ceramic frog.

Anna was willing to bet it was Stella's frog, the one she'd used to scare away shoplifters. She'd been expecting this. Still, her stomach hurt at the confirmation, and the skin on the back of her neck began to crawl.

Evidence. It was what Anna was there for, and once she had it, she could leave. Anna went to the Pez dispenser and wrapped her hand around it.

The beetles were rubbing together, crawling over each other. Their friction created heat, burning Anna's skin from the inside. A red glow poured from her eyes and ears and mouth, colouring everything. Everything smelled of smoke. It was the richest, most seductive smell in the world. The most desirable smell.

She wanted more of it. She was nothing more than the desire to see everything burn. She was an empty place, hollow and glowing. She ached to be filled with smoke.

Anna began coughing, gasping for breath. The Pez dispenser fell to the carpet and she stumbled against the table. She put a hand out to steady herself and felt the cool ceramic of Stella's frog oh god, I'm sorry . . . I'm so sorry . . . let me out . . . let me move . . . just one breath . . . let me go . . . before she was able to draw her fingers away. She went to her knees and rested her forehead against the table until the world steadied itself. She didn't have forever. She knew that. And even if she had been able to take her time, she had no intention of staying in that house any longer than she had to. She linked her hands behind her back and got to her feet. What she needed was something touchable and damning. Maybe a scrapbook or two. She sent her gaze to a set of bookshelves on the right-hand wall . . . and froze. She'd seen something out of the corner of her eye.

"Looking for something?"

The world tilted again, and Anna's stomach heaved. That sure as hell wasn't Collie.

"I asked you a question."

"I heard you." Anna breathed in and out. In and out. Slowly, careful for her balance, she turned to face Anthony Waal.

He did look like his brother, a little. Same sandy hair, same planed features. Same height. He looked like the Identikit drawing, too, in those basic ways. He might even have looked more like the sketch than like his brother, because the sketch portrayed a certain meanness that had never twisted Tim's face. But some things didn't show up in police sketches. It would've taken a gifted artist to portray anger so strong that it flushed Anna's skin with the stinging heat of Mark Ling's fire. No still image could have caught the shadows that skittered across his eyes. He smiled at her, revealing crooked teeth with thin metal strips looped around the incisors. It had none of the charm of Tim's smile, not even the pathos of the outcast. At that moment Anna was certain she heard beetles clacking and echoing inside his skull.

"You disturbed my souvenirs," he said.

He was too thin. Sickly. Anna could have knocked him down with a half-hearted punch. She thought about it and knew that she should do it, but it seemed impossible to cross the room to him. It was unthinkable that she should get so close to him and terrifying to think of her hand grazing his flesh. She swallowed bile and held her ground.

"I should make you put them back," he told her. The idea lit his eyes, and the shadows were thrown into relief. Anna thought she saw an insect's leg. She looked away.

"Did you want to play with my toys?"

With her head turned, she could see the room's left-hand wall. It was covered in photographs, most of them crooked and out of focus. He had no sense of lighting or composition, absolutely no flare, but the subject matter was arresting. The pictures of Eve were there, naturally, but there were others. Pictures of Lou Postnikoff at his home computer . . . Mark Ling filling a gasoline can at some corner Esso . . . Jocelyn in the swimming pool, the back of her shirt still dry . . . and Kate Eby on the floor of her bathroom, cradling her baby.

Anna squeezed her eyes shut and turned her face away. Anthony laughed. "I'm no photographer; I know."

The darkness made the dizziness worse. Anna opened her eyes and saw one of the hallway doors slide open. Collie stepped out, silently, gun in hand. Anna forced her eyes back to Anthony's face.

He opened his mouth to say something, but Collie spoke before any sound came out. "Put your hands up," she said, "or I'll shoot you. I may shoot you anyway."

Anthony threw back his head and laughed. The sound made it hard for Anna to breathe. He spun around and opened his arms to Collie. "Oh, Colette. Would you really shoot me? After all we've been through together?"

Collie's gun hand was shaking. She brought her other hand up to steady it.

"Hold that thought for a minute," he told her. "Keep still. I have some business to discuss with Anna."

Collie's shaking stopped. She was looking at the gun with wild eyes, probably willing herself to pull the trigger. Nothing happened.

Anna couldn't look at that any longer, so she moved her gaze to Anthony.

"Anna," he said, spreading his arms wide. "My true sister. Companion to my soul. Do you have anything you'd like to tell me?"

For an insane moment, Anna thought that he meant it, that she really was his sister. She pictured her mother stepping into the hall and putting an affectionate arm around the magician's hunched shoulders. She shook her head and the image went away. "I'm not," she muttered. "I'm not anything to you."

Anthony cocked his head. He reminded her of a preying

mantis in that motion, and in that moment reminded her of Paul. "You're stupid. You went all the way to Vancouver to see him, and he really isn't anyone to me. Anna. You should know. When you mutate far enough from the rest, you aren't one of them anymore."

He took a step forward. His brown dress shoes squeaked on the white and grey linoleum. She saw him, suddenly, as a talentless imitator, terrified of giving the game away. A bland house in a nice neighbourhood, clothes that were themselves undistinguished imitations of the safest styles. Wouldn't want Them to know there was anything different about him.

"If you're trying to keep a low profile," she told him, "what with the murders and everything, you're doing a shitty job."

Anthony smiled again. Anna resolved to stop making him do that.

"It doesn't matter. They know anyway. They can see us, walking through the hive mind. They don't want anyone else to have that kind of control."

Anna was so thrown by that, she nearly asked him what the hell he meant. As if that was a smart thing to say to a paranoid schizophrenic. She forced her mind back on task. "If I told you to stop what you're doing," she asked, "would it do any good?"

Anthony laughed, making Anna want to scream. He took a step towards her. She wanted to back away, but her muscles clenched to keep her in place. Traitors, all of them. "What if I said the same thing to you?" he asked.

"I don't know what in hell you're talking about," Anna told him.

Anthony blinked mechanically. "You touch and you know. What if I asked you to pick up my souvenirs and not know anything about the people who owned them?"

Anna didn't answer.

Anthony moved closer. One more step and she'd be able to feel his breath, the heat of his skin. "No one says what they really think. They know how sick they are. What he thinks of me . . . there aren't even words. Anna . . . what was in the first mind you touched?"

"I don't understand you," Anna lied.

Anthony smiled. Shadows played against the back of his throat when he opened his mouth to speak. "The mind is a castle. It has one line of defense, and you walk past that line as if it wasn't even there. Once you've fought your way past the walls, everything within will fall to you."

As if it were inevitable, that everything she touched put her one step closer to being Anthony Waal. She didn't believe it, not exactly. But she knew those minds weren't hers to read, and she knew she should never have been inside them. She felt desperately ashamed that Collie was hearing this, that anyone else was in the room.

Anthony studied her face. "Don't look that way. This isn't a funeral. You're finding out what you really are. It's like rebirth."

Anna stared at him and knew she saw it this time, a thin dark leg moving past the iris of his left eye. Could she follow the beetle, go inside, using the path she'd found in Mark Ling's corrupted toy? It seemed not only possible, but easy. Easier to do it than not to. The beetles were getting louder, making her head ache and her stomach roll. Her muscles ached with the effort of keeping her in place when she wanted so badly to run. What was the point of anything if you couldn't get the fucking bugs out of your head? She knew suddenly that she'd rather die. She'd rather Collie died. "It is a funeral," she said.

"I'm sorry to hear that," Anthony told her. His eyes almost looked human, and he did sound oddly sad. "Stay there while I have a word with Colette."

He turned his back on her and she lunged at him, but her limbs paid her no mind. It reminded her of the dreams she sometimes had just before her alarm went off, the ones where she couldn't move or open her eyes or force herself to wake. They made her wonder how a dream that you knew to be a dream could ever end.

"Colette. I apologize. I mislead you when I made you think I'd left the house. And I really do owe you something, because I used to think it was something personal when Jocelyn turned me down. Now I know it wasn't. I feel better."

Collie was pale enough to be a ghost in that hallway. "Shut up," she said distinctly.

Anthony laughed. "We had a better talk in the parking lot. Remember? When you caught me putting Jocelyn's necklace on your car?"

Anna felt as though the ground had dropped out beneath her. Even so, with nothing but air beneath her feet, she couldn't move.

"I didn't," Collie protested, but she wasn't selling it.

Anthony sighed. "It's not flattering," he said, "how quickly the ladies forget me. You even gave me something to remember you by." He hooked a finger into his pants pocket and pulled out a cassette tape.

So the mix tape hadn't run out after all.

"I like your hair," he said thoughtfully. "It's larger than life. I bet you'll photograph beautifully. Why don't you give me that gun?"

Collie moved forward in ungraceful jerks. Her lipstick was dark enough against her skin to look like a streak of blood. She stopped as far from Anthony as she could and held out the gun.

Anna felt a rush of relief that the gun wasn't loaded, which was absurd. Once he figured that out, he'd just kill them some other way.

"Thank you," Anthony said, taking the gun. He turned so that he was standing sideways in the hallway, able to look at both of them. "Now, ladies. . . ." He meant to say something after that. Anna was sure of it. But he shut his mouth instead and stared at the gun as though he'd never seen such a thing before. "Huh." It was more a breath than an exclamation, purely unconscious. His face twisted, and for a moment the play of candlelight on his face made Anna think he was going to cry. "Oh . . . oh God. . . ." His voice was thick enough for tears. He looked at the gun in wonder, then raised his eyes to Anna's. "Angels won't find me now," he said.

He put the gun in his mouth and fired.

At first, Anna thought she was imagining it. She was so accustomed to guns on TV and in movies that she would hear an explosion where there should only have been a click. Of course the gun hadn't gone off. She knew damned well it wasn't loaded. But there he was, the evil magician, sliding down the wall with a trail of blood behind his head and a gun falling from his limp hand.

Someone was breathing in staccato gasps. Anna thought it might be her, but when she looked up from the body she saw that it was Collie.

"A-a-a-anna?" she stammered. "I th– . . . I th– . . . thought you said the gun wasn't loaded."

"It wasn't," Anna said. The ground came up to meet her, jolting her legs, and suddenly she could move. She went to the body and smelled blood.

Blood and gunpowder.

Collie stared at her with wild eyes. "I beg to differ."

Anna wanted to say that she might have been wrong, that she might have put one bullet in, that it might have been loaded when she got it . . . but she couldn't. She knew better. Instead she said, "Let's get out of here."

Collie didn't offer any objections. Before leaving, Anna brushed her fingertips over Stella's little frog. It was smooth, cold ceramic. Nothing more.

Bryan was bent over a ledger as they entered the hotel. Anna didn't think he'd noticed them come in, but as they passed the desk he spoke. "Don't say hello or any—oh. My. God."

"Are we a fright?" Anna asked grimly.

Bryan gaped at her. "No, no, no. We get people who are spattered with blood all the time. Think nothing of . . . oh, Jesus. That's not just blood." As he spoke, he hurried out from behind his desk and took both of them by their arms. "Move. Now."

He propelled them through a door to the left of the front desk and they found themselves in a small concrete stairwell. Anna had loved bare stairwells as a child. She'd always stamped her way up the stairs to hear the echo. As the door swung shut, she heard Bryan calling for the security guard to watch the front desk. The guard said something she couldn't hear.

"Keith," Bryan said, "if you value your private moments with the supply room and a magazine, you can damned well watch my desk for ten freakin' minutes."

It was loud enough to hear through the door, which made Anna wonder just how far that little outburst had carried. Fortunately, there hadn't been anyone else in the lobby when she and Collie had arrived.

"Okay," said Bryan, stepping into the stairwell and pulling the door shut behind him, "I don't want to hear it. You may want to confess, but you're not going to, because I don't want to hear it. Whose room are you going to?"

They looked at each other. Collie shrugged. "Mine," she said. "I guess."

"You're decisive," Bryan told her. "I like that." He pushed past them and headed up the stairs. They followed. When they got to Collie's floor, he stopped between them and the door. "Just tell me one thing. Is this over?"

Anna leaned against the wall. "It's over."

Bryan looked at her. "You get the bastard?"

"He got himself," Anna said.

Bryan thought that over, then shrugged. "It's all good. Ladies . . . it's been a hundred and one tons of fun. The most excitement I've had in years. If anyone asks me about it, I remember nothing." He put his hands on their shoulders and patted them. "You crazy kids take care."

"Thanks for everything," said Collie.

Bryan gave her shoulder another pat. "Anything in the cause of justice." He threw an invisible cape over his shoulder and went downstairs humming something Anna didn't recognize.

"Thank you," she called down.

Without stopping, Bryan raised a hand in salute.

"Who was that masked man?" Collie asked wryly.

Anna put a hand on her back. "Get moving," she said. "We both need showers. This fucking night isn't over yet."

Through the crack under the door, Anna could see the light was still on in Paul's room. She raised her hand to knock, then changed her mind and opened the door as quietly as she could.

Paul and Mark were sitting at the table with a bottle between them. Each of them held a plastic cup with an amber liquid that was probably scotch. Anna stepped into the room and shut the door behind her.

". . . my grandmother," Mark was saying as she entered, "honestly believed it. She once fired a man for having green eyes."

"Didn't she know he had green eyes when she hired him?" Paul asked. The words ran together.

"I guess not. Maybe he wore shades at the interview. Guy shows up for his first day of work, she sees green eyes and *bam!* She cans him." Mark was waving his hand a little as he spoke, slopping his drink onto the table. "Told him she knew what he was. Can you believe that? I can't believe he didn't take her to court."

Paul laughed. Really, it was more of a whinnying giggle. It set Anna's teeth on edge. "Freedom of religion, my friend. That's her defense. I'd love to see a lawyer. . . ." He stopped and looked over his shoulder. "Hello, Anna."

"Hello." She stared at him until he stopped trying to smile.

"Where's Colette?"

"Taking a shower. She said to tell you we got the name of the person who killed Jocelyn. His name is Anthony Waal."

Paul's fingers tightened around his drink. Fine white cracks appeared in the clear plastic. "Interesting. You plan to go get him?"

"No need. Anthony Waal killed himself tonight."

Paul's brow creased. Anna watched as he processed that thought, turning it over in his mind.

"I hadn't heard about that," he said.

Anna said nothing.

Paul finished his drink and set the cup down. "I'll have to get the paper tomorrow. Is there anything else?"

"Colette will have a report for you by Monday. She says you should have no trouble getting another book out of this."

Mark was staring into his drink. Anna felt bad for him. "I think everyone involved would appreciate it," she told Paul, "if you'd show a little discretion in your reporting. Collie seems to think that won't be a problem. Does she have embarrassing photos of you?"

The thin line of Paul's mouth twitched and turned up at the edges. It was a poor smile, but he did seem genuinely amused. "Something like that," he said. "Tell her not to worry."

"Do you understand that she means discreet in general, and not just about her and I?"

"Yes," Paul sighed. "I get that. Anything else?"

"Only that she quits. Respectfully resigns. She will try not to let the door hit her in the ass on her way out."

"Right. When she cools off, tell her to give me a call."

Anna's back hurt in a specific and special way. Of all the things she didn't need that night. "I don't think she's likely to work for you again."

"I know that. I just want to keep in touch." Paul smiled and raised his empty glass to Anna. "Congratulations on a job well done. Pass my compliments on to Collie."

"I'll tell her," said Anna, "but the work was its own reward. By the way, I'll take my cheque now."

Paul laughed. "I wasn't going to stiff you, but let me set your mind at ease." He tugged his jacket off the bed and pulled a chequebook and pen from the pocket. After a moment's thought, he scribbled a figure and held out the cheque. Anna took a few steps forward and delicately pulled it from his fingers.

"Do you think that's fair?" Paul asked. Anna looked at the numbers on the cheque and felt her mouth go dry. It was the most money she'd seen in . . . well, ever.

Of course, Paul thought he was paying for an assassination, so it was only right that he'd be generous. She kept her face impassive and slid the cheque into her coat pocket. "It's fine," she said. "Is my hotel bill taken care of?"

"Yes."

Mark was still staring into his drink. Anna didn't know what he was looking for, but she didn't think it was down there.

"It's been," she said to Paul, and left.

Collie was out of the shower, shivering in jeans and a heavy cream-coloured sweater that fell nearly to her knees.

"I thought you were planning to stay in there until the hotel ran out of hot water," Anna said.

Collie's teeth chattered for a moment. She clamped them together before speaking. "I would have," she said, "but I realized I could shower until morning and what happened tonight would still have happened. I think I got all of . . . him . . . off me."

"Looks like." The bathroom was hidden behind a cloud of steam. It looked like the foyer to heaven. "I think we're done. Aren't we? I don't think we need to see Tim."

"No," Collie agreed. "Not now. He'll hear about it on the news or something. He'll think it was us, but so what? I don't think he'll tell anyone."

"Not the police," Anna said. "And anyone else he told . . . you know, I welcome them to look into it. Maybe they could explain it to me."

Collie had pulled the sweater's sleeves down over her hands. Her fingers were worrying the cuffs. "He's dead. I don't care how it happened. And if Tim really cared what happened to his brother, then I guess he should have come with us. He doesn't deserve an explanation now."

Anna wasn't sure she believed that, but she was too tired to discuss it. "You leave any hot water for me?"

"Maybe."

Anna took her coat off, turned it inside-out, and dropped it on the bed. "Would you happen to have a pad or tampon?"

Collie smiled. "Always. Were you not expecting this?"

"Five days early. Apparently terror kicks things into gear."

Collie's travel bag was open on the bed. She pulled out a pad and a bottle of ibuprofen. "Remember," she said brightly, "at least you're not pregnant."

Anna thought of Kate Eby. She took the pad and the pills and went into the bathroom to wash whatever she could away.

⁂

The smoke rising from their coats was thick and dark, but not bad-smelling. That was, Anna supposed, the benefit of wearing natural fibres.

"You're right," Curtis said. He coughed a little in the smoke and hunched his shoulders under his aviator jacket. "I don't want the gun back."

Anna nodded. "We thought you'd see it our way."

He stared into the smoke for a while. On the other side of the fire, Collie stared back at him.

"You realize," he said, "that what you say happened . . . it's im-fucking-possible."

"So's psychometry," Collie said softly.

Curtis seemed startled by her voice. He met her eyes. "You have a point."

A spark floated towards Anna. She stepped on it, crushing it into the damp earth.

"What did the police say?" Curtis asked. "Did they find a bullet?"

"No," said Anna. "They think someone took it. I guess they can tell he killed himself, so they figure someone came upon the scene and removed the bullet."

"Never mind," Collie said, "that there's no sign anyone dug into his head, and there are no holes in the wall."

"The gun was recently fired, though," Anna said. "I read they checked for that."

Curtis was looking a little ill. "Are the police looking for you?" he inquired.

Anna shrugged. "Not too hard, I think. If we were in Victoria, I guess they'd want a word. But taking a bullet from a suicide scene . . . I don't even know what the charge for that would be."

"And they can't prove it was us anyway," Collie said with a funny smile. Her face seemed unearthly in light that was bent by heat.

"Not now," Curtis agreed. He dropped a handful of twigs onto the fire and stared at them until they caught.

"You don't look well," Anna told him.

"I have rabies," he said. "And smallpox. And polio. I'll be dead by morning."

"Before you go," Anna said, "maybe you could tell us what the story is with that gun."

Curtis looked at the ground. "I'm sorry you had nightmares," he said.

Anna was surprised enough to laugh. "That's really the least of my concerns, Curt. Besides, they stopped as soon as I got rid of the cursed fucking gun."

"Don't chew on my throat," Curtis said. He sounded tired and probably was. They'd been up since sunrise. "All handguns have a history. They exist to shoot people. You could've told me you were having problems." He backed away from the fire. "I'll be back in a minute." He scrambled up the hill to the house. His house and store were the same thing, as was popular in this neighbourhood.

Once he was inside, Collie threw a few more twigs on the fire. "Think he's calling the cops on us?"

Anna smiled. "Maybe just on you," she said.

Collie laughed. "I'll drag you down with me."

It was colder in Seattle than it had been in Victoria, although no snow had fallen. Curtis had given them a pair of siwashes to wear, warm enough as long as the wind stayed down. Collie held her small white hands out to the fire.

"He's right about guns," Anna admitted. She was willing to admit it, since Curtis wasn't close enough to hear. "I don't think I'll touch guns anymore."

"Yeah." Collie rubbed her hands together. "Me neither."

The door to the house slammed. Anna turned to see Curtis stumbling down the hill to the back of the yard, a manila folder in his left hand.

"It's why you got the house so cheap," Anna pointed out as he skidded to a stop beside her. "This stupid yard."

"I'm putting in a ski lift next year," he said. "It'll be huge." He stuck the folder under his jacket and pulled glasses from his pocket, then took the folder out again. "I handle a lot of guns. I had to look this one up."

"And?" Collie prodded.

"Well," said Curtis, opening the folder, "it is pretty bad." He sat down on the dead grass and balanced the folder against his knees. "It was a war pistol. I don't know anything about its history during the war. We can assume it killed a few people." He took a breath and coughed some more. "A good south wind would be nice right about now. Anyway . . . the man who used this gun during the war kept it afterwards. I assume he kept it as a souvenir. Maybe for protection; I don't know."

"Did you buy it from him?" Anna asked.

Curtis shook his head. "No. It was kind of an estate sale."

Anna looked at Collie, who was already looking at her. "You go ahead," Anna said.

Collie turned to Curtis. "Please define 'kind of an estate sale.'"

"The guy was no longer competent to run his affairs, so power of attorney fell to his nephew. The kid sold off a bunch of stuff to cover his uncle's hospital bills."

"How did the uncle wind up in the hospital?" asked Anna. She had a sick feeling she already knew the answer.

"Suicide attempt," Curtis said. "Involving the gun."

"And he failed," Collie said, "but he did manage to improve his life with a permanent disability. That's lovely."

"It's worse than that," Curtis said. "The nephew told me why the old guy tried to kill himself."

Anna raised an eyebrow in question.

Curtis cleared his throat.

"He . . . uh . . . he was diagnosed with Alzheimer's."

It was strange how smoke moved even in the lightest breeze, twisting to form shapes that were nearly human. Shapes that might have been angels with dark grey wings. Anna couldn't move, could barely breathe. The smoke moved effortlessly into her lungs and over her skin. There had been a house once where angels feared to tread, but she couldn't remember where it was. "They took the house away," she said. "They took all my decisions away. If I keep very still, maybe they won't see me."

She felt a hand on her arm and suddenly she could turn her head. She looked down to see Collie standing beside her. Collie said something, but the words didn't make any sense.

"Do you know what the angels want?" Anna asked.

Collie patted her back. "Nothing from you, dear." She steered Anna around until they were facing away from the smoke.

Anna blinked a few times and the angels disappeared. "I understand the dreams now," she said.

"Who needs Jung?" Collie said. It seemed to be a joke, but her tone was flat and her eyes were dark. She turned to Curtis. "Is this guy still alive?"

"After a fashion," Curtis told her. "Why?"

"Could you find out what hospital he's in?" she asked.

"I guess. But—"

"Good. Thank you." Collie pressed Anna's back, pushing her towards the house. "I'm cold. I'm going inside."

"I think you should see him."

Anna was sitting where she'd been pushed, in the antique dentist's chair near the back of Millet Antiques. She was still moving through molasses, and it took her a moment to grasp what Collie had said. "You what?"

"I think you should see him." Collie had picked up an antique metal top and was trying to make it spin on the counter. "I think you need some kind of closure with this guy. Maybe you need to see him to create a separation between him and you."

Anna leaned back in the chair and looked around at Curtis's treasures. Old clothes, early license plates, carnival glass. There was a carousel horse in the corner that hadn't been there when she'd left for Victoria. Curt dusted the place twice a day and still dust floated everywhere, turning gold where the light crept in through melting glass windows. "I don't want to see him."

"You're still too close to him. You need to see that he's someone outside of you."

Anna shook her head.

Collie slammed her hand on the table, rattling countless sets of teacups and saucers. "It might help, Anna. And okay, it might not. But I don't think it's going to do you any serious harm. And I really think you need to cut this connection. You've lived with it long enough."

Anna's head hurt. Her back hurt too, but at least she knew that pain would go away. "If I agree to go with you," she said, "will you stop shouting and busting up my friend's shop?"

Collie picked up the top and gave it a vicious twirl. It spun so quickly that Anna could feel wind move past her face. "Done," said Collie. "I'll get your keys."

They'd taken separate vehicles to Seattle. They hadn't wanted to, but Collie had been determined not to leave her car for Paul. She'd also been determined not to ride in Anna's Jeep, but the fact was that Anna knew Seattle and Collie didn't.

"You drive like a pussy," Collie told her from the passenger seat.

Anna smiled serenely. "Sticks and stones may break my bones," she said, "but a fifty-klick crash in a four-by-four with a roll bar will never hurt me."

Collie grunted and looked out the passenger side window.

Anna reached to turn on the radio, then drew her hand back. "I . . . used to say things," she said.

Collie looked at her. "What?"

"I used to say things. When I was little and didn't know any better. I used to talk about the things I saw."

Collie considered that. "You probably spooked some people," she said.

Anna started to laugh, but quickly stopped. She didn't like the way her laugh had sounded. "You could say that," she said. "Burning witches isn't in style these days, but that doesn't mean people want their kids playing with one. And I think they figured I was saying those things to hurt them. As if I could possibly know what I was saying when I was only three years old."

Collie said nothing. She'd been saying nothing for a while, ever since Anna's heart-to-heart with Anthony Waal. Not one word about the potential for Anna's gift to become Anthony's sickening power. Not one word about Anna's decision that she'd rather let Anthony kill them both than go inside his head. Anna had tried telling herself that Collie had been too scared to hear and understand the things Anthony had said to her, but she couldn't make herself believe it. Still, Anna didn't see the need to discuss the topic. Whatever Collie thought, she had followed Anna to Seattle. God might not be in his heaven and all was definitely not right with the world, but it was close enough. Anna was not going to mess with it.

"My grandmother," she said, "made me a dreamcatcher. They're supposed to filter out the bad dreams and let only good ones in." She gripped the steering wheel harder, until the plastic seam dug into her hands. "It didn't work."

"You're Métis," Collie said. The girl hadn't lost her gift for missing the point.

"My grandmother married a Catholic from Quebec," Anna said. "She used to tell me stories about monsters. They did horrible things to themselves. One of them chewed his own lips off. I think my grandmother felt sorry for me."

"Wouldn't her culture find your gift really valuable?" Collie asked.

Anna shrugged. "I don't know. I never asked. She didn't seem to think of it as anything but a tragedy."

"Oh." Collie was quiet for a few blocks. Then she said, "Maybe your grandmother had visions of her own."

Anna had never thought of that. "Maybe she did."

The driveway to the rest home was coming up on their left. If there was anything else to say, they'd have to say it another time.

It was natural that the hospital would have the quality of a dream. The halls were a little too bright, the sounds soft and thick. Every time a doctor or nurse turned around, Anna thought she saw a blur of wings.

"Are you relatives?" the orderly asked as he led them to the room. He sounded as though he were underwater.

"Friends of the family," Collie told him. Anna marveled again at how easily lies came to her.

The orderly didn't seem to have any other ideas for conversation. They walked in silence, their footsteps muted against the white tile floor.

Anna wondered again what she was doing here. How could it help to look this nightmare in the face? All of her life she'd survived by pretending her dreams were nothing more than dreams, and she saw no reason to drop that tactic now.

It was hard to tell what Collie was thinking. Anna had never seen her face so guarded. The only clues to her state of mind came from the stiff set of her shoulders and back, and the unhealthy tone of her skin. For someone who had wanted so badly to confront the bogeyman, she didn't seem happy to be there.

The orderly stopped abruptly. "He's in here."

Anna waited for the orderly to precede them, but after a few moments it became clear that he wasn't going to enter the room.

"Thank you," she said.

He nodded. "No trouble." He backed away from them a few steps, then turned and hurried down the hall.

"Your friend doesn't seem very popular," Collie commented. She was standing in the doorway, looking inside with unfocused eyes. Anna put a hand on her back and gave her a gentle shove. They went in cautiously. It was a semi-private room with a woman asleep in the far bed. The bed nearest the door had curtains drawn around it. Collie reached up and drew them back.

He was smaller than Anna had expected. Small for a bogeyman. Not more than five foot six by the looks of it, with small bones that were visible through the thin blanket. The heavy machines surrounding the bed made him seem even smaller. Anna stared at them, hypnotized by the flashing red lights and the steady hum of the machines that breathed for him.

Colour drained from the room as if it were water sliding down the walls, and Anna's arms and legs became numb. The humming was the warning of a hive of bees, and it made her sick with fear because she knew she couldn't run away. Behind her, she heard wings.

"Anna! Goddamn it, Anna. . . ."

She looked down and saw Collie shaking her. She looked angry, which Anna read as scared.

"It's okay," Anna said thickly.

Collie was breathing fast. "Get out of here," she said.

Anna stared at her, puzzled. "What?"

"Go!" Collie snapped. "I'll catch up with you in a minute."

Anna went, stumbling down the hall as it swung back and forth as wildly as the deck of a ferry in a storm. Something white swooped in to help her, but she pushed it away. Months or years later, she made it to the door. The ground outside was steady and the air was wonderfully cold. She breathed it gratefully, gulping it down. After a while, she thought she might like to sit down. She found her way to a wooden bench. It was splintered and damp, but Anna loved it anyway. Imperfection was real.

The doors to the rest home opened and a small redhead came out. She looked across the grounds, squinting in the hazy daylight. Anna thought about calling to her, but Collie spotted her before she could speak and came to stand in front of her.

"It's funny," Collie proclaimed. Her eyes shone with tears, but her voice was steady. "I've figured out what bothers me on those winter nights. You know, when it's so perfectly still?"

"I remember," Anna said. "Your songs."

"Yeah. My winter tape. You know what the problem is? When you stand like that and nothing moves or breathes, you become a part of it. Your own skin could turn to ice, and you wouldn't even care. Just for that moment, you forget how sad it is to be dead."

She pulled off her soft leather gloves and dropped them in Anna's lap. "We shouldn't stay too long," she said. "I'll be in the Jeep."

Anna watched her go, then looked at the hospital again. Behind the glass doors, nurses and orderlies were running down the hall, heading for the bogeyman's room. Some of them wheeled more of those heavy and confusing machines.

Collie's gloves were unpleasantly warm on Anna's lap. Anna glanced down and wondered how it was possible for a pair of gloves to look guilty. They were Colette's way of telling her something. She understood that. They were an invitation to take a look inside Collie's mind. But Anna didn't know what the gloves could tell her that she couldn't already see in the panic of the hospital's staff.

Collie had seen to it that neither Anna nor the bogeyman would be having nightmares anymore. Anna didn't need to travel through Colette's memories to the scene of the crime. She would not make that invasion to find out something she didn't even want to know. If Collie had anything she wanted to confess, she could damn well open her mouth and say so.

With her hands in her pockets, Anna stood. The gloves fell to the ground.

She thought about sending a letter to Tim Waal. Maybe paying him a visit. Telling why and how his brother had died. She couldn't say she was sorry about Anthony's death, but she could tell him she was was sorry Anthony had been so far gone. Sorry that dying had been the best thing Anthony could do.

She thought of her grandmother, who might have visions of her own. Maybe Collie would like to visit with her. They'd like each other. Anna knew they would.

Maybe it was time to go home.

ACKNOWLEDGEMENTS

Endless thanks to . . .

Anne Nothof, my most excellent editor.

Amanda Summers, greatest of all beta readers, for knowing what the book needed.

Ryan States, for honesty, support, and a lot of clerical work without which I wouldn't have been able to do this.

Mark Brunsdon, for inspiration.

Chris Stroshein and Jen Woodcock for the photo session.

Lori Forrest, Tom Cantine, Nancy States, Kenn Scott, Jen Harper and Noelle Knoll for advice, encouragment and catching my mistakes.

Everyone at NeWest, for everything.

Everyone else who offered help and comments along the way.

Gayleen Froese was born and raised in Saskatoon, Saskatchewan. She has lived in Toronto, Edmonton, and Prince Albert. She is a graduate of Ryerson University, and is currently working with an initiative to help improve health in Northern Saskatchewan. In addition to her writing, Gayleen is an independent musician with three albums, *Obituary*, *Chimera*, and *Sacrifice*. Gayleen lives with her best friend, two dogs, two degus, and a Siamese Fighting Fish. *Touch* is her first novel.

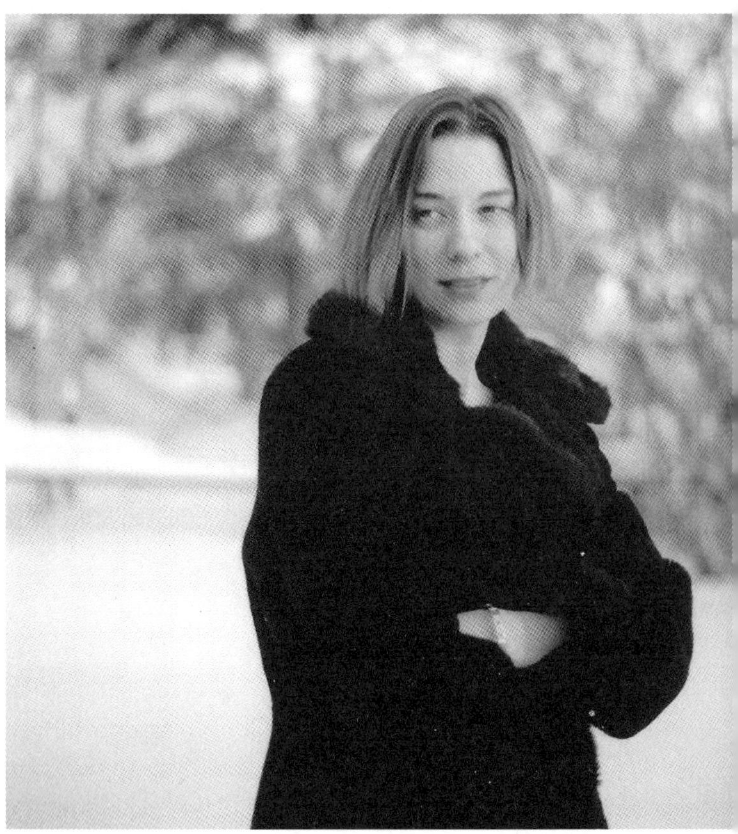